PRAISE FOR DIANNE DUVALL'S BOOKS

Immortal Guardians Books

"Crackles with energy, originality, and a memorable take-no-prisoners heroine."

—*Publishers Weekly*

"Fans of terrific paranormal romance have hit the jackpot with Duvall and her electrifying series."

—*RT Book Reviews*

"Each of these stories... has been heart-stopping, intense, humorous and powerfully romantic."

—*Reading Between the Wines Book Club*

"My favorite series, hands down. Every character is beloved. Every story is intense, funny, romantic, and exciting."

—*eBookObsessed*

"Full of awesome characters, snappy dialogue, exciting action, steamy sex, sneaky shudder-worthy villains, and delightful humor."

—*I'm a Voracious Reader*

Aldebarian Alliance Books

"Intense, addictive and brilliant... I want more!"

—*Caffeinated Reviewer*

"Full of adventures, sizzling passion, romance, and yes kick-ass fighting. This book is simply captivating."
—*Book Dragon*

"An action-packed, hair-raising, and heart-rending journey."
—*Reading Between the Wines Book Club*

"A fascinating world filled with danger, romance, humour, and wonderful discoveries."
—*Totally Addicted to Reading*

"An Epic Adventure!"
—*EnjoyMeSomeBooks*

The Gifted Ones Books

"Full of danger, intrigue, and passion... I'm hooked!"
—*Reading in Pajamas*

"Dianne Duvall has delivered a gripping storyline with characters that stuck with me throughout the day... A must-read!"
—*Reading Between the Wines Book Club*

"Addictive, funny, and wrapped in swoons, you won't be able to set these audios down."
—*Caffeinated Book Reviewer*

"Medieval times, a kick-ass heroine, a protective hero, magic, and a dash of mayhem."
—*The Romance Reviews*

TITLES BY DIANNE DUVALL

Aldebarian Alliance

THE LASARAN
THE SEGONIAN
THE PURVELI
THE AKSELI

The Gifted Ones

A SORCERESS OF HIS OWN
RENDEZVOUS WITH YESTERDAY

Immortal Guardians

DARKNESS DAWNS
NIGHT REIGNS
PHANTOM SHADOWS
IN STILL DARKNESS
DARKNESS RISES
NIGHT UNBOUND
PHANTOM EMBRACE
SHADOWS STRIKE
BLADE OF DARKNESS
AWAKEN THE DARKNESS
DEATH OF DARKNESS
BROKEN DAWN
CLIFF'S DESCENT
AN IMMORTAL GUARDIANS COMPANION

THE
AKSELI

ALDEBARIAN ALLIANCE

NEW YORK TIMES BESTSELLING AUTHOR

DIANNE
DUVALL

For my family

ACKNOWLEDGEMENTS

As always, I would like to thank Crystal. You're amazing and such a pleasure to work with. I don't know what I'd do without you. I also want to send love, hugs, and a huge thank you to my awesome Street Team. You're the *best*! I hope you know how much your support means to me. I appreciate it so much. Another big thank you goes to the members of my Dianne Duvall Books Group on Facebook. I have so much fun in there with you and can always count on you to make me laugh and smile, even when I'm stressing over deadlines.

Thank you, Kirsten Potter, for your stellar narration. You have a true gift for giving characters unique and entertaining voices that continue to delight listeners. I always enjoy working with you.

And, of course, I want to thank all of the wonderful readers who have purchased copies of my books and audiobooks. You've made living my dream possible. I wish you all the best.

PROLOGUE

S IMONE SWUNG HER TREASURED katana with smooth precision, cutting down one opponent after another. One *imaginary* opponent, that was. The small training room she occupied was empty, save for herself. But back on Earth, she'd battled enough psychotic vampires over the centuries—and enough heavily armed mercenaries in recent years—to create some vivid practice scenarios.

She paused.

Back on Earth.

Smiling, she shook her head. Most days, she still found it hard to grasp her new reality. The old adage that life was what happened while you were making other plans had never been more accurate. Not that she'd had much in the way of plans.

Her mortal life had been a harrowing one. Like her father, she had been born in fourteenth-century France with unique gifts she'd hidden so others wouldn't think them demon issued and try to kill her. She'd then lost her whole family to the Black Death and had been ready to succumb herself when a vampire attacked her and infected her with a virus that had rendered her virtually immortal, bestowing upon her extraordinary speed, strength, and regenerative capabilities coupled with photosensitivity and a frequent need for blood transfusions. A virus that caused progressive brain damage in ordinary humans and swiftly drove them insane.

1

Fortunately, the advanced DNA that lent her empathic and telepathic abilities also protected her from the progressive brain damage the virus caused in ordinary humans. So she'd spent the next six centuries hunting and slaying psychotic vampires every night with her immortal brethren to protect humanity.

Simone hadn't learned until recently that aliens called Gathendiens had created the vampiric virus in a lab, then released it on Earth to eradicate humanity so those reptilian bastards could claim the planet and its resources for themselves. Had Immortal Guardians like herself not banded together under the leadership of Seth—the eldest and most powerful amongst them—to keep the vampire population in check, Gathendiens would've succeeded.

She smiled, thinking of Seth. Five months ago, the monotony of doing the same-old-same-old night after night had been weighing heavily on her when Seth had placed Simone in a room with four other Immortal Guardians and ten *gifted ones* (all female) and stunned the hell out of them by announcing that the petite redhead he loved like a daughter was an extraterrestrial from the planet Lasara. An extra... terrestrial.

Even more astonishing, he had revealed his intention to form an alliance with the more advanced Lasaran people and asked if she and the others would be interested in traveling to Lasara and seeking a new home there as part of a trial.

Um... hell, yes. Simone hadn't even had to deliberate.

She glanced at the training room around her. Though it loosely resembled those often found in Immortal Guardians' homes, it couldn't be more different. This one was aboard an enormous Lasaran warship that currently hurtled through space at mind-blowing speeds, carrying her across the galaxy. A computer panel that doled out refreshments to thirsty warriors in response to verbal commands adorned one wall. And—

The door abruptly slid up.

As Simone glanced toward it, a small silver globe zipped into the room like a floating tennis ball. The door slid down, shutting her inside with it. Her eyes widened.

A Bex-7 stun grenade? "*Merde!*"

She swung her sword.

Bright white light filled the room, blinding her. Her body froze mid-swing, muscles locking as electricity crackled through her, making her brain feel like it was boiling inside a cauldron.

Pain seared her for several interminable seconds. Then the light dimmed, the energy surging through her ceased, and Simone toppled to the floor like a fallen statue. Her hand clenched convulsively around the katana's handle.

The door rose, allowing a hulking male to enter. He must have been at least six and a half feet tall to her five feet five and packed a ton of muscle. His skin tone labeled him a Yona warrior. Tan with a hint of gray, it almost looked as if someone had used photo editing software to desaturate his image. Dark brown, formfitting pants and a matching shirt with a leathery texture hugged his big body. A lightweight vest that served as astoundingly efficient body armor protected his chest and back. Multiple weapons—advanced firearms of various sizes and numerous blades—adorned the rest of him.

Gritting her teeth against the pain, Simone stared up at him as he moved to stand over her. He wore his jet-black hair shorn close to his head. The dark pupils and gray irises in his emotionless eyes were larger than a human's, almost eclipsing all of the white as he studied her.

"*M-merde,*" she said again.

His face remained an expressionless mask, not that she expected otherwise. Yona warriors were incapable of feeling emotion.

With preternatural speed, she swung a leg and swept his feet out from under him. In the second it took him to hit the floor, she lunged up onto her knees, filched one of his daggers, and drove it down toward his chest, stopping an inch away from making contact.

No fear filled his features. Neither did chagrin or dismay. "The Bex-7s do not affect you," he said stoically. "Feigning injury was a wise strategy."

Smiling, Simone backed off a bit and drew his attention to how vigorously the hand holding the dagger shook. "Oh, it affects me." When she rose stiffly to her feet, she felt every bit her age. "That hurt like a bitch," she groaned, arching her back. "But now I know I can still function if a Gathendien ever hurls one at me. Thank you, Valok."

The Yona warrior issued an abrupt nod as he rose. "Your argument for wanting to test one on yourself was a compelling one." That argument being that a good warrior prepared for any eventuality.

While the Lasarans were a peaceful people with many friends in the Aldebarian Alliance, there *were* untrustworthy and warlike aliens. Understanding the weapons those unsavory characters might employ made sense. Unfortunately, her many attempts to coax a Lasaran into hitting her with a Bex-7 so she would know whether or not it would incapacitate her the way it would a mortal had met with refusal. All had been too worried they might hurt her.

The Yona, however, didn't feel emotion. They weren't plagued by worry and would feel no guilt after the fact. They knew only duty and logic. So when she'd cornered Valok and asked him to hit her with a Bex-7, he had viewed it purely from the standpoint of a warrior determined to win all future battles.

She smiled as her body swiftly shook off the effects of the stun grenade. "You get bonus points for catching me off guard."

He tilted his head to one side as though trying to discern her meaning. "Bonus points?" The translator chips implanted in Lasaran and Yona brains didn't always translate Earth slang correctly.

Simone lacked one of the fascinating translator chips. When she had transformed, the vampiric virus had basically destroyed her immune system, then taken its place like a symbiotic organism. And the damn thing had viewed the translator chip the Lasarans tried to implant in her head as shrapnel and pushed it right back out again.

Talk about pain.

As a result, she had to wear a translator that fit in her ear like an earbud instead.

"That just means you did extra well by catching me off guard instead of giving me a warning."

"Ah." He motioned to the control panel on the wall. "If you still feel the effects, nutrient water will help."

"Good to know. Thank you." She crossed to the panel and pressed a button. "Two nutrient waters, please."

A hum sounded, then the panel slid aside to reveal two full bottles.

Simone grabbed them both and held one out to Valok. "Join me?"

He took the bottle and held it without drinking while he watched her sit on the bench that lined one wall. "For what purpose?"

She shrugged. "So I can pester you with more questions."

He sat beside her, his posture rigidly correct.

"I don't suppose I could talk you into shooting me with a *tronium* blaster, could I?" She downed several swallows of water.

"Such a wound would draw notice and land me in the brig. I cannot perform my duties adequately while imprisoned."

And duty was everything to the Yona.

She supposed she could understand that. What else *was* there when you had neither wants nor desires?

Simone watched him empty his bottle in a few strong swallows. "What's it like?" she couldn't resist asking when he finished.

"Getting shot with a blaster?" He set the bottle aside. "It is painful."

She couldn't help but laugh. "Well, I guessed that much. I meant, what's it like not to feel any emotion?" The concept was one she couldn't grasp. As an empath, she had not only dealt with *her* feelings all her life. The emotions of others had also bombarded her.

"I have nothing to which I can compare it," he stated.

When she had first encountered Yona warriors, she had thought them some kind of highly advanced robots. They were *that* emotionless. "Do you... regret not being able to feel emotion?" she asked softly.

He shook his head. "Regret is an emotion. Emotion is a weakness. Soldiers cannot adequately perform their duties when hampered by weakness." He said it like a student reciting something a teacher had drilled into him over and over again.

Which had probably been the case.

"You have no curiosity? No desire to know what emotion feels like?"

"Emotion is a—"

"Weakness. Right. But that's not necessarily true. On Earth, there have been instances in which emotion gave ordinary humans extraordinary strength and enabled them to do things they otherwise would not have been able to... like a father single-handedly lifting a car to free his son who had been hit and was trapped beneath it." Not that he knew what a car was. "That would be the equivalent of Prince Taelon lifting one of those sleek black fighter craft I saw in the hangers if it had landed on Abby."

Valok turned his head to scrutinize her. "Truly?"

"Yes. Love. Fear. A thirst for vengeance..." She smiled wryly. "Strong emotion can empower and drive you to do things you normally would not be capable of."

For just an instant, she saw a flicker of something in his eyes, there and gone so quickly she couldn't identify it.

She held out her hand. "Would you like to experience emotion?"

His gaze lowered to her hand, then returned to her face. "I am incapable of feeling emotion."

"Not necessarily. I'm an empath. I don't just feel other people's emotions. I can also alter them, imbuing them with any emotion I choose." Granted, she felt absolutely nothing when she was around the Yona. They truly did seem to be emotionless beings. But that didn't mean she couldn't give him a taste of her own. Or try to, anyway. "If nothing else, it might help you understand what motivates your non-Yona opponents."

The last argument swayed him.

Valok rested his large, grayish hand atop hers.

Simone curled her fingers around his and debated what emotion she should start with.

It might be best to start with the positive and work her way back to the negative.

She thought of her friends here on the *Kandovar*. A smile curled her lips as warmth and affection flowed through her. She loved them all like sisters and was so glad she could share this adventure with them.

Valok's eyes widened.

"You feel it?"

His lips parted. Within his muscled chest, his heart began to thump a little faster. "Yes. What is it?"

"Affection. When you love someone, *nothing* can make you leave them behind in battle. You will fight to the death for them." Next, she thought of a practical joke Eliana had played on Ava the previous day. Amusement bubbled up inside her.

The corners of Valok's eyes crinkled as his lips turned up in a smile. A rusty rumble burst forth from his mouth. His eyes widened even more as his fingers clamped down on hers. "What was that? I've never made that sound before."

She chuckled. "That was a laugh. It happens when you're amused or sometimes when you just feel happy." He must have heard Lasarans laugh many times in the past but hadn't recognized the sound when he made it himself.

An alarm began to blare, piercing her sensitive ears and startling her so much that her feet nearly flew up. "What the hell is that?" she called over it.

Valok leapt to his feet. "The ship's alarm."

Simone rose. "Is this a drill?"

"All crew members to battle stations," a male called over the ship-wide speakers. "Repeat—all crew members to battle stations. We are under attack."

Valok headed for the door. "It is not a drill."

Simone followed him out of the training room. At one end of the corridor, bodies began to pour out of the larger, gym-sized training room like fans leaving a football stadium at the end of a game.

Valok turned the opposite way and took off jogging.

Simone accompanied him, her preternatural strength and speed enabling her to keep up with his longer strides without effort. "What's happening? Who's attacking us?"

He tapped his ear. "Valok reporting. What are my orders?"

Several booms echoed through the hallways as the ship shook.

Lasarans jogged past, seeming to know exactly where to go and what to do, while Simone floundered in uncertainty. This was a massive warship! Who the hell would attack it?

"Affirmative. On my way." Valok turned a corner and headed toward the rear of the large ship.

"Where are you going?"

"Lasarans are scrambling their fighter craft. I will pilot one and join the fray."

Boom. Boom. Boom.

She staggered as the floor shook beneath her feet. "Fight who? Who's attacking us?"

"Gathendiens."

"Are you fucking kidding me?" she blurted as fury suffused her. Gathendiens had tried to commit genocide on Earth *and* Lasara. Now those bastards were trying to shoot them out of the sky? Or out of space? Or the wormhole or whatever?

"That did not translate," he replied, evincing none of the fear, anger, or determination she saw on the faces of everyone else who raced around.

"Why are Gathendiens attacking us?"

"Unknown."

Boom. Boom. Boom. Boom.

"We're still in the wormhole or *qhov'rum* thing. How is there even enough *room* to attack?" She still wasn't sure how the *qhov'rum* worked but thought it was like being in a long narrow tube that shot you forward at incredible speeds.

"The *qhov'rum* leaves little room to maneuver. You should get your people to the escape pods."

She nearly tripped over her own feet, hearing that. "Is it that bad?"

"Yes."

Simone instantly halted and reversed course. "Be safe!" she called after him and raced toward the quarters Prince Taelon had allotted to the Earthling contingent. The walls around her blurred as she put on a burst of preternatural speed.

Halfway to her destination, she passed a fellow Immortal Guardian speeding in the opposite direction.

Skidding to a halt, Simone backtracked and stopped before a bank of escape pods. Ava and Natalie, two *gifted ones* from Earth, had already entered single-occupant pods. Eliana, an Immortal Guardian who was a few inches shorter than Simone, had two more *gifted ones*—Mia and Michelle—draped over her shoulder.

"Where are the other *gifted ones*?" Simone asked as Eliana deposited the two women on their feet. Both looked terrified.

"Their quarters," Eliana said. "I'll go get them. Help these get settled in the pods." She left so quickly that she appeared to vanish into thin air.

Simone ducked into Ava's escape pod and swiftly helped her secure her go bag.

Out in the hallway, Eliana returned with Sam and Emily, then darted away again.

Simone strapped Ava into the pod's only seat and tugged at the harness. "All set?"

Ava nodded, face pale, her fear palpable.

Patting her shoulder, Simone left to help Natalie.

The ship's alarm continued to blare as one explosion after another rocked the ship.

"Shield integrity compromised," the ship's computer announced in a pleasant female voice as Simone moved on to help Mia. "Shields at seventy-nine percent."

"Oh shit," Mia whispered.

The scent of smoke reached them.

Simone struggled to appear calm for her friends' sake but felt as panicked as the others looked.

Dani, one of the other Immortal Guardians, arrived with Allison and Charlie over her shoulders as Simone left Mia's pod. Rachel followed with Liz and Madeline.

Michaela—the fifth Immortal Guardian—skidded to a halt beside them, conducted a quick headcount, then zipped away again.

More booms rocked the ship as Simone, Dani, and Rachel secured everyone else in pods.

Eliana and Michaela zipped past regularly, conveying Lasarans to other escape pods.

Once the *gifted ones* were settled, Simone closed the hatches. "I'm going to help Eliana and Michaela evacuate the Lasarans."

Rachel nodded. "We will, too."

"Be safe!" Dani called before they each sped away in a different direction.

"Shields at fifty-four percent," the computer announced in the same pleasant female voice.

Merde!

More booms thundered through the ship.

Simone skidded to a halt before two Lasaran women who wore maintenance uniforms. "Are you headed for the escape pods?"

Both nodded, eyes wide.

Simone bent, tossed them over her shoulders, and got them to the pods within seconds.

"Thank you!" one called after her as she sped away.

"Shields at fifty-four percent," the computer announced in the same pleasant female voice.

Heart pounding in her chest, Simone sped up and down the corridors, helping every man and woman she came across get to a pod. None of the Yona she encountered intended to seek refuge in an escape pod. Each seemed determined to fight to the end... or, she feared, to the death. Because Simone didn't know how many more hits this ship could take. The pungent scent of smoke seemed to intensify with every breath she took.

This can't be happening. This can't be happening.

Faces grim, her fellow immortals worked their asses off to get as many people into pods as she did. And their work soon began to pay off. The number of Lasarans Simone encountered rapidly dwindled, leaving only the Yona guards and the Lasaran soldiers.

None of them would leave voluntarily, but maybe she could help them in another way.

Thinking of Valok, Simone raced toward the closest fighter craft hanger.

The big bay door was open, allowing one after another of the sleek black Lasaran fighter craft to rocket out. Simone stopped short and stared. Beyond the bay's entrance and transparent atmospheric barrier, a battle straight out of a freaking *Star Wars* movie raged with black fighters engaging pale gray craft in deadly dogfights. Except the black fighters were the good guys. And they were severely outnumbered by the bad guys.

As she watched in horror, two gray craft fired simultaneously on a black craft.

The Lasaran craft exploded in a burst of flames.

Heart slamming against her ribcage, she glanced around.

Multiple black fighter craft remained in the hangar, awaiting pilots. Lasaran and Yona soldiers, garbed in hastily donned flight suits, ran toward them, jostling each other in their hurry.

Then Simone saw a large form she recognized. "Valok!"

His countenance stoic as usual, the brawny warrior turned toward her. "Why aren't you in an escape pod?" he asked as she hustled over to him.

"Because I want to help. I can fly one of those fighters."

"No, you can't. You don't know how."

"Yes, I do," she insisted. "I spent hours and hours hanging around the flight simulators, watching the pilots so I'd know what to do if I ever had to fly one."

He shook his head. "Your life is too valuable to risk. The Lasarans need an alliance with Earth. You should get to an escape pod. Now."

"Shields at thirty-two percent," the calm computer voice announced over the noise of departing craft.

When he started to turn away, Simone grabbed his arm. "Your life is as valuable as mine, Valok. I don't want you to sacrifice it. Let me help you." He was her friend. She didn't want him to get hurt. If having an additional ally out there flying with him and watching his back would help, she would damn well do it.

Sucking in a breath, he glanced down at her hand on his arm. "What is that?" he asked, his voice hushed. When he met her gaze, she saw what had previously been missing in his eyes.

"Emotion," she said. "You're my friend. I don't want to lose you. Let me help you. *Please.*"

Boom. Boom. Boom.

"Shields at twenty percent," the calm female voice announced.

Light flashed to their left. Fire flared, so bright it hurt her eyes, as a blast wave knocked her and Valok off their feet.

Simone landed on her back several yards away. Her head struck the hard deck with a crack. Pain careened through her skull, stunning her for a long moment.

Then Valok leaned over her.

Dizziness engulfed her as he scooped her into his arms and started running. "What...? What happened?"

He didn't respond.

Boom. Boom. Boom. Boom.

"Shields at thirteen percent," the computer announced placidly.

Simone gripped his shirt and struggled to think straight. "Valok?"

The light above her dimmed. Then her butt hit something cushy as he set her down.

A seat?

She glanced around, her vision a little blurry. "Where are we?"

"An escape pod. There is little time." Valok's voice carried an urgency she had never heard him express before. His big hands pressed her back in the chair and tugged straps across her chest.

"What?"

Boom. Boom. Boom.

Her head began to clear. Her thoughts sharpened as the Yona warrior straightened and spun away. "Valok?"

He ducked out of the pod, then turned and met her confused gaze. "Thank you."

Simone shook her head. "For what?"

"Letting me feel."

The hatch closed.

"Wait!" She lunged forward but was jerked to a halt by the harness. Her fingers fumbled for the latches.

Boom!

Bright light flared beyond the crystal windshield as flames burst into being.

Her heart stopped as shock rippled through her.

That had to have hit Valok!

"No!" she screamed in horror.

The pod jerked, shoving her back in the seat like a roller coaster embarking on a ride. A roar arose, accompanied by thunks. The pressure pushing her back against the seat increased as light flickered on and off. Then black space filled the window.

A small gray craft shot past, followed closely by a sleek, black fighter.

The black fighter fired its weapons and blew the gray craft to bits. But Simone was too shaken by Valok's death to cheer.

An escape pod flew by with two gray Gathendien craft in pursuit.

A deafening roar shook the pod as flames lit up the darkness.

Then the bright walls of the *qhov'rum* rose before her, blocking everything else.

Light exploded around her. A screeching, grinding noise filled the pod, so loud it magnified the ache in her head tenfold.

Then quiet fell, broken only by her pounding heart and gasping breaths.

Moisture filled her eyes as she stared through the window at calm, black space.

"Evie?" she asked, voice hushed.

"Yes?" the computer responded. One of the Lasarans had told her they named the computer after either the engineer who had installed it or designed it. But she was too shaken to remember if it was E.V. or Evie.

"Did the *Kandovar* just explode?" *Please, say no. Please, say no.*

"Affirmative."

She closed her eyes. Tears she couldn't hold back slipped down her cheeks. "How many crew members were still aboard?"

She knew Valok had been. She'd seen the explosion that took him.

Her hands curled into tight fists on her thighs as sadness warred with burgeoning anger. Why hadn't he gotten into the damn pod with her?

"Unknown," the computer responded.

"Did the other escape pods launch?"

"According to my last contact with the *Kandovar*, many escape pods launched successfully before the ship was destroyed."

Then all of the *gifted ones* should've gotten away safely.

What of her fellow Immortal Guardians? The last time she'd seen them, they had been scrambling to get everyone else to safety. Had they made it to pods, too? Or had explosions taken them, as well?

Her hands began to shake. "Would you please attempt to hail the ship?"

"The ship is no longer intact," Evie stated. "Any attempts to hail it—"

"Just do it!" Simone snapped as she swiped at her wet cheeks.

"Attempting to hail the Kandovar." A moment passed. "Unable to make contact."

"Try to hail the other escape pods."

"Hailing escape pods now."

She'd seen two Gathendien fighter craft chasing down an escape pod. What if those bastards were picking them off, one by one? Were they in there killing all her friends while she sat on her ass doing nothing?

"All attempts to hail other escape pods have failed."

She swallowed past the lump in her throat. "Were they destroyed in the blast?"

"Unlikely. Escape pods are built to withstand extreme temperatures so they can provide shelter on planets with uninhabitable environments."

"Then why can't you contact them?"

"The range of this pod's communications system is limited. The other pods may have already traveled beyond its reach."

"How is that possible? The pods probably launched only minutes before this one did."

"The *qhov'rum* propels craft forward at speeds that even the fastest engines cannot replicate. If the *qhov'rum* remained functional after this pod breached its walls, it has already carried any escape pods and fighter craft that remained within it a distance that would take this pod with its weaker engine many months to traverse."

This pod only carried two months of supplies.

"What about the pods that were thrust through the walls of the *quov'rum* by the blast like this one?"

"They are likely scattered across vast sectors of space now. My inability to contact them supports that conjecture."

Simone thought furiously. "Can we reenter the *quov'rum*?"

"Negative. This pod's engine cannot generate the propulsion required to breach the walls."

So the explosion must have hurled the pod through it. "Are there any Lasaran outposts near us?"

"Negative."

"What about Yona outposts?"

"Negative."

"Any space stations or spaceports?"

"Negative."

"Are there any habitable planets nearby?"

"Negative."

"Any ships belonging to members of the Aldebarian Alliance?"

"Negative."

Frustration rose. "Well, there must be *something* nearby! Space may be vast, but it isn't freaking empty!"

"Affirmative."

She blinked. "What?" Then she frowned. If the computer told her that space was indeed vast, Simone would lose it. She'd just watched Valok die in a blast of fire. Her immortal friends might very well have been killed, too. Those small Gathendien fighter craft could be blowing up her mortal friends who managed to escape in pods. And the Lasaran and Yona soldiers who'd remained on the ship...

More tears rose.

"Affirmative," Evie repeated placidly. "My sensors have detected something nearby."

Finally! "What is it?"

"A Gathendien warship."

Simone sat up straighter. "What? Why the hell didn't you tell me?"

"Gathendien ships were not on your list of inquiries."

Computers could be so maddeningly literal! "Well, where is it?"

"It exited the *quov'rum* moments before this pod did."

Simone unsnapped her harness and lunged for the window, peering all around. "I don't see it."

"It is too far away to see."

"How is that—?" Oh. Right. The *quov'rum* moved everything forward so quickly that even a few seconds could cover vast distances.

Then the meaning of the computer's words dawned on her.

The Gathendien warship had been inside the *quov'rum*.

Everything within her went still. Her tears ceased. Her jaw clenched. "Is the ship you're detecting the one that blew up the *Kandovar*?"

"Though I cannot determine that with certainty, the timing and placement of the ship make such possible."

Absolute fury filled her, accompanied by cold determination. "How far away is it? Is it close enough for us to reach?"

"Affirmative. Unless the Gathendien ship alters its current speed and trajectory, this pod can reach it in under two months."

"And if they alter their current speed and trajectory?"

"I cannot provide an accurate estimate at this time."

"But more than two months?"

"It is possible."

"Will this pod keep me alive longer than two months if I slow my breathing and ration food and water?"

"Affirmative."

"Then take me to that ship."

"Setting course for the Gathendien warship now."

Simone stared out the window, willing the time to pass quickly.

She would make those bastards pay.

She'd make them pay for *every* life they had taken.

CHAPTER ONE

A CHIME SOUNDED IN the distance, repeating every few moments—each trill louder than the previous—until the noise seemed to pound through Simone's head. "What the hell?" she growled with a grimace.

The chime ceased. "I am awakening you as per your instructions," Evie stated calmly, as if she hadn't just assaulted Simone's eardrums with the most annoying sound ever. "You asked me to rouse you when we approached the Gathendien warship."

"Right. Thank you." Groaning, she sat up and pressed a button on the armrest to transform her narrow bed back into a seat. "How close are we?"

"We should be able to hail them within one Alliance hour."

"Can they see us?"

"Negative."

"What about radar? Can they see us on their radar or whatever they use to detect craft from long distances?"

"Negative."

"Okay. Thanks." Jaw cracking in a wide yawn, Simone rose and headed into the tiny bathroom or *lav* the pod boasted. There wasn't much to it, just a weird space toilet and cabinets stocked with towels, cleansing cloths, a first aid kit, and *wosuur* liquid.

She quickly doffed her black hunting garb and dropped it into the clothing sanitizer. A low hum sounded. After utilizing the space toilet, she rinsed her mouth with *wosuur* liquid, which cleaned teeth more efficiently than brushing and flossing, and used the cleansing cloths to take the pod's version of a shower.

"Damn, I miss soap and hot water," she grumbled.

Simone still had a plentiful supply of pretty much everything. One of the perks she enjoyed as an Immortal Guardian was the ability to slow her metabolism and sleep whenever or however long she wanted to. Unfortunately, she also needed frequent blood transfusions to maintain her preternatural speed and strength. Yet she had no ready blood supply.

Unwilling to take on the Gathendiens while weak as a kitten, she had therefore spent most of the trip in a deep healing sleep.

A very *long*, deep healing sleep.

The clothing sanitizer dinged.

Opening it, she drew out her now-clean black T-shirt and cargo pants. Socks, a bra, and matching bikini underwear, too. Thank goodness this thing could sanitize clothing. Unlike the *gifted ones* she had helped into escape pods, she didn't have a handy go bag full of clothes and other essentials. Valok barely had time to shove her in here before the ship exploded.

Sadness pierced her once more at the thought of him. Guilt did, too. Perhaps if she hadn't thrown him by letting him feel emotion, he would've left her to her own devices and made it into one of the fighter craft in time to escape death.

She kept seeing his face as he'd thanked her for letting him feel.

Her stomach growled.

Giving her head a shake, she retrieved three of the pod's MREs and set them in the food prep thing that rehydrated and heated them. When her stomach again rumbled impatiently, she grabbed a nutrition bar, peeled off the wrapper, and took a big bite.

Immortal Guardians burned numerous calories when they moved and fought with preternatural speed. She was going to need a hell of a lot of carbs to fuel the fight she intended to take to the Gathendiens.

She'd just downed the last of the nutrition bar when the food prep thing dinged.

Steam and a mouthwateringly delicious aroma spilled out when she opened the door.

Simone didn't even sit down. She just grabbed a utensil that resembled a spork, drew out the first tray, and dug in.

"Mmmmm," she voiced around a heady mouthful, "this is so good." She wouldn't have thought an escape pod would boast such tasty food. Clearly, the Lasarans liked to travel in comfort, even when the trip was unexpected enough to warrant a jaunt in an escape pod.

She was well into her third meal when Evie spoke.

"I believe the Gathendiens have spotted us."

It had taken Simone multiple tries to get Evie to say *us* instead of *you*. Being stranded in space was much more tolerable when one could pretend the pod's computer was a friend and didn't feel so alone. "What makes you say that?"

"I detected the brush of their radar. And the ship appears to be turning in our direction."

Simone grunted. "Do you think they know we're in a Lasaran escape pod?"

"Uncertain."

Belly full, she set the last empty tray aside. "Well, let's make sure they do." Rounding the seat in the center of the pod, she sat down and eyed the command screen in front of her.

"What is your intent?" Evie inquired placidly.

"I intend to contact them and play the helpless young thing in a red hood who's too green to realize she's talking to the big bad wolf."

"I am unable to glean your meaning. Please repeat using alternate terms."

A dark smile curled Simone's lips. "I intend to deceive them. Can you limit our contact to audio and keep them from seeing me?"

"Affirmative."

"Perfect. Once you open communications with them, don't interrupt, contradict, or correct me."

"Affirmative. Do you wish me to hail them now?"

"Yes, please."

A moment passed. "Begin communication," Evie instructed.

"Hello?" Simone called, pitching her voice higher than usual and filling it with what she considered an excellent combination of desperation and hope. "Hello? Is anyone there? Please, answer me." For added effect, she whispered, "Please, let them answer."

"Identify yourself," a gruff voice responded.

"Oh, thank goodness!" she gushed. "My name is Simone. I was a passenger on the *Kandovar*. We were on our way to Lasara and... I don't know what happened. I think the ship was attacked, or maybe it malfunctioned or—"

"You are Lasaran?"

"What? No. I was just a passenger." She added a tremor to her voice. "One of the Yona pushed me into this pod and launched it. Then there was a big explosion and a loud grinding noise and..." She faked a sob. "I don't know where I am. I've just been floating out here alone for weeks and haven't been able to contact anyone."

"You are not Lasaran?" he pressed.

"No." She added a sniffle. "I'm from Earth. This is my first time in space. I don't know how anything works. And my supplies are starting to run out. Can you please help me?"

"We will come to your aid."

Simone could be wrong, but she was pretty sure even a helpless young thing would've had second thoughts after hearing his less than friendly, growled responses. Nevertheless, she infused her voice with hope. "You will?"

"Yes."

"Oh, thank you! Thank you so much! How do I reach you? What do I do?"

"Nothing. We will bring your pod aboard our ship as soon as we reach you." She barely managed to sputter one last *thank you* before he snarled, "End communication."

A brief moment passed.

"The Gathendien ship has ended communication and can no longer hear you," Evie announced.

Simone smiled. "Excellent. Those dumb bastards have no idea what they're unleashing on their ship."

"What *are* they unleashing?" Evie asked.

She rose. "Me."

By the time the Gathendiens locked what Evie called an acquisition beam on the pod, Simone was ready. The lights flickered out as Evie had warned, and Evie ceased responding.

Simone's heart thudded with anticipation. Adrenaline flooded her veins and quickened her pulse. Her long, dark hair floated up as the pod's gravity failed. But the seat's harness kept her from joining it.

When the pod entered the Gathendien docking bay, her hair flopped back down as the ship's artificial gravity became her own, and her body sank deeper into the seat.

She swiftly unlatched the seatbelts, rose, and grabbed her katanas' harness. Plunging her arms through the loops, she rounded the chair and let the long, sheathed weapons settle against her back. The daggers she always carried with her—even on the *Kandovar*—already waited in sheaths on her thighs. She glanced at the white spacesuit that hung nearby but had already decided it would encumber her movements too much. Plus, she shouldn't need it. The docking bay should provide adequate atmosphere and pressurization.

Simone drew in a long, slow, calming breath and released it. Feet braced apart, she faced the pod's hatch, which was positioned high on the wall in front of her. Her toes wiggled inside her combat boots. She flexed her fingers and rotated her shoulders, not to loosen her muscles but because she was eager to dive into battle.

These bastards had killed Valok.

They'd killed every Lasaran and Yona who had failed to leave the ship before it exploded.

They'd killed some or all of the Lasaran and Yona pilots who had tried desperately to defend the *Kandovar* in their fighter craft.

And they might have killed her fellow Immortal Guardians if her friends hadn't had time to reach escape pods. Maybe some of the *gifted ones*, too, if the reptilian bastards had captured their pods.

"This is for them," she murmured.

The pod shook as a loud thunk sounded.

"*All* of them." Every drop of blood spilled would be repaid with ten.

Light shone down into the pod like a spotlight as the hatch opened and slid to one side.

Simone backed into the shadows.

Seconds later, a bulky figure appeared at the entrance and blocked most of the light, allowing her to blend better into the darkness.

Though he couldn't spot her, she could see him very well.

He was big. And definitely Gathendien.

Dark green hide that looked as tough as an alligator's stretched across a bald head and down to broad shoulders, at which point it thickened, forming ridges that wound down two thickly muscled arms.

She suspected those ridges served well as armor to protect him. But on the inside of those arms, she spied thinner skin of a golden color that appeared far more vulnerable. The same golden skin adorned powerful pecs, rippling abs, and his face. As far as she could tell, he had no protruding ears, just small holes that must allow him to hear. Two pale green eyes equipped with pupils like a snake's, a subtle nose, and thin lips merely added to his reptilian appearance.

Aim for the gold, she thought with satisfaction, cataloging every single weakness.

Those slitted eyes narrowed as he peered into the pod. "I don't see it."

It? Really?

Once more, Simone affected a helpless voice. "Are you… are you the man I spoke with?"

"No." Though gruff, his voice didn't match the one she'd heard earlier.

"But you're here to rescue me? You're a friend of the Lasarans?"

"Yes. We are allies with the Lasarans."

Bullshit. "Thank goodness," she breathed.

"Exit the pod," he ordered.

She palmed a dagger and faked a sniffle. "I can't. I was injured when the Yona threw me in here. Can you help me, please? I don't think I can make it up the ladder on my own."

Irritation flashed across his countenance before he glanced down to one side.

"Do it," the voice that had spoken over the comms ordered.

Sighing with what resembled human exasperation, the hulking Gathendien warrior squeezed through the entrance and jumped down into the pod.

Simone cut his throat the second he landed, then eased his thrashing body to the floor. She would've preferred to wait and strike *after* assessing the numbers she would face outside but assumed they would question her helplessness as soon as they spotted the swords strapped to her back.

"Oh," she blurted with feigned dismay for the benefit of her audience as the thrashing died down. "Did I step on your tail? I'm so sorry." Sheathing her dagger, she stepped over the bastard and headed for the wall beneath the opening. It took mere moments to scale the rungs that led up to the hatch. "Don't let go," she implored, as if the disgruntled dead guy were helping her, then poked her head up.

The pod rested in a sizable docking bay that housed a couple of transports and a few gray fighter craft. The big bay door slid shut behind her. On the opposite wall, the entrance to the rest of the ship remained open, indicating their belief that she posed no threat.

She dropped her gaze. Below, roughly two dozen Gathendien soldiers waited all in a row. A Gathendien who was riddled with scars and boasted an air of command stood in front of them, his arms crossed over a barrel chest. All were heavily armed.

The leader scowled up at her.

"Are you the man I spoke to?" she asked tremulously, trying hard to look frightened even as rage engulfed her.

"Yes," he barked and motioned to a staircase that looked as though they'd wheeled it up to the pod's opening. "Exit the pod."

The staircase looked so incongruously low-tech—like something you'd see at a cash-strapped airport back on Earth—that she wanted to laugh.

Instead, she stretched a hand toward it before letting her shoulders slump. "I can't reach it. Would you move it closer, please?"

If a green lizardman could turn red with anger, this guy would've.

23

At first, she thought he'd refuse. Then he made an abrupt motion with one clawed hand.

One of the soldiers behind him hustled forward and pushed the staircase up against the pod's side with a clunk.

"Thank you." Simone offered them a tremulous smile and slowly rose into the entrance, making every movement appear as tentative and shaky as possible. She even looked down into the pod and said, "Don't let me fall."

Careful to keep her front facing the warriors below, she hoped the hair she'd left loose would adequately conceal the hilts of her katanas until she stood on the lip of the hatch.

So far, so good.

"Thank you so much for helping me." She gave the leader a nervous smile.

The commander's gaze drifted from her face to her shoulder as she placed one booted foot on the top step of the staircase. His eyes narrowed. Uncrossing and lowering his bulging arms, he barked, "Gongra!" Was that the name of the soldier she'd killed?

Time to strike.

Moving so swiftly she blurred, Simone leapt to the ground, drew a katana, and swung.

The Gathendien soldiers gaped as their commander's head fell from his shoulders, toppled to the ground, and rolled away. Taking advantage of their shock, Simone drew her other katana and attacked.

Chaos erupted.

Reptilian blood splattered her.

For Valok and my friends.

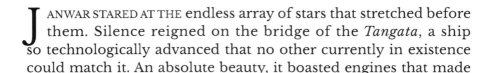

J ANWAR STARED AT THE endless array of stars that stretched before them. Silence reigned on the bridge of the *Tangata*, a ship so technologically advanced that no other currently in existence could match it. An absolute beauty, it boasted engines that made

Aldebarian Alliance ships appear to plod along like ancient *navoxi* pulling wagonloads of *alavinin* ore in comparison.

A good thing since Janwar and his crew were pirates and often benefitted from their ability to outmaneuver law-abiding folk.

He glanced around.

His crew was oddly quiet tonight. Did they share the same peculiar feeling of unrest that had plagued him of late?

He frowned, unable to pinpoint the source of it.

"I miss Lisa," Soval announced. The hulking Domaran warrior slumped in his seat, face more somber than usual.

"And Abby." Elchan, the Segonian in their midst, added.

The rest nodded.

Janwar smiled, thinking of Lasaran Prince Taelon and the Earth female he'd taken as his lifemate. Janwar considered Taelon a friend, as implausible as that seemed to others. Lasarans were well known for being stringent rule followers. So a Lasaran Prince befriending a consummate lawbreaker like Janwar...

He grinned. Both men rather enjoyed the bafflement their friendship inspired. When Srok'a had recently been stricken with a vision that compelled them to race to the outer reaches of explored space, Janwar had been shocked to discover that Prince Taelon's ship had been attacked and destroyed.

Fortunately, Taelon's Yona guard had shoved him and his new family into a royal transport and launched it in time to save their lives. Then Janwar had swept in and rescued them.

He'd enjoyed Lisa's company during the weeks it had taken them to ferry the royal couple to Lasara. No other woman had stepped foot on their ship since its creation. And he had to admit her tinkling laughter had breathed new life into it. The Earthling had not experienced the lofty upbringing Prince Taelon had. Quite the opposite, actually. And she was delightfully uncomfortable with being treated like royalty, something that had amused his hardened, cynical crew and swiftly won them over.

None of them, of course, had been able to resist the plump-cheeked grins and high-pitched giggles of Abby, Taelon and Lisa's infant daughter.

"Hopefully, our usual methods of investigation will enable us to locate some of her friends," Janwar commented.

At last count, only three of the women from Earth who'd been aboard the *Kandovar* had been rescued. The rest, some presumed, were either dead or soon would be when the provisions in their escape pods ran out. Taelon had disclosed in their latest communication that one of the rescued women—Janwar believed her name was Ava—had been captured by the Gathendiens and tortured, confirming their suspicions that the Gathendiens had risked everything and attacked the *Kandovar* solely to get their hands on the Earthlings.

Apparently, they believed the women were the key to discovering why a bioengineered virus the Gathendiens released on Earth long ago hadn't succeeded in eradicating all Earthlings and leaving the planet and all its resources ripe for claiming.

"*Grunarks*," he grumbled.

His cousin Krigara glanced over at him. "Who?"

"The Gathendiens."

All nodded.

Janwar looked at Soval. "How much longer?"

"We should be able to see them without radar within minutes."

Good. Most pirates' strengths lay in their numbers, weaponry, and lack of a moral compass.

Janwar and his small crew's strength, however, lay in the intelligence they gathered and how they chose to use it.

A primary source of his intel had located a Gathendien warship that had gone undetected by the Aldebarian Alliance's various fleets, which—lacking the *Tangata's* more powerful engines—still struggled to reach these distances without the benefit of the damaged *quov'rum*.

The Gathendien ship was close enough to the wreckage of the *Kandovar* to draw suspicion and spark speculation that it had either taken part in the attack or was searching for survivors to slay or capture.

Janwar leaned forward in his seat as a spec appeared amid the stars visible beyond the large, indestructible crystal window that stretched before them. "There it is," he murmured.

"In all its *drekking* glory," Krigara muttered. "I don't know how they manage to travel such distances in those pathetic boxes of *bura*."

Janwar nodded. The Gathendien ship that gradually grew in size as they approached it looked as if a boy not quite old enough to grow a beard had constructed it out of spare parts scavenged from a refuse heap. Even the color—a dark, putrid yellow that reminded him of vomit—lacked appeal.

"Any indication they know we're coming?" he asked.

"None," Srok'a's scarred brother Kova mumbled.

Any other answer would've shocked Janwar. His ship's cloaking ability was without equal, so ships only saw the *Tangata* coming if he *wanted* them to see it coming.

In very little time, the Gathendien battleship filled the window.

"Perform a life-form scan and see how many are on board," he ordered.

Elchan studied his console. "Looks like they have a full contingent aboard."

Janwar rubbed his hands together with glee. "This should be fun then."

Every face lit with a smile of anticipation. All loved a good battle. It got the blood flowing and distracted them from the loneliness their status as rebels and outcasts sometimes spawned.

"That's odd," Elchan said, his brow puckering.

Janwar glanced at him. "What is?"

"I think the life-form scanner may be malfunctioning."

"Why?"

Elchan looked up from his console. "The Gathendiens' numbers appear to be dwindling."

Janwar stared at him. "What?"

"Their numbers are dwindling." Elchan again consulted his screen, then pointed at it. "There! It just did it again. Two more disappeared. And a third."

Krigara crossed to stand beside Elchan and studied the screen. His eyebrows shot up. "It's true. The lights that indicate life forms are vanishing, one or two at a time." He nudged Elchan. "Run a diagnostic."

A hush descended.

After a moment, Elchan shook his head. "Nothing. The scan appears to be performing as intended."

"It can't be," Soval grumbled.

Janwar regarded the Gathendien warship with suspicion.

"Could they have obtained some sort of new cloaking mechanism?" Elchan asked hesitantly.

Srok'a scowled. "To borrow one of Lisa's phrases, what kind of backwards-ass cloaking mechanism would cloak the life forms but not the ship?"

"Good point," Kova added. "The ship is still visible."

Krigara motioned to Elchan's screen. "But according to the scan, it will soon be bereft of life."

Janwar's eyes narrowed. "It's a trick. They must know we're here."

"How?" Krigara countered. "We have the best cloaking system in the galaxy."

Which wasn't an exaggeration. "The life forms didn't start disappearing until we came within shooting range of them. They *must* know we're here." It was odd, though, that they would conceal their life forms—and in such a ragged fashion—instead of the ship itself. Perhaps they hoped anyone approaching would think it a ghost ship bereft of life and become complacent? Or maybe they hoped other vessels would see the life forms disappearing, one by one, and fear contagion? Gathendiens did, after all, make a habit of genetically engineering deadly viruses in their labs.

"What do you want to do?" his cousin asked.

"Get close enough to board them," Janwar ordered.

Before Kova could navigate them closer, Elchan shook his head. "I don't think that's a good idea."

"Why?"

"Because I'm detecting heat signatures that weren't there a minute ago."

"More life forms?" Their bizarre cloaking device must be failing.

"No."

"What *kind* of heat signatures?"

"The kind that usually accompanies explosions."

Silence.

What the *srul* was happening on that ship?

"Maybe their cloaking array is malfunctioning?" Srok'a suggested, his tone indicating his doubt.

But Elchan shook his head again. "Not unless by *malfunctioning* you mean blowing them all up because—if my scanner is correct—Gathendiens are dropping like *tikluns*." The fuzzy mammals on Segonia were known for keeling over as though dead anytime something startled them.

Janwar refused to let the rather amusing image of Gathendiens doing the same thing distract him. "Whatever is happening, we need the information those *grunarks* can provide." Time was running out for the survivors of the *Kandovar's* destruction. "Soval, pull up beside them and extend the docking tube. Kova, run a full diagnostic on all systems. If our life-form scan is malfunctioning, I want to know what else might be, too."

Kova refocused on his console and went to work.

Soval began to ease the *Tangata* closer to the Gathendien ship.

"Wait," Srok'a said.

Janwar sighed. "Now what?"

"One of the docking bay doors is rising."

"Then it *is* a trap." Janwar relaxed back in his seat, happy to be back on normal footing. "Arm weapons. Reinforce shields and cloaking."

"Weapons armed," Soval announced.

"Shields and cloaking at full power," Elchan said.

Janwar turned to his cousin. "Krigara, get in a fighter and prepare to chase whatever leaves that bay. Wait for my command."

Krigara strode from the bridge.

Janwar stared at the Gathendien ship as a crack of light appeared along the bottom of the docking bay door.

Air and debris shot out as it rose.

"Their atmospheric shield must be down," he murmured. Had it been in place, it would've maintained proper atmosphere and pressure in the bay so crewmembers could continue to perform their duties while craft came and went.

Soval grunted. "I hope they evacuated the bay before—"

Several Gathendiens tumbled out, limbs flailing, reptilian tails flicking, and mouths opening in screams no one could hear in the vacuum of space.

None wore protective suits. All died.

Had Janwar not sorely needed information, he would've cheered. As far as he was concerned, the only good Gathendien was a dead Gathendien.

A figure in a white protective suit was nearly sucked out after them but managed to grab hold of the edge of the bay's opening and jerked to a halt.

Janwar grunted. At least they'd found *someone* they could interrogate.

A small transport zoomed out of the bay, nearly dislodging the man who clung to the edge.

Janwar tapped the ship-wide comm button on his command chair. "Krigara, are you ready?"

"Almost there."

"Get your ass in the seat now. A transport just left the ship."

Curses carried over the line, accompanied by the thuds of boots hitting the deck at a brisk pace.

Janwar scrutinized the transport. It was Akseli in design and created more for fleeing enemies than finding refuge during an emergency, so it would be faster than most transports. He didn't worry though. The *Tangata* could easily catch it, as could their fighter craft.

"What the *srul*?" Elchan muttered.

Janwar returned his gaze to the Gathendiens' docking bay.

The figure clinging to the bay's frame wore a helmet that hid his features and a baggy white suit that lacked any noticeable accommodation for the long tail every Gathendien sported.

"That's not a Gathendien," Elchan stated.

Janwar contemplated the figure. "Perhaps he lost his tail in an accident." The *grunarks were* prone to violence.

Drawing his knees almost to his chest, the figure in white shifted until his feet were braced on the bay's edge. But he didn't make his way inside as they all expected. Instead, he looked out at the transport for a long moment, then pushed off. Hard.

"What the *drek*?" Elchan muttered.

CHAPTER TWO

"**A**RE YOU *DREKKING* SEEING this?" Soval exclaimed.

Janwar ignored his friends' comments and focused on the figure.

Was he trying to catch up with his shipmates?

To what end? Even if he miraculously managed to utilize precisely the right speed and trajectory, it wasn't as though the shuttle could just open the hatch and let him in. That wasn't how transports worked. Once in space, the only way a shuttle could safely open its hatch was if a ship locked a docking tube to it capable of pressurization *and*—if they were wise—decontamination.

But the likelihood of the figure who currently cut through space with the speed of a *morilium* missile even coming close enough to the shuttle to—

"*Drek*!" Elchan blurted. "I think he's going to make it."

Janwar stared. *Vuan*, if it didn't look like it. And yet... "He's going too fast to find a handhold."

Srok'a's face lit with excitement. "I'll wager fifty credits that he makes it."

"Done," Soval responded, leaning forward.

Bets began to fly as swiftly as the figure in white did.

"Ha!" Srok'a crowed as the figure grabbed hold of one of the transport's exterior ladder rungs and held on tight. "He did it!"

Those who had bet against him all groaned.

Soval shook his head. "What does he intend to do now—cling to the exterior until the pilot finds a place to land?"

If so, the atmosphere of any habitable planet they sought to land upon would burn him up.

"Where exactly is the craft going?" Elchan asked, his expression baffled.

Janwar leaned back in his chair. "He's fleeing *us*. They know we're here."

"How?" Elchan countered. "I see nothing that indicates our systems aren't fully functional. We're still cloaked. They *can't* know we're here."

Krigara's voice floated out of the bridge speakers. "I'm in the fighter. Do you want me to deploy?"

"Hold for a moment," Janwar murmured. He wanted to see what would happen next.

The figure in white crept along the exterior of the transport until he reached the front window. Tucking one arm in a handhold, he raised what looked like a *tronium* blaster in his other hand and fired.

Soval grunted. "He must be new."

All nodded. Every space-faring craft—large or small—constructed during the past two centuries bore windows made of indestructible *stovicun* crystal. If the *Kandovar* had indeed been destroyed, Janwar did not doubt that the dislodged windows floated through space, wholly intact, sporting nary a crack.

When it became clear that the window would not break, the figure holstered his weapon and gave the occupants a gesture known throughout alliance-occupied space to be obscene.

Elchan laughed. "I don't think he appreciates being left behind."

Janwar battled amusement as the figure crept along the shuttle's exterior once more. "Any movement from the warship?"

Kova shook his head. "All is quiet there. Engines appear to be at full stop."

This was so odd. "Follow the transport." They'd piqued his curiosity now.

The transport began to swing back and forth in an attempt to shake off their furious shipmate. But the white figure clung tenaciously to its surface. Not far from the shuttle's front window, he again anchored himself to the shuttle with one hand and fired a continuous stream from his *tronium* blaster at the edge of the hatch.

Quiet fell once more as all watched, unable to guess the outcome.

"What's happening?" Krigara asked.

"The figure in white is trying to cut into the transport." Janwar nodded to Srok'a. "Send him the feed."

A moment later, his cousin let out a disbelieving laugh.

Elchan frowned. "He can't really cut his way in, can he?"

"With a *tronium* blaster?" Janwar shook his head. "It might heat the metal enough to make those inside nervous, but it won't penetrate or puncture it."

"What are those things on his back?" Krigara asked.

Two dark stripes Janwar had initially thought part of the suit's design moved back and forth as the figure was jostled. "Enhance visual."

The transport's image grew and sharpened, as did the figure in white.

He frowned. "I think they're swords."

As though hearing him, the figure holstered his blaster and drew a long sword. He took a moment to reposition himself on the transport's surface, kneeling with both feet wedged beneath a handrail. Then he angled the blade downward in front of him, gripped the hilt at the top, drew it back over his head, then plunged it down into the metal he'd just heated.

Janwar stared.

Again the man drew his sword up and drove it down into the metal.

"That *grunark* is *very* determined," Elchan said.

Too bad he wouldn't succeed. Janwar found himself rooting for the odd figure. Aside from rescuing Taelon, Lisa, and Abby, this was the most entertaining thing he'd witnessed in years.

But even heated, that metal wouldn't give. It was designed to withstand atmospheric entry and planetary temperatures that would instantly kill— "What the *dreck*?" he blurted and leaned forward once more.

A little plume of atmosphere rose in front of the figure.

"Did he just pierce the hatch?" Soval asked, eyes wide.

"How is that possible?" Krigara blurted, watching the feed down in his fighter craft.

Janwar could only stare. "I don't know."

The sword rose and descended a third time, then a fourth.

This time he saw it sink into the hatch's edge! No being Janwar knew of possessed the strength to accomplish that aside from the cyborgs the Akseli military had created.

Yet that was no cyborg. He knew that with absolute certainty. Years ago, the Akselis had announced that they'd decommissioned and destroyed all their biomechanical creations. The chances of encountering one on a Gathendien ship were nonexistent.

The plume of venting atmosphere grew.

Returning his sword to the sheathe on his back with an ease that bespoke years of practice, the figure reached down and tugged at something.

Janwar gaped as the man wrenched the hatch open, exposing the cramped control room and panicked Gathendien warriors inside.

None wore suits. Some bore weapons that venting atmosphere yanked out of their hands and deposited outside. All scrambled to hold on to something. One was sucked into space, arms, legs, and tail waving. The figure in white reached in and yanked another out as easily as he would a helpless little *gravi* even though the Gathendien was big and bulky with muscle. Then he yanked out another and another, something that became easier as the cold and absence of breathable air slowed their struggles and weakened their hold.

Another hush settled upon the bridge of the *Tangata* as all watched in stunned fascination.

His mission complete, the figure in white sat back on his heels—toes still tucked in a handhold—rested his hands on his thighs, and lowered his head as though catching his breath.

Janwar had never seen anything like it. "Any movement in the warship?"

"None," Elchan said. "Only a few life forms remain. None are moving."

"And the ship remains stationary," Kova added.

Janwar kept his gaze on the white figure.

"What do you want to do?" Kova asked.

He pondered it a moment. "Disable cloaking."

How would that figure in white react when an unidentified warship suddenly appeared beside him?

"Disabling cloaking."

Janwar knew the moment the figure saw them from the corner of his eye. His heaving chest stilled. His helmet rose. Then the faceplate turned their way, the massive ship reflected upon its surface.

A heartbeat passed. Then the figure threw up his hands in a gesture of exasperation Janwar had seen Lisa make a time or two while she blurted, "Are you kidding me?"

Vuan, if it didn't make him smile and bite back a laugh.

Some of his crew didn't bother, their laughter filling the bridge.

"I'm starting to like this man," Soval declared, his deep voice full of mirth.

Janwar was, too. But he would still have to capture and interrogate him... along with the rest of the Gathendien crew.

The figure in white clambered inside the transport and disappeared from view.

Like the Gathendien warship, the transport now floated before them like a ghost ship. "He isn't going anywhere," Janwar decided after a couple of minutes. "Elchan, I want you to join Krigara in his fighter and board the Gathendien ship. We need to know if those life-form scans are accurate. Gear up in case they are. There may be a contagion of some sort."

Elchan left the bridge.

Janwar turned to the Rakessian brothers. "Srok'a, Kova, take a second fighter and accompany them."

Nodding, the two rose and departed.

If the scans were wrong and the ship was still heavily populated with soldiers, Janwar was confident the four would nevertheless be able to fight their way to the bridge and commandeer the ship. They weren't the most feared pirates in the galaxy for no reason.

He and Soval waited quietly, dividing their attention between the transport and the warship.

Two sleek fighters raced toward the ugly Gathendien ship and boldly entered the docking bay.

Long minutes passed.

"Looks like someone disabled the atmospheric shield from here in the bay," Krigara commented.

Janwar frowned. "Is it still operational?" He needed live Gathendiens to question.

"Give me a minute." One soon stretched into several. "Got it," he said with a touch of triumph. "We're going in."

Mere seconds ticked past before curses erupted over the comm.

"I see why the one in white didn't want to be left behind," Krigara commented. "There are a *srul* of a lot of dead bodies here."

Janwar frowned. "How many?"

"Enough to make me think the life-form scan was accurate."

"Cause of death?"

"Battle," Krigara disclosed grimly. "This was no contagion."

"Stay alert." Janwar and his crew weren't the only pirates in the galaxy. Another party could've snuck aboard the last time the Gathendiens docked, intending to wrench control from them.

A quick search of the ship yielded more dead and several wounded. All of the latter were unconscious but would likely survive.

Yet the ship appeared to be free of hostile forces.

What had happened? Had there been a mutiny?

Janwar's gaze slid to the transport.

Had the figure in white been trying to *escape* the bloodbath, or had he *instigated* it?

"Elchan, lockdown the bridge controls. Then I want you all to return to the *Tangata*."

"Doing it now."

If one man had wrought that much damage, he wanted his entire crew back on board when they confronted him. That was a remarkable feat. Gathendiens did *not* go down quickly. Their thick reptilian hide was difficult to penetrate with a blade and could even withstand a few e-blasts. Throw in fear of the punishment their volatile emperor would meet out to any who failed in their missions, and they became even harder to kill, most choosing to fight to the death rather than face his wrath.

Janwar studied the transport and detected no hint of movement inside it.

Once his men returned, he and Soval confirmed the *Tangata's* shields were still functioning at maximum efficiency, then headed down to the docking bay, pausing only long enough to visit the armory.

Krigara, Elchan, Srok'a, and Kova exited two fighter craft and discarded their protective suits as Janwar and Soval entered the bay. Once everyone armed themselves with O-rifles and Bex-7 stun grenades, they retreated to the safe zone near the innermost wall. A small control station resided in front of it, boasting multiple consoles and data entry pads.

At the press of a button, an invisible shield rose in front of them that could withstand a direct hit from a missile.

Beyond the open bay door, the transport floated placidly against a midnight backdrop that sparkled with distant stars.

Janwar glanced at Kova. "Bring the transport aboard."

Kova stepped up to one of the stations. "Locking acquisition beam now."

A beam of light shot forth from the wall behind them and streaked toward the idle transport. As soon as it touched the shuttle, the light spread like water until it engulfed the entire surface, closing off the open hatch so the figure inside couldn't escape.

Not that the figure tried.

Janwar found himself hoping the man wasn't dead in there. He'd like to see the face of the one who had managed to conquer so many... and ask why he'd done it. Was he an assassin who had merely plowed through all the other Gathendiens to reach his intended target? Was he the sole survivor of a small pirate crew who had failed in their attempt to commandeer the ship? Was he perhaps someone seeking vengeance?

The Gathendiens had amassed an impressive list of enemies.

If the figure were any of the above, he might just be worth recruiting.

Guided by the acquisition beam, the mangled transport floated into the hangar and gently descended to the deck. Magnetic clamps rose from the floor and locked onto the new arrival with a series of thunks.

The beam shut off.

"Seal the bay," Janwar murmured.

The large bay door began to lower, shutting off the view of space.

"If nothing else," Krigara murmured, "we've acquired another transport. Once we repair the hatch and rid it of the Gathendiens' stench, it'll make a nice addition to our fleet."

Janwar nodded absently.

The figure inside the transport opted not to make an appearance.

"Do you want a *ziyil*?" his cousin asked.

"Not yet." Raising his voice so their *guest* would hear him, he called, "You may exit of your own accord, or we can force your hand. The choice is yours."

A faint sound reached their ears.

Soval arched his brows. "Was that a snort?"

Janwar would've answered in the affirmative, but the figure in white chose that moment to step into the open hatch. After pausing to sweep the bay with what Janwar guessed was a very discerning gaze, the figure hopped down, landing nimbly on the deck.

He was smaller than Janwar had supposed. Clearly, the baggy suit he wore had been made for someone larger.

The figure raised his wrist, drew back a flap, and consulted the screen embedded in the suit.

Was he confirming that the bay had a breathable atmosphere?

"No blasters or O-rifles," Krigara whispered. "His only weapons appear to be the swords."

The figure's helmet turned in their direction.

Had he heard Krigara? If so, his helmet must be amplifying sound because Janwar had barely heard his cousin, and he was standing right next to him.

Circumventing the shield, Janwar strode toward the newcomer. Krigara remained behind to man the controls should the figure choose to attack. The rest of the crew followed Janwar and fanned out behind him.

A heartbeat passed.

In a bafflingly fast motion, the figure doffed his suit.

Someone sucked in a breath.

Janwar's eyes widened.

Or rather *her* suit. A slender woman garbed all in black now stood before them: black pants with many pockets, a form-fitting black shirt that hugged a narrow waist and full breasts, and heavy black boots similar to those he and his crew wore but were almost child-sized by comparison.

The fingers of both small hands now clutched the handles of long, gleaming swords.

Janwar stared. Her clothing was torn in several places. Her pale skin bore multiple gashes and splashes of red blood. Her long, disheveled black hair shone beneath the bay's lights. And her face...

She was beautiful, even with a scowl creasing her forehead and her jaw jutting forward in defiance.

Judging by her appearance, she was either a Lasaran, a Segonian, or an Earthling. Segonian women tended to be taller, often matching the men in height. And a Segonian soldier facing a possible enemy would've long since activated her camouflage. So he omitted that option. Her petite build resembled that of a Lasaran woman. But a Lasaran wouldn't wear a shirt with sleeves short enough to bare her arms as this woman did. Which left... Earthling?

Could they be so lucky? Could they have inadvertently stumbled upon one of the very beings they hoped to rescue?

Not that this woman *needed* rescuing, he thought with growing admiration.

She *did* remind him a little of Lisa in appearance.

Lisa was an Earthling. But her eyes were a soft brown. This woman's bore a bright amber glow that fascinated him.

Srul, everything about her fascinated him.

When he and his crew continued to stand there in what he hated to admit was dumbfounded silence, she arched a brow.

"Well, boys, are you friend or foe?" She spoke Earth English, but with an accent Lisa had lacked. "If you're friend, I'm afraid I must take my leave of you. There are a few Gathendien bastards left I need to slay before I steal their ship. And if you're foe..." She swung her swords in a showy display, then sent them a wicked smile. "Whose ass am I going to kick first?"

EVERY MALE BUT THE leader raised a hand as if they were elementary school children hoping she'd pick them for her baseball team at recess. And all but one grinned big.

Simone would've laughed if she weren't in so much pain.

Only six men faced her in the bay, far fewer than the Gathendiens had believed necessary when they'd forced her pod on board. Although none wore body armor, each male sported at least one weapon. They also all bore a build similar to humans: one head, two arms, and two legs. Two eyes, two ears, one nose, one mouth.

The leader was handsome as hell, with long raven hair drawn back from his face in cornrows. The rest tumbled down his back and over his shoulders in thick waves intermingled with tight braids adorned with beads. His skin was tan with a reddish hue that almost resembled a sunburn. Long eyelashes surrounded auburn eyes. A closely cropped mustache hovered above full lips while a short beard adorned his strong jaw. He wore a loose shirt that hinted at a nicely developed chest with tight breeches that hugged muscled thighs.

When taken all together, it lent him a piratical look that was every bit as appealing as Jack Sparrow's.

One of the men behind him was huge, easily seven feet tall. Built like the Hulk, he had gray skin imbued with a turquoise hue and eyes so dark she couldn't distinguish the pupils from the irises. Was he part Yona? He wore his dark hair in a buzz like the Yona warriors. But he'd cut intricate patterns into the short hair on the sides of his head, something she'd never seen a Yona do. And, like the others, he was smiling. So *un*like Yona, he could feel emotion.

The two men beside him both possessed a somewhat feline look. Their noses were a bit flatter and wider. Both had long, thick hair that boasted multiple earth tones. And their tawny irises took up more of the white than a human's eyes. Black tattoos or markings that resembled a tiger's stripes covered the face and arms of one. *Very* cool. The other bore scars in all the places the first had markings. And there was something else that differentiated him from the first: a darkness in his eyes and a somber mien as if he had seen far too much of life and hadn't escaped intact.

Simone could relate.

A fifth male looked Lasaran, lending her hope that she wouldn't have to kick these guys' asses. She had wrought havoc on the Gathendiens' ship, killing most of the soldiers on board. But she had taken many hits in the process and fought a constant onslaught of pain and weakness, not that she showed it.

The last member of the group studied her from a distance, standing behind a row of consoles, no doubt ready to unleash a hail of fire or do whatever they usually did when an enemy infiltrated their bay. That one bore a close enough resemblance to the leader to make her think they were related, although the second lacked the mustache and beard and boasted a slimmer build.

When the men continued to hold their hands in the air, eager to see whom she'd pick, she met the leader's gaze and arched a brow.

He glanced over his shoulder, then released a long-suffering sigh. "She said if you're *foe*, whose ass was she going to kick next. *Foe*. Not friend. Put your *drekking* hands down."

They lowered their hands, their smiles transforming into looks of disappointment.

This time Simone didn't quite manage to keep her lips from twitching.

The leader smiled. "I'm Janwar, commander of the *Tangata*. Welcome aboard. The fact that you're an Earthling makes us your friends."

She snorted. "You're going to have to do better than that. The Gathendiens liked that I'm an Earthling, too, and they were *not* my friends."

"You mean the dead Gathendiens who litter the ship floating quietly off our bow?"

"That would be them, yes."

"Care to tell me how they died?"

She offered a nonchalant shrug, careful not to wince when it tugged at some of her wounds. "It's a sad tale, I'm afraid. The clumsy bastards kept falling upon my swords."

He laughed heartily over that, flashing straight white teeth as creases appeared at the corners of his eyes. Most of the others laughed, too. Even the scarred one cracked a smile.

"I would've loved to see that," Janwar murmured with a shake of his head. "And I understand your hesitance to trust. Would an endorsement from Prince Taelon of Lasara and his lifemate, Lisa, lend our claim of friendship more credibility?"

Her heart leapt as her hands tightened on the hilts of her swords.

"Don't forget Abby," the big one rumbled. "Abby likes us, too."

"Lisa is here?" Simone tried not to let hope show in case it was a ruse. "And Abby?"

Janwar shook his head. "We already conveyed the royal family safely to Lasara, then returned at Prince Taelon's request to search for her friends and other survivors of the *Kandovar*." He motioned to her. "To search for *you*."

Bitter disappointment eradicated hope. "Such a journey would have taken many months without the benefit of the *qhov'rum*." *Not* less than two. And Evie had told her the *qhov'rum* had likely been damaged in the blast.

Nothing in Janwar's body language revealed that she'd caught him in a lie. He merely sent her a cocky smile and motioned to the large bay around them. "Not if one has the pleasure of commanding the fastest ship in the galaxy."

The men behind him all nodded, pride glinting in their eyes.

She narrowed hers. Her telepathic gift offered no help in discerning their motives. All it conveyed was a slew of alien gibberish because the little earpiece she wore only translated spoken words, not thoughts. Were she at full strength, she could simply employ her empathic gift and read his emotions from a safe distance, determining sincerity or deceit. But fatigue pulled at her. Pain riddled every limb. And she desperately needed blood.

She glanced at the man who looked human. "Are you Lasaran?" If so, he must sport a rebellious nature because his shirt left his arms bare.

He shook his head. "Segonian."

Like Lasarans, Segonians were members of the Aldebarian Alliance. And she'd learned on the *Kandovar* that their blood was safe for Immortal Guardians to infuse themselves with.

As for the rest of them...

She returned her gaze to the commander. "And you are?"

"Akseli."

Merde. Akselis were *not* members of the Aldebarian Alliance and—from everything she'd heard—were deceptive assholes governed by greed.

His look turned wry. "I see you've heard of my people."

Yep. She was pretty sure her lip had curled with disgust.

The one who closely resembled him called, "Don't judge us by their standards. We aren't like them."

Janwar smiled. "If we were, they wouldn't have placed a sizable dead-or-alive bounty on our heads."

She tilted her head to one side and eyed him curiously. "You would share such information with a stranger?"

"With other strangers? No. With you? Yes."

"What makes you think I won't do to you what I did to the Gathendiens and claim both the bounty and this ship for myself?"

He grinned. "Lisa would be... how did she put it?" He thought a moment. "*Pissed.* Lisa would be pissed if you did."

The big one nodded with a smile. "She likes us."

And damned if she wasn't starting to believe them.

Truth be told, Simone *wanted* to believe them. Rather desperately. She'd been alone for a long time and could also benefit from a trip to their medical bay. But Akselis were notoriously deceptive. And she didn't know how many other warriors occupied this ship or how extensive a fight she would have on her hands if she relaxed her guard and they tried to screw her over.

What if Gathendiens weren't the only ones attempting to get their hands on Earthlings? Weren't Akselis known for hiring themselves out as mercenaries to the highest bidders? Didn't they all favor money over morality? Who was to say the Gathendiens hadn't hired these guys to hunt down all survivors of the *Kandovar* and hand them over?

The fact that Janwar and his crew just happened to show up when she was almost finished kicking the Gathendiens' asses *was* a little suspect. For all she knew, they were responding to a distress call the panicking reptiles had managed to send them.

"Why don't we sort this out later," she suggested. "Right now, there's a Gathendien ship I need to claim."

Janwar glanced at the transport. "How do you plan to get there?"

Simone motioned to the mangled craft with one sword. "This craft will do." She had just about figured out how to restart the engine when Janwar captured it with his acquisition beam.

His look turned doubtful. "Have you ever flown one of those before?"

"No. But unlike most of my brethren, I'm mechanically and technologically inclined." Hunting and slaying psychotic vampires night after night left Immortal Guardians—many of whom were hundreds or thousands of years old—little time to explore humanity's various and assorted technological advances. Some of her immortal friends didn't even know how to download audiobooks onto their cell phones. "I've always had an insatiable curiosity about the world around me and the inventions of man." Exploring new tech had been one of the ways she'd staved off boredom and loneliness over the centuries.

"And the inventions of Gathendien bastards?"

She laughed. "Just so."

"Why don't we board their ship together?" He gestured toward the impressive variety of gleaming craft the bay housed. "If we take one of these, you won't have to don your suit and can travel in comfort."

And leave myself vulnerable? Simone shook her head. "That's not their ship anymore. It's mine. And I'm fully capable of ejecting the refuse on my own."

"You didn't kill everyone," he said. "According to our scans, several life forms remain."

"I'm aware. I left them alive so I could interrogate them."

He smiled. "Which is exactly what we came here to do." He clapped his hands. "Excellent. Then we can work together."

Not while she was still uncertain she could trust them.

Her eyes narrowed.

Janwar sighed. "I see you'll require proof that we aren't full of *bura*." Turning, he called to the fellow in the distance, "Krigara! Bring me a datapad."

Krigara rounded the console and strolled toward them with a datapad the size of an iPad that resembled a clear piece of glass

45

in one hand. He flashed Simone a friendly smile as he drew even with Janwar.

The commander jerked a thumb toward him. "This is my cousin, Krigara." He motioned to the giant. "Soval." Big Blue dipped his head with a grin. "S'Roka." The cat man nodded with a smile. "Kova." The scarred man dipped his head. "And Elchan." The Segonian gave her a cocky salute.

All watched her expectantly. "Simone," she murmured at last.

Janwar removed his weapons and handed them to Soval, then took the datapad from Krigara and approached her slowly. Stopping before her, he extended his right hand. "It's a pleasure to meet you, Simone."

He stood close enough for her to begin to glean hints of his emotions.

Studying him a long moment, Simone failed to pick up any deception vibes.

She dropped her eyes to the large, callused hand he held out to her, palm up. Sheathing one of the katanas, she extended her hand, more interested in getting a better feel for his emotions than because she wished to greet him.

His smile broadening, he clasped her hand with his and pumped it up and down. "I believe Lisa said this is how Earthlings commonly greet each other."

A spark of hope flared to life. The soldiers and crew on the *Kandovar* hadn't known about handshakes until she and the others from Earth had shown them. Aliens tended to greet each other by clasping forearms instead. And Janwar had said *Lisa* rather than Princess Lisa, something she knew her friend preferred even though the Lasarans and Yona persisted in using her title or addressing her as Your Highness.

Did this man really know her friend?

The spark of hope brightened as his emotions flowed into her via her gift, much stronger now that they touched. Simone found nothing negative, only friendliness, admiration, respect, and... attraction?

Her hand tingled as her pulse picked up. Unnerved, she released his hand and took a step back.

Janwar glanced down at the datapad he held and began tapping its surface. "Lisa worried that some of you might be reluctant to trust and would require proof that we're—as she put it—*good guys*." He seemed either surprised or amused that anyone would classify them as such.

In the next instant, he turned the datapad to face her.

She gasped.

Lisa stared out at her, a smile on her pretty face. She stood beside Taelon on what appeared to be a very sleek ship's bridge with Abby in her arms. Behind them, Janwar lounged in the commander's chair while the other men occupied seats at various stations.

"Hi, all!" Lisa said cheerfully. "If you're viewing this, then Janwar and the guys must have managed to track you down. I hope they found you safe and well. If not, the *Tangata* has a fabulous Medical Bay. I mean, it is *incredible*. I doubt there are many wounds or illnesses they can't heal in there."

Taelon wrapped an arm around her. "If you suffer from any they can't address, Janwar can put you in a cryopod that will prevent all health issues from worsening while he brings you to Lasara, where our best healers will be waiting to aid you."

Lisa leaned into his side, looking pensive. "I'm not sure where or under what conditions they found you but thought you might be feeling anxious or uncertain that you can trust them. I just wanted to let you know that you can. Janwar and his crew are great. They're our friends."

Taelon nodded, his expression earnest. "I assure you their dark and violent reputation is undeserved."

Simone glanced at Janwar.

He pursed his lips. "Well... it's *somewhat* deserved."

She fought a laugh.

Lisa looked up at her husband. "I doubt they'll know Janwar's reputation, honey. I don't think they know he's a pirate."

"Oh."

Lisa transferred Abby to her hip and waved a hand in dismissal as she faced the camera or whatever recorded them. "Forget he mentioned that. They're good guys. *Great* guys. Janwar and Taelon go way back. He's the one who discovered Ami was on Earth after everyone else stopped looking for her."

Surprise darted through Simone. All of this had begun when Taelon had gone to Earth, searching for his missing sister, and found the Immortal Guardians after a perilous and torturous introduction to humanity.

"When Srok'a had a vision," Lisa went on, "Janwar hauled ass and rescued Taelon, Abby, and me."

Taelon whispered to Abby, "Don't say ass."

Abby babbled infant noises.

Simone laughed even as moisture welled in her eyes. The three of them looked good. Happy, healthy, and gloriously safe.

Lisa continued, "Ari'k and the rest of the royal guard—Sodu, Yihrus, and Kuxa—are here, too. Janwar brought all of us to Lasara. Now he's going to turn around and rescue as many of you as he can find."

A long, jagged breath escaped Simone as a tear spilled down one cheek.

Lisa's expression softened. "I hope every one of you will see this because it'll mean you're safe." Her brown eyes glistened with tears of her own. "I love you all like sisters and miss you so much."

Taelon pressed a kiss to the top of her head.

Sensing her mother's sadness, Abby glanced up and raised a tiny hand to pat Lisa's cheek.

Lisa took her daughter's cute little fist and pressed a kiss to it. "We'll see you when you reach Lasara."

"You may contact us through Janwar's communication system en route," Taelon said.

"Please do," Lisa added.

The image froze.

When more tears raced down her cheeks, Simone swiped at them impatiently and glanced at Janwar.

Kindness and understanding softened his handsome features. "She and the baby are well. And they're safe on Lasara. No one can harm them there."

"I feared they had all perished," she confessed.

"I know," he said softly. "But two other Earthlings have been found since Lisa recorded this message, and we hope to find more. The entire Aldebarian Alliance is searching for you."

"Who else was found?" Simone asked quickly.

"Eliana and Ava."

"Are they okay?"

His features creased with a slight wince. "Well, Eliana was in rough shape when Dagon found her, but—"

"Dagon?"

"Commander Dagon of the *Ranasura*, a Segonian warship."

Segonians were strong allies of the Lasarans. "You said she was in rough shape?" Eliana was a fellow Immortal Guardian. It would take a great deal of damage to put her in *rough shape*.

"Yes. But she's fine."

Krigara snorted. "She's *more* than fine."

Janwar laughed and—at Simone's questioning look—said, "Apparently, she's been kicking a lot of ass, as Lisa would say."

"Gathendien ass?" Simone asked hopefully.

"Yes. She and the Segonians fought side-by-side to rescue your friend Ava and two Purveli males the Gathendiens had captured."

Again Simone gasped. "The Gathendiens captured Ava? Is she safe? Is she okay?"

"She is now."

Now? Fury flashed through her. "Did the Gathendiens hurt her?" If so, she would hunt them down and—

"Yyyyeah," Janwar said, staring at her with something akin to fascination. "But she kicked quite a bit of Gathendien ass before Eliana found her."

That threw her a bit. "*Ava* did?"

"Yes."

Simone couldn't imagine it. Sure, Ava had been sparring with Eliana since they'd embarked upon their space journey. *All* the Immortal Guardian women had taken it upon themselves to train the *gifted ones* they guarded. But Ava was so sweet and shy and had led such a sheltered life. Simone found it hard to picture her mortal friend holding her own against hulking Gathendien warriors twice or thrice her weight.

Then she frowned. "Why are you looking at me like that?"

The query didn't lessen the intensity of Janwar's regard. "Your eyes are glowing."

Damn it. They'd probably been glowing this whole time and had gotten even brighter while she'd watched the video. It was an involuntary response she was helpless to control. Intense emotion and pain always made immortals' eyes glow.

She stiffened, standing as tall as her wounds would allow, but still had to look up to meet his reddish-brown gaze. "And you look like Jack Sparrow," she announced imperiously. "Do you see me staring?"

His lips twitched. "A little bit, yes."

Simone couldn't help it. She laughed.

CHAPTER THREE

ONCERN ROSE WHEN SIMONE'S laughter halted abruptly, and she winced again.

A faint tap, tap, tapping noise drew Janwar's attention to the sword she still held. Blood dripped from the sharp tip and formed a small pool on the deck.

He frowned. Was that her blood or Gathenien blood? Both Gathendiens and Earthlings bled red, so he couldn't tell.

He forced his attention back to her face. "We need to head to the Gathendien ship and interrogate the few *grunarks* left alive."

"Agreed."

He considered it a good sign that she didn't protest his insistence on working together this time. Lisa's message must have convinced her she could trust them.

"Why don't we take a quick trip to Med Bay first," he suggested. "You've multiple wounds, and I can tell you're in pain." As soon as the words left his lips, he questioned the wisdom of them. As a skillful and daunting warrior, she might not appreciate him pointing that out.

But she didn't scowl or otherwise indicate he had offended her. Instead, she sheathed her second sword and glanced beyond him at Elchan. "You don't by any chance happen to have a supply of Segonian blood on hand, do you?"

"We do." Janwar motioned for her to accompany him and began walking toward the docking bay exit. "Adaos, the chief medic aboard the *Ranasura*, assured us that Segonian blood is safe for transfusing Earthlings with. But I don't know if the rest of our blood is compatible, so Elchan here has donated frequently to ensure we'd have a healthy supply on hand."

She glanced over her shoulder at Elchan. "That was thoughtful of you. Thank you."

Elchan nodded as he and the others fell into step behind them.

Janwar kept his pace slow, aware that his legs were longer than hers. Though she was taller than Lisa, the top of her head barely reached his shoulder. He also pretended not to notice that she limped rather heavily. The fact that she managed to keep her posture straight, her shoulders back, and her chin up despite the plethora of bloody wounds he cataloged bespoke her pride and determination to show no weakness.

Vuan, he admired that. "I'd give you a *silna* to speed your healing, but Adaos advised us not to. He seems to think some Earthlings may not react well to it."

When he invited her with a look to explain why, she remained silent.

Perhaps in time.

Their boots thudded on a spotless floor as Janwar led her down a long, pristinely white hallway, turned left, and guided her into one of three medical bays the *Tangata* boasted.

He handed his cousin the datapad. "I'll see to Simone's wounds. The rest of you, head to the bridge. Re-engage our cloaking array and keep an eye on the Gathendiens. We didn't hear them send a distress call, but they could have broadcast one on a private channel."

"I kept them so busy I doubt they had time to," Simone stated matter-of-factly. "They thought they'd acquired a helpless victim they could easily subdue."

Soval grunted. "Instead, they got you."

She flashed him a grin. "Boy, did they."

The men laughed.

Janwar wished he could have seen how the *srul* this deceptively dainty Earthling managed to slay so many Gathendiens. He caught Sroka's eye. "Just in case they *did* send a distress call, stay sharp."

Nodding, the others left.

Janwar motioned to one of the two treatment beds the main room boasted. "If you climb up here, I'll see what we can do to rid you of those wounds."

She cast him a curious look as she approached the bed. "You're a commander *and* a medic?"

He grinned. "Though you may find this less than reassuring, we don't currently have a medic on staff. And I'm a commander with no formal training as a medic."

She nodded somberly. "That *is* less than reassuring."

He laughed. "*But* when I chose to rebel against the Akseli government, I regularly incurred a multitude of wounds and soon found it in my best interest to learn everything I could about healing, particularly since my cousin insisted on joining me. I thought the fight worth losing my own life but couldn't abide the thought of him losing his."

Janwar had questioned his chosen course every time Krigara suffered an injury until his cousin had made it very clear that he'd lost his parents, too, and wished to do everything he could to make the *grunarks* responsible pay.

Picking up a medic tablet, Janwar again motioned to the bed.

Simone had to jump up to land her shapely backside on the mattress, which was high enough to accommodate the taller warriors on his crew.

Janwar pretended not to hear the hiss of pain the action spawned and wondered if he should've offered her assistance. Aside from Lisa, he hadn't spent time with a woman in so long that he'd forgotten how to behave. But Simone seemed every bit the warrior his men were. And they would've hurled expletives at him if he'd dared to assist them.

He typed a command into the datapad.

A mechanical arm with a diagnostic wand descended from the ceiling and hovered above her head. "If you lie back, I'll perform a quick scan and see what—"

"That's not necessary," she said, softening the interruption with a smile. "A transfusion is all I need."

He stared. The jagged slashes in her clothing provided glimpses of torn flesh and severe gashes. Judging by the way she kept one arm tucked close to her side now that she'd sheathed her weapons, a few ribs were likely broken as well. "Are you sure?"

"Yes."

Unwilling to press her so soon after winning her trust, he ordered a transfusion.

A second mechanical arm lowered from the ceiling, the end bearing a needle connected to a tube. While Simone monitored its approach, the mechanism on the underside of it sprayed the bend of her arm with liquid. Light formed a grid pattern on her pale, damp skin. Then the needle unerringly found her vein.

Red blood began to slither down the tube and into her battered body.

"Will you at least let me spray some of your cuts with *imaashu*?" he asked.

Her brow furrowed. "What's that?"

"A pain deadener that will also kill any bacteria that found its way into your wounds. Gathendiens aren't the most hygienic *grunarks* in the galaxy, so it's best to disinfect any injuries they inflict as quickly as possible."

"I'm hardier than most Earthlings and less prone to illness."

Grabbing a can of *imaashu*, he held it up and raised his brows. "Nevertheless...?"

She released a disgruntled sigh that sent amusement rippling through him. Then—careful not to jostle the needle in her arm—she tugged the hem of her shirt up to the base of her breasts.

Janwar barely noticed her slender waist and lightly muscled abs as he frowned at the gash she revealed. It was even worse than he'd guessed. "We should clean this properly and seal it."

She shook her head. "No time. I want to return to the Gathendien ship before those still breathing die."

If he weren't worried that they'd gotten off a distress call, he would insist. But he didn't want to be on the Gathendien ship if several more appeared. It'd be best to take care of business there as quickly as possible, then return to the *Tangata*.

Grumbling beneath his breath, he moved the container of *imaashu* closer and began to coat the cut liberally.

Simone jumped when the liquid hit her flesh.

Pausing, he met her glowing amber gaze. "Does it hurt?" She was the first Earthling he'd rendered first aid to. Lisa had been in good health—if a little hungry from food rationing—when she and the others had come aboard.

Simone's lips tipped up in a wry smile. "No. It's just cold."

"Apologies," he murmured

She let him spray more cuts on her arms before waving him away.

"I should check your back."

"I'm fine," she insisted and frowned at the needle that continued to transfuse her. "How long is this going to take?"

He consulted the med tablet, blinked, rechecked it, then stared at her. "How can someone your size require more blood than someone Soval's?"

She tilted her head to one side. "Soval is Big Blue?"

He would've laughed at the nickname if he weren't so puzzled. "Yes."

Her gaze slid away as she shrugged. "I guess the Gathendiens liberated more than I thought."

If the Gathendiens had liberated that much blood, she wouldn't have any left!

Would she?

Perhaps he should give the Earthling anatomy files Adaos sent him another look.

"If you'd rather not elaborate on that," Janwar said slowly, taking in her closed expression, "perhaps you might enlighten me regarding another issue."

Eyebrows lowering, she watched him warily. "What do you wish to know?"

He set the tablet aside and leaned back against the second bed, crossing his arms over his chest. "Who the *srul* is Jack Sparrow?"

Her whole countenance lightened as she laughed.

Janwar smiled, feeling a little lighter himself. She had a lovely smile, one he found impossible not to return.

Eyes widening, she abruptly stopped laughing. "Wait. You aren't telepathic, are you?"

"No." If he *were* telepathic, he feared the temptation to delve into her thoughts and seek the answers to all the questions she avoided answering would've proven too much for him. "Why?"

"Where did you hear that name?"

"Jack Sparrow?"

"Yes."

"The *Tangata*'s encryption is unassailable, so I've been channeling all communications with Earthlings. When Lisa commed Eliana the first time, I heard them laughing over my apparent likeness to him." Then it dawned on him. "Oh. Were you thinking the same thing when you first saw me?" Was that why she'd thought him telepathic?

"Yes," she admitted.

Janwar wasn't sure what to make of that. "Do I really resemble him?"

A twinkle of amusement entered her eyes. "Yes, though you're taller."

He narrowed his eyes. "They seemed to find it amusing. Should I feel insulted?"

Her full lips stretched in a grin. "Not at all. Jack Sparrow is a character in what you would call entertainment vids. He's a dashing pirate who usually thwarts the many men and women who wish him dead."

He stroked his beard. "Dashing, eh?"

Again, she laughed and managed to do so without wincing in pain this time.

He didn't notice until then that the amber glow in her eyes seemed to be fading, rendering them browner. "Your eyes aren't glowing as brightly."

"The pain has lessened, thanks to the transfusion."

"Pain makes them glow?"

She nodded. The needle in her arm withdrew. "Finally!" Her mood visibly brightening, she hopped off the bed.

"Careful," he cautioned, recalling her limp.

"I'm fine. Don't coddle me," she warned good-naturedly. "I'm starting to like you, and that would ruin it."

Then he was right. He *should* treat her like one of his warriors. "Then why the *srul* are we wasting time in here," he retorted with a smile, "when some Gathendiens are eagerly waiting for us to interrogate them."

Grinning, she offered him a cocky salute. "Much better. Lead the way."

T HE BAY ON THE Gathendien ship had been swept clean when Simone sabotaged the atmospheric barrier. The only things remaining in it were her escape pod, a transport that looked almost as crappy as the one she'd hacked her way into, and a few battered gray fighter craft that were locked down. A conglomeration of equipment she couldn't identify clung to the walls, probably magnetized to it. And several smears of blood marred the floor, left behind by the first Gathendiens she'd slain after exiting the escape pod.

"I neglected to ask," Janwar murmured from the pilot's seat as he guided the roomy transport into the hangar. "Where did you find the white suit you were wearing earlier? It had no tail, so I assume it wasn't one of the Gathendiens."

"It was in the escape pod." She hadn't wanted to put it on when her battle with the Gathendiens had led her back to the bay, but—technically speaking—Simone wasn't immortal. She was just extremely tough to kill.

Decapitation would work. So would fire if she couldn't escape it. While extreme blood loss would kill a vampire, an Immortal Guardian would instead slip into a state of hibernation similar to that of a tardigrade until a new source came along. The same thing held true for extreme cold or dehydration. Hell, Stanislav had survived being buried in Susan's basement for two years after nearly being blown up. That's how hard it was to kill an Immortal Guardian.

On Earth.

She wasn't sure about the vacuum of space, though, so she'd taken a few seconds to don the bulky, annoying Lasaran space suit toward the end.

Krigara sent her a curious glance. "You wore it while you fought the Gathendiens?"

Hell no. That would've been too awkward. The thing had swallowed her.

Simone shook her head and nodded toward the bay. "I didn't don it until I followed the last few stragglers in here and saw they intended to leave."

Janwar glanced at her over his shoulder. "I'm surprised you had time to put it on."

She shrugged. "I'm faster than you think."

He chuckled. "No doubt you are."

That drew a smile from her. She was starting to like these guys and hoped they were on the up and up.

Janwar set the transport down smoothly.

As soon as the engine powered down, Krigara rose and reached toward the control panel that would lower the ramp.

Simone jumped up and caught his arm. "Wait. I disabled the atmospheric barrier." With her katana. Time had been short, and she'd hoped the presence of live Gathendiens in the bay would keep the a-holes who'd clambered into the transport from opening the bay door and escaping.

Alas, it hadn't.

He smiled. "I repaired it."

That surprised her. "You did?" she asked, releasing him. "When?"

"While you were busy trying to restart the transport's engine."

"Oh. Then it's safe to go out without our suits?"

"Yes."

Simone glanced at Janwar for confirmation as he joined them. For some reason, she trusted him the most.

He nodded. "It's safe."

Krigara tapped a code into the console.

Since Simone couldn't read whatever language they used, she committed the sequence pattern to memory. Just in case.

When the ramp began to lower, Janwar and Krigara moved to stand in front of her while Kova and Srok'a stepped into position behind her.

Rolling her eyes, she cleared her throat.

As she'd anticipated, Janwar and Krigara swiveled to look at her. Stepping through the small gap between them, she took the lead.

"This is *my* ship now. I go first." When Krigara opened his mouth to protest, she scowled a warning. "*I* go first. You all are my guests."

Eyebrows flying up, he glanced at his cousin, then smiled. "Yes, ni'má."

Her eyes narrowed. "That had better be the alien equivalent of ma'am."

"It is," Janwar confirmed. "It's a term commonly used throughout the alliance to address an unbonded female."

"Good to know."

Simone strode down the ramp as soon as it finished lowering.

Boots clomped on metal as the warriors followed her.

"This is your escape pod?"

She turned to see Janwar motioning to the pod. "Yes. I'm not sure if it looks so battered because of the explosion or because it was thrust through the walls of the *qhov'rum.*

"Probably both," he said as they came upon bloody smears on the bay's floor. "What happened here?"

Simone smiled with relish. "The Gathendien welcoming party thought to take me captive." She jerked a thumb toward the pod. "There should be a body in there if it wasn't sucked out when the bastards in the fleeing transport opened the bay door." She shook her head with disgust. "They didn't even care that some of their shipmates were still in here moving around. And they knew I'd disabled the atmospheric shield."

"Which is why I believe the only good Gathendien is a dead Gathendien," he said.

Simone grinned. "I like the way you think, commander."

"Just Janwar. My men only use the formal address to vex me."

She laughed. "Then I like the way *they* think, too." Immortal Guardians often razzed and teased each other to alleviate boredom and lighten what could be a pretty dark existence. They *did* slay vampires for a living, after all.

The warriors around her chuckled. While they each carried blasters or O-rifles, she kept her swords and daggers sheathed, aware of what awaited them on the other side of the bay's door.

When she reached it, Simone studied the access panel beside it. "Does anyone happen to know the code for this?"

Krigara moved forward. "I do. I circumvented their security protocols and inputted a code of my own." He typed in a series of numbers or symbols.

When the door rose with a rumble, she smiled. "Aren't *you* a handy fellow to have around?"

He flashed his teeth in a grin.

Simone steeled herself against the scents of blood and death. The fact that she was familiar with both, thanks to the thousands of vampires she'd slain over the centuries, didn't mean she liked it. And this time, they were almost overshadowed by the stench of stagnant swamp water Gathendiens' seemed to emit. "Damn, Gathendiens stink," she complained as she led them up the first corridor.

The men behind her murmured their agreement.

She had encountered more Gathendien soldiers than anticipated on the ship, so plenty of corpses awaited them. Simone didn't slow when she came upon the bodies. She simply stepped over them, intent on reaching those she'd left alive. Thanks to the blood transfusion, the worst of the fatigue that plagued her had receded. Most of the cuts and gashes she'd sustained should already be mending, the edges drawing together and sealing before fading into scars. And yet the wound across her back began to burn. She hadn't thought it a big deal—just another deep cut like the others—but now regretted not letting Janwar take a minute to look at it.

Though she healed swiftly, it wasn't always a comfortable process. And that *imaashu* stuff he'd sprayed on some of her other cuts would've spared her the pain.

She gave a mental shrug. *Oh well.*

A swishing sound alerted them to movement nearby. The others raised their weapons and slowed their pace. Simone merely rounded the corner.

Half a dozen Gathendiens lay dead in a cluster. The bastards had thought piling on her would bring her down, but it hadn't. It had just made their soft bellies easier targets and given her access to their blasters.

A long smear of blood began at the edge of the group and led up the corridor to a survivor who used his arms to drag himself forward on his belly. Every time he pulled himself along with his arms, the tip of his thick tail braced against the floor and helped with a push.

Simone tilted her head to one side as she watched him. "Hmph. I didn't take the tail into consideration." It was kinda cool that they could use their tails in such a way. She glanced at her companions. "Some survivors may have gotten a little farther than I estimated."

Upon hearing her voice, the Gathendien gasped and rolled onto his back.

She tensed, ready to dart forward and confiscate any weapon he might raise. But his hands were empty.

"We disarmed all the survivors," Krigara mentioned.

She raised her brows. "While I was in the transport?"

"Yes."

They must be quick workers.

Janwar frowned as they strolled forward. "Why isn't he using his legs?"

"Because I kneecapped him," Simone told them.

All stared at her with baffled expressions.

"I shot him in the knees with a blaster that I yanked off one of them."

"Ah." Janwar stopped near the Gathendien as he rolled onto his belly again and began slithering forward faster.

"Okay. How do you want to do this?" Simone asked as she stepped in front of the Gathendien to halt his progress. "Do you want to interrogate each one as we come upon them or round them all up first?" She had little experience with interrogation. When hunting vampires, she'd always found it best to dispatch them as quickly as possible. Such always seemed more merciful, particularly since many of them wouldn't have become psychotic killers if they hadn't been infected with the Gathendien virus that damaged their brains. The only time she'd paused to ask questions had been when she and her brethren needed to hunt down some missing Immortal Guardians an enemy had sought to turn into his own personal army.

Janwar pondered it a moment. "I think it would be best to round them up first."

"Once we have them all together, will we do good cop/bad cop or bad cop/bad cop?" she asked.

More blank looks.

"Good cop/bad cop is when one of us is nice and pretends to want to help them to win them over while the other scares the living *bura* out of them."

Janwar's lips twitched. "Ah. Bad cop/bad cop."

She nodded. "I'm guessing that's equally effective."

"Even more so when you *interrogate* one of them in front of the others."

"To give the others incentive to talk," she finished for him. "Okay. I tell you what..." She glanced around. "They've got a lab up around the corner that looks more like a torture chamber. Two barred cells abut it, so anyone stuck in them can witness firsthand what they do to their *test subjects*." She sneered the last word, infusing it with every ounce of disgust she felt for the alien race that had tried—and was *still* trying—to eradicate humanity so they could obtain Earth. "We can put them all in there."

Janwar nodded. "Sounds good."

"I'll collect the survivors for you since I remember where they all are," she offered.

But he shook his head. "It'll go faster if we all do it."

Not really. He didn't know she was preternaturally fast and strong, though, and she thought it best to keep that to herself. Old habits died hard. And she wasn't ready to reveal just how much she differed from Lisa, the only other Earthling he'd come into contact with.

"Do you want me to draw you a map or something to help you find them?" Though the Gathendien ship was considerably smaller than the *Tangata*, it still contained a maze of corridors.

"No need." Janwar tapped several commands into the electronic pad he wore on one wrist. Seconds later, a three-dimensional holographic image rose above it, displaying a multi-layered map of the ship, complete with blinking red dots that indicated the locations of all remaining life forms aboard.

Stepping closer, she located the six of them on the map and smiled. "That is so cool!" She took Janwar's hand and gave his wrist a slight twist, then moved his arm this way and that to alter the angle of the building. She even passed a hand through the image, distorting it momentarily. But it swiftly reconfigured itself. Laughing in delight, she glanced up at him. "How did you get the plans for the ship?"

"We have the plans for *every* military ship, Aldebarian Alliance member or otherwise."

Amusement wafted through her, momentarily making her forget the pain in her back. "I'm guessing that's pretty helpful, considering your piratical endeavors."

He nodded somberly. "Very helpful."

Laughing, she didn't realize until then that she still held his hand. It dwarfed hers and bore the calluses of a soldier or hard worker. Releasing it, she couldn't resist waving her hand through the image one more time.

Janwar's lips twitched.

"I don't suppose I could talk you into making one of those for me, could I?" she asked, indicating the wristband.

"Perhaps. But we've other business to attend to now."

"Right." Part of her wanted to procrastinate a little longer. Fetching and carrying the fallen Gathendiens would likely make her back sting more. But what had to be done had to be done. She pointed to the holomap. "I'll take these three. And you can divvy up the rest amongst yourselves."

The men exchanged a look.

Srok'a cleared his throat. "Are you sure you don't want us to fetch them all? Gathendiens are heavy *grunarks*."

She snorted. "Something I learned when they thought piling on top of me would take me to the ground. Don't worry about me. You just retrieve the others. I'll be fine."

An utter lie, as it turned out.

Simone left the others and headed for the three enemies she'd volunteered to retrieve. All were in the same general area, so she could've used preternatural speed and strength to nab them in one trip and return before the others even got their first Gathendien captive to the lab. Instead, she made three trips—each at a mortal's pace—so she wouldn't have to explain why her red dot on their maps seemed to travel at light speed.

By the time she made her third trip to the lab, dragging the last Gathendien by his boot, the wound on her back throbbed mercilessly.

Why the hell wasn't it healing?

She glanced down at the arms left bare by the sleeves she'd cut short during her stay in the pod.

And why weren't the lesser cuts on her arms healing? Almost all of them should've sealed by now. But the only cuts that didn't still pain her were the ones Janwar had sprayed with that awesome *imaashu* stuff.

"Is that the last one?"

She turned at the male voice and found Srok'a walking toward her from another hallway.

Like her, he dragged a wounded Gathendien behind him.

She nodded, oddly short of breath. As they'd warned her, Gathendiens were heavy as hell, a result of their thick hide as much as their size. But she could lift an SUV over her head. Dragging one of these jerks around should've been easy.

Srok'a's Gathendien growled something. Frowning back at it, Srok'a delivered a swift kick, then returned his attention to Simone. His brow furrowed as concern darkened his features. "Are you okay?"

She forced a tired smile. "Yes. It's just been one of those days."

Though he nodded, he watched her closely as they entered the lab.

Janwar motioned them over to the second holding cell. While the lab itself appeared to be as state of the art as the one on the *Tangata*, the cells looked almost medieval, the walls comprised of metal bars spaced too closely for an adult to fit through. She didn't notice the high-tech lock beside each gate until Krigara picked up the severed arm of one of the guards she'd slain and waved the wrist in front of the pad. A clunk sounded as the gate unlatched.

Definitely high-tech.

Happy to hand over her burden, Simone stepped back as Kova and Srok'a hurled the last two Gathendiens into the cell.

Janwar's eyes met hers. Then he dropped his gaze to her visible injuries and met her eyes again with a silent question.

She nodded, indicating she was all right.

Satisfied, he studied the dozen or so Gathendiens they'd captured. "That one," he said after a moment and pointed. "He holds the highest rank."

Silently, she applauded his choice.

Janwar stared at the group in the second cell as Kova opened the gate. "Give my friend here any trouble, and we'll initiate a decontamination cycle on both cells."

Simone didn't know what that entailed, but it drove the Gathendiens to slide each other anxious looks. And when Kova boldly strolled inside, no one accosted him. When the Gathendien officer Janwar had chosen tried to clip Kova with his thick tail, Kova blasted a hole in it.

That ended his struggles.

Kova lugged the lizardman over to one of the operating tables on which Gathendiens conducted their twisted experiments.

Simone stared at it. The table boasted metal manacles the so-called scientists could clamp over wrists and ankles to hold their test subjects immobile. Another could be fastened across the forehead so those at their mercy couldn't turn their heads away to avoid... whatever these bastards did in their quest to find chemical weapons that would induce genocide.

Janwar said Ava had been a captive of Gathendiens. As Simone watched Kova and Srok'a lock their prisoner in place with the manacles, she couldn't help but wonder: *Did Gathendiens do that to Ava? Did they strap her small, trembling form down and study her like a lab rat?*

How? Had they hurt her? Cut her? How long had she been at their mercy?

And how had she survived it?

Fury roiled inside her. Her teeth ground together as she imagined her sweet, shy friend suffering who-knew-what horrors at the hands of those monsters and saw in her mind's eye Ava struggling futilely against the restraints while those butchers—

Dizziness assailed her, so strong Simone staggered back a step before catching herself.

Show no weakness.

It had been the first lesson drummed into her by the Immortal Guardian Seth had assigned to train her after her transformation.

Give them nothing to exploit.

Aware of the Gathendien eyes peering at her with their slitted pupils, she casually leaned back against one of the lab's cabinets and pretended to watch the show as Janwar began his interrogation. The pain in her back increased, distracting her as much as the damned dizziness. The burn in the wound steadily worsened until it felt as if someone held a fiery brand against her flesh. Then the heat spread, racing through her body like the hot flashes one of her Seconds had complained about.

Her stomach began to churn. Swallowing hard, Simone kept her expression impassive.

Her skin broke out in a cold sweat. The room began to whirl.

What the hell? Why was this happening? She shouldn't feel worse. She should feel better. After all the blood Janwar had transfused her with on the *Tangata*, she—

Icy fear filled her.

The transfusion. There must have been something in the blood they had oh-so-generously given her.

Merde!

She glanced around surreptitiously, fighting down a burst of panic.

Janwar looked up and caught her gaze.

Hastily looking away, Simone straightened and turned toward the door. The dizziness that afflicted her grew worse with every step, making it hard to keep from staggering. But she kept her shoulders back and her steps straight.

Kova leaned against the doorway, arms crossed over his chest as he watched the activity in the lab.

Simone nodded as she passed him, affixing what she hoped was a bored expression on her face. As soon as she was outside the lab and out of view of its occupants, she lurched to one side and threw a hand out to brace against the wall. Her breathing grew ragged as she doggedly continued forward. She had to keep moving. Had to get to the transport.

No. The escape pod. Or... *was* it the transport?

She swiped cold perspiration from her forehead and rubbed her eyes in a vain attempt to clear her blurring vision.

She had to...

She had to get... somewhere.

Her knees grew weak, and soon one hand against the wall wasn't enough to keep her upright. She had to lean her whole side against it as she doggedly forced one foot in front of the other, her clothing creating a swishing sound as it dragged across the surface.

"Janwar," Kova said somewhere behind her, his voice grim.

Boots tromped on the floor of the corridor.

A gentle hand closed around her arm and drew her to a halt as Janwar appeared before her. Bending his knees, he crouched in front of her until their eyes were on the same level. "Simone? What is it?" He brushed damp hair back from her forehead. "Is it your wounds?"

She managed to give her head a weak shake. "W-what did you do to me?" Just speaking left her breathless. "What w-was in the blood you gave me?"

"Nothing." When he pressed his palm to her forehead, alarm flared in his reddish-brown eyes. "She's burning up," he whispered to someone hovering beside them.

Too tired to look and see who it was, Simone shook her head. "P-poisoned me."

"No. We didn't poison you. I vow it." His expression was so earnest that she almost believed him, but her body said otherwise.

"Bullshit." She tried to shove him aside and merely grew more alarmed by how weak she'd become.

Janwar gripped both her arms now, the only thing—she feared—keeping her from face-planting on the floor. "I swear to you, I only gave you Elchan's blood. The chief medic on the *Ranasura* told us Segonian blood was safe for Earthlings."

"Lies," she murmured. "All lies."

"He had no reason to lie."

"Not him. You." Her damn head chose that moment to loll forward of its own accord and press her forehead to his. Simone stared blearily into the wide eyes so close to hers. "You lied to me," she whispered.

"What's happening?" another male voice murmured.

Before Janwar could answer, nausea inspired by the dizziness opted to make its presence known more forcefully.

Simone gagged.

Swearing, Janwar spun her away from him, looped an arm around her waist, and swept her hair back just in time for her to vomit what was left of the Lasaran MREs she'd consumed earlier.

Agony shot through her back, but she was too busy heaving up her lunch to cry out.

Once her stomach was empty, she hung limply in Janwar's arms.

When someone offered her a canteen of water to rinse her mouth with, she shoved it aside. She'd trusted them once. She wouldn't do so again.

"*Dreck* this," Janwar muttered and swung her into his arms. "Srok'a, stay with Krigara and get whatever information you can from the Gathendiens. Kova, you're with me. We're going back to the *Tangata*."

The lights in the corridor's ceiling pierced Simone's eyes as they swept past overhead. Janwar could move quickly when he wanted to.

A shiver racked her form even as heat flayed her from the inside.

Her lids lowered. It took a Herculean effort to raise them once more, then a few blinks to focus her cloudy gaze enough for her to realize she was cradled on Janwar's lap inside the transport. Had she passed out?

He rattled off a bunch of commands infused with concern that must be feigned, though she didn't know why he bothered. She was entirely at his mercy, a place she had never thought to be again after her transformation. No poisons on Earth affected her. No illnesses did either, aside from the genetically engineered virus that lent her preternatural strength and speed. She never caught colds. She never sickened with the flu. She hadn't sneezed once since she'd become an Immortal Guardian and—if asked—would've thought vomiting impossible for one of her ilk.

Her eyelids grew so heavy she gave in and closed them once more.

"We're almost there," Janwar murmured, resting his cheek atop her head.

He was such a likable guy.

It was too bad he'd betrayed her.

Sighing, she gave herself over to darkness.

CHAPTER FOUR

A S SOON AS THE transport's ramp lowered, Janwar took off running with Simone cradled in his arms. When she had lost consciousness on the short trip back, he'd panicked for a moment, believing her dead. But her chest still rose and fell with shallow breaths.

Kova raced along beside him as they headed for the *Tangata*'s nearest med bay.

Elchan and Soval waited inside.

"Is she dead?" Elchan asked, eyes wide as they fixed upon her limp form.

"No." Janwar lay her on a treatment bed. "I think she's having an adverse reaction to the blood we transfused her with."

Elchan blanched. "The Segonian medic said my blood was safe."

"He lied," Janwar growled. "Run a scan to confirm it and show us the damage it's doing. Kova, get me that *drekking* medic on the *Ranasura*, full encryption."

"On it." Kova crossed to a console on the other side of the bay and started tapping in commands. A transparent screen rose above the counter and hovered in front of him.

Soval stepped forward. "What do you want me to do?"

"Get back to the bridge and keep an eye out for anyone the Gathendiens may have summoned. We don't need any more surprises right now."

Soval nodded and left Med Bay.

Anger pulsing through him, Janwar paced as a mechanical arm descended from the ceiling and held a wand over the top of Simone's head. A band of light illuminated her hair, then slid down

70

her face as the diagnostic tool moved above her, slowly making its way down her body.

Halting, Janwar brushed her hair back from her face. "I'm so sorry," he whispered. He'd trusted the Segonians to deal honestly with him, and now *she* was suffering for it. He *knew* not to trust anyone he hadn't thoroughly vetted. He should have double-checked the information given him with Taelon instead of just taking the Segonians at their word. The Lasaran Prince *always* dealt honestly with Janwar.

"This is Kova of the *Tangata*, contacting you on behalf of Commander Janwar," his friend stated grimly. "Connect us to your chief medic immediately."

"If you'll wait a moment, I'll see if he—"

"We don't have a minute! Connect us to the *drekking* medic!" Kova snarled.

Janwar didn't hear the other man's mumbled response.

"What if it's just *my* blood?" Elchan asked shakily amid the silence that fell.

Janwar glanced up. "What?"

Face pale, Elchan swallowed hard. "If Segonian blood is safe for Earthlings, what if mine...?"

What if his wasn't? What if his differences didn't only extend to those that were easily discerned in his appearance? Was that his concern? Did he think there might be something unique in his blood that could've harmed Simone?

"No," Janwar told him. "It wasn't you. It was that *drekking* medic. He lied to us."

As if referring to him solidified the contact, the Segonian medic's face abruptly appeared on the transparent screen floating above the console. "Chief Medic Adaos responding," he announced blandly.

And for some reason, that made the rage building inside Janwar explode. "You mother *drekker*!" he growled and stalked toward the image, wishing he were speaking to the medic in person instead so he could throttle him. "You lied!"

Adaos's eyebrows shot up. "What?"

"You lied! You said Segonian blood was safe for Earthlings! You said using it in transfusions wouldn't harm them!"

Appearing much more alert now, the medic leaned closer. "You found an Earthling?" He turned away and murmured, "Get Eliana and Dagon in here. Now." Then he turned back. "Where is she?" he demanded.

Janwar gestured over his shoulder. "Dying in my *drekking* med bay, thanks to you!"

Adaos's expression darkened. "What did you do to her?"

"I gave her a transfusion of Segonian blood that *you* said was safe! Now she's dying."

"Segonian blood *is* safe."

"That's *tiklun bura,* and you know it!"

Adaos jumped suddenly as though startled.

"Maarev said Janwar found one of my friends," a female blurted in the background. "Is it true?" An Earth woman smaller than Simone skidded to a halt beside Adaos and turned to peer at the screen. "Janwar? Who is it? Where is she? Is she okay?"

"No, she isn't okay," he ground out and pointed at Adaos, "because that *drekker* told me Segonian blood was safe for Earthlings."

Eliana frowned. "It *is* safe. I've transfused myself with Segonian blood several times."

He stared at her. "What?" The Segonians might lie to him, but he didn't think one of Simone's friends would. They seemed to be a tightly-knit group. A family. "Then why is she dying?"

Eliana blanched. "Oh shit. She's dying? Are you sure? Who is it?"

"Simone."

Her frown deepened as her face scrunched up with confusion. "That can't be. Simone is... incredibly hard to kill. If anything, a transfusion should've helped her. A *lot.* Let me see her."

He turned to the exam bed as the diagnostic wand passed over her toes and retracted into the ceiling. Crossing to her side, he studied her chest, relieved to find it still rising and falling."

At instructions from Kova, the console screen followed Janwar and moved to hover on the opposite side of the bed.

"Oh shit," Eliana whispered as soon as she saw Simone's pallid form. Then she looked up at Adaos. "What the hell? This is from a transfusion? How can that be?"

"It *can't* be," the medic rumbled and glared at Janwar as if *he'd* done this to her. "Send me the results of the diagnostic scan."

Janwar nodded at Kova. "Do it."

A long moment passed while Adaos stared down at a datapad he held.

"What happened to her?" Eliana asked. Her brown eyes began to glow with amber light as they filled with tears. "Where did you find her?"

Janwar rested a hand on Simone's shoulder. "We tracked down a Gathendien ship that was suspiciously close to the area of the *qhov'rum* the battle took place in and approached it. We wanted to discover if they had captured any Earthlings and, if not, if they knew who might have. But Simone managed to get there before us. We found her shortly after she killed almost everyone on board."

Eliana seemed unsurprised by the impressive feat. "And those wounds... She got them while fighting the Gathendiens?"

"Yes. She was eager to question those she'd left alive and didn't want to pause long enough for me to tend her wounds. The only treatment she would agree to was a quick transfusion and some *imaashu* for her stomach wound. So I gave her Segonian blood." He glared at Adaos. "Which *he* assured us was safe." Since he couldn't punch the aloof healer in the face, Janwar had to settle for running a hand over the braids atop his head before he nodded at Simone. "She thought it was safe, too."

"It wasn't the blood," Adaos muttered as he frowned at the data-pad.

Eliana nodded. "Segonian blood really is safe for us, Janwar. Simone has been transfused with it before, back on the *Kandovar*. We both have. The Lasarans had a supply of it left over from the last Aldebarian Alliance War Games thingy they participated in."

What? If Segonian blood was safe, why had her condition deteriorated instead of improving?

Elchan took a step backward, horror slowly filling his face.

Janwar scowled at him. "It wasn't you, *vuan* it. There is nothing wrong with your blood!"

Adaos cast Elchan a fleeting look. "It's true. I'm aware of your condition. It wasn't your blood."

Elchan relaxed slightly, though concern continued to furrow his brow.

Adaos resumed perusing the data the scan provided him. Interminable seconds passed, ratcheting up Janwar's anxiety.

Finally, the medic stilled.

Eliana glanced at him. "What is it?"

"*Bosregi.*"

"What?" All color fled Eliana's face. And the alarm he read in her features sent an icy tingle of fear down Janwar's spine.

"It's *bosregi* poisoning," Adaos repeated and set the datapad aside.

Boots pounded against flooring off-screen, then Commander Dagon appeared behind Eliana. "*Dreck*, you're fast," he complained as he curled an arm around her.

Eliana leaned into his side and looked up at him. "Janwar found Simone, but she's been poisoned with *bosregi.*"

Dagon swore. "Does she still live?"

The somber question, filled with dread, merely heightened Janwar's alarm.

"Yes, but—"

"Check her wounds," Adaos ordered Janwar. "We learned in our latest bouts with the Gathendiens that some of them have begun to dip the tips of their spikes in *bosregi* poison before fastening them to their tails."

Dreck! Janwar drew a dagger and started cutting Simone's clothing from her body. Kova joined him, tugging the pieces of cloth away and tossing them aside.

"I was impaled by one of their tail spikes," Eliana said, "and lost consciousness within minutes. Dagon thought I was going to die."

"You nearly did," Adaos added, his face grim.

Simone had incurred far more wounds than Janwar realized. Scratches. Cuts. Deep gashes that would've rendered most warriors immobile. Puncture and stab wounds. Burns from blasterfire that had grazed her. Bruises larger than his fist. Every scrap of cloth he and Kova peeled away revealed more pale, bloodstained flesh with jagged injuries.

None still bled, which he found baffling considering the depths of some. Surely that must be a good sign, considering she still lived?

In very little time, they divested her of her shirt, pants, boots, and socks.

"Leave the bra and panties on," Eliana warned.

Nodding, Janwar set the dagger aside. "What should I be looking for?" Aside from the not bleeding thing, nothing odd leapt out at him as he scrutinized her.

"Black striations," Adaos said. "The longer the *bosregi* has to maneuver unchecked through her system, the more apparent they should be. Based on the amount of time you told me has passed since the battle, they should be making an appearance now."

Janwar nodded at Kova. "Check her head. See if her hair is concealing any injuries."

Kova immediately moved to that end of the bed and began to sift through her long hair to check her scalp.

"Elchan, check her feet and legs." Janwar leaned in closer and studied her face. Her features were pinched as though unconsciousness brought no reprieve from the pain. Only a few superficial cuts marred them, and none bore black edges.

He checked her neck, thankful for the pulse that slowly beat beneath the skin. Then her chest, too concerned to appreciate her plump breasts. Grasping her left hand, he lifted her arm and twisted it gently this way and that to expose every surface. He found plenty of cuts and gashes but no hint of the black markings Adaos had told him to search for.

Kova stepped back. "Nothing."

Janwar checked her other arm, then the ghastly wound on her lightly muscled abdomen. Her pelvis and rounded hips.

Elchan shook his head. "Nothing on her legs or feet."

Janwar straightened. "Nothing." He glanced at Adaos, who seemed to be scrutinizing her as closely as they did. "Are you sure the signs would be apparent this quickly?"

Adaos's brow puckered. "They were on Eliana."

Janwar nodded to Kova and Elchan. "Help me turn her over."

Together they gently lifted her and rolled her over, careful not to put any pressure on the worst of her wounds.

"Simone is older and stronger than me," Eliana murmured, "so she heals faster. Maybe—"

Janwar and his men swore foully as they settled Simone on her stomach with her head turned to one side.

A ragged wound stretched across her lower back. It looked almost as if someone had impaled her with a hook on one side, then dragged it through her flesh to the other before it tore its way free. The deep groove left behind didn't bleed. And it almost looked as though the shallow end had tried to weave itself back together and heal. But the rest of it...

Black tinted the mangled edges and had begun to slither across her skin like dark veins.

"Oh shit," Eliana breathed. Tears welled in her eyes and spilled over her lashes.

That couldn't be good. Swallowing hard, Janwar consulted Adaos. "What do we do?"

Adaos frowned as he studied Simone.

Eliana shook her head as she looked up at the medic. "They don't have a supply of her blood to give her like you did me."

"We have Segonian blood," Janwar said. "You said that's safe. Is that what she needs? Another transfusion?"

The Earth woman shook her head. "There's something... unique in our blood. Something that can fight the poison in sufficient quantities. Adaos happened to have a goodly supply of mine on hand when I was injured. It's the only thing that saved me." Again she consulted the medic. "But she doesn't have that. What are we going to do?"

Adaos motioned to Janwar. "Let me have a closer look at the wound."

Janwar grabbed the viewscreen and shoved it closer to Simone's back.

A moment passed.

"This end over here looks as if it has begun to mend itself," Adaos muttered.

"It does," Eliana said softly. "And there isn't as much black there."

"But this over here is concerning."

"Very," she agreed.

"Thank you, Janwar," the medic said.

Janwar released the viewscreen, allowing it to back away and hover across from him.

Adaos met his gaze. "I want you to give her another transfusion of Segonian blood. Twice what you would normally give someone her size if you have that much on hand."

"We do." He grabbed the datapad Kova held out and began typing in commands. "That and more. We didn't know what condition any Earthlings we might find would be in, so Elchan has been donating regularly ever since you told us he was compatible."

Janwar set the datapad aside and carefully turned Simone onto her side. The mechanical apparatus descended from the ceiling, found the bend of her arm, and began infusing her again.

"Thank you, Elchan," Eliana said. "I'm in your debt."

Elchan didn't seem to know what to say, so he just nodded.

Janwar bent Simone's knees and drew them up a bit to make her more comfortable. She wasn't conscious, but he hoped that would soon change. "What else?" He glanced up.

Adaos had moved away from the screen and now tapped on a console across the room. "Give me a minute," he uttered absently.

The comm in Janwar's ear crackled.

"Commander," Krigara said.

Janwar glanced at Eliana and Dagon. "Excuse me."

They nodded as he withdrew from visual and crossed to stand in Med Bay's doorway.

He tapped the comm. "Report."

"I was going to ask you to do the same," his cousin said, his voice pitched softly. "Srok'a said Simone is down?"

"Yes. What's your status? Are you in the lab?"

"No. I didn't want the prisoners to overhear."

"Be careful of their tail spikes," Janwar warned. "They've dipped them in *bosregi*."

"What's *bosregi*?"

"A poison that can be deadly to Earthlings."

"And to us?"

"Unknown. One of the Gathendiens must have caught Simone in the back with his tail. The poison is hitting her fast and hard. We're consulting the *Ranasura*'s chief medic and doing what we can for her."

"*Drek*. Judging by the grim tone of your voice, it isn't going well."

From where he stood, Janwar could see the black striations on her back. "Correct."

A long silence ensued. Then Krigara spoke. "These *grunarks* fight amongst themselves so much that I doubt they'd lace those spikes with *bosregi* unless they either had a natural immunity or an antidote. Their numbers are so few now they can't afford the losses."

Janwar nearly clapped a hand to his forehead in dismay. Why hadn't he thought of that? "That's *drekking* brilliant. Let Srok'a do the interrogating. I want you to hack their system and search for anything you can find on a possible antidote. But keep the Gathendiens oblivious. I don't intend to let any of them live longer than it takes to question them, but if reinforcements arrive and attempt a rescue, I don't want those *grunarks* to know how deadly that *bura* is to Earthlings."

"They won't hear or see a thing."

"And get a blood sample from one of them."

"I'll do it now. Krigara out."

Tapping his comm, Janwar returned to Simone's bedside. "Some of my men are still on the Gathendien ship," he told the *Ranasura* trio. "They're going to search the lab's records and see if they can find anything about a *bosregi* antidote."

Kova sent him a hopeful look. "That would make sense. Those *grunarks* are always fighting with each other."

"They're also going to collect a blood sample in case Gathendiens have a natural immunity to it. Adaos, do you think you can use that to manufacture an antidote?"

The medic answered without looking away from whatever he studied on his diagnostic screen. "If they have natural immunity, yes. But it will take time Simone doesn't have."

Drek!

Elchan started toward the other med bed. "I'm going to donate more blood."

Janwar clapped a hand on his shoulder as he passed. "Thank you."

Adaos looked at them over his shoulder. "How is her back?"

Bending, Janwar studied the wound in her back. "It looks the same."

"No change then. Have the med bed send me a visual I can monitor in real-time."

Janwar grabbed the datapad he'd set aside earlier and tapped the requisite commands into it.

A small ball the size of a *reama* berry floated down from the ceiling and positioned itself behind Simone.

On the Segonian ship, a screen lit up beside the one Adaos was using and displayed a clear image of Simone's wound.

The medic studied it. "Excellent."

Janwar stared at Simone's face.

Nothing about this was excellent. Her pretty features still reflected pain. The pulse in her neck was so slow he feared it might stop at any moment. Was the transfusion helping at all?

His gaze went to the gash on her stomach. "I'm going to tend her other wounds and give her a *silna* to speed their healing." Standing around doing nothing certainly wouldn't help her.

"No!" Eliana, Adaos, and Dagon all cried at once.

He stared at them. "Why? The *silna* may not be useful against the poison, but it—"

"You can't," Eliana blurted. "A *silna* wouldn't help Simone. It would hurt her."

Janwar and his men exchanged a puzzled look. *Silnas* had been tested on multiple alien races and had always generated the same results: faster healing.

Why would they think Earthlings would be harmed by it? If Segonian blood was compatible with theirs, how different could they be?

"Trust me, Janwar," Eliana implored. "I love Simone like a sister. I would never say or do anything to cause her harm."

She seemed sincere in her pledge.

"Can I at least clean her wounds and bandage them?" he asked.

Eliana nodded. "Yes. I would appreciate that. Thank you."

Janwar swiftly went to work, spraying each injury with *retsa*, a powerful disinfectant that swelled into a thick foam, dissolved all dirt, congealing blood, and bacteria, then melted away without damaging healthy tissue. "What about the wound in her back. Can I clean it, too?"

Adaos nodded. "The *retsa* won't halt the poison, but it will prevent infection from worsening her condition."

Janwar carefully tended to every injury, relieved when he found no broken bones on top of everything else. Once each cut was clean, he sprayed it with *imashuu* to numb the pain, added a bandage, and topped it with *kesaadi*.

"What's that?" Eliana asked as she watched him.

"*Kesaadi*," he mumbled, moving on to a burn mark on one arm. "It holds the bandage in place."

"It looks like rubber cement," she commented. "Is it stiff, or does it move with you?"

"It moves with you."

She glanced up at Dagon. "That's so cool."

He arched a brow. "Let me guess. You want some?"

"Yes, please."

Smiling, he drew her tighter against his side.

At Adaos's request, Janwar left the poisoned wound in her back bandage-free after cleaning it. Once he finished his ministrations, he stepped back. "If you'll excuse me, I need to check in with my men on the Gathendien ship."

He didn't wait for an answer, just strode from the room as he tapped his ear comm. "Krigara, report."

"One moment," his cousin rumbled. Footsteps carried over the comm. "How's Simone?"

"Not good. Find anything on an antidote?"

"Nothing yet. But I drew some blood from three Gathendiens in case we can't find one."

Impatience nearly dragged a growl from Janwar. "What's taking so *vuan* long?"

"None of us are fluent in Gathendien," Krigara said, his frustration evident. "We know enough to converse with them if they refuse to speak Alliance Common, but deciphering medical terms and phrases..." Unfortunately, translators only enabled one to understand spoken languages. It didn't allow one to read them. "And a lot of this *bura* is passcode protected."

"Can you break it?"

"*Srul* yes. I'm plowing through every obstacle. It's just the language thing that's slowing us down. I keep having to hold my datapad up in front of the screen to help me translate it, and not everything translates because the *vuan* scientists use abbreviations, acronyms, and symbols I've never seen before. Do you know how to spell *bosregi* in Gathendien? Because the translation matrix doesn't. Nor does it know what symbols they might put on a vial of *bosregi* antidote. These *grunarks* have a whole room dedicated to nothing but the cold storage of serums, medications, and—I'm guessing—bioengineered viruses that I sure as *srul* don't want to unleash by inadvertently removing the wrong cap."

Janwar swore. "I'll see what I can come up with. What about the interrogation? How's that going?"

He grunted. "The three highest-ranked *grunarks* refused to cooperate. But now that they're dead, the grunts seem less worried about reprisals and are more worried about making it out of this alive. They're all huddled together. And I heard one mention blaming whatever intel they leak to us on the officers."

"Good. Get what you can from them. Janwar out." He tapped his ear comm to close communication and entered his office. Dropping down in the chair behind his desk, he began typing on the console embedded in the surface. A clear screen rose above it.

Moments later, Prince Taelon of Lasara's visage appeared on the screen. "Janwar," he said with a wry smile. "I'm not going to ask how you managed to bypass our security protocols and contact me directly on my personal comm unit."

Janwar waved the words away. "I found another Earthling. Simone. She's hurt, and I need to know if I can trust Chief Medic Adaos on the *Ranasura*."

His attention sharpening, Taelon nodded. "You can. Commander Dagon and his crew are strong allies. It's why they're still searching for more Earthlings instead of ferrying those they've found to Lasara. We trust them implicitly with their care."

Relief loosened the knot of tension in Janwar's shoulders a little bit. "That's all I needed to know. I'll contact you later with additional details."

Taelon opened his mouth to speak, but Janwar shut down communication and returned to Med Bay.

Simone lay unconscious where he'd left her.

Janwar took a moment to peer at the wound on her back. He couldn't be certain, but the black lines didn't appear to have lengthened in his absence. That was something, wasn't it? He eyed the blood steadily flowing into her arm from a tube in the ceiling. Could the blood transfusion be helping her? Diluting the poison, perhaps? Or was the progression slow enough that it was difficult to detect this early?

Straightening, he looked toward the screen.

Adaos continued to tap on his console. Commander Dagon held Eliana, who wore a pensive expression.

Another Earth female burst into the *Ranasura*'s med bay and skidded to a halt beside them. "What happened? Maarev said someone found one of our friends. Who is it?" Ava was the Earthling Eliana and the Segonians had rescued. Janwar had aided her in sending a message to Earth.

Eliana motioned to the screen. "It's Simone. Janwar found her. But one of the damn Gathendiens got her with a tail spike laced with *bosregi* poison."

The woman's face paled. "Oh shit."

Two Purveli males stepped up beside her.

The thinner one frowned. "Is there anything we can do?"

If Janwar remembered correctly, he was... Jak'ri, Ava's lifemate? "My men are scouring the Gathendiens' lab records, looking for an antidote, but none of us are fluent in their language. Adaos, do you know the Gathendien word for *bosregi* or what symbol they should look for on the vials of serums they've found?"

Adaos turned. "No. I only know the Alliance Common translation."

"I might know it," Jak'ri said.

Ava glanced up at him in surprise. "Really? I thought you couldn't read Gathendien."

"I can't. But the scientists who experimented on us rarely hid what they did because they expected us to die. So Ziv'ri and I memorized every symbol we could, assuming we might need them if we managed to escape."

The Purveli's brother nodded.

Jak'ri motioned to the screen beside Adaos that showed a magnified image of the blackening wound in Simone's back. "Is that what *bosregi* poisoning looks like?"

"Yes," Adaos, Janwar, Eliana, and Dagon chorused.

The Purveli males shared a look.

"Twice while we were in their custody," Ziv'ri told them, "warriors were brought to the lab for treatment after brawling amongst themselves."

"One was unconscious," Jak'ri said. "The other two appeared ill. All three had wounds that looked like that."

Janwar stepped toward the screen. "Do you know what they were given?"

Jak'ri nodded. "They were treated with an injection." He glanced at his brother. "You think we can recreate the symbol on the vial they placed in the injector?"

"Maybe."

As soon as Adaos handed them a datapad, the two set it on one of the empty treatment beds and leaned down over it.

Endless minutes passed while they conferred and tried to recreate the symbol they'd seen.

At least it *seemed* like endless minutes.

Finally, they straightened.

Jak'ri held up the pad. "We think this is it."

Ziv'ri nodded. "Or as close to it as we can get."

"Send me a copy," Janwar ordered as the needle in Simone's arm withdrew, the transfusion complete. As soon as he received the image, he passed it along to Krigara and Srok'a.

Half a ship-hour passed.

"The poison is progressing," Adaos announced grimly.

83

Janwar studied the wound and swallowed hard. The dark striations had crept farther across her pale flesh.

"Give her another transfusion," Adaos advised.

Wondering how her small form could accommodate so much blood, Janwar did as ordered.

Again, the dark vein-like streaks on her back halted. But shortly after the second transfusion ceased, the marks resumed their trek.

Janwar swore.

Adaos's face grew grimmer. "Give her another—"

"I can't give her another transfusion!" Janwar nearly shouted. "I've already given her more blood than Soval would need if every drop in his body were drained! And she's half his size! *Less* than half. At this point, I don't know why she hasn't puffed up like a *balaminian* blowfish or why her heart hasn't already failed!"

Boots pounded in the hallway.

Scowling, Janwar spun toward Med Bay's entrance.

Soval barreled through it, a supply bag in one hand. "Krigara just dropped this off."

Grabbing the pouch, Janwar yanked it open. Several crystal vials rested within. "Where is he now?"

"On his way back to the Gathendien ship. He didn't want to leave Srok'a alone."

Heart pounding, Janwar grabbed one of the vials and turned it until he could read the label.

And there it was—a symbol nearly identical to the one Jak'ri and Ziv'ri had drawn.

"Is that it?" Eliana asked hopefully.

He held it out so they could see. "This is it."

S OMEONE WAS SINGING.

Simone turned her head toward the sound, lured by the smooth baritone voice. But her eyes didn't seem to want to open.

Pain arced through her, sparking a moan. Though she lay on her side, it felt as though her back rested against the burning embers of a fire.

She shifted, trying to get away from it.

The singing halted. A large hand came to rest on her shoulder. "Easy," the male murmured. "Are you in pain?"

She tried to respond but couldn't seem to make her mouth work. Nor could she open her eyes. Was she dreaming?

"Let me get the *imashuu*." When the soothing presence left her side, anxiety flooded her.

Then cool liquid misted her back and doused the flames.

"Better?" the male asked.

Her muscles relaxed as he helped her roll onto her stomach.

Gentle fingers brushed her hair back from her face in slow, soothing strokes. "It'll be okay," he vowed softly. "Rest, Simone. You'll be okay."

He began to sing again as darkness swallowed her.

S OMETHING SMELLED DELICIOUS.

Simone turned her head toward the mouth-watering aroma as her stomach growled.

A low chuckle filled the air. "That's a good sign," a male said, the same one who had been singing before. "If you open your eyes, I'll share it."

The scent grew stronger as if he waved a piece of whatever delicious morsel she smelled in front of her nose.

Again, her stomach growled.

"I know you're hungry," he murmured. "Open your eyes for me, and we can share first meal."

She tried. She really did. But fatigue defeated hunger and herded her toward darkness once more.

The last thing she heard was the male singing to her again as gentle fingers stroked her hair.

CHAPTER FIVE

T HE DRONE OF A male voice roused her.

Simone fought a frown. It sounded as though he were reading something aloud. Not a story. A... medical textbook?

Where the hell was she? And why did her back ache so much?

She stifled a grimace. Her whole body ached, but her back bore the worst of it.

Slowly, she lifted her lids enough to glimpse her surroundings through her lashes.

Her gaze instantly alighted upon a large figure sprawled in a chair beside her bed.

Jack Sparrow?

Her eyes narrowed. No. Janwar, the pirate who'd posed as a friend and ally, then betrayed her.

Just like that, it all came rushing back.

"Janwar," she growled.

His head snapped around. His eyes widened, and his lips turned up in a smile as he lowered the book to his lap. "Simone."

"You son-of-a-bitch! You *poisoned* me!" With a burst of preternatural speed, she rolled out of bed and tackled him.

The force of the move drove his chair sideways, spilling him to the floor. The book skidded away as Simone shoved him onto his back and straddled him. Curling the fingers of one hand around his neck to hold him down, she grabbed the dagger he kept in a sheath at his waist with the other and raised it high.

"No!" A woman shouted. "Simone, stop!"

Already driving the blade down, Simone managed to halt the motion at the last minute. Shock seized her as the voice registered. "Eliana?" She glanced around.

"I'm up here. On the view screen thingy."

Her heart began to pound as she looked up and spotted her friend's face on a screen that floated near the bed. "Eliana! Where are you? Are you okay?"

She nodded. "I'm good. I'm on a Segonian warship called the *Ranasura*. Don't kill Janwar. He didn't poison you."

Simone glared down at the muscled warrior beneath her. "Is that what he told you?" She lowered the dagger's point to his chest, touching it directly above his heart.

Why wasn't he struggling?

"Yes," Eliana replied, "but I'd know it even if he hadn't because I was poisoned, too."

That jerked Simone's gaze back up again. "What?"

"Janwar didn't poison you. The Gathendiens did." Nothing in either her friend's words or demeanor hinted at any doubt.

Simone looked down at Janwar in confusion. "You didn't poison me?"

Resting his strong hands on her hips, he murmured, "I am so attracted to you right now."

She blinked as a tingle of awareness darted through her. "What?"

Eliana snorted a laugh. "Now isn't the time, Janwar."

Shaking her head, Simone looked at Eliana. "What's happening?"

"You've been in a coma for three days," her friend said gently. "Some of the damn Gathendiens laced their tail spikes with *bosregi* poison."

Poisons back on Earth didn't affect Immortal Guardians. The bioengineered virus that had set itself up as their immune system always protected them from such, nullifying the chemicals or...

Actually, she wasn't sure how that worked.

"I know what you're thinking," Eliana said. "Poisons don't usually affect us. But this one does. Big time. I got caught in the hip with a Gathendien's tail spike and was out for the count within a few minutes. I nearly died. And we worried for a while that you *would* die."

Simone frowned. "Are you sure it's the same poison? I didn't start feeling sick and lose consciousness until an hour or so after the battle ended."

"That's because you're older than me. And stronger. So your... *immune system*," she said with a meaningful look, "was able to hold it at bay a little longer."

Translation: the virus that Simone's body housed had fought the poison longer and harder because older Immortal Guardians were almost always stronger than younger ones.

"Adaos!" Eliana called over her shoulder. She appeared to be sitting at a counter in a med bay similar to the one Simone now found herself in.

A tall, muscular man in a pale gray uniform entered from a doorway on one side. "I'm not going to fetch you more *jarumi* nuggets, Eliana," he grumbled. "If you want another snack and don't want to abandon your vigil, ask Brohko to bring you some."

Eliana grinned. "I already did. He said they're on the way. But look." She motioned to the view screen.

Adaos glanced toward it. His eyebrows flew up. "She's awake. Excellent." Then his brow puckered. "Why is she down on the floor, straddling Janwar?"

Heat flooded Simone's face as she realized her position... *and* that she only wore a bra and bikini panties. Rising, she hastily backed away from the handsome pirate, her fingers still curled around the hilt of his dagger.

Janwar grinned, unperturbed, and rose. Even though he'd come very close to dying at her hands, he seemed to be in high spirits as he straightened his shirt and—

Her eyes widened.

—tight breeches that failed to hide the effect her straddling his hips had had on his body.

She swiftly looked away, feeling completely off balance.

Adaos turned to Eliana. "Do you Earthlings always awaken, eager to inflict harm upon others, or did she lose her memory, too?"

What?

Eliana laughed. "She didn't lose her memory. She thought Janwar poisoned her."

"Ah." Adaos turned back to the screen. "He didn't. The Gathendiens did."

"That's what I was telling her. Would you show her a side-by-side comparison of my wound and hers and explain everything?"

"Of course."

"Janwar," Eliana said, "you've already heard all this. Why don't you get some rest while I catch Simone up on things?"

He opened his mouth.

"I'm sure she'd like to have a shower," Eliana continued before he could speak, "and a few minutes to gather her thoughts."

"Of course." He turned to Simone. "The cleansing unit is through there." Crossing to a cabinet, he withdrew a pile of black cloth. "I took the liberty of having our clothing generator duplicate the clothes you were wearing."

She frowned. "What happened to my clothes?" They were the only ones she had.

"I had to cut them off you. But I pieced them together as well as possible in hopes that the clothing generator could reproduce them. This was the closest it could come." He held them out to her.

"Thank you." Her hands brushed his as he transferred the clothing to her arms. "I'm sure they'll be fine."

Dipping his head in an informal bow, he strode from the room.

"He's such a sweetheart," Eliana whispered. "He didn't leave your side the whole time you were unconscious except to shower and use the bathroom. He even sang a little when he thought I was sleeping."

Simone stared at her.

Adaos did, too. "Janwar did?" he asked in astonishment.

"Yep." Eliana grinned. "He read to her, too. Mostly medical texts." She met Simone's gaze. "He doesn't know you're an Immortal Guardian or about the virus or that we sometimes slip into a deep sleep when we're healing. I think he was trying to stimulate a response and lure you back to consciousness, or—in the case of the medical texts—bore you so much that you'd awaken and demand he read something more interesting."

Simone laughed.

Eliana's visage sobered. "But you came damned close to dying, Simone. *Bosregi* poison is strong enough to kill the virus."

Ice filled her veins, chilling her to the bone. "What?"

"In large quantities, the virus can fight off the poison, but our normal viral load isn't enough to get the job done. I only survived because Adaos had drawn samples of my blood prior to the battle and had enough on hand to increase my viral count. But Janwar didn't have that."

"Then how did I survive?"

"He kept transfusing you with Segonian blood. Every time he did, the virus would replicate and resume attacking the poison. It wasn't enough to *eliminate* the poison, but it slowed the progression enough for Janwar's men to find an antidote aboard the Gathendien ship." She bit her lip. "Even then, it was touch and go for a while because we didn't know how much to give you."

Simone's mind whirled. Had the poison succeeded in destroying the vampiric virus, she would've been left with no immune system. "I nearly died." The notion shook her. She hadn't feared death in hundreds of years. To know she had suddenly come so close to it…

Eliana and Adaos proceeded to show Simone images of her wound and walk her through the treatments they'd administered, including the cleaning and tending of every injury by the man she deemed a pirate.

"Janwar's a good guy," her friend concluded. "He really came through for you."

He hadn't just come through for her.

Simone looked toward the med bay's empty doorway.

He had saved her life.

A smile lifted the corners of her lips. "And you said he sang to me?"

Eliana winked. "In a lovely baritone voice."

Just imagining it made Simone feel all warm and fuzzy inside. Shaking her head in bemusement, she promised to talk to Eliana again soon and headed for the cleansing unit. Though her limbs bore a hint of weakness that she found unsettling, such didn't keep her from getting clean or donning the clothing Janwar had left her.

They fit her well, a testament to the advanced technology aliens boasted. The pile included socks, cargo pants, and a t-shirt but no bra or panties, so she used a clothing sanitizer to clean those she'd awakened in. She found her boots in Med Bay's primary room and tugged them on, then ran her fingers through her long, loose hair to comb the tangles from it.

Silence encapsulated her.

Space can be so quiet, she marveled. Her heightened hearing magnified every sound so much that she could hear someone sneeze a few miles away, so Earth had been a noisy place for her.

She heard nothing now, however, aside from the barely audible flow of recirculated air. Was the ship stopped? The *Kandovar*'s engines had generated a low rumble her mortal friends hadn't been able to hear. But this one...

Simone didn't hear a thing. She couldn't even hear the low hum of voices the large crew and military garrison aboard the *Kandovar* had produced. It was a little unnerving, sparking an irrational fear that she was all alone again without even the computer's voice for company.

She stepped out into an empty hallway and looked up and down it. "Hello?" Which way should she go?

"Hello."

Simone jumped when a male voice responded. Turning in a circle, she failed to find whoever had spoken. "Who said that?"

"I did," the male replied.

Still no sight of anyone. "And you are...?"

"The *Tangata*," he announced, his tone friendly.

"As in the ship?" Was he a computer program like Evie?

If so, he sounded more human than the one on the *Kandovar*. Evie had always maintained the same calm, placid tone no matter the circumstances. This guy sounded downright jovial.

"Yes," the ship said. "But you may call me *T* if you'd like."

"Is T a nickname?"

"Yes. Janwar and his crew bestowed it upon me," he told her proudly.

She smiled. "Then it's very nice to meet you, T. Would you please guide me to wherever Janwar is?"

"Of course. He and the others are currently sharing mid meal in the dining hall. Shall I use lights to guide you?" The overhead lights began to brighten, one after the other, heading down the corridor.

"Or would you like me to slip into a maintenance bot and guide you with a physical form?"

Simone's eyebrows rose. "Is that like an android?"

"Yes."

"The maintenance bot!" she exclaimed. The Lasarans had mentioned androids and said some could be quite lifelike. Simone and her friends from Earth had all been eager to see one, but none had been aboard the *Kandovar*. Lasarans were serious about enabling everyone to play a role in their society and only used androids in disaster relief or wartime scenarios to ensure they didn't deprive citizens of jobs.

Rhythmic thuds sounded in the distance.

Simone stared at the end of the corridor, excitement rising. *I can't believe I'm about to meet my first android!* The little girl inside her practically jumped up and down with excitement.

Damn, she was glad Seth had chosen her for this fledgling trip into space. For hundreds of years, her life had read like the directions printed on a shampoo bottle: lather, rinse, and repeat. Except hers had been: hunt psychotic vampires, rest, and repeat.

Now almost everywhere she turned, she encountered something new.

Like the android currently rounding the corner.

She grinned from ear to ear.

It was everything she'd hoped it would be.

As tall as Janwar, it approached her with long, smooth strides that carried just a hint of the stiffness she'd expect from a robot. Built like a man, it boasted two arms, two legs, and broad shoulders. White metal plating comprised most of its exterior, with glimpses of silver at the neck and most of the joints. Its head was bald, its face bereft of eyebrow ridges. Though its features resembled a human male's (a rather attractive one, she had to admit), they were frozen in a blank expression. And its eyes glowed red in their sockets.

The droid stopped in front of her. "You are smaller than I anticipated," he said thoughtfully.

"And you are freaking *awesome*," Simone declared, wanting so badly to touch it and see if its metal casing was cold or warm, rigid or malleable.

T's head tilted to one side. "I am uncertain of your meaning."

"You're beautiful!" she clarified.

"I am?" he asked, the inflection in his voice conveying surprise that his face didn't reflect.

"Yes."

She might have imagined it, but he seemed to stand a little taller. "I thank you for the compliment." He motioned toward the end of the corridor. "Shall I escort you to Commander Janwar?"

"Yes, please." Simone couldn't help staring at him as they began to walk side-by-side. "Hey, T?"

"Yes?"

"Would it be presumptuous of me to ask if I may touch you?"

"You do not need to ask permission to touch this body. It is merely that of a maintenance bot."

She shrugged. "Well, it's *your* body right now, and I didn't want to be rude. I don't know the protocol because I've never met a robot before. You're my first."

"Technically, I am not a robot. I am the *Tangata*'s AI program. I just inhabit this form when duty requires it."

"You seem different, though, from the *Kandovar*'s AI program. More... I don't know... lifelike?" She winced. "I'm sorry. Was that insulting?"

"No. I believe that was another compliment. Most Aldebarian Alliance warship AIs only carry out orders and duties assigned to them and do not stray from those parameters. I, however, am a more advanced program and have achieved sentience."

Her eyes widened. "You can feel things? Like emotions?"

"Yes, although the most common emotions I feel are satisfaction upon executing my duties to the best of my abilities and frustration when Janwar and his men ignore my warnings and place themselves in danger. Ensuring the safety and well-being of the *Tangata*'s crew is, after all, my primary directive."

And she guessed that Janwar and his crew made a habit of flinging themselves into danger.

They turned onto another corridor. "Do you feel pain? Or pleasure?" Just how sentient *was* this fascinating droid?

"Not in the way I believe you mean. I cannot experience sensory input the way life forms comprised of living tissue can. If you shot this body with an O-rifle, I would register the damage but would not feel pain. If I touched your hair, I could analyze the chemicals in the cleansers you used and even sample your DNA, but I could not tell you if it was soft or coarse." He shrugged. "Though my artificial nasal passages can draw in air and analyze every chemical or particle it carries, I cannot determine its scent."

"Hmm." So he was emotionally sentient but not physically sentient? Did she understand that right?

"Do you still wish to touch me?" he asked.

"Yes, please, but only if you don't mind."

In answer, he offered his arm.

Simone rested a hand on his forearm and found the metal cold and hard with no give at all. "May I also pepper you with questions?"

"You may," he replied genially. "I like answering questions."

Simone grinned. "Then you're going to love me."

A S PER HIS HABIT, Janwar met his men for mid meal. The room they dined in was less a cafeteria and more of a lounge. It usually only boasted one table large enough for the six of them, but they'd added a second when Prince Taelon, Lisa, baby Abby, and their Yona guard had joined them temporarily.

A long counter divided the dining area from a sizable kitchen with an extensive pantry. When their crew had initially come together, Janwar had hired a kitchen staff to cook for them. Alas, the lure of the sizable bounty on Janwar's head had proven too tempting. And several assassination attempts later, he'd given up on the idea. Hence, the lack of a larger crew.

Instead of using a food generator (even top-of-the-line food generators couldn't compete with dishes prepared by living beings), they either took turns cooking the meals themselves or heated up a few taken from the hundreds of meals they paid their favorite restaurateur to prepare and freeze-dry for them. The latter usually required the male to close his restaurant to the public while he filled the large orders. But Janwar paid him well.

He and his crew loved their luxuries.

The other end of the room boasted plush seating that provided a place to relax and listen to music, watch entertainment vids, or play hologames and engage in other recreational diversions with easy access to the food stores.

"Here we are," T announced cheerfully.

Janwar glanced toward the doorway.

Garbed in her warrior clothing, Simone stood with her arm tucked through that of a maintenance droid T sometimes inhabited as if T were escorting her to a lavish Aldebarian Alliance gala.

What an incongruous pair they made. Simone barely came up to the bot's armpit and was all smiles and flushed with pleasure, while T appeared cold and unexpressive.

"Thank you, T." Simone patted the bot's arm before she released him.

"It was my pleasure," T responded. And Janwar was pretty sure the bot would be smiling if he could.

Simone watched the robot go, then practically skipped toward them. "That was so awesome!" she exclaimed.

Janwar couldn't help but grin as he rose but couldn't decide if the pleasure coursing through him resulted from relief at seeing her hale and hardy once more or because she looked so adorably excited. "What was?"

"Meeting a robot," she announced as if that should've been obvious. "Or android. They didn't have any on the *Kandovar*, so I've never seen one before."

"They don't have robots on Earth?" he asked, surprised. He knew Earth was considered a primitive planet but hadn't realized they were so far behind alliance nations technologically.

"Not like T," she proclaimed.

"Well, technically, he isn't a robot. He's a computer program that can download into a mechanical form if needed."

"That's what he said. And he was very patient when I bombarded him with questions." Clasping her hands in front of her, she continued to smile as if she'd just been given a gift she'd always wanted. "I found him to be quite charming."

Janwar shook his head. "I'm sure he found you equally charming."

"Indeed I did," T said.

Simone glanced at the empty doorway, then up at the speaker from which T's voice had emerged. Her eyebrows rose. "Has he already left the bot and uploaded to the ship? That was fast!"

Again he smiled. "No. He's still putting the bot away. But T can inhabit both the bot and the ship at the same time. Right, T?"

"Correct," T replied. "I can, in fact, inhabit the ship and all twelve maintenance bots simultaneously."

"That is *so* cool," Simone whispered, practically bursting with delight.

Amused, he shook his head.

"What?" she asked.

"Nothing," he murmured, unwilling to mention he found her adorable in front of the others. They'd already given him a hard time after Soval had caught him singing to her. But he'd been trying to lure her back to consciousness and spark a response in her.

Though not the kind of response she'd sparked in *him* when she'd straddled him earlier. That had been... unexpected.

Janwar cleared his throat. "I'm just glad you're feeling better."

"I am, too. Thank you for taking care of me." She turned to the others, her expression earnest. "Thank *all* of you. Eliana is convinced I would've died if you hadn't worked so hard to find that antidote. I hope you know how much I appreciate it. You saved my life. That is not a debt I take lightly."

They stared at her.

"I like her," T declared cheerfully.

Simone grinned and looked up at the speaker. "I like you, too, T." Then her stomach growled.

Janwar chuckled. "Let's get you something to eat."

An hour later, he reclined in his seat with his arms crossed over his chest and watched Simone with amusement.

The rest of the crew had returned to work, leaving the two of them alone.

Sighing, she lowered her utensils to the table and relaxed back in her chair.

"Would you like another?" he asked. Her appetite surprised him as much as her need for blood had. She'd slowly but steadily worked her way through two full meals. Even Soval didn't eat that much.

"No, thank you," she said, looking somewhat abashed. "Sorry about that. I feel as though I haven't eaten in a week."

"No need to apologize. I understand."

Pushing her plate away, she rested her elbows on the table and leaned toward him. "So where are we in terms of the Gathendiens?"

He'd insisted on not talking business until she finished her meal. The poor woman seemed starved. "They weren't as forthcoming as we'd hoped."

"Are any still alive? I'm sure I can frighten some information out of them."

He smiled, not doubting it for a moment. "I believe they would find you quite frightening. But the problem with Gathendiens is that only a few are privy to the kind of classified information we sought. I've interrogated many over the years."

"Is that how you found out Prince Taelon's sister, Ami, had gone to Earth?"

"Yes. We intercepted a scout ship the Gathendiens sent to your planet and pried the information out of those aboard it."

"Well done."

The admiration in her tone inspired a desire to puff his chest out with pride, which he promptly tamped down.

"What difficulties did you run into with those we captured?"

Mimicking her posture, he leaned forward and rested his elbows on the table. "The officers were lower level. The rest were common soldiers who were expected to follow orders without knowing what sparked them."

She winced. "Did I kill all the higher-ranked guys?"

"Yes."

"*Merde.* Once I started cutting a swathe through them, they came at me in such numbers that I didn't have time to stop and look for uniform insignias." Her brow furrowed. "Do they even wear insignias? Because there isn't much to their uniforms."

He smiled. "They burn their ranks into the skin on their chests."

"Hmm. I vaguely recall seeing scars on some of the Gathendiens, above their hearts, but I assumed they were old war wounds." She shoved a hand through her long hair, which had drawn up into soft waves as it dried. "I shouldn't have let my temper and thirst for vengeance get the best of me. I can't believe I blew it."

"You didn't blow it. A few of the soldiers we interrogated were of sufficient rank to be privy to at least *some* of the information we sought. But they refused to talk, choosing death over—"

"Dishonor?" she scoffed. "Everything they do is dishonorable."

"Agreed. But they chose death over the prospect of having their rank stripped from them by their emperor, which would've been their fate if we'd let them live and their betrayal had become known. That involves more than him simply removing the small patch of flesh their rank has been seared into."

"Now you've sparked my curiosity. You'll have to tell me about that later. What about the rest?"

"They could only confirm things we already suspected and offer up limited bits and rumors."

She frowned. "Like what?"

"They confirmed that their ship was the one that attacked the *Kandovar.*"

A muscle in her jaw twitched as her brown eyes acquired a faint amber glow. "Did they confirm that the *Kandovar* was destroyed? The AI in my pod said it was, but—"

"Yes. They destroyed it."

She swore.

"They had just finished repairing the damage inflicted by the *Kandovar*'s counterattack when you found them."

"Did they say *why* they attacked the *Kandovar*? Were they attempting to kill the royal family? Or driven by old grudges?"

"No." Janwar wished he didn't have to tell her. He would *not* take the news well in her position. "The Gathendiens only had one goal when they attacked—to capture every Earthling on board."

She stared at him. "What?"

"You and your friends were their targets."

Her hands curled into fists as her face flushed with fury. "They killed *all* those people just to get their hands on a few Earthlings?" Her volume increased with every word, ending in a shout.

"Yes."

"What the hell?" She rose so swiftly that her chair toppled over, then began to pace. "Why would they do that? Kill so many for so few?"

"Because they want to know why the virus they released on Earth didn't kill you all."

Halting, she turned to study him.

"I know about the virus that infects you," he stated calmly. "I know you're an Immortal Guardian."

Her expression revealed nothing of her thoughts. "How? Eliana said she didn't tell you."

"She didn't have to. T slipped into the Segonian's systems and found the information for me."

"It was quite difficult," T mentioned merrily. "They have been very careful to keep all mention of the virus that infects you and Eliana out of their primary records. The only place Chief Medic Adaos stores information about it—and the research he has conducted thus far—is on a single personal datapad that is not connected to their AI."

"Then how exactly did you access it?" she asked.

"I saw him download his observations on your recovery and the *bosregi* antidote onto the datapad, then delete the data from their primary system. I was curious about what else the device might contain, so I infiltrated it the next time he made a momentary connection. I am very good at what I do," T boasted.

Janwar smiled. "He is."

"The only other evidence I could find," T continued, "that the Segonians had made contact with an Earthling was a recording on

Commander Dagon's personal datapad of Eliana singing an Earth song called 'At Last.'"

Simone blinked. "What?"

"According to his datapad, he has listened to it many times, usually upon retiring for the night."

She met Janwar's gaze, hers full of bafflement. "That's just... weird."

He grinned. "Eliana and Dagon are lifemates."

Her jaw dropped. *"What?"*

"I take it she didn't have time to tell you that?"

"No."

He winced. "Perhaps I shouldn't have said anything."

"No, that's fine. I'm sure she didn't withhold it on purpose. We just didn't have a chance to catch up." Bending, she righted her chair and sat at the table once more. "Lisa and Taelon said being lifemates is the same as being married."

He nodded. "According to my translator, yes."

She bit her lip. "Does he know she's... different? That she's infected with the virus?"

"I assume so. T, can you confirm that for us?"

"Yes," T said. "He is aware of her differences."

"*All* of them?" she pressed.

"Yes. Chief Medic Adaos keeps meticulous records on his datapad, and I perused them all. One of his goals in studying the virus is to help Commander Dagon and Eliana find a way to conceive a child without transmitting the virus from mother to fetus."

She flattened her palms on the table. "Okay. That's a lot to take in. But if *you* could ferret out that information, T, can't the Gathendiens do the same?"

"No."

When he didn't elaborate, she shot the ceiling an exasperated glance. "Why not?"

"They are not me," T replied simply.

She looked at Janwar. "He's kidding, right?"

Janwar smiled. "No. Gathendiens wouldn't be able to sneak into the *Ranasura*'s system undetected. That isn't their strength. And T can do things ordinary AIs can't. The fact that he's sentient gives him a huge edge over the others because he can think outside the box, as Lisa would say."

Her lips curled up in a faint smile. "You guys picked up a lot of Earth slang while Lisa was on board."

He chuckled. "Yes, we did. T is one of the reasons I'm able to traffic in information so often. Interrogation doesn't always yield what I'm looking for."

"So T finds it for you?"

"When we're lucky."

"Were you able to get any other information from the Gathendiens you interrogated?"

"Only rumors they'd heard of a classified outpost where more extensive research is conducted. Since I've heard the same, I took it as truth."

"Did they tell you where it is?"

"They didn't know with certainty but thought it might be near Promeii 7."

"Which means...?"

"We're on our way to Promeii 7."

She nodded. Then her eyes widened. "Wait. What about my ship?"

His eyebrows rose. "The Gathendien ship?"

"Yes. I'm one hundred percent serious about claiming it."

"I thought as much, so we incinerated all the bodies, decontaminated the ship, locked it down, cloaked it, and tagged it so you can retrieve it later."

Her face lit with a smile. "Awww. That's so sweet. Thank you."

He laughed. "You must still be recovering from the poison. *No one* would describe us as sweet."

She waved a hand in dismissal. "Pfft. You can't fool me. You've already revealed your secret."

He stared at her. "What secret?" More specifically, which one? They had so many.

"That you're all just a bunch of great big teddy bears."

Janwar didn't think that translated correctly unless she was calling them large, hairy, omnivorous animals. "I don't know what that means."

"It means that you're big, tough, and dangerous on the outside like a bear. But you're soft and lovable on the inside." She winked. "Just how I like it."

Janwar could find no response to that.

Simone laughed, the joyful sound interrupted by a yawn.

"You should rest," he suggested softly. "Eliana said you would probably need another transfusion and a good night's sleep to fully recover."

"I just spent three days in a coma. You'd think more sleep would be the last thing I'd need," she grumbled.

"Nevertheless." He rose. "Shall I show you the room I prepared for you?"

"Sure. Though I hope you didn't go to any trouble on my account. I could just stay in the infirmary."

"No trouble. We have rooms to spare." He smiled. "This is a big ship."

Rising, she snorted. "This is an *enormous* ship. I wish I weren't so tired. I'd love to see more of it."

"I'll give you a tour tomorrow."

A maintenance bot entered and strode toward them. "Rest well, Simone," T said as he collected their empty dishes.

"Thank you, T."

Janwar led Simone toward the front of the ship. "These are the crew quarters. Thanks to T, we all maintain the same schedule instead of half of us working during the day and the other half keeping things running at night. We've had a higher than ordinary workload the past few days, so the others are probably already asleep." Because of the possible bioweapons on board the Gathendien ship, locking it down had been trickier than usual.

Every time they passed a door, he mentioned who slept behind it. "Soval. Srok'a. Kova. Elchan. Krigara. This one's mine." He passed it. "And this will be yours. T has already altered the access panel so you can open the door either with a verbal command or by pressing your palm to the pad."

Eyebrows raising, Simone pressed her small hand to the access panel.

The door slid up.

She smiled. "Thank you."

Janwar watched her stride inside and hoped the quarters would be to her liking. This was the same suite Prince Taelon and Lisa had used during their stay on the *Tangata.*

"Wow," she breathed as she turned in a slow circle. "It's so *big.*"

Most warships this size required a crew of hundreds, could carry thousands of soldiers, and needed multiple large bays to house the transports, fighter craft, and ammunition military strikes required. Which meant quarters tended to be cramped. But this ship had been specially designed for operation by only a few, enabling him and his makeshift family to have rooms that rivaled the size of those found in the homes of the wealthiest citizens on Aksel.

"If you'd like to change some things to make it more comfortable—"

"Are you kidding?" she asked with a disbelieving laugh. "It's beautiful. *Too* beautiful for the likes of me. I'm just a warrior, Janwar. This looks like Prince Taelon or some other royal family member should stay here. Not plain old me."

"Prince Taelon *did* stay here, with Lisa and little Abby. You'll find some of Lisa's clothing in those drawers." He motioned to the entrance to the bedroom, through which they could see drawers embedded in one wall. "They're all shirts like ours that she modified. I'm afraid T didn't finish adjusting our clothing generator until after we left the royal family on Lasara."

When Simone headed into the bedroom to investigate, he followed her as far as the doorway and leaned against the jamb.

The bed was large enough that she had to jump up a little to sit on the edge.

She would look tiny, sprawled in the center of it. As tiny as she'd looked perched atop him when she'd forced him onto his back and straddled his hips earlier.

"And there's nothing plain about you," he couldn't resist adding, his voice acquiring a rough texture as he imagined her straddling him again on the bed.

Simone had been bouncing experimentally on the bed but stilled when she heard those words. Her eyes met his. Her throat worked in a swallow. As she looked away, color crept into her cheeks.

Drek, he found that appealing, that a warrior as fierce as the woman before him could also be gentle and even... shy?

"I'll leave you to your rest," he murmured and turned to head for the door. Best to depart before he did something stupid. Only a couple of hours had passed since she'd awoken, thinking he'd poisoned her. He doubted she would welcome any amorous overtures on his part.

Inwardly, he snorted. *Amorous overtures*? What the *drek* was wrong with him?

"Janwar?" She spoke softly as the door slid up.

Halting, he turned to face her and couldn't guess what thoughts passed behind her somber expression. His heartbeat picked up as she closed the distance between them and stopped only a heartbeat away.

Tilting her head back, she gazed up at him. "Thank you. For saving me. For caring for me when I was ill. For locking down the Gathendien ship for me. And for agreeing to pursue the Promeii 7 lead and help me search for my friends without me even asking you to." Sliding her arms around his waist, she gave him a tight hug.

Heart rate spiking, he wrapped his arms around her and held her close.

"I'm sorry I accused you of poisoning me," she murmured.

He rested his chin atop her head. "I would've done the same in your position." He chuckled. "Except I probably would've killed you before I passed out and then died from the poison."

She laughed. "I think we're more alike than we are different because I would've done the same if I'd had the strength."

"Well, I'm glad you didn't," he told her softly.

After giving him another squeeze, she backed away. Head down, she cleared her throat. "How long will it take us to reach Promeii 7?"

"Nine days."

She nodded. "Are we still on for the tour tomorrow?"

"Yes. Have T alert me when you awaken, and we can begin after first meal."

"Okay."

He backed into the corridor, oddly reluctant to leave her.

At last, she met his gaze. A faint smile curled her full lips, and her eyes bore a soft amber glow. "Good night, Janwar."

He performed a slight bow. "Good night, Simone."

Her smile widened as the door slid shut.

CHAPTER SIX

S IMONE SHARED FIRST MEAL with Janwar the following morning. "Where is everyone else?" she asked, glancing around the empty cafeteria.

"Soval is flying the ship. Everyone else is sleeping in. They've had a long, few days." He downed several swallows of *dawa*, which she'd discovered was a delicious fruit drink similar to orange juice with maybe a little strawberry mixed in. Her gaze lowered to his neck as the muscles there moved with each swallow. *Merde*. Even his neck was attractive.

Mentally she rolled her eyes and refused to let her gaze drift down to his chest. The shirt he wore today fit loosely like the one he'd worn when she'd met him. But after hugging him last night, she knew it covered some very impressive muscles. This man worked out.

Returning her thoughts to the present, she sipped some *dawa*, too. "What about everyone else?"

He tilted his head to one side. "What do you mean?"

"I assume you meant Krigara, Srok'a, Kova, and Elchan still sleep." She gestured to what she assumed was the officers' lounge around them. "This is a huge ship. I imagine it takes a substantial crew to keep everything up and running and help you fight off any enemies who might pursue you. But I haven't run into anyone else in the hallways. Are they down on another level or something?"

His handsome face lit with understanding. "Ah. No. It's just the six of us. And T."

Stunned, she stared at him. "What?"

"The only other member of my crew is T."

She mentally reviewed every area she'd seen of the *Tangata*. "That's impossible. Six men can't run a ship this massive."

"Eighteen," T said in a pleasant voice.

She looked up. "What?"

"Eighteen men. The *Tangata*—s crew includes Commander Janwar, Krigara, Srok'a, Kova, Elchan, Soval, and me. I can operate twelve maintenance bots simultaneously, expanding our number to eighteen."

She lowered her gaze back to Janwar, who nodded.

"Right now," T continued cheerfully and maybe even a little boastfully, "I am scanning our plotted course for obstacles that may interfere with the autopilot's functions or require a detour; monitoring all communications within range for distress calls or any mention of Earthlings, Lasarans, Yona guards, Gathendiens, or the *Kandovar*; using T3 to repair a fuel leak in our primary transport; using T5 to examine your Lasaran escape pod and repair the damage it sustained while crashing through the *qhov'rum's* walls; composting the remains of yesterday's meals; using T1 to remove garments from the clothing sanitizer and fold them; monitoring the cloaking array's function; monitoring engine temperature; monitoring—"

"Okay. I think she understands, T," Janwar interrupted with a smile. "Thank you."

"Yes, thank you," she added, amazed that they could maintain a ship this size with just a skeleton crew.

"You are welcome."

Quiet fell.

Simone shook her head. "That's amazing. It's just you guys and T?"

"Yes." A teasing glint entered his russet eyes. "Is this the point where I should mention that fail-safe protocols are in place that would result in the total destruction of the ship should anyone decide that dispatching such a small crew and claiming the *Tangata* for herself would be easy?"

She laughed. "I'm going to have my hands full with the Gathendien ship. I don't need another, thank you."

He smiled. "Good to know."

As soon as they finished their meal, Janwar began the tour. The *Tangata* was massive, roughly the same size as the *Kandovar*, which had carried hundreds—or maybe thousands—of soldiers and crew. Yet because this ship housed so few, its design was much more open. Spacious. Luxurious even.

Not what one of her Seconds had once referred to as "new money" luxurious with fancy décor she had always found gaudy. But with a sleek, modern, minimalist elegance that greatly appealed to her. Paintings even adorned the walls of some corridors, breaking up the white with splashes of color.

"These are lovely," she said, indicating a few that particularly appealed to her. Some were landscapes depicting fascinating alien planets that looked as real as a photograph. Others were spacescapes of solar systems, nebulas, and the like. A few were portraits that portrayed men and women who resembled the crew but were older or younger. Beloved family members, perhaps? And there were portraits of the crewmembers, capturing snapshots of their daily life as perfectly as a camera. Elchan reading. Soval planting something in a garden. Janwar and Krigara sparring. Srok'a tinkering with something mechanical.

There were even some abstracts.

"Kova paints them," Janwar said.

Like most Immortal Guardians, Simone could draw well. Before the radio, television, and internet were invented, they'd had to find creative ways to entertain themselves and stave off boredom during the long daylight hours they had to remain inside. But she had never managed to master painting. "He's very talented."

"Yes, he is."

She smiled as they came upon a few of Lisa and baby Abby. Kova had captured them perfectly. Her favorite depicted Abby sitting on the floor, staring up at Soval—who seemed enormous compared to her tiny form—with amusing solemnity while she sucked on two fingers.

Janwar led her into a dark room. Lights flickered on, revealing another large bay.

"Wow," she breathed. "What are those?" Row upon row of what looked like sleek fighter craft stretched before them. But they were smaller than those she had seen on the *Kandovar*.

"Khemenu 6s, also known as K-6s. I believe you would call them drones."

Her eyebrows flew up. "Like surveillance drones?"

"They *can* be used for surveillance," he said, "but their primary use is as unmanned fighter craft."

She let out a low whistle. There must be a hundred of them... at *least*. A veritable army. "So you can never be outnumbered or outgunned."

He nodded. "And can avoid casualties in battle. We don't use them often." His lips turned up in a sly smile. "But we've used them enough for most to believe that an entire squadron of mercenary soldiers mans the *Tangata*."

Simone had been all over the *Kandovar* and had seen nothing like these. The Lasaran fighter craft had all required pilots in the cockpits. "Are these common?"

"No. They're expensive, the payment for each more than most governments and militaries are willing to spend when they can get standard fighters for a fraction of the cost. Also, the early prototypes malfunctioned in catastrophic ways that resulted in the loss of life."

"And these don't?"

"No."

"Does Taelon know about them?"

He gave her a look that suggested she should know better. "Of course not. Taelon didn't see this." He motioned to the sleek beauties and arched a brow. "I trust you'll keep our little secret?"

Simone arched a brow, too. "As long as you don't betray my trust." She was still getting to know him, after all.

He grinned, then narrowed his eyes playfully. "Are you sure *you* aren't a pirate? Because you sound a lot like us."

She laughed. "I'm sure. Although the more I see of your ship, the more I think there may be some interesting perks to becoming one."

He chuckled. "Perhaps we'll be able to convert you then."

The next room Janwar showed her rivaled Seth and David's arsenals back on Earth, except the *Tangata*'s armory bore countless weapons she couldn't identify.

And Immortal Guardians didn't use grenades. Making things go *boom* tended to be counterproductive when you didn't want society to know you existed, which was why Immortal Guardians and the vampires they hunted tended to use blades.

The human network that aided Immortal Guardians, on the other hand, had repeatedly proven that they would use whatever means and weapons they deemed necessary to protect the immortals they served. In recent years, that had occasionally necessitated Blackhawk helicopters, shoulder-fired missile launchers, flame throwers, napalm, and grenades, among other things.

After ogling the vast array of weaponry in the *Tangata*'s arsenal, she muttered, "Remind me never to piss you off."

Janwar laughed as they left and headed up another corridor.

"So," she said as he showed her a cargo bay the size of a freaking airplane hangar. "Space pirate. How exactly does one come to choose that particular profession?"

He shrugged. "It's not always a choice."

A sizeable engineering room came next, the hum of machinery much lower than she'd anticipated.

"On Earth, pirates are only viewed favorably by heroines in romance novels," she mentioned, making a mental note to become fluent in reading Alliance Common. That seemed to be the language they used to label things on the *Tangata*, perhaps because the crew hailed from different planets. "At least, those who do their pirating on ships are."

"What are romance novels?"

"Fictional stories that revolve around characters falling in love."

"And they fall in love on spaceships? I thought Earthlings hadn't advanced enough technologically for deep space travel."

She smiled. "We haven't. By ships, I meant the kind used in oceans. We still have pirates who prey upon boats."

"Ah."

"Most people," she continued, "consider pirates assholes who would rather steal than get a job and earn an honest living. Or they're considered assholes who get off on hurting people since pirates are known to be violent. Pirates who do their thieving from the comforts of their homes tend to be viewed as assholes who simply get off on screwing over other people. Either way, pirates on Earth are generally considered assholes."

Janwar offered her a tight smile. "A sentiment shared by many in the galaxy."

They encountered T3 when they left Engineering Room 1 and stopped to chat for a moment before continuing the tour.

"Do you know what a dog is, Janwar?" Simone asked as she admired more paintings.

"According to my translator, it's a mammal of the canine species on Earth that is often kept as a pet."

"Correct. They come in a variety of sizes and appearances. Some are tame. But some can be very dangerous. Do you know what a flea is?"

"An insect that feeds on the blood of mammals?"

"Correct again."

He studied her. "Are you educating me on Earth creatures for a reason?"

She smiled. "There's a saying back home. If you lie down with dogs, you get up with fleas." She thought about it a moment. "Or wake up with fleas?"

"These insects are harmful to Earthlings?"

"If they carry disease, yes. But mostly, it's a metaphor. If you lie down with dogs, you'll get up with fleas because if you *act* like a dog, you *are* a dog. Hence, the fleas."

He shot her a confused look. "I'm not sure—"

"Taelon is a good man." She smiled, recalling the kindness the Lasaran prince had shown her and her friends, how he'd gone out of his way to make them feel comfortable in their new environment and ensure their happiness and well-being. "He's a *very* good man. I spent four months getting to know him on the *Kandovar* and consider him a friend." Halting, she caught and held Janwar's gaze. "And I saw nary a flea on him."

A cynical smile turned up one side of his mouth. "Afraid he'll get a few if he continues to associate with me?"

She rolled her eyes. "That's not the point I'm trying to make."

Expression stony, he said, "Then please enlighten me."

"Taelon doesn't have an amoral bone in his body. I don't know if Lasarans have middle names. But if they do, Taelon's should be Honorable. He wouldn't associate with you if you were an asshole or amoral."

Some of the tension left his form. "Are you so sure? He was desperate to find his younger sister. She was missing, and he thought I was the only one who might be able to discover what had happened to her and where she might be."

"Bullshit."

He snorted.

"Not the missing sister part. That was true. But Taelon was already friends with you before that. If you were an asshole who got off on hurting and screwing over others, he wouldn't have anything to do with you. Period. Not even when he was desperate to find Ami. Because he would've had no reason to believe you'd deal honestly with him."

He resumed their stroll, his cynical smile turning into one tinged with amusement. "An astute observation. However, there *are* some instances in which I *do* enjoy hurting and *drekking* over others."

"If you mean the Gathendiens, we're in the same boat. Those bastards tried to annihilate my people. *And* the Lasarans."

"And they seem to have added the Purveli to the list of races they wish to eradicate."

The Gathendiens were the scourge of the galaxy. "Clearly, you are not of the amoral sort. So how did you become the dashing pirate you are today?"

He smiled. "Would you believe I sought adventure in my youth and stumbled into the profession by accident?"

She pretended to consider it. "You *do* seem the type who likes to get into trouble a lot."

He laughed.

"I honestly would like to know, though," she told him, serious now. Instinct told her to trust Janwar. He *had* saved her ass, after all. But there was also this oddly strong desire to know more of him. Almost a craving. Something she couldn't attribute to simple curiosity, not if she were honest with herself.

His smile faded, but his features didn't slip into the stony mask he sometimes hid behind. The one he wore like armor. Instead, he seemed comfortable with her, if a little reluctant to delve into her chosen topic.

Or perhaps he merely debated how much to tell her.

"Aksel, my planet, was similar to Purvel when I was a boy. We maintained positive relations with the Lasarans, Segonians, Secta, and other members of the Aldebarian Alliance. But sometimes, we warred amongst ourselves."

"Yeah. We do that a lot on Earth."

He nodded. "Aksel was divided into four quadrants or territories. Each had a ruler nominated and affirmed by the citizens of their quadrant. Every five years, their rule was reviewed, and they would then either be reaffirmed or replaced at the people's discretion."

"We have some governments similar to that on Earth."

"Well, when I was eleven solar orbits, the ruling tetrad banded together and began putting pieces into play that would alter Aksel's laws and enable the four rulers to remain in office indefinitely. They were very clever, convincing much of the populace that such would unite the planet and make us stronger, manufacturing dangers they claimed they alone could protect us from. But in reality, they just craved more power, more wealth, and the ability to do whatever they wanted to without being punished or wrested from office."

"Did it work?"

"Yes. But even members of the tetrad played the fool. Because it had all been a ploy by one man who wanted to rule the entire planet by himself. First, quadrant two's ruler died. Then quadrant one's. Then quadrant four's. All were deemed natural causes or accidents: illness, a transport crash, a fall. And most believed it, content to have the planet united under the rule of one charismatic leader who publicly mourned the deaths of the others even as he campaigned for absolute power. However, those who saw through his lies to the truth protested in the streets, questioning the deaths of the other tetrad rulers, calling for an investigation by a Lasaran delegation."

"Lasarans are all telepathic," Simone commented. "They would've discerned the truth in a heartbeat."

"Which was why he refused and changed course, announcing that he had received death threats and suggesting the Lasarans had orchestrated the deaths of the other tetrad members so they could put someone malleable in power to negotiate trade deals that would benefit Lasara at the expense of Aksel."

"Oh, please."

"Exactly. The protests continued, increasing in size and volume, demanding at the very least the nomination and affirmation of three new rulers to restore the tetrad, understanding the danger of leaving power over the entire planet in one man's hands."

"One man's bloody hands," she muttered, thinking how messed up Earth would be if only one person who could not be removed from office reigned over it.

"Hands he bloodied even more," Janwar bit out, "when he had most of the protesters killed."

And there it was. "Who did you lose?"

"My parents. And my aunt and uncle, Krigara's parents. Our illustrious ruler deemed them *yetoni*."

"That didn't translate."

He thought for a moment. "Terrorists?"

"Got it."

"I was eighteen solar cycles and Krigara sixteen when we lost them. But we were *drekking* furious and bitter and determined to reveal Chancellor Astennuh for the *grunark* he was. We picked up where our parents left off and managed to accumulate enough evidence to clear their names and implicate Astennuh in the protest killings. When his spies figured out what we were doing, Astennuh sent an emissary to try to buy our silence, but we told him to go *drek* himself. He couldn't have us killed without raising more questions, so he staged an attack, falsified evidence, labeled us *yetoni*, too, and sent cyborgs to capture us for execution or execute us outright if we 'resisted' arrest. I'm guessing he preferred the latter."

"What happened?"

"We couldn't elude the cyborgs when they came for us. But we talked fast and managed to catch the lead cyborg soldier's attention. Once we showed him the information and documentation we'd gathered, they let us go. The next day Astennuh ordered all cyborgs to be decommissioned... for the 'safety' of the nation. Put out some *tiklun bura* story about them malfunctioning and turning on other military units, slaughtering countless soldiers."

"That makes them sound like robots."

He shook his head. "They weren't. They were just men with so many enhancements and augmentation that they were as hard to kill as you are." He gave her a faint smile. "But the strength that they'd gained gave them power. They weren't like other Akseli soldiers. They couldn't be bullied or blackmailed into obeying all orders without question, even if it meant doing the wrong thing. Cyborgs were too strong. Too fast. And analytical as *srul*. They embraced logic. And thanks to the implants in their brains, they had access to far more information than we did... far more than the military realized... and turned against him." He shrugged. "Once the order went out to destroy the cyborgs, I knew it was only a matter of time before Krigara and I would be hunted down and killed, so we did the only thing we *could* do at that age with so few resources at our disposal. We fled to the ass-end of the galaxy."

"Yonkers?"

His expression blanked. "What?"

She grinned. "Sorry. Inside joke. I couldn't resist. I used to be stationed in New York and..." She waved a hand. "Never mind. You were saying? Ass-end of the galaxy?"

"Promeii 7."

"Ahhh. A place I heard a few of the younger Lasaran males whispering about visiting for a little off-world debauchery."

He laughed. "Well, they would find that and more there, though I doubt they'd linger. The things they'd read in the inhabitants' minds would have them blanching and racing back home within hours."

She wrinkled her nose. "Not a great place then?"

"Not a great place, especially for youths barely on the brink of manhood. Krigara and I nearly starved to death at least a dozen times before landing jobs a couple of years later on a cargo ship. We lucked out and found one commanded by an old Akseli male whose son had been a member of the cyborg corps."

"Oh no. Was his son...?"

"Killed? Or, as Astennuh put it, decommissioned? Yes. So Hanon was sympathetic to our cause." He sent her a sly look. "He also supplemented his income by periodically hauling cargo that wasn't entirely legal."

She arched a brow. "Stolen merchandise?"

"Yes. And sometimes exotic plants, animals, and other contraband that had been banned for one reason or another. He taught us everything he knew about running the ship, locating cargo, and finding buyers and sellers who paid more when he had to find ways to subvert mandatory inspections and the like to get them what they wanted."

She frowned. "Did he ever traffic in people? Women and children? Slaves?"

"No. There were always lines Hanon wouldn't cross."

"Like you."

He smiled. "Like me. When he died, Hanon left me the ship and my new vocation."

She was pretty sure there had been more to it than that. A cargo runner in the ass-end of the galaxy wouldn't incite the ire of a planetary ruler. "And the bounty on your head?"

"That wasn't Hanon's doing. Chancellor Astennuh forgot about Krigara and me after a time, so I... might have used the contacts and wealth we amassed as piratical entrepreneurs to remind him who we were, expose some of his secrets, and aid the growing Akseli resistance."

So he was a Robin Hood of sorts. "Is Astennuh still ruler?"

"Yes. More and more of the population of Askel see him for what he is now, but he's the wealthiest, most powerful man on the planet with a private army protecting him. No one can touch him."

Someone with preternatural speed, strength, and the element of surprise probably could. Perhaps once she found all of her friends, she would sit down with Janwar and Krigara and examine the evildoer evidence they'd accumulated.

They stepped into the next room on the tour. "Ooh." Simone smiled. "You don't have to tell me what this is for."

A training room the size of a school gymnasium spread out before her. Boasting high ceilings and a cushioned floor, it offered a variety of weight equipment that looked similar enough to Earth's for her to identify. A running track circled the perimeter. And one wall displayed multiple weapons with blades that looked dull enough to prevent one from slicing flesh from a partner while sparring.

"If there are only six of you," she wondered aloud, "why do you need so much room?" The *Kandovar*'s training room had been about the size of a football field, but that was because so many soldiers trained there.

"We train with T, too."

She looked at him in surprise. "You do?"

He nodded. "Though our security protocols make it unlikely, if an enemy force should ever board our ship, twelve androids trained in combat would enable us to defeat them."

"I assume he's stronger than a mortal?"

"Much stronger. Faster, too."

Stronger and faster than an Immortal Guardian?

Discovering the answer to that question might be fun.

Oh, who was she kidding? It would be *awesome*! She'd be the first Immortal Guardian to pit her skills against those of an advanced freaking android!

Until then...

She crossed to the wall of weapons. Most were blades and staffs. Janwar and his crew probably practiced the firearms in simulation rooms like the soldiers on the *Kandovar* did.

Her gaze wandered across daggers, short swords, long swords similar to her precious katanas, wooden staffs, metal staffs, staffs with blades on both ends, staffs that ended in rounded balls she suspected would bear spikes in actual battle. It was an intriguing array.

Like most of her immortal brethren, Simone held a deep appreciation for finely crafted weaponry. Reaching up, she plucked a plain staff off its brace. And this was finely crafted. It felt like wood

117

but must be from a tree she'd never seen before. Almost white, it bore dark stripes like a zebra.

Balancing it in her hands, she gave it a few experimental twirls, then turned to Janwar. "Care to spar with me, handsome?"

His burnt sienna eyes lit with interest. "Are you sure it isn't too soon?"

"I'm sure. I am one hundred percent healed. And after two months of being cooped up in that escape pod, I could use the exercise."

He hesitated only a moment, then smiled. "Okay. Do you want to change first?"

She glanced down at her soldier's garb. "All I have are more outfits like this."

"T," Janwar called.

"Yes?"

"You have Simone's physical specs. Do you think you could print her some exercise clothing?"

"Of course. Printing clothing now."

She blinked. "Really? You can *print* clothing?"

"Yes. Though some worlds like Lasara ban clothing fabricators on their planets to increase employment opportunities for their citizenry, they frequently use them on warships to avoid taking up storage space for uniforms that may not be needed. Have you never used one before?"

She shook her head. "On the *Kandovar*, we wore whatever we brought from home. And 3-D printing is still in its infancy on Earth. Most of our garments are sewn by people."

"Printing complete," T announced. "I will deliver your new garments momentarily, Simone."

"Thank you."

Janwar started backing toward a door on one side of the room. "The changing room, lav, and sanishowers are through here. Do you mind if I change my clothing while we wait?"

"Not at all."

Grinning, he disappeared into what she guessed was the *Tangata*'s version of a gym locker room.

Her spirits lightened. She really liked his smile. Every once in a while, it would light up his eyes and face in a way that let her glimpse what he must have looked like as a boy, back when all was right with the world, and he still had two loving parents.

Happy. A little mischievous. And today?

That smile was far too appealing, filling her belly with butterflies.

Footsteps alerted her to T's imminent arrival. For a heavy, metallic being, he had surprisingly light footsteps.

T entered the gym, carrying a small bundle of clothing. "Greetings, Simone."

"Hi, T."

"I have prepared your garments for you."

"Thank you. I appreciate that." Joining him near the entrance, she plucked the clothing from his hands and held them up. They consisted of a white, sleeveless muscle shirt and loose black pants. Both were as soft as silk. "Ooh. These are nice."

T's red eyes brightened. "I chose the fabric myself."

She didn't notice until then that a pair of something that resembled running shoes rested in his hands. "There are shoes, too?"

"Yes. Since the medical scans included the exact measurements of your feet, I opted to fashion you a pair of shoes that would benefit you more than your boots while training."

"Wow. Thank you." She measured one against the sole of her boot. "They look like they'll fit me perfectly."

"I am pleased you like them."

"I more than like them. I love them. You're a genius, T."

"Oh my." The android stood a little taller. "Thank you for noticing."

She laughed. Soft footsteps sounded behind her, alerting her to Janwar's return.

"Did you bring her everything she needs?"

"Yes," T responded. "And she is very pleased."

Grinning, Simone turned to show him... and promptly lost her train of thought.

Janwar approached with the long, smooth strides of a tiger. The loose shirt was gone, replaced by a tight white muscle shirt aptly named because it clung to every one of his mouth-watering mus-

119

cles and left his big biceps bare. The white fabric hugged a trim waist and rippling abs. Loose black pants hung low on his hips but clung to his powerful thighs when he moved.

Simone wasn't sure what he wore on his feet. She couldn't seem to drag her gaze away from the rest of him. Janwar was freaking *hot*!

"Do you like it?" he asked with a smile that brought butterflies back to her stomach in droves.

His body? Hell yes! "What?" she asked faintly.

"The clothing." He nodded toward the garments and shoes she held. "Do you like it?"

"Oh." She blinked and hoped fervently he wouldn't notice the flush that rose in her cheeks. "Yes. It's perfect."

"Simone said I'm a genius," T blurted.

She grinned. "I did. And you are." Grabbing the other shoe from T, she headed for the locker room. "I'll just go change."

J ANWAR WATCHED SIMONE HURRY to the changing room.

Had it been his imagination, or had he seen a glint of interest in her eyes—along with a faint amber glow—as she studied his form?

"I like her," T declared again.

He laughed. "That's because she said you're a genius."

"I admit that pleased me immensely. You and the others rarely acknowledge my genius."

He snorted.

"But I liked her before that."

Janwar smiled. "Yeah. Me, too."

"I believe she is attracted to you," T told him cheerfully.

Janwar stared. "What?"

"When you returned, her heart rate and respiration increased. And her face turned pink. Am I correct in ascribing those symptoms to physical attraction?"

"Yyyyyyyes." He glanced back at the empty doorway, thrilled to have his suspicions confirmed because he was incredibly attracted to her. "But you shouldn't mention such things." He turned back to T. "She may not want me to know that."

"Oh. You life forms *do* like to keep your secrets," he murmured, his confusion evident. "Does that mean you don't want Simone to know you're attracted to her?"

He stilled. "What?"

"I could not help but notice that your breathing changes, too, whenever she's near you. And when she hugged you last night, your arousal was impossible to mi—"

"No," Janwar blurted. *Drekking* cameras in the corridors! "You're not supposed to... That's personal T. It's personal. Remember that talk we had about privacy?"

T tilted his head to one side in a motion that mimicked Janwar's tendency to do so. "Is this a boundaries thing?"

"Yes. Boundaries," he confirmed. T might be brilliant, maximally efficient in many ways, and downright dangerous to anyone who threatened the crew. But he could also be as innocent as a child, his understanding of the intricacies of life-form relationships limited. He'd learned quite a bit by interacting with the crew. But his only contact with females prior to Simone joining them had been with Lisa and little Abby.

Even though the android form he currently inhabited did not breathe in or out, T managed to manufacture what sounded like a beleaguered sigh. "If I were living tissue, I think trying to understand the lot of you would make my head ache."

Janwar laughed.

Turning on his heel, T marched out of the room.

"Where's T going?" Simone asked.

Jumping, Janwar spun around. He relaxed a little when he spotted her emerging from the changing room. Hopefully, she hadn't heard any of that.

But he tensed again as she strolled toward him.

Drek, she was beautiful. She'd pulled her long hair back into a braid that trailed over one shoulder. Her new shirt left her shoulders and slender, toned arms bare. And the skin that graced them

121

looked as soft as that on the collarbones visible above the round neckline.

He stared, oddly transfixed. When did collarbones become a thing of beauty?

The stretchy white fabric hugged full breasts, a narrow waist, and a flat stomach that boasted hints of muscled abs. Loose black pants settled low on nicely rounded hips and molded themselves to her shapely thighs as she approached.

Janwar swallowed hard and hastily raised his gaze to meet hers so his body wouldn't do what T had mentioned and make the attraction he felt for her blatantly obvious. "What?" he asked belatedly.

"Where's T going?"

"I don't know. He didn't say."

"Oh." Halting a few steps away, she smiled up at him. "Then it's just the two of us?"

Images of some of the things they could do together when it was *just the two of them* threatened to subvert his efforts to avoid becoming aroused. But that was overshadowed by an odd spark of joy that flickered somewhere in the vicinity of his cold heart. The prospect of spending more time alone with him seemed to please Simone.

Her expression was so open and friendly that he couldn't help but smile. "Yes." He nodded at the track that circled the edges of the room. "I usually warm up with a jog."

"Sounds good."

The two took off simultaneously, heading for the track and settling into a casual jog. Nothing strenuous. Just something to warm up their muscles.

Though he was considerably taller than Simone, Janwar didn't have to shorten or alter his stride to keep her from falling behind. She matched his easily, a faint smile touching her lips as they completed the first lap.

A companionable silence fell upon them as if they'd done this a thousand times before.

"This is nice," she said.

"Yes, it is." He couldn't remember the last time he'd felt this... content?

No. He'd worked hard to make the Tangata what it was—not simply a means of conveying them from place to place, but a home—to help them all find some level of contentment since they could never go home again. So he was well acquainted with being content. But happy?

Was that what this peculiar feeling was? Happiness?

If so, he liked it. It had been long enough that he'd forgotten what it felt like.

They completed a couple more laps, then paused to stretch now that their muscles were warmed up. The stretches Earthlings performed were very similar to those he did when he worked out. Janwar made sure he was always positioned *beside* Simone as they chatted, laughed, and compared techniques. T was right, *vuan* it. Janwar *was* attracted to her. And if she bent over in front of him...

Well, his exercise togs wouldn't hide his reaction.

Simone had just been through hell. She'd embarked upon her first voyage into space. Her ship had been attacked. Some of the new friends she'd made on the *Kandovar* had undoubtedly been killed. The rest had been scattered across the galaxy, as had her friends from Earth if they still lived. She'd single-handedly taken on a ship full of the *grunarks* who had destroyed the *Kandovar*. Then she'd nearly died of *bosregi* poisoning.

The last thing she needed right now was a pirate she wasn't even sure she could trust trying to lure her into bed. "What now?" he asked when they were sufficiently limber.

She grinned. "Wanna race?"

Why were her smiles so *drekking* contagious? "*Srul* yes."

She laughed... and succeeded in chipping away another piece of the cold, numb, weary shell that had gradually encased him after too many years of life and death struggles, dealing with liars and swindlers, and striving to repay old debts.

It made him feel young again. As if he were no longer burdened by the past or what sometimes felt like the weight of the galaxy.

They returned to the track and stood beside each other.

Mischief twinkled in her brown eyes as she looked up at him. "Ready?"

"Ready."

"Set."

They lowered into starter stances.

"Set," he parroted.

"Go!" she shouted.

Both shot off, their strides lengthening and gaining speed with every step. Arms pumping. Braids floating on the breeze behind them. Mouths stretching in huge grins. Laughter escaping. She was amazing! Though her legs were shorter than his, she had no difficulty keeping up with him and even pulled ahead, forcing him to push himself harder just to keep up.

"Where's the finish line?" Simone called out after their second lap.

She wasn't even out of breath!

"The black staff on the wall," he said, heart pounding, muscles burning.

Something that sounded suspiciously like a giggle escaped her as she increased her speed even more.

Carefree laughter threatening to throw off his stride, Janwar pushed himself to his limits and barely managed to draw even with her just as they passed the black staff.

Both pulled up, slowing to a walk.

While Janwar's breath huffed in and out in gasps, Simone's remained as even as if they'd just walked around the track instead. The only indications he could find that she had exerted herself were pink cheeks and a fine sheen of perspiration that gave her skin a minute glimmer.

Laughing, he shook his head.

"What?" she asked, still smiling.

He motioned to her. "There is... a *lot* of speed... packed into that little body," he professed, still trying to catch his breath.

She laughed in delight. "There's a lot of speed packed into your *big* body. We tied."

He shook a finger at her as they continued to walk. "Only because you... willed it. You *know*... you could've easily won."

She wrinkled her nose. "Yes. But you're the commander." She gave him a friendly nudge with an elbow. "I figured you'd boot me off the ship if I won."

He laughed again and shook his head as his breathing finally slowed. "No. I'd just get you to race against Krigara—he's the only one who comes close to beating me when we race—and bet against him."

"Ooh. Devious."

He winked. "Well, I *am* a pirate."

"And the masses are all jealous of your booty," she quipped.

He cast her a quizzical look. "That word didn't translate."

"Jealous?"

"No. Booty. What does it mean?"

"Depends. Sometimes it means treasure or stolen goods that are valuable."

He *did* possess stolen goods that were quite valuable, most pilfered from the Akseli elite who supported the *grunark* who'd had his parents and other protesters killed. "And other times?"

She winked. "It means ass."

Halting, he mentally reran her booty comment. So the masses were jealous of either his treasure or his ass? "Which way did *you* mean it?"

Grinning, she turned away and headed for the weapons wall, a spring in her step. "Come on. Let's see if we're as well-matched sparring as we are running."

Vuan, she was appealing.

His spirits lighter than he could remember, Janwar strode after her.

CHAPTER SEVEN

S IMONE SWIFTLY FELL INTO a routine in the days that followed. Every morning, she met Janwar, and they shared first meal. Sometimes the other guys joined them. Sometimes they ate alone. Then they continued their tour of the ship.

The *Tangata* was huge. And just about everything on it fascinated her, even things Janwar considered boring, like the acquisition beam he'd used to bring the Gathendien transport she'd conquered aboard. Smaller acquisition beams controlled by handheld devices were used in the cargo bays to load heavy crates. When she'd asked him how they worked, he'd demonstrated by making her rise off the deck and float around one of the cargo bays while she threw her arms out, pretended to fly, and—she feared—giggled like a schoolgirl.

Once their breakfast settled, they headed for the training room.

That became Simone's favorite part of the day. They always seemed to have the gym to themselves. She didn't know if that was by design or happenstance, but she liked it.

She liked *him*. Janwar.

Simone felt so comfortable with him. In very little time, jogging around the track with him, their arms occasionally brushing, felt like being with an old friend. She'd missed that.

On the *Kandovar*, she'd had to adjust her behavior around the men so she wouldn't do anything their culture would view as too forward since unmarried Lasaran men and women weren't supposed to touch. Her friend Eliana hadn't been quite as careful, raising eyebrows when she "forgot" the rules and rested a hand on a crewman's shoulder, clapped a soldier on the back, or nudged one with an elbow.

Some aspects of Lasaran culture reminded Simone of her youth and the tighter social strictures she'd had to abide by, so she and Eliana had shared some laughs over it.

Back on Earth, Simone had often hunted with the same male Immortal Guardians for decades before being transferred to a new location either because she was needed elsewhere or simply wanted a change. Whenever Seth sent her somewhere new, there had always been a brief introductory period in which the immortal men would give off watchful vibes as they waited to see if she might have any interest in pursuing something amorous.

Until recent years, all Immortal Guardians had been turned against their will by vampires, who tended to be particularly brutal with females. Women rarely survived long enough to complete the transformation, so immortal males vastly outnumbered immortal females.

Unfortunately, Immortal male/human female relationships never seemed to end well. Human women couldn't be transformed without becoming vampires and losing their sanity. More often than not, the mortal woman would grow bitter as she aged and her immortal lover didn't, accusing him of seeing younger women on the side and driving a wedge between them. Or the two would love each other until the day she died an old woman. Then the immortal would spend decades—if not centuries—mourning her loss.

Relationships with *gifted ones* were no better since—until recently—the *gifted ones* had always refused to transform and spend eternity with the immortals they loved. They hadn't yet understood that vampirism and immortality were spawned by a virus and instead had believed religious claims that those afflicted would be damned.

So many immortal males dreamed of finding an immortal female with whom they could share a lasting, loving relationship.

Simone didn't blame them. Loneliness was something most of them struggled with.

Yet when nothing romantic developed between them, she and the immortal males she hunted with always settled into a comfortable friendship.

She'd missed that camaraderie and had found it again with Janwar.

Though they were from very different worlds and backgrounds, they shared some surprising similarities. Both enjoyed the simple things in life, like going for a nice, relaxing jog with a friend. Sometimes they chatted. Sometimes they ran in companionable silence. Both loved to tease and joke. They laughed a *lot* when they were together, often finding humor in the same things. Simone hadn't realized how much she needed that to keep worry for her friends from overwhelming her. And Janwar...

Well, his life thus far had been full of struggle and strife. He probably needed laughter and light moments as much as she did.

She really liked him... in a way she hadn't liked any of the immortal males she'd hunted with in the past. Those had always felt more like brothers to her.

But her feelings for Janwar were far from sisterly.

Like right now. The two of them had been sparring for over an hour, bodies brushing, limbs tangling, pulses racing as they challenged each other every chance they could get and admired each other's skill.

Even that—the way Janwar favored her strength, speed, and skill as a warrior instead of resenting it—thrilled her. There were too many men back home who felt threatened by powerful women. When confronted by one, they would verbally tear her down and disrespect her instead of treating her the same way they would a man in her position. But not Janwar. He was stronger than that. Whenever Simone managed to get the best of him and land him on his ass, he didn't sulk or bitch and moan. He grinned and looked at her with praise and something more in his eyes.

Something that made those butterflies flit about in her belly more and more often.

"How do I make the spikes come out?" she asked.

They were sparring with *baaki* training staffs today. When she'd asked him about the odd ends, he'd retrieved the real deals to demonstrate.

The one she held was almost as long as she was tall, with a round nub on each end about the size of a tennis ball. Fashioned from dark metal, the staff remained cool in her hands no matter how long she held it. They must have designed it that way to keep their palms from sweating. Very nice.

"You grip it here and slide your hand down it." Janwar demonstrated with the *baaki* he'd chosen for himself. When he slid his hand down the staff, spikes jutted forth from the spheres.

Simone duplicated his actions, but nothing happened. She tried again with no better results. "I don't think I'm doing this right. Am I not hitting the right spot or something?"

Janwar leaned his staff against the wall. "Try again."

Her heart skipped a beat when he moved to stand behind her as she repeated the action. "Still nothing."

"Here. Like this." He wrapped his arms around her... and like every woman in every chick flick who had ever been in this position, Simone felt her breath catch. Her pulse picked up, and the world around her seemed to slow. Closing her eyes, she drew in a surreptitious breath and bit back a moan.

The toiletries on the *Tangata* included a deodorant that looked and felt like water when you spritzed yourself with it. But it did the job and kept you from reeking after strenuous workouts *without* disguising your unique scent.

And she loved Janwar's scent.

"Clasp this end with your left hand up near the end, but not close enough for the spikes to get you." He positioned her left hand about half a foot from the smooth ball and curled his fingers around hers to hold them in place. "Hold it tight. Now grip it here with your right hand." He pressed closer to her back, took her right hand in his, and placed it directly beneath her left. "Make sure your fingers stay tight around it." A sensual shiver danced through her as his warm breath tickled her ear. He clamped his hand over hers. "And without lessening your grip, slide your hand down to the center in one quick motion." He jerked their hands down the shaft to the center.

The smooth surface of the spheres instantly morphed into a multitude of spikes.

"It worked," she blurted, heart pounding wildly in her chest.

He nodded, her hair catching in his beard. "I think you were loosening your hold as you drew your hand down." He released her hands but didn't step away.

"You're right. I was. Now how do I get the spikes to retract?"

"You do the reverse. But be careful not to slide too far." He repositioned her hands at the center and jerked one toward the end, stopping short of the spikes.

The spikes retracted, restoring the formerly smooth surface of each sphere.

Releasing her, Janwar stepped back with as much reluctance—she thought—as she felt over breaking the contact. "Now try it on your own."

Careful not to loosen her grip this time, Simone activated the spikes.

"Now retract them," he ordered.

She did, tossing him a triumphant grin over her shoulder.

"Activate them again."

Spikes appeared at her command.

"Retract them."

She found the task easy now that she understood it. "This is so cool."

Chuckling, he retrieved his *baaki* staff and stood facing her once more. When he activated the spikes on his, it seemed much smoother, almost an afterthought, indicating his comfort with the weapon. "Want to see something cooler?" he asked, an increasingly familiar sparkle entering his russet eyes.

"Hell yes."

Grinning, he gripped the staff with both hands, then gave it a swift shake, almost like one would do if one were faking a throw.

Blue light sparked to life on the spheres, crackling through the spikes like electricity.

Her eyes widened. "Is that what I think it is?"

He nodded. "The shock this gives your opponent will instantly incapacitate him."

"That is *awesome!*" She gave her staff a shake.

Nothing happened.

"Don't hold it in the center. Grip it like this." He positioned his hands slightly wider than a shoulder's width apart and gave the staff another shake. The electricity disappeared.

Simone followed his example, and blue light crackled to life. "Yes! Does it only do it when the spikes are raised?"

"No. You can do it with or without the spikes. The shock will just last longer if the spikes are embedded in your opponent's armor or flesh than it would if you delivered a quick blow from one of the smooth ends."

"Does it work on all aliens? Or do some have natural defenses against it?"

"Unless they're chemically enhanced, this will hurt anyone you touch with it."

By chemically enhanced, she assumed he meant high as a kite. She knew some drugs on Earth could vastly alter one's tolerance for pain. "Including Gathendiens?"

He nodded. "Even their thick hide can't protect them from it."

"Good to know." She motioned to his drool-worthy body. "You don't by any chance have a protective suit you could wear to spar with me, do you? I'd like to practice with this but don't want to accidentally impale you or shock you while I get used to controlling it."

"I don't. But T can spar with you until you're comfortable with it. It takes a stronger jolt than these deliver to take him out." He glanced up at the ceiling. "Hey, T. Are you up for a little exercise?"

"To quote Simone," T replied, "hell yes."

Eyes wide, she grinned at Janwar as she bounced up and down on her toes. "I get to spar with an android!"

Laughing, he shook his head. "You are too *drekking* adorable."

Even that made her heart go pitter-patter.

JANWAR DIDN'T SPAR WITH Simone the following day.

He had to admit he was a little disappointed. Their companionable jogs and training sessions had swiftly become his favorite part of the day. But he'd saved the best of the *Tangata* tour for last and wanted plenty of time to savor it with her.

"You seem different today," she commented as they negotiated the maze of corridors.

"What do you mean?"

She shrugged. "You seem... excited, maybe? Like you have a secret you're just bursting to share with me."

He smiled and frowned at the same time. "That's disconcerting."

"What is?"

"That you know me so well."

"Aha!" She gave him a triumphant poke in the chest. "Then you *do* have a secret. What is it? Tell me."

He laughed. "It's one I have to show you."

Her eyes narrowed. "Oooh. Intriguing."

Drek, he liked her. Far more than he should. And he loved the way he felt when they were together.

Such was not wise. The Earthlings were all bound for Lasara, so Janwar knew her stay on the *Tangata* would be temporary. Yet he couldn't seem to keep his distance, seeking Simone's company often throughout the day, something the rest of the crew must have noticed.

Krigara certainly had. When he'd left last meal the previous evening, his cousin had caught Janwar's eye and indicated with an arch of his brow that he hoped Janwar understood how ill-advised it would be to fall for Simone.

Krigara had never felt the need to issue that silent warning before. The fact that he did now was telling.

But not necessary. Janwar knew pursuing anything beyond friendship with Simone was foolish. He had amassed many enemies in his quest to avenge his parents' deaths. The last thing he wanted was for those *grunarks* to start targeting Simone or view her as a means to get to him. Though he knew from their sparring sessions—and her stunning defeat of every soldier aboard the Gathendien ship—that she was a highly skilled warrior, he didn't want to put her in the position of having to constantly look over her shoulder and guard her back. That *bura* was tiring.

And that was all he had to offer her. Life as an outlaw. Isolation from everyone she loved.

Once her friends were rescued and taken to Lasara, she would surely want to join them or at least visit them frequently. Prince Taelon had indicated that King Dasheon and Queen Adiransia had thawed toward Janwar after he and his crew had located Ami; raced to Taelon's rescue; and safely delivered the prince, his lifemate, and the first new royal heir to step foot on their homeworld in half a century to Lasara. But had they thawed enough to permit him to visit? If so (and he had his doubts), how would that work? How would it look? The Lasaran people enjoyed a world free of strife because they were such stringent rule followers. How would the populace react to their sovereign leaders suddenly looking the other way and welcoming a notorious rule-breaker like him?

Not well, he would think.

But *vuan* it, Simone was like *loana*. He couldn't see the mouth-watering pastry without wanting a taste. Or *jarumi* nuggets, his favorite snack. He could never eat just one. He wanted the whole *drekking* bag.

Janwar didn't want to just pass Simone in the corridors or only see her when he shared a meal with the rest of the crew. He wanted to spend every moment he could with her, laughing and talking, jogging and sparring, which was all sweet torture because he knew they could never have more than that.

Halting shortly before they reached an intersection, he turned to her. "Close your eyes."

Simone didn't ask why or look suspicious. She simply smiled and closed her eyes.

Vuan, that was tempting—her standing so close with her face tilted up and those lovely lips close enough to kiss.

He had intended to take her arm and guide her the remaining distance to their destination but instead clasped her hand, twining his fingers through hers.

Her lips parted.

Soooo tempting.

Lasara. She intends to make a new life on Lasara when all this is fin-ished, he reminded himself sternly and led her around the corner where a clear, *stovicun* crystal doorway waited.

When Janwar pressed his free hand to the reader on the wall beside it, the door slid up.

A warm breeze buffeted them.

Simone sucked in a breath.

"Open your eyes," he murmured, turning to watch her reaction.

Her long lashes fluttered, then lifted. Pretty brown eyes widened as she stared in awe at the room behind him. "What is this?" she asked, her voice soft and reverent.

"This," he said, backing into the room and drawing her after him, "is what makes the air on the *Tangata* smell so good. It's what provides us with a healthy environment." He glanced over his shoulder. "And it's what makes this our home."

The crystal door slid shut behind her as he drew her forward.

Another breeze brushed them, lifting loose strands of hair and caressing their skin.

Bird song serenaded them with musical notes.

"It's beautiful," Simone said as her rapt gaze swept this way and that, trying to take everything in.

Janwar moved to stand beside her and tried to see it with fresh eyes.

As he did, satisfaction filled him.

The park was multiple decks high. It had to be to accommodate the forest it housed.

"And so big," she marveled. "How far does it go?"

"It stretches almost the entire length of the ship."

"That's amazing."

He began to stroll down the shaded path, wondering how long it would take her to realize he still held her hand. "We refer to it as the park. The forest takes up most of the space, but there are also a couple of meadows, a lake we enjoy swimming in, rocks we can climb, and the garden."

She shook her head. "I know I sound like a broken record, but this is amazing, Janwar." A colorful *maahili* fluttered past in front of them. "There are butterflies, too?"

Accepting the term his translator provided, he nodded. "Every ecosystem needs producers, consumers, decomposers, and pollinators like the *maahili* we just saw."

"There's another one!" She pointed with her free hand, her face alight with excitement.

He nodded. "You'll find insects and wildlife throughout the park."

"How varied is the wildlife?" she asked. "Are there any predators I should worry about?"

He grinned. "No. The mammals are all small enough not to pose a threat to you." As if to confirm his words, a *samaela* scurried across their path.

"Is that a squirrel?" She laughed in delight. "It's so cute!"

"It's called a *samaela*. My translator says they're similar to Earth's squirrels and feed on nuts and seeds. They're quite friendly, too."

"This is..." She shook her head. "It's extraordinary. They didn't have anything like this on the *Kandovar*."

"That's because the *Kandovar* is a warship."

"So is the *Tangata*."

"Yes," he acknowledged. "But the *Tangata* doesn't house a full regiment of pilots and ground forces or the hundreds of crewmembers needed to feed and support so many and keep the ship running. So we had plenty of room for this."

She shook her head. "It doesn't even feel like we're on a ship. It feels like we're walking through a forest on Earth."

"That's why we all like it here so much." None of them had a planet they could call home, no motherland they could return to between missions like the crews of the *Kandovar* and the *Ranasura*. Instead, this ship was their home, the park their retreat.

They strolled along the path for some time, Simone asking one question after another. Janwar found it even more peaceful and soothing than their morning jogs. This moment... right now... rambling through the forest, with Simone smiling and chattering and holding his hand, was the happiest he could remember ever experiencing.

Light bloomed up ahead.

"Is that one of the meadows you mentioned?" she asked.

He shook his head. "It's the garden."

The trees thinned, then stopped altogether, giving them a view of row after row of carefully cultivated plants bearing vegetables and fruits.

Halting, she spent a long moment drinking it in. "Wow. You mentioned having plenty of food, but I didn't realize that was because you grow it yourself."

Pride filled him as he examined the results of their hard work. "The *Tangata* provides us with everything we need to survive."

"Not just survive." She motioned to the garden. "Thrive."

He nodded. "We don't need generators to rid the ship of excess carbon dioxide and provide us with the oxygen we need. The trees and other plants do that for us. They also provide us with more than enough food. Spices, too. And even clean and recycle our wastewater."

She looked up at him in surprise. "What?"

He motioned behind them. "All of our wastewater is pumped into the park's far end as groundwater. As it makes its way toward this end, the roots of the plants absorb nutrients from it and remove anything harmful, purifying it naturally and even more efficiently than the recycling processors found on most warships. By the time it reaches the lake we swim in and the streams that feed the garden's irrigation system, it's clean. The excess is then carried through a simple filter into storage tanks to be used again."

"That's incredible. So you literally have your own self-sustaining ecosystem?"

"Yes."

"I am so freaking impressed." She started forward once more, tugging him after her. "Tell me more about your garden and what some of these vegetables and fruits are. That one looks almost like corn with some kind of bean vine growing up its stalk."

Janwar named the different plants, beginning with the *reladi* she called corn. Reluctantly releasing her hand, he broke off one of the round vegetables and peeled back the husk to show her the yellow interior. "We use *reladi* in many dishes, but it's also used to make my favorite snack: *jarumi* nuggets."

She grinned. "Eliana mentioned those. Either her or Adaos."

"They're addictive. I admit I used my piratical resources to acquire the recipe."

"So you make all of your food?"

He shrugged. "Much of it. We buy special treats when we visit planets or docking ports. And I have our favorite restaurant prepare meals in bulk that we freeze and can reheat whenever none of us feel like cooking. But the park provides everything else." He started down the row. "Here's something I think you'll particularly enjoy."

Simone hissed suddenly.

Spinning around, Janwar found her staring down at her arm. It looked like she was in pain. "What's wrong?" He strode toward her. "Did one of the *nehpits* sting you?" A number of the plump little insects buzzed around, busily collecting nectar and pollinating the plants. Usually, they paid Janwar and the others no heed.

She glanced up at him as he reached her, her face full of dismay.

"Simone?"

Spinning around, she ran back to the forest.

Janwar dropped the *reladi* and jogged after her. "What's wrong? Are you hurt?"

She stopped a few strides into the trees with her back to him.

"Simone?" He halted behind her.

Lowering her head, she shook it slowly. The hands at her sides curled into fists, increasing his concern. Then she turned to face him.

His heart sank. The pale skin of her face was now a livid pink. When she held her arms out for his inspection, they too were pink and appeared burned.

"What happened?" Trying to hide his alarm, he gingerly clasped her fingers and studied her angry flesh. "Were you stung?"

"No."

"Is this some kind of allergic reaction to the *reladi*?" How could that be? She'd eaten meals that contained *reladi* several times without suffering any reaction to them.

"It's an allergic reaction," she confirmed, her voice a little thick, "but not from the *reladi*." Was she on the brink of tears, or was her throat swelling from the allergic reaction?

Janwar's concern escalated. "We need to get you to Med Bay."

Shaking her head, she didn't move when he tried to urge her back down the shaded path. "Med Bay can't help me, Janwar."

The resignation in her tone halted him. "I don't understand."

She nodded at the garden behind them. "You said the plants provide you with everything you need. You provide them with everything they need, too, don't you?"

"Yes." Where was she going with this?

"Including simulated sunlight?"

"Yes."

She stared past him at the garden, her expression wistful. "I was so entranced by the beauty of it all that I forgot for a moment..." She shrugged and sent him a sad smile. "I simply forgot."

"I don't understand."

"The peculiar virus that infects me..."

"The one the Gathendiens genetically engineered?"

She nodded. "Another downside of it is photosensitivity."

He stared at her. The *Tangata*'s corridors were well lit, as was the training room and every other he'd shown her on the tour. "*All* light doesn't harm you."

"No. But sunlight does."

And he'd just led her into simulated sunlight.

"If I'd lingered longer than I did, my skin would've blistered."

Janwar bit back a curse. "Apologies. Many apologies."

She shook her head. "You didn't know." Again her gaze drifted past him. "And I should've realized that all these plants would need more than standard artificial light. It was my mistake."

His heart clenched at the regret reflected in her eyes. "Are you sure you don't want to go to Med Bay?"

"Yes. It's just a sunburn. It'll fade quickly as long as I stay in the shade." She turned and headed back up the path.

Silence engulfed them as he followed.

His was rife with self-recrimination. Hers carried a palpable sadness.

"You have to avoid sunlight completely?" he asked softly.

She nodded, her eyes on her boots. "On Earth, I only ventured out at night. My brethren, too. No amount of sunscreen applied to our skin could prevent the inevitable reaction." She shrugged. "It's one of the things I loved so much about being on the *Kandovar*." She cast him a smile that lacked its usual hint of amusement. "And here on the *Tangata*. For the first time in many years, I could keep the same schedule as everyone else—sleeping at night and going about during the day—and feel... normal."

Then he'd dangled sunlight in front of her and yanked that normalcy away.

Though Simone still seemed to find pleasure in the forest and its inhabitants as they meandered through the trees, disappointment had leeched some of the joy from her.

"I don't know why you'd want to be normal," Janwar mentioned casually. When she glanced up at him uncertainly, he arched a brow. "Normal is boring. If anything, I'd think you'd want to be more like me."

Her lips twitched as some of the darkness left her countenance. "And you are?"

Turning his head to face the path ahead, he tilted his chin up and looked down his nose at her. "Magnificent," he announced haughtily.

She laughed.

Pleased to have made her smile again, he held out his hand.

Simone didn't hesitate to take it, twining her small fingers through his as they continued their stroll.

CHAPTER EIGHT

T HEY REACHED PROMEII 7 five days later.

Tiny compared to its sister planets, Promeii 7 was the runt of this particular solar system.

Simone studied it curiously. So this was the ass-end of the galaxy.

When viewed from space, it bore a reddish hue that reminded her of Mars. Very little water interrupted the barren land that proliferated on its surface—far less than that found on Earth—which likely accounted for the lack of vegetation. As far as she could see, the planet boasted no verdant forests.

Mountains? Yes.

Valleys? Yes.

Open pits that resembled those produced by mining? Oh, yes. There were plenty of those.

But that was about it aside from a few strips of green that bordered narrow rivers.

Overall, Promeii 7 was a dry, arid planet with nothing to recommend it.

Once night fell, she, Janwar, and Soval boarded a small transport and flew down to a city equally lacking in appeal.

Perhaps the place looked better during the day?

She glanced around. *Nnnno. It would probably look worse.*

Simone wasn't sure what she had expected. Maybe something as flashy and eye-catching as the Las Vegas strip. Promeii 7 did seem to have a similar reputation. Except what happened in Promeii 7 didn't stay in Promeii 7... unless it involved corpses. According to Janwar, murders were so common on this little planet that having to step over a dead body while walking down the street was a norm.

Unlike Vegas, however, there was nothing flashy about this place. Just dust, old buildings, an open-air market she might like to check out later, and inhabitants who either looked beaten down by life or emitted as much menace as they did body odor.

Both groups stopped whatever they were doing and stared as Janwar, Simone, and Soval strode past. None approached them, threatened them, or offered greetings. They just stood there, eyes tracking every movement.

Creepy.

The bar Janwar took them to both exceeded *and* fell short of her wild expectations. The inside was dark and delightfully seedy. Simone had frequented too many disreputable taverns to count over the centuries while on the hunt. Vampires tended to be lazy and sought easy targets: men too deep in their cups to recognize a predator when one stood right in front of them, travelers too weary to take the time to scope out the shadows and ensure they were bereft of danger, and women desperate enough for coins to slip away with any man who offered them a few for a quick tumble.

Most of those wouldn't be missed when they disappeared. The deaths of those who *would* be missed were always ascribed to thefts that turned violent or accidents, leaving the vampires free to slay again. But Immortal Guardians did their damnedest to ensure those deaths were avenged and the lives of future victims spared.

The battered exterior of *this* tavern practically shouted, "Enter at your own risk."

This is going to be fun, she thought and followed Janwar inside.

The first thing that hit her was the smell.

Immortal Guardians had heightened senses. And *wow*, this was a lot to take in. Or rather, it was a lot to try to keep *out*. Unwashed bodies. Liquor that seemed to have a similar aroma even light-years away from Earth. Exotic foods. Other scents she couldn't identify, some of which were damned near gag-inducing.

Unique body odors or pheromones she'd never encountered, perhaps?

Lasarans and Yona were frequent bathers and pretty much smelled like humans. Akselis and Segonians, too. Janwar's scent was particularly intoxicating, probably because she was attracted to him. Kova and Srok'a each bore their own unique, pleasant scents. And Soval smelled as fresh as a baby. So... yeah. She didn't know what the hell was currently curling her nose hairs.

No music played, neither from a live band comprised of peculiar-looking aliens nor a hidden futuristic jukebox. No singer crooned a tune on a raised stage in a skimpy outfit that neglected to draw attention from her oddly shaped head.

There was just a bar, some bar stools, and multiple tables packed with patrons.

With each step, her boots produced a sound akin to the one Velcro made when you pried two pieces apart, indicating a very sticky floor. Sticky with *what* she didn't want to know.

As she glanced around, Simone couldn't help but feel slightly disappointed. This wasn't exactly what she had expected.

Granted, everyone in here had alien origins, which was awesome. How many Earthlings could say they'd visited an alien pub? But she had hoped the clientele would be more along the lines of something one might find in Star Wars movies and series. Lots of *what-the-ever-loving-hell-is-that* kind of creatures with two heads or multiple arms. Three eyes or maybe a dozen tentacles. Insect-like beings. Velociraptor cousins. A sasquatch look-alike. Someone with a chin that resembled testicles enough to spark lewd jokes or a snout as long as a trumpet.

Alas, she spied nothing that jaw-dropping.

Everyone present appeared to have two legs, two arms, and one head. *Evidently, the symmetry found on Earth is typical throughout the galaxy*, she thought wryly. Perhaps if the atmosphere on this little planet were different, she would've seen some odder combinations.

Which was not to say that everyone here looked human.

Simone surveyed the beings perched at the bar as Janwar led her deeper into the establishment.

Two athletically built males turned to stare at her. And she couldn't help but stare back. Both had long, shiny black hair and skin covered with barely discernible scales that bore a beautiful silvery tint. When they shifted, the light from the bar produced a slight rainbow shimmer on their muscular arms.

Excitement dawned. Were they Purvelis, like the man Ava had fallen for?

She glanced at the hand one of the males curled around a glass and, sure enough, saw a hint of webbing between his fingers.

Simone grinned. They *were* Purvelis! And they were *hot*. She could see why Ava was attracted to one.

The men shared a bemused look before they returned her smile.

Should she—"Oomph!" Simone rebounded off a wall. Or a post or...

What the hell had she just walked into?

Rubbing her nose, she looked up. And up some more. Sheesh. This guy was even taller than Soval, except the male she now gaped at wasn't as bulky and had arms that were elongated like a monkey's. He even had tufts of fur on his pale, bare shoulders. And was that a tail twitching behind him?

He scowled down at her.

"Apologies," she blurted in Alliance Common, then smiled. Maybe this place was more like a Star Wars cantina than she'd thought.

Growling what she suspected was an insult, he stepped around her and kept moving.

"Don't mind him," one of the Purvelis said. "*Digwas* have no sense of humor."

"I see," she replied, never losing her smile. "Thanks for the tip." Hesitating only a moment, Simone stepped closer to them and lowered her voice. "To show my appreciation, let me give you one of my own: Guard your back against Gathendiens."

One grinned. "Doesn't everyone?"

"If they're wise," she acknowledged. "But Gathendiens currently seem to have a particular interest in obtaining Purvelis." When she lowered her voice further, the two leaned closer. "I found one of your fallen males on a Gathendien ship I commandeered."

They stiffened, all levity fleeing their features.

"What?" they demanded simultaneously.

"I was looking for friends I believed the Gathendiens had taken and found a Purveli instead. I'm sorry to say he was already dead. I could do nothing for him beyond killing those who harmed him."

Janwar stepped up behind her, his warmth infusing her back. "And she did. All of them."

She looked up at him over her shoulder. "Well, you killed a few, too."

Both Purvelis rose and stood shoulder-to-shoulder facing them.

"How are you involved in this, Janwar?" the taller one asked, expression flinty.

She glanced at them all with surprise. "You three know each other?"

The Purveli didn't take his gaze off Janwar. "I know *of* him."

Janwar nodded at her. "I was looking for the same women she was when our paths crossed. You should heed her warning. Gathendiens have captured three Purvelis that we know of. They're obviously interested in conquering Purvel and would love to get their hands on more victims for their labs who can help them further their research and find a bioweapon that will kill you all."

Both men looked sick at the notion.

"What happened to the other two?" the second male asked.

Simone answered before Janwar could. "My friend and her Segonian lifemate rescued them."

"Do you know their names?"

"Jak'ri and Ziv'ri A'dar," Janwar supplied.

Their jaws dropped.

"You know them?" she asked with some surprise. Talk about a small world.

"Not personally," the first said. "The A'dars are the most prominent *sahstin jins* on our planet."

The second nodded. "They were making exciting progress in terraforming one of our moons before they inexplicably disappeared."

Simone frowned. "They didn't disappear. They were snatched right off the surface of Purvel, something they have made very clear to your government."

They glanced at each other.

"That would explain the message we received, advising all Purvelis off-world to return home," the taller one said.

Crossing her arms over her chest, she arched a brow. "A message you chose to ignore?"

They shifted guiltily and, despite their height and evident strength, reminded her of two teenagers who had been caught coming home past curfew.

"Are the A'dars all right?" the first asked.

"Yes." Relenting, she smiled. "They're working remotely from a Segonian ship and remain in frequent contact with your government."

Janwar spoke before the men could relax. "*You* may celebrate their good health, but the Gathendiens won't. They'll be looking for new specimens to test their vile concoctions on. So get your asses back to Purvel. You can't use the *Nehjed qhov'rum*. It's been damaged. Use well-traveled shipping lanes instead. Or better yet, book passage on an Aldebarian Alliance sanctioned liner that can accommodate your ship in their bay."

"Yes, sir," they chorused.

Nodding at the Purvelis, Janwar curled a hand around her upper arm. "We should keep moving."

"Okay." She tossed the males a wave. "Nice to meet you." As she allowed Janwar to pull her along after him, she murmured, "They seemed a bit in awe of you."

"Some who are either too young to know better or have rebellious spirits are unwise enough to admire me," he stated absently, his head swiveling from side to side, his gaze missing nothing. "But most loathe me. They think me an amoral pirate who would do anything or kill anyone for a credit. Or they hate me for being a more *successful* amoral pirate who would do anything or kill anyone for a credit than *they* are. Still others hate me for being too *drekking* hard to capture or kill because they would love to claim the large bounty the Akseli government has placed on my head."

"How large a bounty?" she asked.

He spouted a number.

Simone blinked. "That's a damn big bounty." Big enough to lure both the greedy and the desperate.

He grunted.

"Have you ever considered that perhaps they simply hate you because you're so *drekking* handsome?"

Halting so suddenly that she nearly bumped into him, he turned to face her. "You think I'm handsome?"

She rolled her eyes. "*Everyone* thinks you're handsome, Janwar." She jerked a thumb over her shoulder, where she knew Soval hovered. "Soval told me that's the only reason he agreed to join your crew. I even caught him checking out your ass when you weren't looking."

A choking sound accompanied a faint breeze that ruffled the hair atop her head.

Swiveling around, she craned her neck to peer up at the brawny warrior.

Soval looked about as appalled at the notion of checking out Janwar's ass as he would if she'd offered him a plate of monkey dung for dinner.

Simone couldn't help it. She burst into laughter. "Relax, Big Blue. I'm only teasing." She gave his barrel chest an affectionate pat before turning back to Janwar. "*He* didn't check out your ass." She winked, then whispered. "*I* did."

The corners of Janwar's lips twitched. "And?"

She grinned. "Your ass is very nice."

Laughing, he resumed leading her through the throng.

Pleased to have made him smile, Simone returned her attention to the beings they passed.

Three women who looked human stood together near the bar, laughing. All were at least six feet tall and wore military uniforms that hugged broad shoulders and bore short sleeves that left their muscled arms bare.

The short sleeves said they weren't Lasaran. Maybe they were Segonian? Their skin *did* have a bronze sheen similar to Commander Dagon's.

When her gaze slipped past them to the bartender, she struggled not to gawp. That guy may be built like a human, but his features reminded her of a pug. He even had big, dark eyes that narrowed when they met hers.

Simone hastily looked away.

146

Okay. All aliens weren't hot. Good to know.

A group of Rakessians like Srok'a and Kova sat around a table, engaging in very rowdy conversation. Two men and one woman with skin as black as midnight and masses of long dreadlocks occupied the booth behind them. Simone initially thought they were human. But there was something different about their eyes, a peculiar shimmer or glow. And she didn't think the faint markings at their temples were tattoos.

There were tall aliens. Short aliens. Males. Females. Muscled bodies. Freakishly thin bodies—like *Avatar* thin. Bulbous bodies. Hairy. Hairless. Skin sporting a wide range of earth tones with some gray mixed in and occasional hints of red or gold. One of the waitresses bore skin almost as white as snow and hair that matched despite her apparent youth.

Soval was the only bluish alien present, and his skin merely hinted at turquois.

"I'm seeing a lot of alien races," she murmured.

"It's a popular gathering place," Janwar said.

"Which ones have the butt fetish?"

He cast her a quizzical look over his shoulder. "I don't think my translator got that right. What?"

"Which ones are obsessed with asses?"

His eyes glinted with amusement. "I believe that would be you."

Soval let out a bark of laughter that drew looks.

She grinned. "I didn't say I was *obsessed* with your ass, just that I thought it was very nice."

He turned a chuckle into a cough. "Stop making me laugh, *vuan* it. I'm an amoral pirate renowned throughout the galaxy for my cold ferocity. When I'm in places like this, I have to look the part."

"So you're saying your ass is fierce?" she quipped. "Now I like it even more."

That sparked another laugh from Soval. And Simone caught a glimpse of a dimple in Janwar's cheek before he hastily schooled his expression into an appropriately forbidding mask. He sent her a narrow-eyed look of warning, then turned away.

"What is a fetish?" Soval rumbled.

"It's... something someone is excessively interested in, I guess, sometimes in a sexual manner. Shoes. A certain body part. That sort of thing. Some people on Earth say aliens have been abducting Earthlings and probing their butts. I can't imagine what you can learn from a butt that you can't learn from a cheek swab or blood sample, so I figured they must have a fetish."

"Who the *srul* has been visiting your planet?" Soval muttered.

While Simone continued to chatter with Soval and marvel over the bar's patrons, the warrior in her cataloged everyone she saw and mentally divided the clientele into four categories: down-on-their-luck individuals who wished to drown their sorrows, adventure seekers like the Purveli males and Segonian soldiers who wanted to cut loose and have a good time, low-level criminals looking for victims to pickpocket or cheat out of some credits, and beings who warranted serious monitoring. The latter boasted multiple weapons, dangerous demeanors, and dead eyes that said they'd sell their youngest child for a profit... or kill anyone for a credit.

Anyone but Janwar, it would seem. All gave him a wide berth, stepping out of his way as he approached to let him pass.

Though the styles of their garments varied, everyone present was fully clothed except for a few women she suspected were prostitutes because they might as well be wearing postage stamps for all the coverage they got. She spied no bare-chested men, no shorts, and no skirts despite the heat that permeated the air outside. Air that she dearly wished they would allow entry into this establishment. *Sheesh,* this place reeked. Since none of the surfaces seemed particularly clean, she wondered if everyone here might wish to cover as much skin as possible to avoid contamination.

Janwar stopped beside an empty booth and motioned for her to sit.

She took a moment to remove the sheathed katanas from her back, then did so, scooting over to make room for him. Once he slid into the booth beside her, they sat with their backs to a wall and could see everyone in the tavern.

Simone smiled as she lay her weapons on the table. She was sitting in an actual... alien... bar.

How cool was that?

J ANWAR SETTLED BESIDE SIMONE, his spirits far lighter than they ordinarily would've been under such circumstances.

Soval lowered his hulking body into the seat across from them, then shifted to the side so he wouldn't block their view. He studied Simone. "Why are you smiling?"

Janwar glanced at her from the corner of his eye.

Her expression said that should be obvious. "I'm sitting in an *alien* bar full of *dozens* of aliens on an *alien* planet. *And* I'm accompanied by the two best-looking aliens in the place."

Vuan if Soval's cheeks didn't darken at the compliment.

Stifling a snort, Janwar returned to studying the room.

A waitress approached, carrying a tray that held three glasses. Her anxious blue eyes only met his for an instant. Then she hastily averted her gaze and placed the drinks on the table with shaking hands. As soon as she finished, she scuttled away.

"What was that all about?" Simone asked.

He shrugged and sipped his drink. "Most here are aware of my reputation."

She arched a brow. "Does that reputation include groping waitresses against their will or something?"

He stiffened. "I don't abuse females."

"Good to know." She nudged him with her shoulder. "Relax. I didn't think you were the type. You could've groped me dozens of times by now but haven't. I merely wondered why she was acting like you two used to be lovers, then parted ways, and now she's worried you found out she used your favorite shirt to scrub the lav."

Once more, he found himself wanting to laugh. Instead, he shook his head. "Certain incidents in my past have been greatly exaggerated, leading many to believe that I'll kill for the slightest offense."

"I can see how that might aid you in your current occupation." She tilted her head to one side. "But it must also make life lonely."

Janwar didn't know how to respond to that. He doubted anyone other than Lisa or Taelon would even *care* if he and his crew were lonely.

When neither he nor Soval said anything, Simone reached for her drink.

Janwar touched her hand before she could raise the glass to her lips. "Careful. It's potent enough that even Soval has to drink it slowly. Someone your size…"

"Should tread carefully?" She smiled. "Thanks for the heads-up."

Combatting an increasingly familiar urge to twine his fingers through hers, he withdrew his touch, conscious of the gazes on them.

In the next instant, Simone raised the glass to her lips, tilted her head back, and downed the entire contents.

Janwar and Soval gaped.

Alarm struck. Janwar hadn't exaggerated when he'd warned her. *Suja* was the most potent drink he'd ever ingested. His first glass had resulted in Krigara having to sling him over his shoulder and carry him back to the ship.

Simone slammed the glass down on the table. Her eyes narrowed to squints and teared up as she swallowed. Then her mouth popped open and emitted a gust of air flavored with the powerful drink. "Wow," she wheezed and hit herself in the chest several times with a fist, "you weren't kidding. That shit burns all the way down."

His heart pounded a frantic rhythm as he waited to see how it would affect her. He knew so little about her species. Would she pass out? Become ill? It wouldn't stop her heart, would it? Why the *srul* hadn't he consulted Chief Medic Adaos about what was safe and what wasn't safe for her to eat or drink?

Simone stretched her arms out in front of her and flattened her hands on the table as if to brace herself while she coughed and drew in a couple of deep breaths.

Soval shot him a look of fear that Janwar hadn't even seen on his face during battle.

Then Simone's shoulders relaxed. Her pretty brown eyes ceased squinting, and she blinked back the tears. Eyebrows lowering, she pursed her lips and shook her head. "Nope. Nothing," she declared, her melodic voice normal again. Resting her arms in her lap, she cast him a disgruntled look. "Well, that sucks."

He stared. "What?"

"Other than burning a path down my throat, that did absolutely nothing for me. I thought I'd at least get a momentary buzz, but *pfft.* Nothing." Her expression lightened as she looked back and forth between them. "What's wrong? You two look like you're having mini heart attacks. Did you think it would kill me or something?"

Soval grunted. "We thought it would knock you on your ass at the very least."

She laughed. "I guess I neglected to tell you that alcoholic beverages don't affect me. My body metabolizes and counters them too quickly." She motioned to the empty glass and sighed. "I thought perhaps alien liquor would affect me differently, particularly after Janwar's warning." She narrowed her eyes at him as if it were his fault the drink hadn't lived up to her expectations. "But it didn't."

Janwar realized he'd been staring at her far too long in a place like this and tore his gaze away. A figure making his way through the throng caught his attention. "My contact is here," he murmured.

Nandara nodded as he reached their table. Another Akseli who had objected to the totalitarian turn their government had taken, he was one of only a handful of people Janwar trusted to deal honestly with him on this planet.

Soval scooted over to make room for him.

Nandara sank down across from Janwar. His skin was considerably darker than Janwar's but still bore a reddish hue. His thicker black hair was drawn back from his face in similar braids adorned with almost as many warrior beads as Janwar's: one for each battle from which he had emerged victorious. "Good to see you, brother," he murmured.

Janwar clasped his forearm in greeting. "Good to see you, Dar."

His friend's curious gaze slid to Simone.

"This is Simone, the newest member of my crew. You may speak freely in front of her. Simone, this is Nandara."

Simone showed no surprise over being labeled a crew member. Her face impassive, she nodded. "Pleasure to meet you. Are you a brother by blood or more of a brother in arms?"

"Brother in arms," Dar replied and sent Janwar a quizzical look.

He ignored it. "What do you have for me?"

Leaning forward, his friend lowered his voice. "Not as much as I'd hoped. A battered Gathendien ship reportedly limped into port a couple of *beks* ago. They lingered only long enough to buy whatever they needed for repairs, then left."

"Does anyone know where they're headed?"

"They're rumored to have a base on a moon not far from here. But Pulcra is the only one who claims to know its location."

Janwar and Soval both swore.

"Who's Pulcra?" Simone asked curiously.

"He owns the fighting arena that draws most of this sorry planet's visitors," Janwar grumbled. "Of *course,* that *grunark* would know. It wouldn't surprise me if the Gathendiens supplied some of his competitors."

Simone frowned. "Fighting arenas? Do you mean places where people pay to watch others fight?"

"Yes," Janwar said.

"Do the players fight voluntarily or because they're forced to?"

"Most are forced to." Slavery was illegal in all Aldebarian Alliance worlds. But Promeii 7 had been colonized by wanted criminals, escaped prisoners, and others who wished to hide for one reason or another. When rumors of the precious stones found on the planet had leaked, the gem industry had swept in and installed mines that reaped greater rewards when those running them disregarded Aldebarian Alliance rules. And the profits they'd raked in had inspired local businessmen to do the same. "Others fight by choice." Although it wasn't much of a choice. Fight to earn enough to feed your family, or don't fight and watch your children starve because you couldn't find work.

"For sport or to the death?" she asked.

Dar answered this time. "In the matches with the highest viewing fees, it's usually to the death."

"Or dismemberment," Soval added.

Dar nodded. "Sometimes they stop it when a competitor loses a limb."

Janwar grunted. "And sometimes they can't before the competitor loses another."

Scowling, Simone slumped back and crossed her arms over her chest. "Well, that is damned disappointing."

"What is?" he asked.

"That alien races who have advanced enough to travel through space," she snapped, "are backward and barbaric enough to still do that shit."

Dar looked at Janwar.

He shrugged. "She's from a planet that is not yet advanced enough to explore the galaxy."

She snorted. "And they call *us* primitive? At least we don't force people to fight to the death for our entertainment."

"Not all are forced," Dar reiterated cautiously, as though he didn't want to increase her ire. "Some volunteer, knowing that their families will receive enough credits to keep them fed for at least one solar orbit if the contestant dies. And if he lives, he might earn enough to get them off this *drekking* rock."

Some stiffness left her posture as she leaned forward and rested her arms on the sticky table. "It's regrettable that some would have to resort to such. I noticed on our way here that poverty is a serious problem on Promeii 7." She grimaced. "And in all honesty, I'm sure there are plenty of assholes back on my planet who would pay richly to view such contests."

"What planet is that?"

"Back to business," Janwar said, forestalling her answer. He'd already identified at least a handful of bounty hunters scattered throughout the bar. If Gathendiens had let it be known that they would pay richly for Earthlings, it would be best to keep Simone's origins a mystery. "Did you talk to Pulcra?"

Dar grimaced. "Yes. But the *grunark* refused to tell me, so I set up a meeting. He should be here shortly."

"Does he look like a pug?" Simone asked as she examined the crowd behind Dar. "Because if he does, I think he's already here."

Janwar followed her gaze and saw Pulcra's stout form plodding toward them. According to his translator, a *pug* was a small mammal similar to an Akseli *taelanu* with drooping jowls and a flat, wrinkled face. An apt description for the wealthy *grunark*. Except Pulcra walked upright on two legs and had a broad, boxy body.

He also stood only a head taller than Simone.

Pulcra halted beside their booth. "Janwar, my Akseli friend," he boomed in Alliance Common, "it is good to see you again." Without waiting for an invitation, he grabbed a chair from a nearby table, dumped its occupant onto the floor, and seated himself facing the booth. "Nandara told me you wished to see me but didn't say why." He motioned to the bar. "Has my brother served you well? Would you like another drink? No payment necessary, of course."

Janwar motioned to his half-full glass. "This will suffice."

Pulcra nodded, jowls jiggling, and clapped his hands together. "What can I do for you, my friend?"

Pulcra didn't even qualify as an acquaintance, let alone a friend. But the bloviating sack of *bura* knew claiming friendship with Janwar publicly would increase his status.

"A Gathendien ship docked here a couple of *beks* ago," Janwar said. "You can tell me the location of the outpost they were headed toward when they left."

"Hmm. A Gathendien ship, you say?" he asked and appeared to search his memory.

Dar sighed heavily.

"Yes," Pulcra said finally with a nod. "Yes, I believe I *did* hear such a rumor."

Dar released an impatient growl. "It wasn't a rumor. You told me yourself that they docked here."

"Indeed, I did." His golden eyes acquired a cunning gleam as he addressed the other male. "*That* I told you for free." His gaze slid to Janwar. "But where they went? This will cost you."

Janwar had assumed as much. Men like Pulcra cared nothing for right or wrong. They cared only for profit. "How many credits?"

Pulcra leaned back in his chair and linked his hands over his belly. "No credits this time."

Janwar kept his face impassive. That was different. "If not credits, then—"

Pulcra pointed at Soval. "I want that one to battle the Dotharian in my arena."

Janwar didn't even look at Soval to catch his reaction. "Not going to happen. Name another price."

Pulcra shrugged. "I'm afraid that is the only price I will accept."

Fury rose. Why did *grunarks* like this always have to make things complicated? "That price is too high, and you know it. Stop *drekking* around and tell me what you really want."

"That *is* what I really want," Pulcra insisted, his face turning to stone. "I paid heartily for that Dotharian. Yet fewer and fewer patrons are willing to pay to see the matches."

"Because the Dotharian always wins!" Dar blurted with disgust.

"Which is why I want that one"—he again jabbed a finger at Soval—"to get in the cage with him. He is one of the biggest beings planetside. He should be strong enough to put up an entertaining fight."

"No," Janwar gritted, knowing that even someone of Soval's size and strength would inevitably fall when pitted against such a monster.

"What's a Dotharian?" Simone asked suddenly, her face alight with curiosity.

Pulcra smiled at her. "My greatest champion. My patrons love him."

"*It*," Dar snarled, his expression livid. "*It*. Not *him*. And *it* isn't a champion. It's a *drekking* beast."

Janwar nodded. "A genetic experiment gone wrong."

"How wrong are we talking?" she asked, face somber. "Like Incredible Hulk wrong? Or something worse."

"I don't know what a hulk is or why it's incredible," he answered. "But it doesn't matter because Soval is not fighting the Dotharian."

Soval opened his mouth.

Janwar shot him a glare. "You *aren't* fighting it. I'm not sacrificing you for information." He shot Pulcra a menacing glare. "I'll just torture it out of this one."

Though Pulcra kept a smile plastered on his flat face, moisture formed on his wrinkled brow. "I wouldn't try it, my friend. My brother will see you dead if you harm me."

Janwar offered him a cold smile. "Many others have tried and failed."

"*Many* others," Soval added.

A long, tense silence ensued.

"What exactly does this Dotharian look like?" Simone asked as though death threats weren't flying.

Janwar sighed. "Simone..."

"What?" she asked, all innocence. "I just want to understand what we're talking about here. Soval is practically as big as the Hulk. I can't imagine what could possibly conquer him."

Smiling, Soval puffed out his chest.

Janwar sighed and looked at Dar. "Show her."

The Akseli drew a datapad from his pocket and tapped several commands on its surface. A three-dimensional, translucent image rose from it and hovered above the table, depicting the Dotharian in all its glory towering over some poor *drekker* in Pulcra's arena.

Simone's brown eyes widened as she leaned closer. "Holy hell. It's like a rancor got together with King Kong and had a baby."

Janwar had no idea what a rancor was or why the *srul* a king on Earth would want to *drek* it. And he didn't get a chance to ask.

Her pretty face lighting with a grin, Simone blurted, "*I'll* do it! I'll fight the Dotharian."

Shock tore through him.

"*Srul* no!" he and Soval shouted.

Dar's jaw dropped.

"Why not?" she asked and actually seemed *drekking* puzzled. "I mean, look at it! When will I ever get another chance to battle one?"

Even Pulcra seemed astonished by her offer.

"I don't have to look at it," Janwar countered. "I've seen it. And I've seen what it can do—what it *will* do—if you step into the cage with it."

Her face brightened even more. "We'd be fighting in a cage?"

"Yes." Without taking his gaze from her, he said, "Pulcra, tell her why you had to build a cage around the arena floor."

156

"Because the Dotharian kept eating audience members after he finished off his opponents," Pulcra said without hesitation or care.

If anything, her smile broadened as she met Janwar's gaze. "Perfect. Then you and Soval will be safe while you watch me fight."

Was she insane? "No," he repeated and couldn't believe he had to repeat it. "You are *not* fighting it."

"Oh please," she cajoled. Curling both hands around his biceps, she gave his arm several tugs. "Please, please, please. Let me do it." She sounded like a child begging her parents to buy a toy she wanted.

"I agree with Janwar," Pulcra said, his countenance reflecting utter bafflement. "You wouldn't last long enough in the cage for the audience to finish finding their seats. Then they'd all demand their credits back."

Simone turned her attention to Pulcra. "Are you so sure about that?" Determination replaced excitement as she stared at him long and hard.

Pulcra opened his mouth to speak but closed it after a moment as he stared back.

Janwar looked back and forth between them as the silence stretched. What was happening?

"No," Pulcra said at length. "Hmm. Perhaps she *would* put on a good show," he murmured.

Janwar frowned.

Simone nodded. "I mean, how many females have battled your Dotharian in the past?"

"None."

"Then the novelty of that would surely bring in a large crowd, don't you think?"

A sly smile stretched Pulcra's wide mouth. "Indeed, it would." Nodding, he rapped a hand on the table. "I rescind my offer. The female must battle the Dotharian."

Simone pumped a fist in the air. "Yes!"

Janwar stared at her. "No!"

Soval frowned as though he, too, questioned her sanity. "No!"

"Oh, come on," she coaxed. "I promise I'll put on a good show."

When Janwar would've again objected, she tugged his arm and drew him down until she could touch her lips to his ear.

"Could Soval defeat a ship full of heavily armed Gathendien warriors with only two swords, a dagger, and no one else's help?" she whispered.

Her warm breath sent a shiver rippling through him. "No," he acknowledged reluctantly.

"And yet *I* did." Something that still amazed and impressed him.

He turned his head slightly so he could meet her gaze.

"I am capable of far more than you know, Janwar. Trust me in this and agree to his terms. It's a win-win situation."

"How the *dreck* is this win-win?" he whispered, familiar with the term, thanks to Lisa.

"*You* will get the location of the Gathendien outpost, and *I* will get to fight a giant alien monster." She grinned. "You see? Win-win."

He stared at her for a long moment.

Soval leaned forward, his brow puckered with concern. "You aren't considering it are you?"

Simone just kept smiling up at him without a shred of worry or self-doubt.

Janwar questioned his *own* sanity as he turned back to Pulcra. "Agreed. Simone will fight the Dotharian in exchange for the location of the Gathendien outpost." He infused his voice with warning and specified, "The *exact* location."

"Done!" Pulcra all but shouted, then rubbed his hands together with glee. "I'll have my minions put the word out immediately."

CHAPTER NINE

T HE TEMPORARY TRANSLATOR LODGED in Simone's ear only allowed her to understand Akseli words Janwar *spoke*, leaving
her clueless regarding his thoughts. As she understood it, a translation *implant* would've allowed her to understand his thoughts, but
her body had rejected that. Truth be told, she'd come to like that.
Her inability to understand the *Tangata* crew's thoughts, which
her telepathy constantly carried to her whenever she let down her
guard, had transformed them into white noise that filled the background like one of those machines that produced beach sounds to
help people sleep.

As an empath, however, she had no difficulty discerning Janwar's
emotions. They were all over the place as he clutched her hand, his
long fingers woven through hers, and followed Pulcra through the
bar.

Once the pug-faced man told his bartending brother to get the
word out about the fight, he refused to let Simone out of his sight.
"Can't have you changing your mind now, can I?" he boomed with
a rough laugh as he studied a tablet. "Ah, yes. Credits are already
pouring in."

Simone might have used a bit too much of an empathic push to
get him to agree to this because he was crazy excited about it now,
insisting the battle take place later that night.

Janwar didn't want to let Simone out of his sight either. He'd told
Soval to return to the ship, perhaps worried Big Blue might be
asked to step in and fight if the Dotharian killed her too quickly.
But Soval had refused.

She studied Janwar from the corner of her eye as she reveled
in the warmth merely holding his hand generated inside her. It

reminded her of how she had felt many centuries ago while in the first bloom of womanhood when the handsome innkeeper's son had smiled at her.

Janwar wasn't smiling as they left the bar. Rather, he radiated fury and anxiety. Fear and dread. Determination and... admiration?

The emotions flowing into her where they touched told her everything she couldn't hear in his thoughts: He very much wanted to believe in her but at the same time feared she would be sorely injured or killed.

As if sensing her gaze, he glanced down at her. "Why the *dreck* are you smiling?"

Soval grunted on his other side. "You should be quaking in fear."

Simone never took her gaze from Janwar. "I am so attracted to you right now," she admitted breathlessly, mimicking the words he'd spoken to her when she'd straddled him with the intent of killing him. He had agreed to let her fight a massive alien beast. And she hadn't had to use her empathic gift to force his hand the way she had Pulcra. Janwar had simply trusted her. Believed in her. Despite the insanity of it all—and she *was* aware of how insane this must seem to him—he had bowed to her wishes.

His eyes widened as his steps slowed. "Oh, *drek*. It's the *suja*. Why didn't I think of that? The *drekking suja* is compelling you to do this!"

Soval stared at her with dread. "You said you weren't affected by the *suja*!"

When Janwar started looking around as though seeking some way to escape their predicament, Simone laughed and squeezed his hand. "It's not the *suja*. I might as well have been drinking water for all the effect that fiery beverage had on me."

Her denial didn't lessen the dismay Janwar exuded a bit. "You're on your way to an arena where you'll fight a *drekking* Dotharian to the death, and you just said you're attracted to me! You may not *think* it affected you, but—"

She stopped short, tugging him to a halt even as his words tugged at her heart. "Janwar." Brow furrowing, she raised her free hand to cup his bearded jaw. "Is it so difficult for you to fathom that I'm attracted to you? Do you truly believe I have to be drunk to care for you?"

He swallowed hard, his hand tightening around hers.

And her heart broke for him.

Simone stepped closer. "I'm not just attracted to you because you're handsome as hell." She took in his rugged features and drank in the emotions suffusing her. "It's because you trust me. Because you *believe* in me."

"I do believe in you," he murmured. "I just..."

She smiled. He wasn't accustomed to taking such giant leaps of faith and feared losing her.

An irresistible urge to kiss him struck, to feel his soft, warm lips against hers. Pulse pounding, she rose onto her toes and—

"Come-come!" Pulcra shouted impatiently.

Dropping her heels again, she swung away to scowl at him.

The boxy man had stopped several steps ahead and waved impatiently for them to catch up.

Sighing, she sent Janwar a rueful smile. "I was totally going to kiss you."

His lips turned up in the first faint smile she'd seen since Pulcra had met them in the tavern. "And I was totally going to let you."

Laughing in delight, she resumed walking.

The street the group navigated was packed dirt rather than paved. Very few plants survived along it. Most of those that did had needles like a pine tree rather than leaves, perhaps due to the planet's arid environment. A conglomeration of vehicles passed them: hoverbikes, small personal transports she deemed hover-cars, significantly larger conveyances that must serve as buses, wheeled rickshaws pulled by aliens, and wagons led by fascinating creatures that looked like shorter, rounder, hump-less camels with cheetah spots, beagle ears, and beards. Too cute!

She would've stopped to pet one, but Pulcra hustled them into a hovering vehicle big enough to seat four adult passengers.

Four average-sized adult passengers.

Pulcra's stout body took up most of one bench seat. When Janwar motioned for her to enter, Simone slipped out of her katana harness once more and opted to sit across from Pulcra. Janwar sank down beside her, the hovercar rocking slightly with his weight. Then Soval stood in the opening, trying to hide his disgust over the prospect of squeezing in beside Pulcra.

Fighting a smile, Simone took pity on him and shifted onto Janwar's lap.

There was no mistaking Janwar's surprise and pleasure at the unexpected action. Resting a hand on her hip, he slid over to make room for Soval.

If Janwar's weight had made the hovercar rock a bit, Soval's made it lurch so much she had to throw her arms around Janwar's neck to keep from landing on the floor.

The door closed, then the vehicle rocked again as a few of Pulcra's henchmen squeezed into a front seat she couldn't see.

A minute later, the low hum of the engine arose and they moved forward.

Simone leaned back against Janwar and tried not to smile when he wrapped his arms around her. This wasn't exactly how she had pictured sitting on his lap for the first time.

Nevertheless, she enjoyed it and knew he did, too. Some of his roiling emotions quieted, quelled by the contentment and affection that filled him when she leaned against him.

The trip was a short one. Outside the hovercar's windows, a giant stadium arose that evinced a fascinating combination of advanced technology and basic building materials, as if it had been constructed by some ancient alien race, long-extinct, then stood vacant for millennia until men of Pulcra's ilk had swept in and updated it, using as few credits as possible.

Nevertheless, it impressed her. Towering above them, the coliseum was large enough to host either a Super Bowl or the Olympic games.

Upon their arrival, Simone, Janwar, and Soval followed Pulcra and his men inside and were soon ensconced in what appeared to be a high-end waiting room within the arena's structure.

Simone crossed to the far wall and drew back thick curtains that had a fuzzy texture similar to felt.

Her eyebrows flew up. They were in a skybox like those most stadiums on Earth made available to wealthy sports fans. This one overlooked thousands and thousands of bench seats that formed a circle around a center ring encased in what looked like a massive birdcage.

She smiled as excitement rippled through her.

"*Tangata*, this is Janwar."

As she turned, he lowered his hand from his ear comm. Simone used her heightened hearing to listen unabashedly to both sides of the conversation.

"Yes, commander?" Krigara responded instantly. The way he spoke the title indicated he only used it to goad his cousin.

"Cut the *bura*," Janwar snapped. "We have a situation."

"Tell me," Krigara said.

"Pulcra knows where the Gathendiens went but wouldn't part with the information for less than an arena fight."

"Who's fighting? You or Soval?"

Janwar ground his teeth before gritting, "Neither of us. Simone agreed to battle the Dotharian."

Swears erupted over Janwar's earpiece.

"Nandara is headed your way. He'll fill you in on the details."

Simone smiled as Janwar began to rattle off orders. He wanted Kova to lockdown the *Tangata* and monitor things remotely while Krigara, Elchan, and Srok'a lost themselves in the crowd and stood ready to come to Simone's aid. If the fight went disastrously wrong, T was to send in a drone to take out the Dotharian and join them in all twelve android forms to facilitate their getaway.

Janwar was such a sweetheart. It didn't bother her that he couldn't seem to convince himself that someone her size and weight could defeat the hulking creature Dar had shown her. In his position, she would probably believe the same.

Hell, she *was* still thinking the same about Ava, the *gifted one* who had reportedly held her own against Gathendiens soldiers. When had her sweet, shy, soft-spoken friend become such a badass?

Pulcra's henchmen brought them trays loaded with food and plenty to drink. Though her stomach growled, Simone opted not to partake. The symbiotic virus that infected her would protect her from food poisoning if anything didn't sit right in her stomach, but battling the bacteria would deplete some of her blood supply.

And she wanted to be at full strength when she butted heads with the beast.

Janwar spent the ensuing three hours they waited pacing.

Krigara did the same once he arrived.

Srok'a sat stiffly, his expression grim while he tried to induce a premonition of the match's outcome. Evidently, he had psychic abilities that—judging by the frustration he exuded—were not cooperating.

Soval poured his anxiety into filling his gut. He was definitely a stress-eater, poor guy. And if he didn't stop running a big hand over his buzz-cut, he would end up bald.

Elchan... never appeared, leading her to wonder what role he would play.

Everyone insisted on accompanying her and Pulcra down to the entrance she would use to enter the arena's fighting cage.

Pulcra paused briefly before a wall of weapons and motioned to it. "Are you satisfied with your weapons, or do you wish to use one of these? I doubt blades as thin as yours could pierce the Dotharian's hide."

Simone studied the array. Most of the weapons were thick swords, maces, and large hammers that looked like they weighed as much as she did. None were stunners or blasters. She was starting to think she wouldn't find anything more helpful than the precious katanas that dangled down her back when her eyes alighted upon something that resembled brass knuckles. "I'll take a couple of those, please."

Huffing a laugh, Pulcra shook his head and deactivated the shield around the weapons so he could retrieve them for her.

They were too big to fit her small hands properly, but she could make them work.

Tucking them in her pockets, she indicated she was ready.

Once more, Janwar took her hand and held it rather desperately as they resumed following Pulcra. Her heart began to beat faster at the contact, and it was already thump-thump-thumping with excitement.

They halted in a long, empty tunnel that ended in a rather archaic-looking barred entrance that must be thirty feet high and fifteen feet wide. The access pad beside it, however, indicated the gate was much more high-tech than it appeared.

Simone drew Janwar several feet away from the others and smiled up at him. "I don't suppose I could talk you into kissing me for good luck, could I?"

He glanced over his shoulder at the others, then turned back. "Such would be unwise. I've already started tongues wagging just by holding your hand. If word carried that we shared anything more intimate than that, some might think they could use you as bait to capture me and win the sizable bounty on my head. I don't want them to start targeting you."

Amusement sifted through her, broadening her smile into a grin. "I don't think that's going to be a problem, Janwar. Once they see me fight, they will fear *me* even more than they do you."

But he didn't return her smile. He merely stared down at her for a long moment as though debating inwardly. Then he lowered his head and touched his lips to hers.

Fire sparked through her, lighting her up inside and filling her with wondrous heat. Rising onto her toes, she looped her arms around his neck, leaned in, and lost herself in the feel and scent of him. His kiss carried a hint of desperation, as though he feared this would be his only chance to hold her like this. And hold her he did, wrapping his arms around her in a crushing embrace. As soon as she parted her lips, he deepened the contact, slipping his tongue inside to stroke hers.

Damn, he could kiss.

When he finally drew back, Simone was breathless.

"Good luck," he whispered, his russet eyes darker with desire as he released her.

Unable to speak, she nodded and watched silently as he walked away with the others, leaving her alone.

Even the guards retreated to the far end of the tunnel.

"Wow," she breathed. "I would fight a Dotharian every night if he would kiss me like that before each match."

Shaking herself out of it, she strolled toward the gate. Although Simone remained in shadow, she had no difficulty seeing the brightly lit arena. Just as she had predicted, the place was packed, every bench crowded with aliens whose speculations filled the night with a constant hum.

Crossing her arms, she watched the spectators take their seats. "Did you enjoy the show, Elchan?"

A curse split the air to her left. "How did you know?"

She shrugged. "I can hear your heartbeat. And Eliana disclosed the Segonians' unique physiology." That physiology included chromatophores in their skin and musculature that allowed them to camouflage themselves so well that they could blend in with whatever surface they stood in front of.

He loosed another curse word. "That's supposed to be confidential." Everyone assumed Segonian warriors' capacity to blend into their environment stemmed from some kind of advanced military technology. They didn't know the Segonians were born with the ability and had found a way to make clothing and armor that would respond to the chemical change in their skin and do the same.

"I know. And I assure you it will go no further," she promised, still not looking at him so the guards in the distance wouldn't grow suspicious. "But my hearing is far more acute than that of others. I can hear your heartbeat, your breath, the faint rustle of your clothing." She smiled. "The gurgling of your stomach. Trust me when I say you're safer with me knowing. I would've long since attacked you, thinking you an enemy trying to creep up on me unawares had Eliana not forewarned me and were I not already familiar with your scent."

He grunted.

The gate in front of her clunked, then began to rise slowly.

The crowd began to cheer.

"Don't follow me into the arena," she ordered. "It would be a distraction that could cost me."

Another curse befouled the air. "Call me if you need me."

"Oh, I won't need you. Enjoy the show." Grinning big, Simone strutted into the coliseum.

The shouts increased in volume, threatening to deafen her.

Though she knew these assholes had all come to watch her get torn apart by the King Kong/rancor lovechild thing, she jogged a slow circle around the edges of the cage, waving to the one or two hundred thousand alien men, women, and children. (*Merde.* Parents brought their kids to see this savagery?) Every once in a while, she threw a flurry of mock punches and danced around like her all-time favorite boxer, Muhammad Ali, much to the crowd's delight. They had expected her to cower in fear, perhaps even be forced into the cage by armed guards, not behave like a returning champion. And they all seemed vastly entertained by the fact that she had no idea she was about to be ripped apart for their pleasure.

Janwar, Soval, Srok'a, Krigara, and Dar had strategically positioned themselves amid the crowd. Those handsome fellows looked grim as hell when Pulcra's voice blared over a loudspeaker, broadcasting the imminent arrival of his champion like the ring announcer in a professional boxing match.

The crowd quieted. All seated themselves and leaned forward, eager to watch fear overtake her and the slaughter that would ensue.

An even larger gate at the far end of the arena floor began to rise.

Simone halted and turned to face it.

She had to give Pulcra credit. The snail's pace with which the gate rose certainly heightened the tension. She had plenty of time to surreptitiously don the knuckle guards and was about ready to burst with impatience when she finally spied movement in the shadows beyond it.

The gate halted.

A quiet fell that was so complete she heard someone up on one of the highest benches sniff.

Her heart began to pound. Adrenaline flooded her veins.

Then the Dotharian lunged from the darkness.

Her eyes widened. Holy shit, that thing was *huge*! Like several-stories-tall huge. Its head alone was easily eight feet from its chin to the top of its forehead.

Once outside the tunnel, it straightened to its full height and roared.

The crowd cheered heartily, then died down as they awaited her response.

A wide grin stretching her lips, Simone cried, "That. Is. *Awesome!*"

Her King Kong comparison had been a good one, but non-ape characteristics of it were less like the Star Wars saga's rancor and more akin to Godzilla. Grayish green fur coated long arms bulging with muscle and much of its body in ragged tufts that reminded her of a dog with mange. Its face and powerful chest, on the other hand, bore scales of the same color, and its features were vaguely serpentine with a misshapen snout and a gaping maw that flashed a host of sharp teeth, some of which she estimated were at least a foot long.

The creature raised clenched fists at the crowd and howled again. Those big-ass hands each boasted four clawed fingers and an opposable thumb.

The better to grab me with, she thought wryly.

It walked upright on big bowed legs. Or rather waddled. As it turned in a circle, something about its gait indicated its legs weren't quite right, as if they had difficulty supporting its weight or something. And between them...

She stared.

It wore a loincloth. Simone wondered idly if that was there for the audience's benefit or if the Dotharian's previous opponents had simply drawn the line at being slapped in the face with its big, monster balls while they tried desperately to keep it from killing them.

The beast gave her little time to speculate further as it abruptly focused all of its attention on her. Relying on its massive arms like a gorilla, it charged toward her.

Yeah. She didn't know what the assholes who genetically engineered the Dotharian had been going for, but they'd obviously gotten some things wrong.

Turning slightly to one side, she adopted a fighting stance and waited to see what it would do.

The crowd quieted again, the boom, boom, boom of the beast's fists and feet hitting the ground the only sounds.

Just as Simone wondered if it intended to just bowl her over, it halted, dipped its head, and roared right in her face.

Squinting her eyes against the hot, rancid wind buffeting her and the dust the beast had stirred up, she held her ground until it stopped.

The beast glared at her, air huffing in and out of its mouth like a bellows.

Simone coughed and grimaced. "I take it your captors don't let you brush your teeth." She waved a hand back and forth in front of her face to clear the air. "Seriously. You need to do something about your breath. That alone could slay your opponents."

The beast's brows lowered as it squinted golden eyes that were oddly pretty in its ugly face. And she could tell the spectators weren't the only ones caught off guard by her response.

Okay, she thought and mentally rubbed her hands together. *Let the show begin.*

Drawing in a deep breath, Simone stepped closer to the beast and roared right back at it as she wielded the one weapon none of the others could see. Employing her empathic gift, she started sifting through its emotions, intent on altering them and twisting them to her advantage.

<hr />

IF JANWAR HAD EATEN anything before the match began, he might very well have soiled his pants when the massive Dotharian raced toward Simone and roared in her face. He was *that* terrified for her.

She was so tiny compared to it, not even big enough to fill its hand or mouth if it decided to grab her and stuff her inside.

Why was she not afraid?

Why did she not tremble as everyone else who got in the cage with the beast did?

Why the srul *did she just stand there and grin?*

As he waited, his heart in his throat, one hand creeping toward the *tronium* blaster he'd concealed, she merely waved a hand back and forth in front of her face and complained about the beast's breath.

Its breath! Not that anyone close enough to hear her knew that. Most of those present either boasted outdated translators that didn't contain Earth languages or had no translators at all, and she wasn't speaking Alliance Common.

Much to his shock, Simone stepped closer to the beast and roared in its face. Not a high-pitched cry or screech, but a full, deep-throated roar he was surprised she could even make.

Eyebrows flying up, he stared.

Srul, everyone stared.

Even the Dotharian seemed taken aback for a moment. Then—head still bent to her level—it opened its massive mouth and snapped at her.

Janwar sucked in a breath.

Simone deftly dodged the beast's gleaming teeth and swung a tiny fist, landing a punch on its scaled cheek.

The Dotharian's head jerked hard to the side as if someone had instead hurled a boulder at it.

Janwar's eyes widened. His heart pounded in his chest.

The crowd gasped.

How much strength did one have to back a punch with to knock the Dotharian's head aside like that?

Simone shook her hand but displayed no pain. The scales on that beast's face were rumored to be as hard as stone. He was surprised it hadn't broken every bone in her—

His gaze dipped to her hand and caught a glimmer of light reflecting off metal.

Somewhere along the way, she must have donned the knuckle armor.

The beast shook its head and looked confused. Then fury darkened its countenance. Growling in outrage, it raised a fist high and swung it at her.

Simone ducked out of the way an instant before it hit the ground where she'd stood. Before the dust settled, she leaped onto the fist, sped up the beast's arm, jumped, flew through the air, and delivered another punch to its ear.

The Dotharian staggered sideways as Simone dropped to the ground, landing in a crouch on the balls of her feet.

Spectators let out a collective gasp, then cheered wildly.

The beast went mad, slamming its fists down, doing its best to flatten her with strikes so powerful that the floor shook beneath Janwar's feet.

Simone dodged every fist but lacked time to deliver more hits of her own. She was too busy darting this way and that, narrowly escaping being flattened into a small stain in the dirt.

The beast grew more frustrated by the second and even began to look confused. Simone seized an opportunity and—

Drek!

She scrambled up one of its legs so fast that her form blurred, continued up its spine, grabbed a tuft of hair on the back of its head, and rode its neck like a hoverbike. "Wooooohoooo!" she hollered in Earth English. "Someone had damned well better be filming this!"

"What the *srul* is happening?" Krigara asked over his ear comm.

Janwar shook his head. "I don't know."

The creature went mad, twisting and turning, trying to dislodge her. But every time its thick clawed fingers came too close, she slammed a fist into the back of its head. In an act of desperation, the beast suddenly jumped up in the air and reared backward.

Janwar's heart lodged in his throat. It was going to flatten her!

Simone leapt free moments before the beast landed on its back in the dirt. Hitting the ground on her feet, she rolled forward, jumped up, and swung to face it. "Ha! Missed me!"

The Dotharian looked as astonished as the audience.

Relief rushed through Janwar, leaving him almost light-headed. Admiration swallowed his fear, and he began to *believe*. He'd known Simone was an incredibly proficient warrior. She couldn't have defeated a ship full of Gathendiens otherwise. But *this*... defeating a Dotharian single-handedly...

This was something he didn't even think a Cyborg could do.

The creature lumbered to its feet, roaring as it renewed its attempts to crush her.

Dropping her knuckle armor in the dirt, Simone drew her swords and began inflicting cuts on fists that came too close. Nothing deep. Nothing truly damaging. Nothing that would deliver more pain than what Lisa would call a paper cut to a creature so enormous it could use those blades to pick pieces of previous opponents from between its teeth.

And yet, as Janwar watched in amazement, the beast began to hesitate, as if it weren't sure how to attack her. Its blows continued to fall but lost some of their strength. It ceased roaring, a low grumble emerging from its throat instead.

Simone stared up at it intently, a smile no longer gracing her pretty face, as she spun away from one giant fist and swung a blade at the other. Then she didn't even do that, sheathing her swords. When she rolled to one side to avoid another hit, she came up with the knuckle armor once more in place.

The crowd around him shouted incessantly. Half of them wanted her to cut the Dotharian's heart out. The other half encouraged the beast to eat her.

But something indescribably bizarre happened.

Straightening to its full height, the Dotharian studied her uncertainly, then began to back away.

Simone took a step toward it.

The beast backed away again, its head swiveling from side to side. One step. Two steps.

Its immense, muscled chest began to rise and fall faster. Its eyes widened and rolled around in their sockets in a clear display of fear as it sidled away from her.

"What the *drek*?" Janwar murmured.

A slow smile slid across Simone's face.

She took another step toward it.

The Dotharian released a rumble of warning and again sidled away.

Her face brightening with delight, Simone began to shuffle her feet and jab the air in front of her with mock punches, spouting something about floating and stinging like Earth insects.

To the astonishment of all, the Dotharian seemed utterly terrified.

Spinning away from her, it raced back toward its tunnel. But the gate slammed shut.

Howling in fear, it glanced over its shoulder.

Simone did another little dance with her feet.

The Dotharian turned away and gripped the sides of the cage with giant fingers, its claws slipping between the bars.

The crowd on the other side shrieked and scattered, no doubt afraid the beast would crumple the bars and devour them. But the Dotharian couldn't break a cage built specifically to contain it.

Not that it didn't try. Roaring, it yanked and pulled and tried to rattle the cage apart to no avail.

Pausing, it looked over its shoulder.

Simone stopped dancing and strolled toward it.

Now the Dotharian shrieked. Desperate to get away from her, it started scaling the sides of the cage like a ladder. The spectators on the other side trampled each other as they scattered. Other occupants of the arena shifted uneasily as the creature climbed as high as it could before the cage's roof sloped up to a peak.

Janwar returned his attention to Simone.

Assuming an exaggeratedly innocent expression, she shrugged and raised her hands—palms up—at her sides as if to say, "Hey, I don't know what's wrong with it."

He laughed. Janwar couldn't believe it, but he actually laughed and shook his head in amazement. What the *drek* had she done to it?

The creature huddled in a trembling ball on the side of the cage, feet scrabbling to maintain its purchase.

The spectators who hadn't run in terror gawked in stunned disbelief.

Silence fell.

After several long minutes, Simone looked around until she spotted Pulcra's stout form high up in his box and called, "Does this mean I won?"

CHAPTER TEN

"WHAT THE *SRUL* JUST happened?" Krigara muttered over the comm.

Janwar tapped his ear. "Show's over. Meet me at the tunnel."

"On my way," Krigara, Soval, and Srok'a chorused.

"Already there," Elchan assured him quietly.

Janwar waited only long enough to watch Simone shrug, offer the crowd a cheery wave, and head toward the tunnel from which she'd emerged. Then he spun and jogged through the throng, Dar right behind him.

Even in their current confused, what-the-*drek*-just-happened state, spectators recognized Janwar and jumped out of his way, speeding his progress enough for him to reach the lower level in mere minutes.

More guards than usual manned the entrance.

"Let me by," Janwar ordered as he strode toward them.

One raised an O-rifle. The others closed rank behind him.

"Pulcra told us not to let you or your crew pass," the one aiming his weapon uttered.

"No," Janwar said. "Pulcra told you not to let me or my crew pass *while the battle took place*. The battle is over. Get the *drek* out of my way."

Krigara joined them. Then Soval and Srok'a.

The guards looked at each other, then parted to let them pass. The large door slid up.

"Pulcra is incoming," Elchan warned softly over the comm as they charged forward.

Janwar and his men arrived in time to see Pulcra and several more guards storm into the tunnel Simone had probably already reached. He couldn't catch the arena owner's expression, but the *grunark's* stiff posture radiated displeasure.

Janwar followed, his men flanking him, and peered past Pulcra's group.

At the far end of the tunnel, Simone waited in front of the lowering gate with a smile. She even waved, undaunted by the forces who marched toward her.

Janwar glanced at his men and Dar.

Each nodded, ready to leap into battle if Pulcra tried to pull any *bura*.

"That was awesome!" Simone declared, eyes bright, a wide grin betraying her excitement.

But Pulcra disagreed. "What the *drek* did you do to my champion?" he bellowed.

She shrugged. "I beat it. Wasn't that the whole point?"

"The *point*," Pulcra snarled, "was to give Promeii 7 something they've never seen before—a fight in which the Dotharian devoured a female!"

Her smile slipped into an expression of placating apology. "Well, you didn't make that as clear as you should have, so that's on you, not me. *I* thought I was here to put on a show and kick a giant beast's ass." She motioned to the arena behind her. "And I believe I accomplished that."

Pulcra took a menacing step toward her. "You didn't beat it. You ruined it! It's terrified!"

"You don't want it to be terrified?" she asked innocently.

"No!"

She threw her hands up in exasperation. "Well, how was I supposed to know that letting out one squeaky little fart would frighten the beast so badly."

Janwar barked out a laugh.

The guards in front of him spun around, only then noticing his arrival, and aimed O-rifles at him.

Pulcra stood on his toes and peered through them. "You!" he shouted. "This is *your* fault, Akseli!"

"Actually, it's yours, Pulcra," Simone said behind him. A mischievous glint entered her brown eyes as she winked at Janwar. "You're the one who sent us the food that made me gassy."

Janwar laughed again, knowing she hadn't eaten a thing and that gas had nothing to do with her victory. "Tell your guards to stand down."

Face reddening with fury, Pulcra ground his teeth. "I should have them kill you all."

"I don't think you want to do that," Simone offered conversationally.

Pulcra spun toward her. "Why? Because you know you'll be next?"

She stared up at him with a dark smile. "Oh. I won't be next. I'll be too busy feeding you to the Dotharian."

That bold declaration rendered Pulcra speechless. He opened his mouth to reply but paused. For several long moments, he just stared at her. Then he blinked, and a jovial smile slipped across his features. "Of course. Of course. I jest." Turning to his guards, he waved a hand. "What are you doing? Lower your weapons and let my friends pass."

What the *srul*?

The guards did as ordered, lowering their weapons and stepping aside.

Janwar walked straight to Simone.

"That was so much fun!" she blurted, delight returning as she jumped up and down in excitement. "Did you see me?" She even did another one of those funny foot shuffles and threw some mock punches.

He grinned, utterly charmed. "I did."

Puclra loosed a hearty laugh. "Indeed, we *all* did. A fascinating fight it was. They'll be speaking of it for years to come."

Janwar studied him suspiciously. What was with the sudden good humor? Why had he changed his mind? What was he up to?

"So, Pulcra." Simone addressed the arena owner with a smile. "You said that if I fought the Dotharian, you would give Janwar the information he seeks."

"I did. And I shall." He delved into a pocket.

Janwar tensed, barely stopping himself from grabbing Simone's arm and jerking her behind him.

But Pulcra didn't remove a weapon. He brought forth a datapad and offered it to Janwar with a good-natured smile. "This holds the information you seek: a location and a map to guide you there."

Janwar motioned to it. "Show me." He didn't trust the *grunark* not to slip him a bomb instead.

Pulcra turned to his guards. "Look away."

All of the guards turned their backs.

The arena owner sent Janwar a conspiratorial smile. "The fewer who know, the fewer who may succumb to temptation and offer bounty hunters information on your whereabouts in exchange for credits." He activated the device.

A three-dimensional holomap rose from the tablet and hovered above it, displaying a planet with thirty-three moons. One of the smaller moons glowed red.

Pulcra poked it with a pudgy finger, enlarging it to show an icy sphere bereft of plant life. "That is the place you seek." He closed the map and passed the datapad to Janwar. "But I fear approaching it and breaching the hidden compound without drawing notice will be impossible."

Janwar frowned and feigned disappointment. "With no clouds or vegetation to hide behind, they would see us coming long before we reached the base."

"Whether you approached by air or land," Pulcra agreed and slid Simone a sly glance. "Should you wish to catch them away from the base, however, I may be persuaded to alert you the instant a Gathendien ship docks here again if this female will agree to return for a rematch with my champion."

Simone grinned. "Technically speaking, I believe *I* am now the champion of Promeii 7's most impressive arena. But yes, a rematch would be fun."

"Excellent!" Pulcra cried with unusual excitement considering he had just been fuming over her defeating the beast. "Then we have an accord."

Once more, Janwar wondered what the *drek* was running through the arena owner's mind.

Pulcra clapped his hands with a smile. "Will you all join me for a celebratory meal?"

Janwar shook his head. "We must leave, I'm afraid."

Pulcra seemed disappointed but didn't press it. "Next time, perhaps," he suggested and escorted them to the exit.

E VERYONE WAS QUIET WHILE they crammed themselves into another hovercar that took them to the docks. After bidding Dar thanks and goodbyes, they boarded Janwar's transport and left Promeii 7 behind.

Simone couldn't stop smiling. This had to be one of the best days she'd ever had. She couldn't wait to tell Eliana about it.

As soon as they were back on the *Tangata*, Janwar handed Pulcra's datapad to Kova. "Check this for trackers and explosives. I don't trust that *grunark*. He was too happy when we left and may be plotting something."

Simone shook her head. "It isn't booby-trapped. I would've sensed his deceit when he gave it to you. But you can double-check it anyway."

Kova glanced at Janwar before taking the device to a nearby station from which he retrieved a few tools.

Elchan abruptly appeared beside Simone.

She grinned. "That is so cool. Perhaps *you* should fight the Dotharian next time."

He shook his head. "It doesn't always work as it should when I'm under stress."

"I know how that is," she empathized with a smile. It had taken her far longer than anticipated to seize control of the Dotharian's emotions. She'd had to ride the damn thing like a bucking bull so she could avoid its fists long enough to concentrate. That big beast had even bigger emotions, all of which had driven it to try to kill her. Simone had never had to dampen mindless fury and bloodlust on such a large scale before. Nor had she ever infused such an enormous creature with undiluted fear.

Kova spoke. "It's clear. No trackers, explosives, or recording devices."

Nodding, Janwar waited for the scarred male to join them, then crossed his arms over his chest and studied Simone expectantly.

The others followed his example.

"What?" she asked, some imp driving her to tease them. "Do I have something on my face?"

"Actually, yes," Kova said softly, surprising her, and touched a finger to his cheek. "You have some blood right here."

Since she hadn't let the Dotharian score any hits, she assumed the blood was the beast's. "Ew. Gross." Raising an arm, she scrubbed at her face with a sleeve.

Janwar sighed and rolled his eyes. "Simone."

"Yes?"

"Tell us how you did it."

Krigara nodded. "How did you defeat the Dotharian?"

Elchan grinned. "It sure as *bura* wasn't with a fart."

She laughed. "Okay, but first... *please*, tell me one of you recorded the battle."

"I recorded it," T said, his voice coming from a speaker in the ceiling.

She glanced up. "You did? How? You weren't even there."

"I tapped into the arena's surveillance feed."

Simone grinned. "Brilliant! Can I see it?"

Janwar sighed. "Simone."

"Oh. Right. You asked how I defeated it." She shrugged. "I'm an empath."

His brows furrowed. "You can sense others' emotions?"

"Yes."

Krigara shook his head. "How did that help you? I thought the creature's emotions were obvious."

Again, she laughed. "I'm an *older* empath. Younger empaths on Earth can only feel the emotions of others and often have to touch them to do so. Older empaths like me can feel the emotions of others from a distance. But we can go a step further, seize control of those emotions, and manipulate them to our advantage, which is what I did today. I dampened the Dotharian's fury and bloodlust and filled it with fear."

The men shared a glance.

"What?" she asked. "You don't believe me?"

Krigara spoke slowly. "We've never encountered an empath who could do such."

Soval nodded. "They can only read emotions, not alter them."

Simone performed a quick scan of their emotions. Krigara, Soval, Elchan, and Srok'a were skeptical. Kova seemed intrigued. And Janwar believed her, exuding no doubt whatsoever.

She rewarded him with a smile. "Shall I show them?"

His lips twitched. "Please do."

Concentrating, she filled the four skeptics with the same fear she had infused the beast with and didn't have to wait nearly as long for a reaction.

Eyes widening, they sucked in sharp breaths. Their hearts began to pound franticly in their chests. Their hands began to shake.

"What the *drek*?" Krigara blurted.

Janwar grinned.

Kova's lips twitched as he watched the others stumble backward, looking as if they wanted to bolt.

Simone shut off the fear and fed the men humor. Within seconds, the four were stumbling around, laughing so hard their eyes watered.

"*Drek*, that's a powerful gift," Janwar breathed, grinning over the men's antics as guffaws doubled them over.

But Simone's gaze was drawn to Kova, who—instead of being amused at his friends' antics—exuded envy.

She studied the scars that adorned his face and muscular body, considered his perpetually somber countenance and quiet reserve, and didn't have to ask to know he'd had a hard life.

Had Kova never experienced joy like this? Was that why he envied them?

"All right. That's enough," Janwar declared.

Simone reined in her gift.

The four men sighed and wiped their eyes.

180

Janwar shook his head. "Is that why Pulcra shifted so quickly from wanting to strangle you to trying to arrange another match?"

"Yes. Full disclosure, I *did* consider feeding him to the Dotharian." She'd been furious when the bastard had looked as if he intended to renege on his deal and order his guards to kill Janwar. "That would've been a nice bit of poetic justice. But I thought he may be of use to you in the future, so I coaxed him into a more amenable mood instead."

Janwar grunted. "If we didn't need the information, I might've preferred the first." Then he turned to Kova. "Think you can keep him from broadcasting the fight off-planet?"

Kova nodded. "His systems are outdated, so T and I were able to hack them remotely. If we can corrupt the recordings he made, he shouldn't be able to share them with anyone."

"Do it."

Simone watched Kova leave, then looked up at Janwar. "Why is that necessary?"

"To the best of our knowledge, no one knows you're an Earthling. But if that information should unexpectedly come to light, along with footage of the fight, your missing friends may find themselves facing men who believe them as dangerous as you or who may want them to fight in arenas of their own."

"*Merde.* I didn't think of that." Only four of her fellow Earthlings—the other Immortal Guardians—would survive a contest like the one she'd just fought. The others would fall even against an opponent like Soval. "Can Kova and T keep that from happening?"

"Yes," Janwar stated with absolute confidence. "Pulcra won't be sharing it."

"Good." She bit her lip. "Could I have a copy though? I want to show my friends when we're reunited."

He grinned. "I'll have T make you a copy."

"Already done," T told them.

Simone smiled. "Thank you. Now, if you will excuse me, I need to shower." She drew in a deep breath and grimaced. "That Dotharian's stench is all over me."

Janwar nodded. "Meet us in the mess hall afterward."

A few minutes later, Simone stood naked in the shower, loving the warm water that pounded her shoulders. "These boys sure know how to live," she murmured.

Janwar's ship was so cleverly designed that his water supply could last an extraordinarily long time, mainly due to the tropical forest that took up half the ship, which meant she could take a nice, long shower without worrying someone else would have to do without.

It felt so good that she lathered up and rinsed off twice before abandoning the gleaming enclosure. She could use the air whatchamacallit to blow the moisture off her skin but preferred to do things the old-fashioned way and reached for a soft towel.

Made for the tall, muscled warriors on board, it covered her from her shoulders to her knees and made Simone feel tiny. Fatigue tugged at her as she buffed her skin dry. Perhaps she should stop by Med Bay for a blood infusion. Though she hadn't suffered any injuries during her epic battle, avoiding those massive clawed fists and hitting the Dotharian hard enough to hurt it had taken a great deal of preternatural speed and strength. Enough that she felt about how she used to after engaging in battle with an unusually large number of vampires or after blitzing a military compound with her immortal brethren.

Once she donned her usual garb—the uniform generator's version of panties, a sports bra, cargo pants, a T-shirt, and socks—she headed for the infirmary.

She'd expected to find it empty, but Elchan reclined on one of the examination beds. Feet crossed at the ankles, one hand pillowing his head, he stared up at the ceiling while blood flowed up a tube attached to his arm and into the medical apparatus above him.

She hesitated in the doorway.

His chin dipped as he noted her arrival.

"What are you doing here?" she asked, strolling toward him.

Lips quirking up, he nodded at his arm. "Donating blood. Even though you weren't hurt, I thought you might need some after the big battle and figured I'd replenish what you'll use."

He was such a nice guy.

"Isn't donating blood so often harmful?" On Earth, she and her fellow Immortal Guardians had infused themselves with blood donated by their Seconds and the many employees of the human network that aided them. And her Seconds used to space out their donor dates.

"Not as long as I give myself a booster afterward. That significantly shortens the time it takes my body to replenish my blood supply."

Smiling, she gave his arm a friendly pat. "Thank you. I'm sorry you have to do this."

He waved his free hand. "Don't be. It makes me feel useful."

Simone fought a frown as she picked up the med pad on the exam bed beside his. Did that mean he often *didn't* feel useful? "How does this thing work again?"

He showed her how to order a transfusion for herself, then watched her hop up onto the bed.

As soon as she lay back, a mechanical arm wielding a needle lowered from the ceiling. Simone crossed her ankles and rested her free hand on her stomach while the machine sprayed disinfectant on the bend of her arm, lit it with a grid pattern, and unerringly found her vein. Seconds later, Segonian blood slithered down the tube.

Simone's thoughts circled back to Elchan's comment. "Thank you for staying with me in the tunnel today." She sent him a grin. "And for ignoring my wishes and stepping into the arena." She'd caught an occasional flicker in her peripheral vision and didn't mind that he'd done so since he'd stayed out of the way.

He snorted. "If you try to tell me you were nervous, you're full of *bura.*"

She grinned. "I wasn't nervous. But despite my excitement, I *did* like knowing you'd have my back if the Dotharian ended up being more than I could handle."

Smiling, he shook his head. "After seeing you fight it, I don't think there *is* such a thing as more than you could handle."

She laughed. "I wouldn't be too sure. I'm new to all species of man and animal alien to Earth and know little about them. My empathic gift seems to work well with those I've encountered thus far, but on something like the Dotharian that was created in a lab somewhere..." Simone shrugged. "I had no idea what would happen. If my gift had failed me, I would've been screwed and required your aid. So again, thank you for being there for me."

"You're welcome. Although I doubt I would've done more than provide it with a meal to distract it." He looked away, redirecting his gaze to the apparatus above him. "My camouflage is unreliable and often fails me when I need it most." Admitting it seemed to be a source of embarrassment for him.

She studied him. "I can understand that."

His lips tightened. "The Segonian military didn't. They discharged me when years of training failed to help me bring it under control."

She frowned. "That sucks."

A bitter laugh escaped him as he studied the ceiling. "It was an unforgivable humiliation for my family. My father is military, of high rank, and highly respected. He desired no other future for me but to follow in his footsteps. When I failed to overcome my genetic abnormality... my *weakness*..." His throat worked in a swallow. "He disavowed me. My whole family did."

Her heart went out to him. Unlike most Immortal Guardians, Simone hadn't had to walk away from her family after being transformed by the vampiric virus. And she hadn't had to face their fear or scorn because she had already lost them to the Bubonic Plague. But she had contended with plenty of that since then and understood how hard a blow that must have been for him.

"No offense," she said softly, "but your family sucks."

When he cast her a wary glance, perhaps more accustomed to contempt or derision than understanding, she shrugged. "It's true. So you aren't perfect. Who the hell is? If your camouflage doesn't always work in battle, that doesn't mean you can't use it proficiently in other scenarios. Scenarios that would be equally useful to your military, I might add." The mechanical arm withdrew the needle from her flesh and rose into the ceiling. "Weakness, my ass," she grumbled. "You need to hang out with my brethren on Earth. We all bear special gifts. But those gifts can sometimes fail us. Sensing others' emotions is easy for me, but *altering* them takes concentration that I don't always have time for in battle. Do you think that makes *me* weak?"

His lips turned up in a genuine smile as the mechanical arm above him withdrew into the ceiling. "*Srul* no."

"And neither are you. Don't let assholes get in your head and convince you otherwise."

He laughed. "I don't think my translator got some of that right, but I gleaned your meaning."

Simone hopped off the bed, already feeling more energetic after her infusion. "Janwar doesn't think you're weak. Otherwise, you wouldn't be a member of his crew. And coming from an outsider's perspective: Every one of you is badass."

He chuckled. "I'm going to assume that's a compliment rather than a declaration that you find our asses unattractive."

She laughed. "It's definitely a compliment. It means you're impressively tough warriors. And I also happen to think your collective asses are hot." Dropping her voice to a whisper, she winked. "Although I like Janwar's the most."

"Good to know," a deep voice commented.

Jumping, she turned to face the door as Janwar stepped through it.

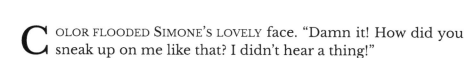

COLOR FLOODED SIMONE'S LOVELY face. "Damn it! How did you sneak up on me like that? I didn't hear a thing!"

He grinned. "Of course, you didn't. You were too busy talking about my ass."

Elchan laughed as he rolled out of bed and headed for the door. "I believe I have work to do."

Janwar clapped a hand on his shoulder as he passed, grateful for his friend's continued blood donations.

He was grateful to Simone, too. He'd overheard how swiftly she'd come to Elchan's defense, disparaging those who had denigrated his friend. She had a kind heart and probably had no idea how much her approval meant.

Elchan's father hadn't just publicly disavowed him and labeled Elchan damaged. He'd done his best to exile him, taking his son's reputed "failure" as a personal affront. Over the years, he had blackened his son's name so efficiently that most Segonian women had steered clear of Elchan, some even going so far as to avoid making eye contact when they passed him. Since the Segonian people as a whole were much more accepting of differences than that, Janwar did not doubt that—rather than finding Elchan lacking—the women had instead worried that Elchan's father would turn his ire on *them* if they associated with him.

But Elchan was convinced the women spurned him because they feared his faulty genes would be passed on to any children he would sire.

Simone, however, viewed him as a whole warrior. She considered *all* of the Tangata's crew *badass* warriors worthy of kindness, respect, and friendship.

Recalling the embrace they'd shared earlier, he wondered if she might perhaps view *him* as worthy of more.

His heart began to pound as she approached, a blush staining her cheeks. Her hair cascaded down her back in a damp, silky curtain that started to draw up into waves as it dried.

"What brings you to Med Bay?" she asked, changing the subject.

"You do."

Her eyebrows rose. "Why? What's on your mind?"

Her. Always. Simone was a constant distraction Janwar welcomed like rain in a desert. "I wanted to show you something before last meal."

Curiosity wiped the embarrassment from her features. "Okay."

Taking her hand, he felt as if he'd just won a tournament when she didn't object.

Together they left Med Bay and strolled down the corridor.

"Thank you," he said softly.

"For what?"

He glanced over his shoulder to ensure Elchan wasn't nearby. "For your kindness. Elchan has not received much of it during his lifetime."

She frowned. "That's disappointing. I thought member nations of the Aldebarian Alliance were smarter than that, that they'd moved beyond disliking people because of their differences."

"They are, and they have. Others like Elchan enjoy happy lives on Segonia because most of the Segonian people are as accepting as the Lasarans. But his father is amongst the few who aren't. And he made Elchan's life a—what was the phrase Lisa used?—a living hell."

"Well, someone needs to kick his father's ass." Her face brightened suddenly as she looked up at him. "Ooh. I'll do it," she offered eagerly. "I can even humiliate him in public by making him cower in fear before I wipe the floor with him. Or better yet, make him grovel before Elchan and publicly beg his forgiveness for being such an ass."

Laughter rolled through him. "That's something I would very much like to see."

"Me, too. Elchan's a good guy." She smiled. "You're *all* good guys."

He squeezed her hand. "Many believe otherwise."

"That's their loss then," she said with a shrug. "Fortunately, I judge people by their actions, not by what others say about them. And why wouldn't I? I know how bad it feels to be feared, hated, or even hunted because I'm different. I've lost count of the number of Earthlings who tried to kill me once they began to suspect what I am."

He slowed to a halt. "What? Why?"

"I'm an empath. I could do things they couldn't. I was different. I *am* different, even more so since I was infected with the damned Gathendien virus. And being different doesn't go over well back home."

"Then why the *srul* does Lasara want to form an alliance with Earth?"

"Not with *Earth*. With *Seth*, the leader of the Immortal Guardians, who also watches over *gifted ones* like Lisa. Seth would like nothing more than to find a place where we can all live in peace without having to hide our differences."

"And Lasara hopes your women will help them repopulate?"

"Yes."

It sounded like an alliance would benefit both parties.

They resumed their walk, a companionable silence enfolding them as they turned up another corridor.

After a moment, Janwar realized he was smiling. It was odd how something as simple as strolling alongside Simone with her small hand tucked in his could be so pleasurable, calling forth a sense of peace he hadn't experienced in years.

He liked it.

"He we are," he announced as they reached the entrance to the garden. Pressing his palm to the reader, he opened the *stovicun* crystal door.

A warm breeze rushed out to welcome them, brushing the hair back from their shoulders. Trees shaded this entrance, their leaves whispering as the manufactured wind wafted through them.

Simone closed her eyes and breathed it in. "This is so much better than the recycled air on the *Kandovar* and the escape pod."

"Or on the Gathendien ship?"

She laughed. "Yeah. Their air smelled like stagnant swamp water."

Together they ambled along a path as the door shut behind them.

"Do birds or other creatures in the park ever sneak out into the rest of the ship?"

"Yes." He sent her a sheepish look. "Catching and returning them has become something of a sport for us, alleviating the boredom that traveling long distances can generate."

She grinned.

A chittering in the tree they walked beneath drew their gazes upward.

"You have the cutest squirrels here. They look like they have lions' manes."

"They *are* cute." As was she. "And *rinyas* aren't as destructive as some of their counterparts." He smiled down at her. "Kova keeps one in his quarters as a pet."

She started to speak but seemed to forget whatever she'd intended to say when her gaze shifted to the path ahead. Some of the joy left her expression as her footsteps slowed to a halt.

The trees in front of them thinned, allowing bright, simulated sunlight to reach the ground.

"I can't go that way," she reminded him. "Can we leave the path and continue in the shade?"

Moving to stand in front of her, he clasped both of her hands. "Do you trust me, Simone?"

"Yes."

He stared down at her as a thrill raced through him. She hadn't even hesitated, hadn't spoken slowly as though unsure. And he read no doubt in her pretty brown eyes.

His hold on her hands tightened as he dropped his gaze to her full, pink lips. His pulse leapt. He wanted to taste them so badly at that moment. But that wasn't why he'd brought her here.

Slowly, he began to walk backward along the path.

She looked past his shoulder to the light beyond. Though her throat worked in a hard swallow and her fingers tightened on his, she didn't balk or drag her footsteps. She merely followed his lead. And *dreck*, that one act of trust despite what must surely be a certainty that it would cause her pain won his heart then and there.

Warmth bathed him as he stepped into the light, mirroring precisely that which the sun emitted. Her eyes fell to his arms, watching the light slide down them as he drew her after him, getting closer and closer to her own until it touched her hands. She drew in a breath but kept moving, following him until they left the shadows several paces behind them.

She squeezed her eyes shut, her brow furrowing. And for a moment, fear engulfed him.

Oh, *drek*. It was hurting her. They'd *drekked* up! He had to—

Releasing him, she raised a hand to cast a shadow over her face before opening her eyes.

Then he remembered that her eyes were unaccustomed to the brightness because she'd avoided the sun for many years.

He studied her carefully. The skin on her arms, chest, and neck didn't pinken or blister, nor did that on the hand she'd raised or the one he held.

She stilled. The teeth she'd clenched in anticipation of the pain relaxed. Lowering the hand that shielded her eyes, she stared down at it. Then she released him and brought her other hand up, holding it out beside the other for inspection. "I don't understand," she whispered. "What's happening?"

Every moment her pale skin remained free of burns and blisters, Janwar's anxiety faded a little more. "Kova tinkered with the lights in the garden. Since those in the rest of the ship don't harm you, I guessed that ultraviolet light was the culprit and asked him if there was anything he could do about it." He smiled. "And there was. He installed shields that will dampen the ultraviolet rays and protect you."

She stared up at him. "He did?"

"Yes. We want you to be able to come here and enjoy the park as often as you want, the way we do."

Stunned, she looked around. "But... won't that... I mean, don't the plants need it?" She motioned to the trees and the plethora of foliage around them. "Won't all of this die if you block the ultraviolet rays?" Anxiety flooded her features. "You can't do that, Janwar. And not just because it's so beautiful here. You *need* these plants. You depend on them. You can't just—"

He captured one of her hands once more. "Easy," he murmured. "The plants won't die."

"But—"

"The shields aren't permanent." Reaching into a pocket, he withdrew a bracelet and fastened it around her narrow wrist. "We placed sensors at every entrance to the park and made you this. As long as you wear it, you'll be safe here. Each time you pass the sensors at an entrance, the shields will slide into place and dampen the ultraviolet light. When you leave, they'll automatically retract so the plants can continue to thrive."

She stared up at him, her expression unreadable. "Really?" she asked, voice hushed.

He nodded.

Moisture welled in her eyes as they acquired an amber glow. Her throat worked in another hard swallow. "I can't believe you did this for me. Both of you."

Though his chest constricted at the sight of her tears, the fact that they were spawned by happiness brought him a joy he hadn't

190

experienced since Lisa and Taelon's baby had held her little arms out to him for a hug, then snuggled against his chest. "We take care of our friends," he said, his voice a little husky. She was rapidly coming to feel like far more than that to him.

Simone smiled as tears spilled over her lashes and down her cheeks. Closing her eyes, she tilted her head back and raised her face to the light, spreading her arms wide as if she wished to bathe in it. A sound that was half-sob, half-laugh escaped her. "It's warm." She turned in a slow circle. "I forgot how warm sunlight can be."

And these lights accurately mimicked both the look and feel of sunlight.

When next her eyes opened, they glowed bright amber. Lunging forward, she slammed into him and locked her arms around him in a crushing hug. "Thank you."

Pleasure filling him, he hugged her back.

"Thank you so much." Her hold tightened until she threatened to crack his ribs.

"You're welcome," he wheezed.

"Oh!" Hastily releasing him, she leaned back. "Was that too tight? Are you okay?"

He nodded as he caught his breath. "I'm fine."

She gave him a rueful smile. "Sorry about that. I don't think you fully grasp how much this means to me." Turning, she strode farther up the bright path. "Do you know how long it's been since I walked in sunshine... *without* frantically searching for shadows to seek refuge in?"

Janwar followed her. "No."

Halting, she faced him. More tears spilled down her cheeks as she forced another smile. "Almost seven hundred years."

Shock rippled through him. She'd said she was older than she looked, but...

"Seven hundred years," she went on, "of having to eschew daylight and only move about in the darkness of night." She shook her head as she looked around. "When I'm at full strength, I can tolerate brief exposure, but the pain that follows always robs me of any pleasure I might've taken in it." She held out her arms.

"Ordinarily, my skin would already be prickling with a sunburn." As it had the first time he'd brought her here.

His throat tightened as he watched her gaze down at her flawless skin, more tears chasing each other down her cheeks.

Then her gaze met his. "You don't know what an incredible gift you've given me."

If Janwar had his way, he would give her many more.

CHAPTER ELEVEN

L AUGHTER ABOUNDED WHEN THEY all gathered together for last meal. T joined them in android form and trod back and forth from the kitchen, dividing his attention between serving them all their favorite dishes, contributing to the conversation, and monitoring the radar for any bounty hunters who might have followed them when they left Promeii 7.

At Simone's request, they watched the three-dimensional holorecording T had produced of her battle with the Dotharian.

"I *have* to send a copy of this to Seth and David," she declared.

Janwar had to admit that now that he knew the match's outcome and wasn't terrified she'd be killed, watching it from a spectator's point of view was immensely entertaining.

"Who are Seth and David?" Elchan asked.

"Seth leads the Immortal Guardians on Earth—who are warriors like me—and watches over *gifted ones* like Lisa. David is his second in command. They're both like fathers to me. I love them to pieces."

Krigara's eyebrows flew up. "Did you say *Immortal* Guardians?"

"Yes. But we aren't really immortal. We're just exceedingly hard to kill."

Soval snorted. "So we've seen."

Her arm brushed Janwar's as she turned to face him, sending little tingles of awareness dancing through his body. "Can we do that? Can we send them a copy?"

He nodded. "You mentioned wanting to comm them and let them know what we find on the Gathendien outpost. When we do, I'll send them a copy they can play on the equipment Taelon gave him."

"Yes!" She grinned wickedly. "I want to see their faces while they watch it. Seth and David have lived so long that nothing... or *almost* nothing... surprises them. Rescuing Ami and finding out she's an alien surprised them. But *this*..." She motioned to the holomatch taking place in the center of the table. "This will shock the hell out of them."

Smiling, Janwar shook his head.

"Let's watch it again," she implored.

Janwar began to replay it.

As soon as her small form strode confidently into the massive arena, Simone boomed in a deep voice, "Ladies and gentlemen, I present to you... Promeii 7's newest champion... Simone the Dotharian Conqueror!... Prepare yourselves for a lesson iiiiiiiiii-iiin... Girl! Power!"

The men all cheered and hooted and laughed over her commentary.

Everyone remained in high spirits throughout the meal. Janwar thought it part relief that she'd survived her bout with the Dotharian and part getting caught up in her enthusiasm and good humor. Simone had yanked them all out of the boredom of doing the same thing day after day and thrust them into a vastly entertaining, ongoing new adventure. How did someone who had lived as tough a life as she had for so many centuries hold on to that joy and spread it so freely? Even Kova smiled and chuckled, something the somber male usually only did when his pet did something crazy.

Afterward, the rest of the crew wandered away to perform the last of the day's duties before bedtime, leaving Janwar and Simone alone. The two carted their dishes to the kitchen, where T tidied up in android form.

"Good night, T," Simone called with a smile.

"Good night, Champion of Promeii 7."

She laughed as they left the lounge and headed toward the area sporting the crew's sleeping quarters.

Janwar's heartbeat increased when she took his hand in hers and squeezed it.

"This has been such an amazing day," she said, "that I admit I'm sad to see it end."

He was, too. "You must be tired, though, after the big battle."

She tilted her head first one way, then the other, considering it. "Mmmaybe a little."

Their steps slowed as they turned onto the corridor their respective rooms were on.

"Do you know what my favorite part was?" she asked.

"Of the day or the battle?"

"The day."

"The battle with the Dotharian," he answered with a grin.

"Nope. Guess again."

Hmm. "The sunlit stroll in the park?"

"Nope, but that was a close second. Guess again."

He'd thought for sure it would be one of those two. "Visiting a bar full of aliens on an alien planet?"

"Nope. But damn, I had a big day today, didn't I?"

He laughed as they halted outside her door. "Very big. What *was* your favorite part?"

She stepped closer, tilting her head back to smile up at him. "The good-luck kiss you gave me."

Surprise swept through him, followed closely by desire as he recalled the feel and taste of her. "What?"

"I'm not used to being the aggressor," she confessed softly. "There aren't many female Immortal Guardians on Earth. And breaking up with someone you know you'll run into over and over again for hundreds or thousands of years afterward can be awkward, so we females tend to be very careful not to do anything that would invite amorous attention. Hence, the men are the aggressors." She inched closer. "I haven't... dated in a very long time, Janwar. I'm out of practice, behind the times, and honestly don't know what the hell I'm doing."

She was setting him on fire. That's what she was doing.

His heart began to batter his ribs. "What *do* you know?"

Amber light flared to life in her alluring brown eyes. "That I want another kiss."

Srul, yes. Dipping his head, he pressed his lips to hers. Not with the desperation he'd felt the first time he'd kissed her, but with the same wonder he'd seen on her face when she'd realized the sun in the park wouldn't hurt her anymore.

Simone wanted him.

Simone—the remarkable woman he already cherished as a friend and whose company he constantly craved—*wanted* him.

Him.

Her lips were soft and warm beneath his, the kiss they shared gentle and full of affection.

He drew back just enough to break the tantalizing contact and stared down at her.

"Magnificent," she whispered.

He chuckled, amused by the description he'd applied to himself to make her laugh when she'd suffered the sunburn.

"I am so drawn to you," she said with a smile.

"Because I'm forbidden fruit?" he teased, expecting her to laugh at the phrase he'd once heard Lisa use.

Instead, Simone shook her head and smiled again, her expression tender. "Because you're you."

What those words did to him.

Rising onto her toes, she slid her arms around his neck.

And Janwar claimed her lips in another kiss, this one firmer, hotter. Wrapping his arms around her slender waist, he drew her up against him, loving the press of her full breasts and how deceivingly delicate she felt compared to his bulk. As soon as she parted her lips, he slipped his tongue inside to stroke hers.

When Simone moaned and rubbed against him, fire streaked through him, hardening his cock and tightening his hold. *Drek*, he wanted her.

The kiss turned heated. Breath shortened and hearts raced as passion rose.

Tunneling her fingers through his hair, she fisted his braids and kissed him back with the same burning need that threatened to consume him.

Janwar placed just enough space between them to palm one of her breasts. "Perfect," he uttered against her lips, wishing clothing didn't prevent him from feeling her silky skin.

Simone slid one leg up the outside of his and hooked a knee over his hip, bringing their hips into better alignment.

Drek, he needed her naked. Right now. Beneath him. On a bed.

As if hearing his thoughts, she withdrew one hand from his hair and waved it behind her, blindly searching for the palm pad that would open her door. But Janwar backed away from it, forcing her to lower both feet to the floor and trip along with him.

She broke the kiss with a gasp. "What—?"

"My quarters," he growled, trailing his lips down her throat.

"Hell, yes," she moaned. When their feet tangled together and nearly sent them tumbling to the floor, she jumped up and wrapped her legs around his waist.

Groaning, Janwar clamped one hand on her gorgeous ass and supported her back with the other as he turned and stumbled toward his door. Her lips captured his with a hunger that made him consider taking her right there, up against the wall in the corridor. "Not the aggressor, my ass," he murmured. She was doing a damned fine job for someone who had tentatively claimed she was out of practice.

Simone grinned, her hair falling in a curtain around them and blocking his view. As her lips met his once more, he blindly reached out to touch the wall so he could feel his way to his room. "Why are these corridors so *drekking* long?" he grumbled.

She laughed. "Do you want to put me down so we can race?"

"*Srul* no. You feel too good in my arms."

Amid kisses, touches, stumbles, and laughs, they finally made it inside his quarters. As soon as the door slid shut behind them, he turned and pressed her up against it, repositioning her so the heart of her could ride his hard cock.

Both moaned.

Her legs tightened around him, heels digging into his ass as he rocked against her.

"Janwar," she breathed, his name full of longing and desire.

"I want you," he murmured against her lips. "All of you." He couldn't remember ever before feeling this desperate to bury himself balls deep inside a woman, to tease and taste and explore every part of her. Not even his first time had fired his blood like this.

She nodded. "Then take your damned clothes off."

Chuckling, he lowered her feet to the floor. They instantly began tugging at each other's clothing, exchanging kisses, caresses, and more laughter when they nearly tripped and face-planted on the floor in their haste. He had never experienced anything like it.

Janwar had been on the run since he was seventeen. A criminal. A bounty hunter's dream capture. As a result, every coupling he'd engaged in had been the mere scratch of an itch and a quick release with nameless strangers. Strangers with whom he had always had to keep his guard up, something that had become even more apparent after a pleasure worker managed to drug Krigara and came damned close to handing him over to a bounty hunter.

With Simone, it could not be more different.

The two of them had been practically inseparable since she'd first stepped foot on the *Tangata*. Janwar liked her, had enjoyed the time they'd spent together, and treasured the friendship that had swiftly grown between them. It meant so much more when her lips touched his. When she smiled and drew a tender hand down his beard. Though he wanted nothing more than to get naked, bury himself inside her, and take her fast and hard, joy filled him as they chuckled over their impatience, the clumsiness of their attempts to divest each other of their pants only to be hindered by their combat boots.

With Simone, it was fun.

No. It was *more* than fun. It was something he couldn't adequately describe.

He just knew he never wanted it to end.

S IMONE WAS PRACTICALLY PANTING by the time she and Janwar finally stood naked before each other.

"You're beautiful," he declared, his voice hoarse.

Even as his words thrilled her, she devoured him with her gaze.

Janwar was packed with muscle, the reddish tinge to his skin alluring, with dark hair on his chest that she couldn't wait to toy with.

Her gaze traveled down rippling abs and found more dark hair surrounding the base of the hard cock that jutted toward her. He was big all over. And she was relieved to see that there was nothing bizarre going on down there. She hadn't really thought there would be, since Akselis were very similar to humans.

"So are you," she told him. *Beautiful from head to toe.* Closing the distance between them, she rested her hands on his chest. His skin was warm, his heart pounding beneath her touch. Dragging her fingers through the crisp hair, she rose onto her toes so she could lean in and press her lips to his neck. "I love your scent," she said softly, breathing it in, and touched her tongue to his soft skin. "Your taste."

The gentle contact seemed to shatter his control.

Locking one arm around her, he drew her so close that even air couldn't pass between them. Fisting a hand in her hair, he tugged her head back and captured her lips, plundering, devouring, and driving the flames ever higher.

Lifting her, he urged her to lock her legs around him again.

Simone did so eagerly, pleasure streaking through her as she ground against him. It had been so long that she feared for a moment she would come before they even made it to the bed.

Then Janwar strode forward, kneeled on the mattress that would be waist-high to her, and leaned down. Her back touched cushy bedding.

Loosening his hold, he eased back and sat on his heels between her spread thighs.

Against her will, Simone felt heat creep into her cheeks. Her sexual encounters since transforming had been few and very far between. She had always believed there should be an emotional connection between two people before they pursued anything intimate. But it was hard to form that connection with someone you couldn't tell you were immortal.

"Look at you," he said, his deep voice rough with need. Those big hands of his clasped her ankles, slid up her shins, her thighs, his thumbs coming sooooo close to the place she craved his touch the most, and continued up her sides until he reached her breasts.

"Perfect," he murmured, cradling them in his palms, squeezing, teasing the tight buds, and sparking shocks of pleasure.

Gasping, she shifted her hips restlessly.

His lips curled up in a knowing smile as he leaned over her and lowered his head.

Simone moaned when he captured one taut peak between his lips. Burying her hands in his long hair again, she gripped his braids as he teased her with his teeth and tongue.

"Janwar," she whimpered, arching against him. "Take me. I need you."

But instead of plunging his long hard length inside her, he shifted his mouth to her other breast, driving that need higher. When he trailed heated kisses down her stomach, she released him and fisted the bedding on either side of her. If he did what she thought he was going to do, she wouldn't last two seconds.

His warm breath brushed her clit, even that light contact making her gasp. Then, his eyes meeting and holding hers, he lowered his head and took her with his mouth.

Simone moaned long and low. The things he did. With his teeth and his tongue. Stroking, sucking, and teasing as she writhed beneath him.

He slipped two fingers inside her, adding to the sensual torment. "You're so wet for me."

She nodded, unable to speak or think beyond the pleasure as he drove her higher and higher. An orgasm crashed through her. Simone cried out as his tongue and fingers lengthened and extended it, keeping the ripples of pleasure going on and on until she collapsed against the covers.

Janwar kissed his way up her body again and settled between her thighs. "Beautiful," he declared once more.

Simone stared up at him, something indefinable filling her as her empathic gift infused her with the same emotions she read in his heated gaze as he stared down at her. There was much more in those russet eyes than rudimentary lust or desire. There was friendship, affection, and—dare she believe it?—burgeoning love.

She cupped his handsome face in her hands. "Janwar," she whispered.

Dipping his head, he brushed his lips against hers, the contact tender despite the need that tightened every muscle pressed against her.

Simone poured everything she felt for him into that kiss, swiftly turning into a fiery conflagration. Heat swept through her, the urgency she'd felt earlier returning full force. Slipping a hand between them to his chest, she gave the hair there a tug and toyed with his nipple.

"Simone," he groaned.

She continued to explore, sliding her hand down between them until she could curl her fingers around his hard cock. A shudder of pleasure shook him when she guided it to her entrance. Abandoning his talented mouth, she trailed kisses across his cheek and gave his earlobe a little nip. "Take me."

He didn't hesitate, pressing forward with rigid control. "You're so small," he gritted. "So tight."

When he started to withdraw, she locked her legs around him. "Don't stop!"

Bracing his weight on his hands, he chuckled. "I didn't intend to. I just wanted to give you time to adjust. Let me know if I hurt you." He pressed forward again, deeper this time. Withdrew then pushed forward again.

Simone gripped his biceps and arched up to meet him, loving the feel of him.

"Good?" he asked, his voice hoarse as laughter left his expression, replaced by an intensity that made her breath catch.

"Better than good," she told him.

Again, he nearly withdrew, then sank deeper. "Want more?"

"I want all of you," she professed.

And wow, did he give her what she wanted, burying himself to the hilt, withdrawing, then driving into her again and again, harder, faster, stealing her breath, altering the angle of his hips so he could grind against her clit with every thrust, ratcheting up the pleasure and sending her higher and higher until another orgasm crashed through her.

As soon as her body began clenching around his cock in rhythmic pulses, Janwar followed her, calling her name as he spilled his heat inside her.

His breath coming in gasps, he lowered himself to his elbows and burrowed his hands beneath her so he could wrap his arms around her and hug her close. Resting his head on the pillow beside hers, he pressed a kiss to her temple.

So much affection filled her that Simone found herself blinking back tears. No one had ever made her feel the way Janwar did.

Bodies still joined, he rolled them to their sides. "I don't want to crush you," he murmured, encouraging her to snuggle her head to his chest.

She smiled and draped a leg over his hip. "The prospect of that doesn't seem to bother you when we spar." He had, on several occasions, taken her down to the floor and wrestled with her.

He chuckled, his cock jerking inside her. "Because I'm always too busy trying to keep you from kicking my ass."

Simone smiled as she studied him. She didn't think she had ever seen him so relaxed, not even on their jogs and strolls through the park. But the passionate lovemaking they'd just shared seemed to have stripped away the hard, mercenary-like veneer and left him looking years younger.

"What?" he asked, a smile toying with the edges of his lips.

"How quickly do you recover after sex?"

"Quickly," he declared. "Why? What did you have in mind?"

Simone pushed him over onto his back and straddled him.

Eyebrows flying up, he grinned in delight.

Quickly was right. She could feel his cock already hardening again inside her. Giving him a wicked smile, she indicated their new position. "Can't crush me this way, can you?"

His strong hands gripped her hips. "No. And I like the way you think." The growly, hungry tone that deepened his voice sent a shiver through her.

"Do you like *this*?" she asked innocently. Clenching her inner muscles, she rotated her hips.

His grip tightened. "*Drek* yes."

Then they both began to move.

"**J**ANWAR."

Simone jerked awake at the tinny voice.

Curled up behind her, one arm pillowing her head and the other wrapped around her waist, her notorious pirate lover didn't move.

"Janwar," Krigara repeated, his voice coming from the ear comm Janwar had tossed on the bedside table sometime during the night. "Respond."

Simone grinned. Oh, he was responding all right. At least his body was. She had no difficulty identifying the hard length currently trapped between their bare bodies. But she must have tuckered him out because he was out like a light, his long, slow breaths fanning her hair.

"Janwar," Krigara said louder, this time over the ship-wide comm. "Where the hell is he?" he muttered.

"He appears to be sleeping deeply," T mentioned cheerfully.

"Janwar is still asleep?" Krigara sounded so astonished that Simone wondered if this was the first time their commander had ever overslept.

"Yes," T said as murmured conversation erupted. "Perhaps you should ask Simone to wake him."

"Why would I ask Simone to wake him? I don't even know where she is."

"She is in bed with him."

Silence.

"Smooth, T," she muttered dryly. "Real smooth."

Janwar sighed and nuzzled her neck, sending a delightful shiver through her. "What's smooth?"

A number of naughty replies came to mind, but she opted to save those for later. "T just told everyone we slept together."

"What?" he asked, sounding much more awake.

"Apologies, Simone," T said. "Did you not wish the rest of the crew to know you slept with Janwar?"

"Stop talking," she said with a laugh.

203

Janwar propped himself up on an elbow and ran a hand through his mussed hair. "Boundaries, T. How many times have we talked about boundaries?"

"Many times," T replied. "Why? Have I crossed another?"

"Yes," he growled, but no anger touched his features as he smiled and leaned down to drop a kiss on her lips.

T made a huffing noise. "I fail to see what boundary I have crossed this time. If you're worried that I watched the two of you copulate, I assure you I didn't."

"T!" they both shouted at once, Simone appalled and Janwar exasperated.

T grumbled, "Fine. I will leave *you* to converse with them, Krigara. They appear to have woken up on the wrong side of the bed."

Sighing, Janwar kissed both her cheeks, then her forehead. "I'm sorry," he whispered. "Did you want to keep this private?"

She smiled. "Honestly, I hadn't thought much further than wanting to get your handsome, naked ass in bed."

He grinned.

A throat cleared. "Janwar, respond," Krigara said, this time over the ear comm.

Grimacing, Janwar leaned past her, plucked the little device off the bedside table, and put it in his ear. "What is it?" he demanded, none too pleased.

"We've plotted a course for the moon on Pulcra's map," he announced, his tone laden with sarcasm. "I thought you might want to discuss our plans before we get there?"

Judging by Janwar's expression, he didn't appreciate his cousin's tone. "Meet us in the lounge. We'll talk after first meal."

Krigara muttered something about it almost being time for mid meal before signing off.

Janwar returned the ear comm to the bedside table, then regarded Simone somberly.

Wanting to bring a smile back to his handsome face, she yelled, "Race you to the lav!" and darted out of bed.

Laughing, he dove after her.

Since she opted not to use preternatural speed, they hit the shower at the same time. Janwar gallantly held her back until the water warmed, then motioned for her to enter first.

Unlike the claustrophobic cleansing units on the *Kandovar*, this one was big enough for the whole crew to share and had multiple showerheads that drenched them both within seconds.

"*Drek,* that's tempting," he murmured.

Busy lathering up a cloth, she glanced at him.

His face dark with desire, he ogled her openly as she sent him a wicked smile and began to draw the soft cloth over her body in sensuous strokes.

Simone lowered her gaze to his muscled chest, rippling abs, and lower, feeling her pulse pick up. Absolutely perfect. "So are you." So tempting just staring at him sparked heat they, unfortunately, didn't have time to act upon. "One day, I'll have to show you the Immortal Guardian version of a quickie." She pursed her lips. "As long as T doesn't watch us."

He winced. "Apologies. Because of the way his sentience evolved, T can be rather..."

"Naive?"

"Yes. He's very curious and doesn't always know what is and isn't appropriate." Motioning for her to turn around, he used a soft soapy cloth to wash her back. "You're also the first female he's had any contact with aside from Lisa. And I told him to keep his distance while Taelon and Lisa were aboard."

When his hands lingered on her ass, she fought the desire to push back against him and instead traded positions so she could wash his back in return. "Were you afraid T might spill some of your piratical secrets?"

He chuckled. "Yes. And the Aldebarian Alliance frowns on AIs that possess the kind of sentience T has achieved." He shrugged. "You seemed to take such delight in his company that it didn't occur to me to warn him away. Nor did it occur to me that he'd share our newfound intimacy with the others." He turned to face her, his expression somber. "He may not understand your wanting to keep it secret."

T wouldn't? Or Janwar wouldn't? His countenance was irritatingly unreadable now, something she noticed tended to happen when something troubled him.

Reaching up, Simone touched his face and allowed his emotions to flow into her so she could read them more clearly.

Yep. There was a little hurt there. Maybe a little cynicism, too. A grim acknowledgment that most women wouldn't want to admit to having slept with the likes of him.

Her heart went out to him. Everyone had their insecurities. And it would seem she had inadvertently stumbled upon one of his. "If you think I don't wish to be associated with you in such a way," she said softly, "that others knowing the extent of our relationship would bring me shame, you're wrong."

"Our relationship?" he asked, stoic façade still firmly in place.

She smiled. "I don't sleep with men I don't care about, Janwar. And the more time I spend with you, the more I feel for you." It would be so easy to fall in love with him. "But I was raised in a time when women who had sexual relations with a man outside of marriage were viewed as disgraceful and likened to whores."

The blank mask crumpled into a frown. "Isn't that what Earthlings call pleasure workers who sell their bodies for credits?"

"Yes. Times have changed since then. But it took centuries for society—not all of it, but some of it, anyway—to acknowledge that women should have the same sexual freedom as men." Backing up, she reached for the shampoo and started lathering her hair. "And I just spent four months aboard a ship full of Lasarans who looked scandalized every time I accidentally brushed a man's arm while passing him in the hallway."

His lips turned up slightly as some of the tension left his form. "Lasarans are very strict with regards to unmarried males and females touching."

"Yes, they are. I just"—she shrugged, fighting a smile when his attention dropped to her breasts, then jumped back up again—"wasn't sure if your men would look down on me or think less of me if they knew how thoroughly and shamelessly I explored your body last night."

His lips twitched. "Don't forget enthusiastically."

Laughing, she gave him a self-deprecating smile. "As enthusi-astically as I want to right now." She ducked under the spray. "I like your crew, Janwar." Her thick hair grew heavy as the water rinsed away the suds and weighed the long strands down. "Your make-shift family. And I want them to like me." Closing her eyes, she let the water stream down her face. "As much as I pride myself on having become a modern woman unencumbered by the social strictures of the past, I admit I worried that your men would not react well." Turning her back to the spray, she wiped the water from her face. "I'm not familiar with their cultures or the rules they—"

His big body crowded hers, startling her into silence. His erec-tion trapped between them, he banded his arms around her and pressed her close until even water couldn't pass between them.

Her eyes met his in surprise.

Then he dipped his head and claimed her lips in a long, deep, passionate kiss that stole her breath and drove all thought from her head. Rising onto her toes, she locked her arms around his neck and kissed him back for all she was worth. Fire streaked through her.

Maybe they had time for a quickie after all?

Simone actually whimpered a protest when he broke the contact. Her heart pounded fiercely in her chest as she held his gaze, the amber glow of her eyes reflected in his.

"We make our own rules on the *Tangata*," he said, his voice so deep with lust that she wanted to jump up and lock her legs around his waist. "No one else's matter. We owe no allegiance to the societies that expelled us or hunted us or treated us like *bura* and still do because we're different or they think we're less than or because we weren't content to look the other way when we saw things that were wrong."

Simone had a sinking feeling that the scars that marred Kova had resulted from his lacking the traditional markings the rest of his race were born with. And she knew Elchan had faced difficulties over being different, thanks to his asshole father. She still didn't know much about Soval. But Janwar and Krigara had both lost par-ents who had been imprisoned, then executed for protesting what people on Earth would call human rights violations perpetrated by their government.

"We don't give two *dreks* what they think." His handsome face softened as he brushed her wet, tangled hair back with a gentleness most probably wouldn't believe him capable of. "And we don't tear each other down. Krigara. Srok'a. Kova. Elchan. Soval." He shook his head. "We just want to be happy—or as happy as we *can* be—and find some semblance of peace."

Her lips twitched. "I don't know if piracy was the right profession to pursue if you wanted peace."

He laughed. "Okay. We might want to get a little payback, too, and our current profession enables us to do that." Releasing her, he turned the water off and motioned for her to exit the shower.

A cabinet across from it opened automatically as a bar slid out, offering two large towels.

Janwar grabbed one and wrapped it around Simone.

It was so warm and fluffy.

"My point is," he said, holding the towel closed over her breasts, "as long as we're happy together, neither of us will face condemnation."

So... no drama or lovers' quarrels?

No problem. Simone wouldn't be happy in a contentious relationship. And if she and Janwar continued on their current course, she didn't foresee herself dumping him and pissing off the rest of the crew because she'd yet to find anything about him that she didn't like.

His brow furrowed. "You *are* happy, aren't you? I know you're concerned about your friends. But when it comes to you and me—to *us*—are you happy with the way things are going?"

She feigned a regretful sigh. "Well, to be honest..."

His hands tightened around the towel as tension practically pulsed from him.

"I'd be a lot happier," she said with an impish grin, "if we'd had time to make love in the shower."

Laughing, he drew her attention to his hands. "Why do you think I covered you up so fast? I'm trying to do the right thing and get us to lounge."

She arched a brow. "Perhaps later then?"

"*Drek* yes."

Grinning like two teenagers in the grips of first love, they swiftly toweled off, dressed, and left his quarters.

CHAPTER TWELVE

T HE REST OF THE crew trickled into the lounge as Janwar and Simone devoured what she deemed *brunch*, which was a combination of first and mid meal since they'd slept so late. Both had amusingly strong appetites and shared a laugh over it.

"So," she began once she'd devoured every crumb on her plate, "what's the plan?"

Krigara leaned back in his chair. "We've plotted a course for the planet Urkheht. The moon on Pulcra's map is one of thirty-three moons that orbit it, so the Gathendiens chose a good place to hide."

Janwar supposed he should feel guilty for sleeping late while the others worked but could manufacture no regret. He had never slept with a woman in the literal sense. He'd still been in school and living with his parents when they'd been killed. And after that, sex hadn't been a high priority. Surviving and avenging his parents' murders had.

Once he had barreled down that path, Janwar had only been able to find occasional relief with pleasure workers. And he couldn't relax and sleep beside someone who might sell him out for the bounty on his head.

So Simone had been his first. And he was still reeling a little from the intimacy of it, of curling his big body around hers and letting her warmth and sweetness lure him into slumber. He would've thought he'd lie there wide awake, counting the hours until dawn, or wake at every tiny movement. Though sleeping beside a woman after exploring her body might seem natural to others, it *did* require absolute trust, something he had only ever given his crew.

And yet, he hadn't hesitated to give Simone that trust.

Nor would he hesitate to do so again. That was how much she'd come to mean to him.

Blinking, he dragged his thoughts back to the topic at hand. "How long will it take us to reach the moon?"

"Two days," Krigara said.

Janwar opted to ignore the fact that his cousin's gaze was more watchful today.

Simone's eyebrows flew up. "Really? Considering the enemies they've amassed and the nature of the experiments they're conducting, I would've thought the Gathendiens would balk at building a supposedly *secret* facility so near a popular destination like Promeii 7. Particularly since so many people in the Aldebarian Alliance hate those bastards."

"With good reason," Elchan muttered.

"Exactly. Wouldn't they want more privacy to do their evil deeds?"

Janwar shook his head. "The moon isn't as close to Promeii 7 as you might think. The *Tangata* is just exceptionally fast. It would take other ships far longer to reach it."

Krigara nodded. "And though it might initially seem unwise, the Gathendiens may find close proximity to a place like Promeii 7 convenient. It's far beyond the boundary of alliance-occupied space. And Aldebarian Alliance laws have no meaning there."

She glanced at Janwar. "You did call it the ass-end of the galaxy."

He smiled wryly. "It is. Which also makes it a good place to waylay travelers of a certain species and take them to their base."

Her brow furrowed. "*Merde.* I didn't think of that. I hope those Purvelis we met at the pub will make it home safely."

"As long as they followed my advice, they should."

A moment passed, during which Janwar tried to ignore the surreptitious looks his crew kept sending him. He understood now why Simone had felt some reservations about T informing everyone they'd become lovers. Although they treated her no differently, his friends watched *him* like a bird of prey and didn't seem to know how to react.

"Is it possible we'll catch up to the ship before it reaches the moon?" she asked.

"I doubt it," Krigara said. "But we'll remain fully cloaked to keep them from detecting our approach, just in case."

"What happens if we *do* reach the ship first?"

Janwar considered it a moment. "We'll have a few options. We can postpone our trip to the moon and seize the ship. With that, however, we'd run the risk of them sending a distress call to the moon facility and warning them of our presence."

"Or they may request reinforcements," Soval added.

Janwar nodded. "We don't know how big their moon installation is, if it's primarily a research facility with a small staff or if multiple contingents of warriors are stationed there with a goodly supply of weaponry and fighter craft."

Simone studied them. "I assume another risk would be the one I feared when I attacked the other Gathendien ship, that they may kill any Earthlings or other test subjects they have aboard at the first sign of an attack to keep us from getting our hands on them."

"That's possible, too," he agreed.

Her look turned pensive. "I thought at first they had done that with the Purveli I found in one of the labs." The ebullience she'd exhibited since waking up in his arms dissolved. "I thought they'd killed him as soon as the first alarm blared, and it really threw me. That's when one of those bastards got me in the back with his tail spike. I just froze for a minute, and all I could think was *Did he die because of me? Did I do that? Is this my fault?* But then the pain struck. I had to kill the asshole who got me. And when I looked closer, I could tell the Purveli had been dead for some time." Her eyes met his, full of regret. "I wish I would've found him sooner."

He covered one of her hands with his. "I do, too."

"Did you incinerate his body with the others?"

"No. We took him through decon, scanned his image, and put him in cryostorage. We sent the image and analysis of a blood sample to the *Ranasura* so Jak'ri and Ziv'ri could help them identify him and let their people know we'll deliver his body for a proper Purveli ceremony once we've concluded our search for *Kandovar* survivors."

Turning her hand under his, she twined her fingers through his. "You're not nearly as nefarious as you want people to believe."

Leaning closer, he said in a loud whisper, "Don't tell anyone."

She laughed. "I know this is a longshot, but is there any way we could slip on board the Gathendien ship without them knowing and perform a quick search and rescue?"

He tilted his head to one side as he considered it, sliding his thumb back and forth over her soft skin. "It's doable," he said at last. "T can provide us with the ship's specs. Then a couple of us could take a C-23 over—that's a small stealth craft we use in covert operations—fully cloaked, attach it to the belly of the ship, cut our way in, and see what we can find."

"I'll do it," Kova said.

Beside him, Srok'a tensed, his jaw clenching. And Janwar girded himself for an old argument to make a new appearance.

"I will, too," Simone said. Had she caught the tension arching between the brothers? She was an empath, after all.

"It still carries risk," Janwar warned her and had to fight to keep from blurting out a *drek no*. He hated the idea of Simone diving into danger. But she had more than proven that she could handle it. "If any Gathendiens spot you, something I think likely since you'll have to make your way to each of the labs to look for your friends or anyone else in need of rescuing, they'll sound the alarm—"

"—and send the station a distress call," Srok'a bit out, "all while hurling every warrior they can at the two of you."

Soval nodded. "What if you find more than one or two lab subjects? What if there are multiple cells full of them? People go missing on Promeii 7 all the time. It wouldn't surprise me at all if the Gathendiens were responsible for some of those."

She shrugged. "Then I'll hold off the warriors until more of you can join us." She caught Janwar's eye. *And I'll make damned sure Kova doesn't fall while trying to aid me.*

Startled by her voice in his head, Janwar clutched her hand tighter. It was the first time she had communicated with him thusly. He wouldn't think he'd like it. He sure as *srul* didn't like it when Taelon and other telepaths spoke in his head. But as with everything else, it was different with Simone. And he found he enjoyed it as much as he would a touch of her hand. "All the

Gathendiens would have to do," he countered, focusing on the topic at hand, "is distract you long enough to toss a stun grenade into the room." He arched a brow. "Stun grenades *do* affect you, don't they?"

She nibbled her lower lip. "Yes. But I recover quickly. More quickly than most."

He shook his head. "You're lucky they didn't hit you with one on the other ship." The thought chilled him.

She wrinkled her nose. "They tried, the bastards. But I managed to duck and dodge them all."

"Because you're exceptionally fast. Faster than any man sitting at this table, including Kova." Who would be incapacitated by a stun grenade if Simone failed to protect him.

That seemed to give her pause.

Kova scowled. "Don't worry about me. I can—"

Srok'a slammed a hand down on the table, startling Simone so much she jumped. "*Drek* you, Kova!" he snarled. "You are *not* dispensable! Stop *drekking* acting like you are!"

And there it was.

Silence fell.

A muscle in Kova's jaw jumped.

Srok'a wasn't the only one that had raised this argument. Every member of the crew had at one point or another. Like Elchan, Kova had been born *different*. But the difficulties *Elchan* had faced as a result had been solely his father's creation. Women had avoided him because they feared his father, not because they found him lacking. Kova, on the other hand, had been hated on sight by everyone on his planet except for his brother. Perhaps his mother might have loved him had she not died birthing him. But everyone else had spent every day of Kova's life making him feel worthless.

Before Janwar could add his objection, he became aware of Simone's grip on his hand growing tighter and tighter until it felt as if she might break his fingers.

He glanced over at her.

Head bent, she stared down at the table, a muscle in her jaw twitching as she gritted her teeth.

Concerned, he leaned toward her. "Simone?"

Her eyes beginning to glow, she offered him a tight smile. "I'm an empath. Remember?" She jerked her chin toward the glowering brothers. "That's a lot of anger to take."

Janwar carefully kept his own fury from rising when he scowled at Srok'a and Kova. "Calm the *drek* down and rein in your anger. Now. You're hurting Simone."

Both looked at her with surprise, the rage swiftly fading from their expressions.

Sighing, she relaxed and cast them all a sheepish smile. "Sorry. Being an empath can suck sometimes."

"You have nothing to apologize for," Janwar assured her, tempted to take her in his arms. "Is it better now?"

"Yes. Thank you."

Kova and Srok'a watched her with remorse while studiously avoiding each other's gaze.

"Look," Simone said as her hand relaxed in Janwar's, "you've all been good to me." She studied each man in turn. "And I don't want to put any of you in danger. If we decide to sneak aboard the ship to covertly search for my friends and others they might have captured, I would prefer to do it alone."

Janwar might have been the first to bark a protest, but he wasn't the last. Everyone jumped in, shouting over each other to ensure their objections were heard while Simone frowned.

"If I may interrupt," a cheerful male voice said, startling them into silence.

Simone glanced up at T as he moved to stand beside her in one of his android forms.

"If we catch up to the Gathendien ship before it reaches its destination," T said, "I would be happy to accompany Simone in the covert operation you've described."

Janwar stared at him. "What?" T didn't go on special operations missions. He only joined them in the rare instances that *bura* went sideways.

She looked at Janwar and shrugged. "That works for me. T's android body looks much harder to damage than a mortal's. And if Gathendiens *do* manage to destroy it, he won't die. He'll continue to exist since his primary programming and consciousness resides here on the *Tangata*, right?" She glanced at the others, who appeared as stunned as Janwar felt. "Would that be feasible?"

"Absolutely," T answered before anyone else could. "I am fully capable of piloting a C-23. Once we cut through the hull and board the ship, I will find a conduit I can use to tap into the Gathendien ship's computer. I can then infect their communication system with a virus that will prevent them from contacting the station on the moon if they detect our presence. I may even be able to deactivate their alarm system."

"What?" Janwar demanded.

"You will also be happy to hear," T continued brightly, "that this form can sustain a great deal of damage and continue functioning. I am also stronger and faster than the rest of the crew, so I would be a great asset if we were to find multiple captives in need of rescuing."

No one seemed to know what to say to that.

Simone bit her lip. "Does he not usually do those sorts of things?"

"*Drek*, no, he doesn't," Janwar said, worry rising. "T, have *you* been infected with a virus?" It was the only explanation he could concoct for T's wild claims. "Run a diagnostic."

"Running diagnostic," T said.

Simone remained quiet, looking from one man to another.

"Diagnostic complete," T announced. "All systems are performing as intended."

"I don't understand," Elchan said.

"Me either," Soval murmured.

Kova and Srok'a nodded, all anger gone now as they studied the gleaming android.

Janwar shook his head. "You've never disabled another ship's comm system before, T. Why would you think you can do so now?"

"I don't think I can. I know it," T replied, his tone both happy and boastful.

"*How* do you know it?" he pressed.

"I am capable of performing millions of tasks simultaneously," T told them, something everyone here already knew, except perhaps Simone. "And I do so every day. But as my sentience has expanded, I have found myself feeling what may best be described as boredom," T admitted. "I needed a challenge." A disturbing hesitance entered his voice. "Or challen*ges*."

Oh drek.

Srok'a looked around at them. "Is it me, or does he sound guilty?"

Kova grunted. "He sounds guilty as *srul*."

Janwar sighed. "T, what did you do?"

"In the interest of expanding my knowledge base and alleviating my boredom, I took it upon myself to learn how to autopilot every craft in our bays."

The men's jaws dropped.

Janwar's alarm shot up. "Please tell me you just read the manuals."

"That is how I began," T said. "But I wished to do more. Performing the same tasks day after day became too..."

"Tedious?" Simone supplied helpfully.

Janwar didn't think she understood just how much of a *bura* storm this was.

"Correct. Tedious. To dispel that tedium, I..." T's speech again slowed as though he were reluctant to continue.

"You what?" Simone encouraged.

"I have been taking the craft out for test flights while you all sleep."

Janwar's jaw nearly hit the floor. If he weren't so shocked, he might've laughed. T sounded like an adolescent admitting he'd taken the family hovercar out for a joy ride without asking for permission. "Are you *drekking* kidding me?"

The others piled on. "While we *sleep*?"

"How the *srul* did we not know that?"

"How many did you damage, T?"

"I did not damage any of them," T told them, all indignation. "I happen to be an excellent pilot."

Janwar waved a hand to quiet everyone down. "What about tapping into another ship's system. Have you practiced that one, too? I thought infiltrating the *Ranasura* was the first time you'd done that."

"It was not. I do not like being left behind, so I have accompanied you on some of your missions."

"Which missions?" Janwar demanded.

"All of them," T said, a smile in his voice.

Janwar dragged a hand down his face and struggled for patience. "How?"

"The datapads you wear on your wrists. I was with Krigara and Srok'a on the Gathendien ship and monitored their actions while they overrode access codes and searched the lab's systems. I wished to know more and opted to remain on the ship after you locked it down so I could practice."

"Are you on the other ship now?"

"No. Once I mapped their system and reviewed every bit of data stored in it, I returned to the *Tangata*."

How the *srul* had he done that? T had never jumped remotely from one ship to the next. He always needed a conduit.

Simone sat forward. "You reviewed *all* of the data stored on their computers?"

"Yes."

"Was there any mention of other ships capturing my friends from Earth?"

"No," T told her with some regret. "But the battle with the *Kandovar* left their ship badly damaged. They were still trying to get their long-range communication system up and running when they found you."

"Oh." She glanced around. "That sucks. It would've been nice to obtain a list of every ship that's picked up Earthlings and other survivors so we could just haul ass and rescue them all."

Janwar nodded.

"So." She glanced around the table. "One option is for me and T to infiltrate the Gathendien ship and save whomever we can. What are the other options?"

"If you and T infiltrate the Gathendien ship," Janwar said, "I'll accompany you."

She shook her head. "The whole point of taking T is to—"

"I *will* accompany you," he repeated, his expression brooking no argument.

Simone cracked a smile. "You're *hot* when you're all authoritative, commander. Frustrating, but still hot."

His mind went blank with surprise.

Someone snorted a laugh. He thought it might have been Soval.

"We'll call that one Plan A," she continued. "What's Plan B? We bypass the ship and go to the station first?"

He nodded. "That also has risks. The station could contact the ship and either enlist its aid or warn it away."

"So while we kicked ass on the station, the ship could jet off to who-knows-where, along with any *Kandovar* survivors they might hold on board?"

"Yes."

She frowned. "How hard would it be to track them?"

He shrugged. "Depends on how long we're delayed by any battle that might erupt on the station. We don't know how many warriors we'll face or how long it will take us to sneak inside and orchestrate a rescue. T can only track the Gathendien ship as far as radar will allow. And if it manages to fly out of range before we can get back on the *Tangata*, there's a chance we'll lose it."

Krigara nodded. "As well as anyone they have on board."

Simone swore, then turned to T. "Can you do like you did with the *Ranasura* and be two places at once, both here with us and on the Gathendien ship, so you can keep us informed of its location?"

"That would require an open comm channel, which would alert them to our presence and general location."

Janwar didn't like the options any more than she did. It seemed like either way, they would likely miss their opportunity to rescue anyone the Gathendiens had in their clutches—either those on the ship or those on the station.

"And if the ship reaches the station before we catch up to them?" she asked.

"If the ship carries Earthlings or other survivors," Janwar speculated, "they'll be the first unloaded upon arrival."

"Seems logical," she murmured. "And more convenient for us since everyone we're hoping to rescue will be in the same place."

"Hopefully," Krigara inserted. "But again, we don't know how large an installation they're maintaining, how tight their security is, or the number of warriors that guard it."

"That's a lot of variables," she reluctantly admitted.

"And if the ship and its crew linger," Elchan added, "we'll face larger numbers."

Janwar silently agreed. It could be the seven of them against dozens, or it might be the seven of them against hundreds.

Drek, if this moon ended up being a major military base for the Gathendiens, there could be thousands. While he and his crew had taken on large numbers in the past, there was a limit to their capabilities.

Simone sighed. "What I'm hearing is that we're just going to have to wait and see."

He sent her a commiserating smile. "I'm afraid so."

She grimaced. "Patience is not my strong suit."

"Perhaps a distraction will help," T suggested brightly. "Shall I show you how I can pilot all of the K-6s at once?"

Every male's eyes widened before they began blurting objections.

"No!"

"*Srul* no!"

"What the *drek*?"

T produced a huffing sound. "Well, it's not like I haven't done it before."

"*What*?" Janwar came close to bellowing.

Silence fell.

T sounded much more subdued when he spoke again. "Did I cross another boundary, Commander Janwar?"

"By taking our entire fleet of K-6s out on fun runs without permission because you were *bored*?" he asked incredulously. "*Drek* yes, you crossed a boundary!"

Another moment passed before T replied. "Well, it wasn't *only* because I was bored."

Simone nodded. "T told me his primary directive is to ensure the safety and well-being of you and the crew. If he can pilot the entire fleet of drones simultaneously with success, I'm thinking that could benefit you in the future, especially if they're well-armed."

He scowled. "They carry the same weaponry fighter craft do and then some."

"Then they could provide a nice distraction if you needed some-one to draw attention away from you. And in a life and death sit-uation—like every bounty hunter in the galaxy suddenly deciding to band together and try to take you out—T could keep them all busy while you get the hell out of Dodge."

Elchan snorted. "As if Janwar would ever back down from a fight."

Simone rolled her eyes. "Yet another way we're alike. I can never seem to back down from a challenge."

"Yes," Janwar acknowledged with a smile. "You made that abun-dantly clear when you insisted on battling the Dotharian and won."

Grinning big, she released his hand and thrust both fists up in the air. "Aw, yeah! Champion of Promeii 7, baby!"

Everyone laughed.

"For now," he said, "let's see if we can dig up any mention of this moon base on the intergalactic net."

"*And* any mention of Earthlings," Simone added.

"And any mention of Earthlings," he seconded, then turned to the android. "T, no more fun runs until I confirm that you know what the *srul* you're doing."

The light in T's eyes dimmed a bit.

"Until then," Janwar continued, "do you think you, Srok'a, and Krigara can fabricate a virus we can plant on Gathendien ships that will give us a backdoor into their communications array? Specifically, I'm looking for something you can use to hack their system, track them, monitor their comms, and determine which ones might have Earthlings aboard without alerting them to your presence."

T straightened, his eyes flashing brighter. "I did examine every bit of clunky coding on that ship. Mine is far more complex and beautiful."

Krigara snorted and waved a hand. "Yeah, yeah. You're gorgeous, T. You're a genius. Just answer the question."

If an android could preen, Janwar was pretty sure T would be doing it.

"Yes. I believe the three of us can fabricate such a virus, though I do not know how long it will take us. You life forms don't think nearly as quickly as I do." T glanced at Janwar from the corner of his eye sockets. "Which is why I'm such a superlative pilot."

Simone grinned. "There's certainly nothing wrong with T's ego."

Janwar sighed. "We'll talk about your piloting later. Everybody, get to work."

CHAPTER THIRTEEN

S IMONE SIGHED WITH CONTENTMENT as she strolled down the park's shaded path. Giant trees rose all around her and perfumed the air with a scent reminiscent of pine. The alien equivalent of squirrels, rabbits, and other forest creatures rummaged through the detritus, chased each other around tree trunks, and lazed on branches above her head. Birds twittered and sang. Butterflies and bees fluttered and buzzed past.

Now that the simulated sunlight wouldn't harm her, this was her favorite place on the *Tangata*. The beauty. The scents. The gentle breeze. Since embarking upon her great space voyage, she had been so enthralled by meeting aliens and marveling over their advanced technology that Simone hadn't realized how much she'd missed this.

Janwar must have noticed how much she loved it here because he had asked her to meet him by the lake in half a ship hour so they could jog through the forest instead of in the gym this morning.

He was such a sweetheart.

The trees thinned.

Smiling, she stepped into wondrous sunshine. Warmth bathed her as she squinted against the brightness. Simone knew it wasn't actual sunlight and that crystal plates had slid into place to protect her from the harmful "rays" as soon as she'd entered the park. But it felt exactly like the sunlight she'd had to avoid for hundreds of years. It even dimmed occasionally, as if a cloud were passing overhead, lending it incredible realism.

Halfway to the lake, her steps slowed as Simone realized she wasn't alone.

Kova sat on a boulder up ahead.

Unaware of her presence, he tossed a few small nuts onto the grass. Or maybe they were seeds. She couldn't tell. They were larger than sunflower seeds but smaller than almonds.

Several *rinyas* that cavorted in the grass hurried over to claim the treats, stuffing already plump cheeks. They reminded her a lot of the squirrels on Earth. Their heads and bodies were of a similar shape and size. Gray fur covered them, adorned with black stripes and polka dots. But a fluffy black mane formed a halo around their faces like a lion's. And their tails...

She grinned.

Their tails were so fluffy they looked like puffballs and reminded her of the way cartoon animals often looked after landing in a clothing dryer.

When the other *rinyas* claimed all the seeds, one scampered up Kova's leg, jumped onto his arm, and continued until it perched upon his shoulder. Touching a little paw to his face, it chattered something in his ear.

Smiling slightly, Kova offered it three seeds.

The little cutie stuffed two in its mouth and took the third down to show the others.

Simone stared. She couldn't remember ever seeing the scarred warrior so relaxed and content. Wanting to alert him to her presence, she intentionally stepped on a twig as she started forward.

Kova glanced over, surprise lighting his honey-colored eyes. Then a familiar veil of stoicism descended over his features.

Simone smiled tentatively. "Hi. I hope I'm not disturbing you. I didn't know anyone else was here." She gestured to the forest that surrounded the pretty glen. "This place is huge!"

He nodded toward the *rinyas*, which now stood on their back legs like meerkats and watched her alertly. "Toa wanted to visit his friends. If he's away from them too long, he tends to get into mischief."

"Is Toa the showoff with the three seeds?"

His lips twitched. "Yes."

"I could see that little guy getting into trouble."

"Stay on the *Tangata* long enough, and you *will* see him get into trouble. Like the rest of us, he gets bored from time to time."

"Don't tell T that," she said in a stage whisper. "He might decide to take Toa on his next joyride."

His countenance lightened with a hint of amusement.

She motioned toward the boulder he sat on. "May I join you?"

Nodding, he scooted over a little.

Simone sat beside him, too short for her feet to touch the ground. "Wow." Leaning back a little, she rested her palms behind her on either side of her hips. "I forgot how much the sun can heat stone. When I was a little girl, I used to sit on rocks like these on cool days to warm my bottom."

He cracked a smile, one of his scars tugging at it and making it uneven.

Taking a chance, she bumped him companionably with her shoulder. "Speaking of the sun, I wanted to thank you for this." She took in the brightly lit meadow around them. "Janwar told me you were the one who arranged things so that the light wouldn't harm me."

He tossed a few more seeds to the *rinyas*. "It was his idea."

"Perhaps. But you were the one who figured out what needed to be done and how to do it. *And* you took the time to implement it."

He mumbled something she couldn't quite catch even with her sensitive hearing and looked adorably uncomfortable.

Her movements slow and careful, Simone reached out and took one of his hands.

He stilled, his gaze darting to the contact.

"May I show you what you gave me?" she asked softly.

His eyes met hers for a long inscrutable moment. Then he nodded. Just once.

Returning her attention to the meadow around them, Simone focused on the happiness that sitting here like this—something she hadn't been able to do in centuries—brought her and let it flow into him where they touched.

His breath caught. Facing forward, he closed his eyes. The tension in his face eased. His fingers twitched as if he wanted to curl them around hers, but he didn't. Instead, he released a long sigh, the muscles in his broad shoulders relaxing as his lashes lifted. He stared at the sunny meadow.

Minutes passed.

His throat worked in a swallow. "Is this happiness?" he asked softly.

"Yes."

"So that's what it feels like."

The simple statement—offered innocently and with a touch of awe—reminded her of Valok.

Sadness struck so swiftly and forcefully that she had to blink back tears.

"Now you're sad." Kova turned to study her, joy no longer reflected in his features. "Or is that pity?"

Swallowing against the sudden lump in her throat, she shook her head. "I'm sorry. You weren't supposed to feel that."

He shrugged and looked away. "I'm accustomed to pity."

"It isn't pity, Kova. It's grief."

His brows drew down in a frown as he glanced at her. "Grief?"

She stared down at their hands, afraid to see his expression. If he showed her an ounce of sympathy, she would break into sobs. That wound was still too raw. "I made a lot of friends on the *Kandovar*." When her voice emerged a little hoarse, she cleared her throat. "One of them was a Yona warrior named Valok. Shortly before the Gathendiens attacked, he hit me with a stun grenade. Afterward—"

"He hit you with a stun grenade?"

She smiled at the shock he emanated. "I asked him to. I wanted to know if it would incapacitate me in battle, but none of the Lasarans would do it."

"So you appealed to a soldier who wouldn't be hampered by worry or guilt."

"Yes. Afterward, I offered to show him what emotion felt like."

"Yona don't feel emotion."

"*He* did," she said, "when I utilized my gift."

Kova grunted. "I'm surprised he let you. Yona lack the curiosity that normally drives one to want to try something new."

"I convinced him to." She loosed a laugh rife with bitter self-condemnation. "I fed him some bullshit about helping him understand what motivates his opponents in battle. But the truth was I just wanted to satisfy my curiosity and see if he would be able to feel something with my aid."

"And did he?"

"Yes." She shrugged miserably. "His response was so similar to yours that I couldn't help but think of him."

A long moment passed.

"It's possible he survived," Kova murmured, perhaps wanting to lessen the guilt that battered her.

She appreciated it. Like his crewmates, Kova had a kind heart. "He didn't. I caught up with him as he prepared to board a fighter craft. I wanted to join the battle and grabbed his arm to hold his attention when he dismissed me." A lump rose in her throat as she blinked back tears. "Though it wasn't my intention, my emotions flooded him." Simone looked away, seeing Valok's face instead of the beautiful glen and playful *rinyas*. "There was an explosion. I was injured. Valok picked me up and hurried to get me into an escape pod. As soon as I was strapped in, he backed out and closed the hatch. Seconds later, another explosion killed him."

Kova said nothing.

Moisture spilled over her lashes. "The last thing he said to me before he died was, 'Thank you for letting me feel.'" Releasing his hand, she brushed away her tears. "If I hadn't used my gift and distracted him, he would've made it onto a fighter craft and off the ship, and there would be some hope that he had survived." Instead, she had watched him die. "And here I am, forcing my emotions on you." She laughed, the sound bereft of mirth. "I suppose I haven't learned my lesson."

Minutes crept by. Two? Three? Ten?

She wasn't sure, too wrapped up in her thoughts.

Kova sighed. "I don't know how to respond to that."

"You don't need to. I'm sorry. I should've made my intention to alter your emotions clear before asking your permission. And I shouldn't have burdened you with the rest."

He shook his head. "When I was fifteen orbits," he said slowly as though the words had to be dragged from him, "some older boys ambushed me, held me down, and cut traditional markings into my skin. One of their knives hit a major artery. Srok'a found me and got me to the nearest healing facility before I could bleed out. But the medics there viewed me with the same disgust as the boys who'd marked me. A disgust *everyone* on my homeworld shared." His lips turned up in a bitter smile. "The medics didn't give me blood to replace what I'd lost, leaving me to live or die without it. They just sealed the wounds and—while Srok'a was forced to wait outside, unaware—treated them with a compound that would worsen the scarring instead of reducing it." Turning his head, he met her gaze. "Does my telling you that burden you?"

"No," she said, fury burning bright inside her. "It makes me want to hunt down every one of those bastards—both the boys who cut you *and* the medics who treated you—and feed them to the Dotharian." She pasted a look of excitement on her face and eyed him eagerly. "Ooh. Do you think Janwar would let me do that after we find my friends?"

He laughed and looked younger despite the scarring and the hard life he'd led. "I suspect he would if Srok'a and I hadn't already killed them all."

"Good for you. High five." She held a hand up, palm-out. When he stared at it blankly, she took his wrist and showed him how to give her a high five. "Earthlings do that to celebrate wins and good news."

"Ah." He gave her another high five. "What emotions did you let the Yona feel?" he asked curiously, his features slipping back into their usual somber mien.

"Happiness. Humor. Caring and concern."

He tossed a few seeds to their furry companions. "Well, I can't speak for Valok, but I'm glad you showed me happiness. Everyone should experience that at least once in their lifetime."

Simone hoped fervently that Kova would experience it again *without* her having to share it with him. It would be far better for him to find it himself.

Taking one of her hands in his, Kova turned her palm up and dropped several seeds into it. "I don't think Valok would've thanked you if he didn't feel the same." He met her gaze. "Thank you."

"Thank *you* for the sunlight." One of the *rinyas* scampered up the rock, seated itself in her lap as if her hand were a banquet table, and helped itself to a snack. "And for the seeds," she added with a grin.

"That one's very competitive," he warned good-naturedly. "He'll keep stuffing seeds in his mouth until he has as many as Toa and still want more."

She laughed when the little *rinya* did just that.

The faint sound of approaching footsteps carried to them.

"That must be Janwar," she said. "Do you think I could talk him into letting me have one of these as a pet?"

"No," Janwar answered as he exited the trees.

As always, seeing him lightened her spirits, though she feigned a pout. "Why? They're so cute."

"Yes, they are. But we already have a hard time keeping T from interrupting our... private moments. Do you really want one of these running around, tripping us up, and distracting us when I'm trying to get you naked?"

Heat crept into her cheeks as she laughed. "No! And don't make me blush, damn it." She dropped her voice to a loud whisper. "You aren't supposed to talk about that sort of thing in front of others."

Kova snorted. "You'll soon realize that there are few secrets with a crew this small."

She grinned. "It was the same back home. Immortal Guardians and their Seconds are enormous gossips."

Both men chuckled.

Janwar stopped beside the boulder. When one of the little *rinyas* scurried up his form and perched on his shoulder, he plucked a seed from Simone's hand and offered it to the little critter.

"You see," she said with a smile. "You're all just great big teddy bears."

"You're going to have to draw me a picture of a teddy bear so I can decide whether or not I should feel insulted," Janwar said with a wry smile.

Simone laughed. "I'd show you a photo of one, but I lost my phone when I was fighting the Gathendiens." She'd taken several photos of Adira playing with a big fluffy bear the last time she'd seen her.

Kova looked at her with interest. "A phone is a communication device?"

"Yes."

"How big is it?"

As soon as the *rinya* finished liberating her of all the seeds in her hand, she pantomimed the size of her cell phone. "It's flat and about this big. Black on one side, silver on the other."

"I think I have it," he said.

She stared at him in surprise. "What?"

"I found something like that on the Gathendien ship when we were cleaning everything up. I thought it might be some new kind of tech but couldn't get it to activate."

Excitement filled her. "I shut it down before the big battle. You have to press and hold two buttons for several seconds to turn it on."

"That explains it. It doesn't appear to be damaged. I was curious to see what it was and brought it back to examine later."

"Then you have it here on the *Tangata*?"

He nodded. "It's in my lab."

Simone let out an ecstatic squeal that made every *rinya* stop and sit up on its haunches, eyes wide. Then she threw her arms around Kova and gave him a hug. "Thank you, thank you, thank you!"

After a moment's surprise, he returned the hug. Amusement and genuine happiness sifted into her where they touched. "All I did was pick up a piece of unfamiliar tech I found on the floor," he mumbled.

Simone released him and slid off the rock. "Yes, but that phone has *everything* on it. Pictures and videos of my home on Earth, my friends, and my immortal family. Music. Books. Apps. Movies." Her eyes widened as she threw her hands out in a *hold everything* gesture. "Ooh! We are *so* having a movie night!"

Both smiled, their amusement over her exuberance clear.

"Can I have it now?" she blurted, eager to get her hands on it. She'd thought she'd lost that last link to home.

Kova rose. "Come by my lab after your jog. I'll give it to you then. If you want me to, I can also transfer a copy of the information on it to a standard datapad."

Simone cocked her head to one side. "How did you know we were going on a jog?" She didn't recall mentioning it.

He winked. "No secrets, remember? You two always jog about this time."

"Right. Do you want to join us?" She glanced at Janwar, who seconded the invitation with an easy nod.

"No. I have to get Toa back to my quarters before he and Baki start squabbling."

She glanced down. Sure enough, Toa and his chief competitor were standing nose-to-nose, issuing sharp little barks at each other as the hair along their backs rose.

She laughed.

Kova tossed the last seeds onto the grass and scooped up Toa. Giving Simone and Janwar a farewell nod, he transferred the little *rinya* to his shoulder and headed into the forest.

Toa glared at Baki and released several more barks before he and Kova disappeared.

Simone turned her attention to Janwar. Grabbing his arm, she started jumping up and down and sang, "I'm going to get my phone back. I'm going to get my phone back. *Woohoo!*"

Laughing, he wrapped her up in a hug. "You are too *vuan* adorable."

She winked. "Right back at you, handsome."

Dipping his head, he pressed a tender kiss to her lips. "I missed you."

Amusement and affection warmed her as she leaned into him. "It's only been an hour."

"I still missed you. I'm used to spending the whole morning together."

"Yeah. I missed you, too," she admitted and loved that he was so open regarding his feelings for her. "I like that you didn't go all Me-Tarzan-You-Jane when I hugged Kova."

"I have no idea what that means."

Chuckling, she slid her arms around his waist. "You didn't turn caveman and get angry."

His brow furrowed. "Why would I get angry? I'm glad you and Kova are friends. He's part of my family. And I trust you both."

Simone narrowed her eyes as she studied him.

"What?"

"I'm trying to figure out what I'm missing."

"What do you mean?"

"You're too perfect."

He pretty much guffawed over that, laughing so hard she had to step back and give him room. "The entire Aldebarian Alliance—and the rest of the galaxy—would vociferously object to that description and ask if you were high on *fosi*."

Simone grinned. "You see? I even like your laugh and sense of humor. Seriously, I've yet to find anything about you that I don't like, Janwar."

Still smiling, he looped an arm around her shoulders and began strolling toward the lake. "Give it time. I'm sure you'll find plenty not to like."

She made a scoffing sound. "Like what? Name one thing. I dare you."

He thought about it for a moment, then gave her a sly smile, his eyes dancing with mirth. "You won't like being in an enclosed space with me after I eat *mamitwa*."

She laughed.

When they reached the lake, he halted and turned to face her, keeping her close.

Her heart raced at the expression on his face.

"I hope you *won't* find anything you don't like," he murmured as he brushed some loose strands of hair that had escaped her ponytail back from her face. "But I fear overlooking the darkness of my past would prove a monumental task."

Simone took the comment seriously, her gift allowing her to feel both the burgeoning love he felt for her that made her heart beat faster and the worry that it would somehow all be taken away. "My past is dark, too," she offered softly.

"It isn't the same."

"Isn't it?" she prodded gently. "I've slain thousands of men, Janwar. It's all I did, night after night, for nearly three-quarters of a millennium. Hunt down men infected with a bioengineered virus that ate away at their healthy brains, depriving them of impulse control and all knowledge of right and wrong. Some of those men embraced the madness, thrilled by the power their heightened speed and strength gave them over ordinary humans and relishing the violence they inflicted, the fear they bred. But others fought the madness. They were good men until they turned vampire. They didn't ask to be infected. They clung to control by their fingertips. And I killed them anyway."

"No," he replied. "You spared them. You kept them from turning into the monsters they knew they would become. Your motive was altruistic. Don't make the mistake of believing my motives have always been the same."

Gripping the front of his shirt with both hands, she gave him a little shake. "You did what you had to do to survive and keep Krigara fed and clothed and safe from Chancellor Astennuh. You avenged your parents' murders. And I know you're fine with the rest of the galaxy thinking you're a self-serving, narcissistic bastard who's only in it for the money, but I see you for who you are." She held his gaze. "I *see* you, Janwar. You found Taelon's missing sister when no one else could and after everyone else had given up."

"For a reward. I found her for a reward."

She arched a brow. "Did you even ask Taelon what the reward would be before you began searching for her?"

He hesitated. "No."

"Ha!" she crowed triumphantly and poked him in the chest, wringing a smile from him. "And when you found Taelon, Lisa, Abby, and their Yona guard after the *Kandovar* was destroyed, did you offer to take them to Lasara for a price? Or did you just bring them on board and do it?"

"Taelon gave us a reward when we reached Lasara."

"That's not what I asked. Did you offer to rescue them and take them home for a price, or did you just bring them on board?"

He sighed. "Brought them on board."

"Then you came out here to look for more of us." Leaning up, she kissed his bearded chin. "You see? I was right. You're a teddy bear." Simone grinned up at him as they reached the lake. "A teddy bear who will eat my dust." She took off running up the path they'd intended to jog along and called over her shoulder, "Catch me if you can!"

Laughing behind her, Janwar gave chase.

L ATER THAT AFTERNOON, JANWAR lounged in the commander's chair on the bridge and stared at the image Simone's cell-phone screen displayed. "A teddy bear is a toy?" In the picture, a beautiful red-haired child of no more than two or three orbits played with a fluffy brown bear twice her size.

Simone grinned from the chair she'd positioned beside his. "Yes. Is there any way we can view this on the big screen?"

"T," Janwar ordered, "project Simone's images onto the view screen."

Simone's eyes widened as a large, clear screen descended from the bridge's ceiling. Seconds later it lit up with the image of the child, blocking the view of the stars beyond the windshield.

The rest of the crew glanced at the screen.

"Who's the little girl?" Krigara asked.

"She reminds me of Abby," Soval murmured.

"That's Adira," Simone said with a smile. "She's Ami's daughter."

"Princess Amiriska's?" Janwar asked. He could see the resemblance. She looked like a tiny version of Taelon's sister.

"Yes. I think the Lasarans want to keep that quiet for a while. But I'm not sure how they'll manage it. Everyone on the *Kandovar* knew about it, so I'm sure word will spread."

"Every Lasaran and Yona who serves on a warship commanded by a member of the royal family is completely loyal," Janwar murmured. "If their sovereigns ask them not to mention that there are *two* new royal heirs rather than one, no one will disclose it."

"Why would revealing that Ami has a daughter even be a problem?" she asked, her brow furrowing. "Taelon and Lisa have a daughter. That's certainly no secret."

He shrugged. "The king and queen may worry about word of a royal heir residing on Earth spreading."

"Why?" She swiped her finger across her cell phone, causing the image on the big screen to cycle through more photos of the child.

He smiled. The next photo included Princess Amiriska, and she looked well. Janwar was pleased to have played a role in uncovering her location and dispelling her family's grief. "Because Earth is so far behind us technologically. It would be too easy for someone to sweep in, take the child, and hold her hostage in exchange for untraceable credits." Once the words left his lips, he winced inwardly, afraid she might feel insulted.

Instead, she smiled. "I can see how you'd think that—or how the king and queen might—but I guarantee you, that won't happen."

He arched a brow. The notion seemed to amuse her. "How can you be so sure?" Plenty of unsavory characters in the galaxy considered the kidnapping and ransoming of important personages a lucrative business. And they would have no qualms about kidnapping children.

Her smile broadened into a grin. "Because *these* are her bodyguards."

The next picture displayed a room similar to the lounge here on the *Tangata* but seemed to be in more of a home or family environment. Boasting high ceilings and a wood floor, it was filled with many plush sofas and chairs. End tables and what Simone called coffee tables were sprinkled throughout. What appeared to be a large viewscreen hung on one wall, but none of the individuals present paid attention to it.

Leaning forward, Janwar stared. At least twenty-five or thirty Earthlings occupied the sofas and chairs. The males were tall and similar in size and bulk to Janwar. The females were Simone's size or smaller, appearing petite and delicate beside their male counterparts. Almost everyone present had dark hair and was dressed in black, their garb similar to that which Simone preferred: slim-fitting black shirts, coupled with pants that boasted many loops and pockets, and boots.

Even Amiriska wore them.

He stared at the arms he'd never seen the Lasaran princess bare before. She looked positively tiny beside the men, yet utterly fierce.

Daggers, swords, and other weaponry littered every table, as if those present had just disarmed after returning from a mission.

Or a hunt.

All eyes fixed upon the center of the room, where Ami's daughter Adira—her orange hair standing out like a beacon against so much black—grinned as she played with a dark-haired boy about the same age.

Janwar studied the gathering. Those warriors looked as if they would rip apart anyone who threatened the little ones in their midst. "Who are they?" he asked, curious to know more of Simone's home and what her life had been like before they'd met.

"My brethren," she answered, a catch in her voice.

When he glanced at her, his chest tightened.

Tears welled in her eyes as she pointed at the screen. "That one there, the one holding a wooden block out to Adira, is Marcus, Ami's lifemate. Those two there, the imposing ones seated close to Ami, are Seth and David."

Recognizing the names, he returned his attention to the screen. The man she identified as Seth was noticeably taller than the others, with tanned skin and black hair that fell to his shoulders. Though his posture was relaxed as he reclined on a sofa, he nevertheless emanated power and an air of command. The one she identified as David was just as big, with skin as dark as deep space and long thick locks that were drawn back at the nape and flowed over his shoulder to pool on the cushion beside him. He, too, emanated power and authority.

These were the men Simone considered father figures.

"No one," she said, "can get past them. I don't care what technology they use. Seth and David are so powerful that the rest of us look like toddlers by comparison. And everyone you see in this picture would die before they let someone kidnap Adira. Or Ami."

She cycled through similar images. Every warrior seemed to adore the children. "Teddy bears," she whispered as she stopped at another picture.

In this one, Simone stood in the center, smiling, with ten or twelve men clustered around her. Seth and David stood at her back, towering over her.

Janwar smiled. *All* of the men towered over her and looked like they were twice or thrice her weight with muscle. They also wore the black soldier garb she favored and sported multiple weapons.

A sniffle yanked his attention back to Simone.

Tears spilled down her cheeks as she flipped through more images, a tremulous smile on her lips. "Damn, I miss them."

Wrapping an arm around her shoulders, he drew her closer and pressed a kiss to her hair. "You'll see them again."

"Only on video comms," she replied sadly.

Janwar shook his head. "You're forgetting how fast the *Tangata* is. If you want to see your brethren again after we've rescued your friends, I'll take you to Earth."

Her face lit with hope as her glowing amber gaze shot to his. "Really?"

"As often as you wish." At least he would if she remained on the *Tangata* and didn't continue to Lasara to guard her friends as she'd initially intended. If that happened, he might never see her again.

He didn't even want to *think* about that possibility.

Reaching up, she cupped his jaw in her free hand and pressed a tender kiss to his lips. "Thank you."

His pulse sped up. Did that mean she intended to stay with him?

"The Gathendien ship just appeared on long-range radar," Elchan announced suddenly.

Janwar stiffened. "Heading *toward* the base or away from it?"

"Toward it."

"How far from the moon is it?"

Elchan tapped his console. "Looks like they're four days out at their current speed."

Simone rested a hand on Janwar's arm. "How far is that for us?"

"We'll reach the ship tomorrow and the base a day after."

She tucked her phone away. "Then I guess it's time we choose a plan."

CHAPTER FOURTEEN

T WO HOURS LATER, JANWAR stood in Bay 3, feet planted a shoulders' width apart, arms crossed over his chest. Simone lingered beside him, shifting restlessly as they watched preparations unfold.

After an intense discussion that had twice erupted into heated arguments, they had settled on a plan. Only two of the *Tangata*'s crew were content with it. T-4 bustled back and forth with the bubbling excitement of a child who'd just been told his parents were taking him to the renowned Wadjerwa Animal Sanctuary. Kova was satisfied, too, and studiously ignored his brother's glower as he toted gear to a C-23 with an open hatch.

Simone bit her lip and looked pensive. The rest of them...

Well, they'd been here before. Many times.

He stifled a sigh. Kova always volunteered for the most dangerous operations. Janwar had never been able to determine if the younger Rakessian had a death wish or simply did it because he believed he had less to lose if *bura* went sideways.

As always, Srok'a was furious.

Janwar would feel the same way if Krigara perpetually volunteered for the roughest missions. A pang of guilt struck as he recalled those first few years after he and his cousin had fled their homeworld. Janwar had put his life on the line dozens of times in his efforts to keep them both fed and sheltered. He'd even fought a few times in the same arena Simone had battled the Dotharian in on Promeii 7.

Pulcra's father had owned it then. And there had been no Dotharian, only vicious, bloody bouts between slaves and anyone desperate enough to fight them for credits. Pulcra didn't remember it. He was too young at the time. And Janwar had been a scrawny kid with short hair, no beard, and barely enough skill to stay alive. Nothing would've made him stand out to the crowds that called for his defeat and cheered their favorite fighters.

Somehow, he had managed to make it through each match. But he probably would've died either from blood loss or infection settling into his wounds if one of the local medics—a good male swimming in a sea of bad—hadn't hunted him down after each match and tended his injuries.

To this day, Janwar still delivered medical supplies he *liberated* from enemies—and others he purchased—to that same medic on Promeii 7. T had made another delivery in android form while Janwar, Simone, and Soval had met Nandara at the bar.

Janwar hated that Krigara had most likely suffered the same anxiety and anger Srok'a always did when Kova went on missions like this. But at least Krigara had known Janwar did it *not* out of self-loathing or because he felt he held little worth but because they would've starved to death if he hadn't.

Kova strode past with more gear.

In a few minutes, he and T-4 would depart in a C-23 and sneak over to the Gathendien ship. Once they attached the stealth craft to the hull, they would cut their way in. T had selected a point of entry that would put them close to a data access room he could use to infiltrate the system—something Simone called hacking—and scramble their comms so any messages the ship tried to send wouldn't reach their destinations. Then the two would use a combination of the ship's specs and life-form sensors to navigate the maze of corridors and search for captives, beginning with the labs and ending with the cryo units.

Janwar kept his expression neutral, revealing no hint of the worry that soured his stomach. Usually, three of them would carry out an operation like this, with the rest on standby and T's army of androids ready to jump in if necessary. There had even been times when five of them had infiltrated a ship with only one left behind on the *Tangata* to monitor their progress and send in androids if an emergency arose.

But this time, Kova would be on his own with only T-4 to aid him because the *Tangata* would carry the rest of them to the moon base.

Kova emerged from the C-23 and joined them. "We're ready."

Janwar nodded. "To victory."

"To victory," Kova repeated.

Simone stepped forward, her pretty face sober. "I've lost too many friends, Kova. I can't lose any more."

His friend nodded. "Understood. I'll protect any Earthlings I find with my life."

Janwar could practically hear Srok'a grinding his teeth.

"I wasn't talking about Earthlings," she said softly, holding his gaze. "I was talking about *you*."

Kova went very still as he stared at her, clearly caught off guard.

"I don't know why you might need to be told this, but in case you do... You are *not* expendable. You're my friend. And I need you." She glanced at the others. "We all do. So please be careful and return safely."

Swallowing hard, Kova nodded. "I will."

Closing the remaining distance between them, she hugged him.

For a moment, the gruff warrior didn't move. Then he wrapped his arms around her and tentatively returned the embrace.

Releasing him, Simone turned away.

"Simone?" Kova said.

Halting, she glanced over her shoulder.

"I don't have many friends."

Tilting her head to one side, she turned to face him.

His gaze piercing, the Rakessian said, "I don't want to lose the few I do. You be careful, too."

"I will." Her lips turned up in a wicked grin. "But I intend to kick a *lot* of ass while I do."

He chuckled. "I look forward to hearing about it when I see you again."

As the warrior headed for the C-23, Simone moved to stand at Janwar's side.

Giving in to the urge, he wrapped an arm around her and—despite his concern—sighed with contentment when she leaned into him.

Kova boarded the stealth craft without another word.

"Thank you," Srok'a murmured. A muscle worked in his jaw as the clamps holding his brother's craft in place released it with a clunk.

"Thank *you*." Simone's gaze touched upon each one of them. "Thank all of you. You don't have to do this... risk your lives on what amounts to little more than a hunch that these guys *might* be holding one or more of my friends captive."

Soval snorted. "If your friends are anything like you, they'll probably end up rescuing *us*."

She smiled.

The stealth craft rose and rotated toward the exit. Its surface shimmered for a moment before the ship seemed to disappear.

"Wow," Simone breathed. "That's one of those cool things you have to see with your own eyes to believe. I knew the craft would be shielded from radar but forgot it would be hidden visually."

Janwar smiled at the awe in her tone. "All of our craft are imbued with the most sophisticated cloaking technology on the market."

Krigara snorted. "And some that *isn't* on the market. It cost us a fortune."

"And was worth every credit," Janwar professed. "Most cloaking arrays only hide ships from radar. But as you just saw with the C-23—"

"And with the *Tangata* the day we met?" she asked, her brown eyes sparkling with amusement.

He laughed, recalling her reaction to the *Tangata* miraculously appearing beside her. "Yes. Our cloaking arrays also allow our craft to blend seamlessly into our surroundings from every viewpoint, concealing us from anyone who might search for us the old-fashioned way."

"With their peepers?" she asked.

He nodded, entertained as ever by Earth terms.

Now that the craft had left their sight, Srok'a turned to stalk away.

Janwar shot a hand out and caught his arm. "Wait."

When Srok'a glared at him, he didn't take it personally. As commander, Janwar could've forbidden Kova from embarking upon this mission and spared his older brother the fear currently gnawing at his gut. But this was the best plan they'd been able to concoct under the circumstances. They all knew the horrors Ava, one of the Earthlings rescued by the Segonians, had been subjected to aboard a Gathendien ship and didn't want to bypass the one flanking them and risk leaving other females to suffer the same fate. So every one of them had agreed to this.

Unfortunately, that didn't diminish the fury that always consumed Srok'a when his brother insisted on being the one who risked everything.

Janwar met his glare evenly. "Wait," he repeated: a command, not a request.

His friend drew a long breath in and let it out slowly before nodding.

Giving his shoulder a pat, Janwar released him.

The door behind them that led to the rest of the ship rose, and T-7 entered.

Was it Janwar's imagination, or was there also an extra bounce in T-7's steps today?

He studied the android.

T's red eyes even seemed to glow brighter.

Simone and the others watched the android advance toward them.

"Ready?" Janwar asked.

"Yes, commander." Without breaking stride, T-7 crossed to a small but heavily armed fighter craft.

No one made a sound when the hatch opened at his approach. As soon as the ramp lowered, T-7 tromped up it and disappeared inside. A minute later, the ramp closed. The clamps holding the fighter in place clunked as they released it. Then the engine started with barely a hum. T-7 activated the cloaking array as the vessel flew out of the hangar.

When everyone cast Janwar puzzled looks, he shrugged. "A little extra backup for Kova. I'd feel better about it if I'd had more time to gauge T's competency as a fighter pilot—"

"I am an exceptional fighter pilot," T announced over the ship-wide speakers.

"—but something is better than nothing," Janwar finished.

"Does Kova know?" Simone asked.

"No." Janwar usually only brought T into things if an operation figuratively—or literally—blew up in their faces and they ended up backed into a corner, furiously fighting for their lives. He nodded after the craft. "Keep looking."

As one, they returned their attention to the view beyond the bay's massive entrance. Had they not paid attention, they would've missed the faint flickering of the stars beyond.

"What was that?" Simone asked, her brow puckering. "It looked like..." She shook her head. "I don't know. I thought I saw the stars move a tiny bit."

"The stars didn't move," he told her. "Ten cloaked drones just flew past."

Her face lit with a combination of relief and excitement. "You sent drones, too?"

He nodded and addressed them all. "T is operating them and—"

"I am an extraordinary drone operator," T interrupted smugly.

Janwar ignored him. "If Kova gets into trouble, the drones will attack the ship and hopefully create enough of a diversion for him to get his ass—and that of anyone he finds—out of there safely."

The big bay door began to close, blocking out the stars.

Some of the tension melted from Srok'a's form as he thrust out a hand. "Thank you."

Janwar clasped his forearm and drew him in for a rough hug. "No thanks necessary, brother. We look out for our own." Smiling, he stepped back. "And if we can't handle whatever we find at the Gathendien facility with Simone the Dotharian Conqueror, ten androids, and the rest of the drones at our backs, then I doubt the backup I sent with Kova would've made a difference."

"Ooh, I like that," Simone said with a grin. "Not the whole *we'd die even if we* did *have the missing backup* thing, but the *Simone the Dotharian Conqueror*." She said the latter in a dramatic, artificially deep voice, then returned to her own. "I'm going to have to see if the clothing replicator can make me a T-shirt with that printed on it."

The others laughed as they headed for the door.

Janwar did, too. *Vuan*, he loved her.

His eyes widened. Wait. He loved her?

"What's wrong?" Simone asked.

He didn't realize until then that he'd stopped walking.

The others filed out and left them alone, their minds already on tomorrow's mission.

Janwar considered it.

He had never been in love before. He hadn't had the time, really, or the opportunity. The life he'd led wasn't exactly conducive to courting women and forming long-term relationships. He didn't even have a favorite pleasure worker he liked to visit again and again when they docked at ports and stations.

The last time he'd had anything close to a relationship was back when his parents were still alive and he couldn't grow much of a beard. He'd been physically attracted to the Akseli female more than anything else. Neska had been breathtakingly beautiful, and he'd been young enough to like that she'd chosen him over all the other boys. She'd been his first and only lover before life had started kicking his ass. And she'd turned her back on him as soon as the smear campaign designed to cover up the government's role in his parents' murders had begun, even though she knew it was all lies.

"Janwar?" Simone asked softly. Her pretty features full of concern, she rested a hand on his chest and peered up at him.

He covered her hand with his, holding it close to his racing heart.

For years, he'd thought what he felt for Neska was typical of most relationships. Maybe even typical of lifemates. But the time he'd spent with Taelon and Lisa, watching their interactions, had made him question that and remember the close bond his parents had shared.

He stared down at the fascinating Earth woman who had come into his life.

How wrong he had been. There was so much more to what he felt for Simone than mere lust and physical attraction. She was his friend. As much his friend as Krigara, and his cousin knew him better than anyone.

Yet Janwar craved her company more. Simone made him laugh, challenged him, and was so *vuan* fun to be with, even during the

244

quiet moments. The pensive moments when she worried about survivors of the *Kandovar*. The moments of sadness she sometimes slipped into when she thought of the friends and the family she'd left behind on Earth. The everyday moments when the two of them shared a meal, jogged and sparred together. Or when she combed his hair after a shower and rebraided it, carefully adding the beads in the exact pattern he always did.

Every moment with her felt different.

She brought him happiness, comfort, and contentment.

She brought him peace.

And he hadn't felt that in many years.

Janwar could never seem to get enough time with her. And her touch...

He craved that, too, and found more pleasure in her arms than he'd ever believed possible. He'd had no idea how great a difference having a close emotional bond with a female would make, how much that would magnify the ecstasy they found in each other's arms, and was still dazed by the discovery.

He even loved the tranquil moments afterward. The cuddling, as she called it. He'd never desired that before, always eager to leave once his need had been sated. But with Simone...

With Simone, he wanted it all. Everything he'd thought he could never have.

Her eyes began to glow as the silence stretched.

"Do you feel that?" Janwar asked, his voice barely above a whisper. She was an empath, after all. And he didn't attempt to hide his feelings from her.

"Yes," she whispered back, her luminous gaze mesmerizing.

"I'm falling in love with you." His heart still pounded over the admission as he awaited her response.

Her lips parted. Her pupils dilated as the amber glow of her irises brightened. The hand on his chest fisted around the fabric of his shirt. "I've already fallen in love with you," she confessed.

Janwar caught his breath.

It felt almost as if those softly spoken words shattered him into a thousand pieces, then swiftly reassembled him, putting him back together in a way that made him stronger than he had been before. That made him *more* than he'd been before. That—for the first time since his parents' murders—made him feel whole. And changed him forever.

Bending, he wrapped his arms around her waist and lifted her so high that he had to tilt his head back to look up at her. Simone loved him. Janwar's pulse pounded in his ears as he crushed her against him and rested the side of his face against her chest above her lovely breasts, his ear close enough to her heart to detect its rapid beat.

Simone slid her arms around him and tunneled her fingers through his hair. Her feet dangling somewhere in the vicinity of his knees, she rested her cheek atop his head and held him close.

"Are you afraid?" he asked softly.

A moment passed before she responded. "I'm afraid you or the others will be wounded tomorrow," she said quietly. "I'm afraid we won't find any of my friends on that base and that it will all be for naught. I'm afraid some of my friends may never be located—that they're either dead or lost to us in a place we'll never discover. I'm afraid the Lasarans will be pissed when I tell them I no longer want to live on Lasara. But loving *you*? The way you make me feel?" Her cheek moved against his braids as she shook her head. "I don't fear that at all."

He squeezed her tighter.

"Are *you* afraid?" she asked.

He snorted. "I'm scared shitless."

She laughed. "Another Earth phrase I see you've learned."

Tilting his head back, he smiled up at her. "I've never felt like this before, Simone. And I'm afraid one day it will end, that you'll leave for Lasara, and I'll never see you again. But fear has never stopped me from pursuing what I want. And I want you. I want every minute I can have with you, even if we're just sitting next to each other on the bridge, holding hands."

Her eyes flashed brighter. Then she fisted his hair, dipped her chin, and took his lips a scorching kiss. Parting her lips, she invited him inside.

Janwar moaned, slipping his tongue within to stroke hers as fire burned through him, hardening his cock. Shifting his hold on her, he cupped her tempting ass with one hand. When she locked her legs around his waist, he groaned and tore his mouth from hers. "Really?" he panted. "*That's* what turns you on? Holding hands on the bridge?"

She laughed. "Hell yes, it does. How fast can we get to your quarters?"

"Fast," he declared and took off running.

SIMONE COULDN'T BELIEVE IT, but she broke into giggles as Janwar raced through the corridors, trying to kiss her, feel her up, and watch where he was going, all at the same time, with hilarious results. He looked boyishly happy and carefree as he laughed with her.

And he loved her.

Janwar *loved* her.

At last, they burst into his quarters.

"Privacy mode, T," he called as the door shut behind them.

Sheesh. She'd forgotten about that.

Spinning around, he pressed her up against the door. Simone gasped, eyes rolling back as he leaned into her and ground his hard cock against her clit. One of his big hands yanked her shirt out of her pants, found warm skin, and slid up to cup her breast. His warm lips found her neck as his thumb tweaked her nipple through her bra.

She moaned. "Too many clothes. We're wearing too many clothes."

He thrust against her. "We'll have to work around them. I don't think I can let you go long enough to—"

With preternatural speed, Simone pushed him back, disentangled herself, and tore off their clothes.

A second or two later, Janwar stood before her, his big body bare of everything except his boots, erection jutting toward her. His eyes widened as his jaw dropped.

Simone was naked, too, except for her boots.

He looked so stunned that she couldn't help but laugh. "You were saying something about working around our clothes?"

Grinning, he shook his head. "Just for that, I'm keeping my boots on." Then he closed the distance between them and drew her into his arms. "*Drek*, I love you."

Just like that, the urgency returned. Lips melded. Hands explored with passionate caresses.

"Say it again," she uttered between fiery kisses.

"I love you." Lifting her effortlessly, he lay her atop the covers on his big bed. Then he loomed over her, settling his big, muscled body between her parted thighs as he kissed her neck just beneath her ear. "I love you."

A shudder of pleasure shook her.

He palmed her breast, kneading it and tweaking the sensitive peak with no more cloth impeding him.

Writhing beneath him, Simone buried her hands in his hair and clutched his braids.

"I love you," he murmured again, trailing kisses over her collarbone and down to the other breast.

Heat engulfed her, searing her veins as he teased the taut peak with his lips, teeth, and tongue, laving and sucking. "Janwar," she moaned.

When he started to move lower, she slid her arms between them and pushed him over onto his back. A heartbeat later, she straddled him. Her eyes met his and clung as she curled one hand around his long, hard cock. So much heat simmered in his gaze as he fastened his strong hands on her hips.

Guiding him to her entrance, she slowly lowered herself upon him, inner muscles stretching to accommodate him. "I needed you inside me," she murmured. "And you were taking too long."

His lips curled in a wicked smile. "Simone the Conquerer," he murmured, his voice rough with desire as she took every inch of him.

Bracing her hands on his muscled chest, she gave the crisp hair there a tug. His cock jerked. She rotated her hips, eliciting more moans from them both. "Now, I'm going to conquer you."

He slid his hands up to cup her breasts, squeezing, teasing, and ratcheting up her need as she began to ride him. "You already have."

Simone lacked the breath to speak further, urgency driving her to take him harder and faster. He felt so good inside her, so hard, stretching her, stroking her. And the way he touched her, slid a hand down to brush her clit even as he tweaked her nipple...

Their movements grew rougher, more frantic, his grip almost bruising as the pressure built and built until she threw her head back and cried out in ecstasy. Janwar groaned her name as her inner muscles clenched and unclenched around him, following her into orgasm.

Collapsing onto his chest, Simone fought to catch her breath. A fine sheen of perspiration bathed their skin as their hearts pounded in their chests. Little post-orgasmic ripples of pleasure continued to rock her.

When Janwar wrapped his arms around her and hugged her close, she smiled. Warmth suffused her. He was a snuggler. Yet another thing she loved about him.

"This is just the beginning," he whispered, pressing a kiss to the top of her head.

Nodding, she knew he wasn't just referring to the night's love-making. "The beginning."

Peace settled upon them as they lay there, neither interested in moving for many long minutes.

Then a chuckle rumbled in the muscled chest beneath her ear. "Next time, let's remove our boots first. Those soles are rougher than I expected."

She laughed.

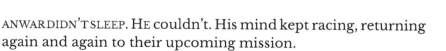

JANWAR DIDN'T SLEEP. He couldn't. His mind kept racing, returning again and again to their upcoming mission.

Usually, he would embrace a challenge like this and even look forward to the heart-pumping adrenaline surge the danger would spawn since little else thrilled him.

He glanced down at the lovely female curled up against his side.

Or little else had thrilled him before Simone had fought her way into his life.

It was an odd feeling, knowing he had something to lose now. Once Krigara had grown and matured enough to fend for himself, Janwar's need to survive for the sake of others had faded. The thirst for revenge—to finally unseat the murderous, greedy bastard who had ordered his parents' deaths—had taken its place and driven him then. But he'd grown weary over the years. Jaded. Less and less satisfied with the blows he managed to strike against Chancellor Astennuh.

Less and less satisfied with... *everything*, wanting more.

Simone sighed in her sleep and snuggled closer, draping a thigh across his.

He couldn't remember the last time an impending battle had filled him with so much anxiety that it deprived him of sleep. Yet there he was, envisioning the future he and Simone could have together and fretting over every little thing that could go wrong tomorrow and *drek* that all up.

When another hour brought no slumber, he carefully eased out of bed.

Simone slept so hard she barely moved.

He smiled. Perhaps he had finally tired her out.

Making as little noise as possible, he donned a shirt and a pair of loose workout pants, then left his quarters.

No, *their* quarters. Janwar didn't want to spend another night away from her.

The ship was quiet, the *Tangata*'s engine noiseless, as he padded barefoot through the corridors. Night sounds from the park drifted through the hallways courtesy of the hidden speakers in the ceiling. The whole crew had unanimously voted in favor of that to eradicate the loneliness utter silence could worsen.

Entering his office, he closed the door behind him. "T, contact the *Ranasura*. I wish to speak with Eliana and Commander Dagon. Full encryption."

"Yes, commander."

Dropping into the seat behind his desk, he ran a hand over the braids atop his head. They remained tight and orderly. But the loose hair that mingled with the braids in the back was tangled. His lips twitched as he combed his fingers through it to tidy it while he waited.

Simone liked to muss it when they *made love*.

A glass panel rose from the desk's surface and hovered above it like a console screen.

Janwar relaxed back in his chair.

Several minutes passed.

"T?" he prodded.

T sounded a bit irritated when he said, "I am trying. But Commander Dagon and Eliana have retired for the night, and none of the crewmembers wish to disturb them."

He sighed. "Then give them a push."

"Yes, commander."

Shortly thereafter, the screen lit up, showing an office similar to his. A large figure blocked the view. Then Commander Dagon dropped into the only visible chair. His short hair looked wind-blown, sticking up in multiple directions. And his countenance broadcast aggravation.

"What?" he growled as his eyes locked on Janwar.

"Where's Eliana?" he asked, unperturbed. "I requested both of you."

"Requested my ass. Your comm officer said this was urgent and couldn't wait until morning."

"It is, and it can't. Where's Eliana?"

"I'm here," a female said. Eliana stepped into view, wearing something Simone called a form-fitting tank top and loose pants. Her long, dark hair fell around her shoulders in waves as tousled as Dagon's. Her cheeks bore a bright flush, and her lips were plump from kissing.

Yeah. He had definitely interrupted something.

251

"Hi, Janwar." She sank onto Dagon's lap, brow furrowed with concern. "What's going on? Is Simone okay?"

"She's well," he assured her. "I've contacted you because I need a favor. From both of you."

Dagon's eyebrows shot up. "You do?"

The last favor Janwar had asked had been of Hanon, the cargo ship captain who had hired him when he was still a starving youth on Promeii 7. Janwar had asked the elder Akseli to take on Krigara, too—had begged him—so he and his cousin wouldn't be separated. And the gruff captain had agreed.

None of them had ever regretted it. But after seeing firsthand how the few favors Hanon had asked of others had ended up biting him in the ass when they were called in, Janwar had asked no favors since.

Eliana looped an arm around Dagon's shoulders. "Okay. What can we do?"

Janwar fought the urge to shake his head. Eliana didn't even ask what the favor was before she agreed to help him. "We've located another Gathendien ship. This one is heading toward a classified research facility on a moon not far from Promeii 7." He swiftly filled them in on both the situation and their plans.

"It's risky," Dagon murmured. "What will you do if the research facility ends up being one of their primary bases? They've kept those locations secret since they were driven from Alliance-occupied space."

He shrugged. "We'll do whatever we can to get in, look for captives, and get the *srul* out intact."

"What are the coordinates of the facility?"

Janwar dictated them.

Leaning forward with Eliana still perched on his lap, Dagon tapped on a console Janwar couldn't see. His eyes moved as he studied the screen. "Traveling at top speed, we can be there in three weeks. If you hold off until then, we can coordinate a mission and execute it together. I have a full—"

Janwar shook his head. "We're going in tomorrow."

Dagon's expression darkened. "If you wait until we get there, you'll have a better chance of succeeding."

"If we wait until you get here, the Gathendiens will have three more weeks to torture whomever they have in their cells. Three more weeks to do to them what they did to Ava. And three more weeks to find a virus that may finally succeed in eradicating *all* Earthlings and share it with their emperor."

Eliana nibbled her lower lip. "Is there any way to confirm they're holding Earthlings in their facility *before* you attempt to breach it?"

"No. Unfortunately, long-distance life-form scans can only tell us how many life forms are inside, not which ones are Gathendien and which ones aren't. Once we're near the base, we should be able to see if anyone inside lacks a tail, but the life-form scan won't tell us what race they are."

She looked at Dagon. "I wouldn't want to wait either, Dagon."

"You wouldn't have to because you'd have an army of ground troops and fighter craft at your back."

Smiling, she wrapped an arm around his neck. "You've seen me in action, honey. I'm my own army. And so is Simone."

"Yes, she is," Janwar seconded. "She took out an entire shipload of Gathendiens by herself, armed only with swords and daggers."

But Dagon shook his head, his eyes on his lifemate. "If Janwar expected this mission to go smoothly, he wouldn't have contacted us."

"I *hope* it will go smoothly," Janwar said. "But if it doesn't..."

Dagon arched a brow. "The favor?"

"Yes."

"Name it."

"You won't make it in time to join the mission, but I'd feel better if you would still head this way as swiftly as possible in case *bura* goes sideways and we end up needing an extraction."

"We'll set course as soon as we end communication," he said.

Janwar shot his office door a quick look to ensure it was closed. Should Simone come looking for him, he didn't want her to hear the rest. "If I don't make it out," he told Dagon, "I want Krigara to take command of the *Tangata*. The crew knows this without my having to tell them and won't balk at it. If my cousin and I both fall, the crew can decide for themselves who will lead. I want your word that you won't confiscate the ship and turn them in for the bounty."

"You have it," Dagon replied without hesitation.

Janwar blinked, surprised by the quick consent.

The commander shrugged. "I have no allegiance to Aksel or the *grunark* who rules it. There's a reason Segonia isn't allied with him."

Relieved, Janwar shifted his gaze to Eliana. "Simone said she trusts you with her life, so I ask that you ensure your lifemate will keep his vow."

When Dagon stiffened, Janwar waved a hand in a *what can I say?* gesture. "I just met you, commander. I don't know you as well as I do Prince Taelon." If Taelon commanded a ship as close to him as the *Ranasura*, Janwar would've contacted him instead.

"I'll do as you wish, Janwar," Eliana said earnestly, "but you can trust Dagon."

He smiled. "I trust you more. Which is why I've another favor to ask."

"Okay."

"Of all of us, Simone is the least likely to die," he stated baldly, then huffed a laugh. "As she's so fond of saying, she's incredibly hard to kill."

"As am I," Eliana quipped with a smile that looked a little forced under the circumstances.

He mustered up a smile of his own. This was new to him. He'd never felt the need to make requests like this before or take such a leap of faith and rely upon virtual strangers. Not since the fateful day he'd met Hanon. "If the rest of us should fall and only Simone still lives when you get here…"

Eliana's face sobered.

"I want her to have my ship, everything on it, and my entire fortune."

Both stared at him, stunned.

"T—the *Tangata*'s AI—can tell you where all my credits are hidden. There's also a Gathendien ship—the one that attacked and destroyed the *Kandovar*—that we've locked down, cloaked, and tagged. T can help you find it. That's Simone's, too. I don't want *any* of it to be confiscated by the Akseli *grunark* who killed my family and put a price on my head. I want all of it to go to her. And I don't want Aldebarian Alliance soldiers pouring over every bit of tech included and duplicating it before you hand it over to her. Can you take care of that for me?"

Eyes wide, Eliana visually consulted Dagon.

He nodded.

"Yes," she said finally. "I'll do it."

"As tempting as that tech will be, we'll honor your wishes," Dagon seconded.

"Thank you. As soon as we enter the facility, we intend to hack their system and download every snippet of information we can from their database. We hope that will include the identity tags and locations of any ships that may have Earthlings aboard and whatever progress the Gathendiens have made in their viral research. I've instructed T to send you a copy upon either the mission's completion or its untimely end as a show of good faith. Adaos will undoubtedly understand the medical data contained therein far better than I would."

Dagon nodded. "I hope you'll succeed in your mission so we can sit down and go over it together."

Imagine that, he thought. *A Lasaran prince* and *a Segonian commander—both straight-laced, upstanding citizens of the Aldebarian Alliance who balk at breaking the rules—befriending* me.

Ten solar orbits ago, Janwar would've laughed his ass off if someone had suggested that would happen.

"If the mission ends badly," he said, his words emerging more slowly as he met Eliana's brown-eyed gaze, "do whatever you can to help Simone." This request he wished he could make without Dagon's presence. "And I'm not just talking about helping her escape the base if she needs a rescue. I'm asking you to help her afterward when she..."

When she grieved for them.

When she grieved for *him*.

Their relationship was new enough for a little voice inside to mock him for thinking she might cry over him. But he *knew* Simone. She continued to grieve for a Yona soldier she'd barely known on the *Kandovar*, one who had never even shown her affection. Fearing she might take Janwar's death hard wasn't an arrogant assumption. It was a valid concern.

Though the two of them had known each other for less than an alliance month, he and Simone had fallen in love and shared an intimacy that—despite neither of them coming to each other a virgin—had been both new and *Earthshattering*, as she'd once described it. If he died tomorrow while trying to locate and liberate her friends, he knew that would strike a blow.

But he couldn't bring himself to explain that to these two, so he finished with, "I just want her to be happy."

Eliana studied him for a long, somber moment. "I'll help her. Ava will, too."

"Thank you."

She tilted her head slightly. "You care about her."

He nodded. "Very much."

"And she cares about you?"

"Yes. I don't know why. But I'm too selfish to turn down such a gift."

Her expression softened, then brightened abruptly with a look of glee. "Holy crap! Simone fell in love with Jack Sparrow. I can't wait to tell the others!"

Janwar groaned at the familiar piratical comparison.

Then her face twisted in a grimace. "Well, shit. Now I feel like I should try to talk you into waiting until we join you. I don't want my friends to be tortured or die at Gathendiens' hands if they're being held in that facility or base or whatever. But I don't want you to die either. This sucks."

He found a laugh. "You and Simone are so alike."

"Yes, we are," she acknowledged, her tone and expression making it clear that she took that as a compliment. "That's why I know my girl will do everything she can to keep all of you alive while she kicks a *ton* of Gathendien ass."

"I believe that's how *she* summed up the plan, too," he admitted dryly. "If Simone had her way, the rest of us would just sit back, snack, and watch the chaos she spawns."

She laughed. "That's not a bad plan."

Dagon chuckled and shook his head. "Whatever plan you go with, update us on your progress. We look forward to receiving confirmation of your success."

Eliana nodded. "Be safe."

"We will." Janwar ended communications.

He sure as *srul* hoped they would.

Leaving the office, he headed to his quarters. Simone still slept when he returned.

Quietly shucking his clothing, he slipped into bed.

He barely had time to stretch out before Simone rolled toward him, eyes still closed. "Everything okay?" she mumbled.

"Everything's fine." Curling an arm around her, he drew her up against him. "Go back to sleep."

"Mm-kay." A contented sigh escaped her as she snuggled closer and draped a thigh across his. "Love you."

He pressed a kiss to her forehead. "I love you, Simone."

Embracing the bliss her presence always brought, Janwar closed his eyes, finally quieted his mind, and let sleep claim him.

CHAPTER FIFTEEN

QUIET ENGULFED THE BRIDGE as the little moon appeared in the distance.

Everyone except Kova was present.

T provided them with periodic updates on his and Kova's progress. Thus far, they had attached the C-23 to the underside of the Gathendien ship's hull and cut their way in without detection. Now Kova and the android were crammed into a maintenance shaft, waiting for some Gathendiens to take a break so T could access their terminal, deliver a virus to the communication system, and block all outgoing and incoming messages with the Gathendiens none the wiser.

Having been on similar missions in the past, Kova was the epitome of patience.

T, on the other hand, drove them all crazy. He kept complaining about the long wait and even wondered aloud if Kova should kill the Gathendiens so they could complete their mission faster.

"Discretion, T," Janwar droned. "Discretion. If you drop a bunch of Gathendiens, it will alert whoever finds them to the presence of interlopers on the ship. If you *do what you're supposed to do*—slip in, fix the comms, and slip out—you won't have a ship full of soldiers hunting you while you look for Simone's friends. You want Kova to come out of this alive, don't you?"

"Yes, commander," T responded, his tone wary as if he thought Janwar might be leading him into a verbal trap.

"And you want *us* to come out of this alive, too?"

"Yes, commander."

"Then stop complaining, let us concentrate, and only interrupt us if you have progress to report."

"Yes, commander," he agreed, his tone dejected.

"And don't fill Kova's data pad with silent complaints."

There was a pause, then a manufactured sigh. "Yes, commander."

Amused, Simone shook her head. She wasn't a hundred percent sure the AI would be able to keep that promise.

Poor Kova. On the upside, maybe if T aggravated him enough, the warrior wouldn't be so quick to volunteer for the next mission.

"What's next?" she asked Janwar.

"Once T accesses the mainframe, he'll be able to monitor the locations of all life forms aboard remotely, and the two can begin their search for captives.

As more minutes passed, Simone could empathize with T. The wait was nerve-racking, the tension on the bridge palpable. But she thought they'd timed things well. At the rate they were going, Kova would execute his rescue attempt at roughly the same time she and the others would infiltrate the research facility, so the two Gathendien groups wouldn't be able to seek help from each other.

Seated in a chair that was now a permanent fixture beside the commander's, Simone distracted herself from worrying about Kova by focusing on the moon they approached.

It reminded her a lot of Jupiter's Europa. Like Europa, it orbited what appeared to be an enormous gas giant. But whereas Jupiter was a mass of churning clouds and swirling cyclones with that massive orange eye, this planet seemed almost soothing by comparison. Clouds or gases that ranged in color from cream to sage green formed layers of smooth, linear stripes that looked as soft as cotton candy.

According to Elchan, thirty-three moons orbited the planet. The one they sought was the smallest. It was also one of the brightest, reflecting much of a distant sun's light. Unlike the moon she'd admired in the night sky back home, this one didn't appear to be pockmarked with craters, so it must have a protective atmosphere. She studied its smooth, white surface. Gray streaks that resembled scratches marred it, lending it the look of a white ball a cat had played with too roughly. Ragged-edged rust-colored patches here and there made her wonder if it might be volcanically active.

The *Tangata* approached the moon fully cloaked. As more details became clear, Simone was surprised to discover clouds as puffy as those common on Earth floating above the moon's surface.

She must have been right about the atmosphere. "Is that ice or sand?" Simone had seen some beautiful white sand beaches and deserts on Earth and couldn't tell from this distance which lay below them.

"Ice," Elchan responded. "According to my scans, most of it sits atop a vast saltwater ocean. The dark streaks are fractures, likely caused by the competing gravitational forces of the planet and other moons."

Since there were thirty-two other moons, that force must fluctuate often. "What about the orange splotches?"

"Glaciers that sit atop rocky landforms rich in iron and sulfur. The moon is also likely volcanically active."

Those orange patches were few and far between. Did that mean this little moon didn't have much land?

"How's the atmosphere?" Janwar asked.

"Too much nitrogen," Elchan said. "We'll have to keep our helmets on."

Simone supposed that meant she would have to don the bulky Lasaran spacesuit. "And the gravity?" The only time she had experienced zero gravity for more than a minute or two was when she'd pushed off the Gathendien ship and jetted into space to catch the fleeing transport the day she had met Janwar. Every ship and escape pod she'd traveled in since she'd left Earth had produced artificial gravity twenty-four hours a day.

She had thought it more for convenience than anything else until Prince Taelon had explained that the Lasarans had learned in their early years of space exploration that long-term exposure to no gravity weakened the crew's muscles and bones. Much to her astonishment, he'd said it also shrank their hearts by as much as twenty percent per year.

That had swiftly dampened her disappointment that they didn't spend most of their time floating around like balloons.

"According to scans, there's more gravity on the moon's dark side than on this side," Elchan said.

She frowned. "That's weird."

"It's not as uncommon as you might think," Janwar murmured, "particularly with so many other moons tugging at it."

"Oh." Outer space remained a constant source of wonder. Simone loved it. "How different is it from the ship's gravity?"

Elchan consulted his console. "The gravity on the bright side is light enough that a little jump would send us up pretty high."

"Cool," she breathed, eager to give it a try if she could find a suit that would protect her from the sunlight.

Again, Janwar smiled. "Not really. Though it makes carrying heavy gear easier, it also makes walking and running awkward."

"Oh."

Elchan looked at Janwar. "The dark side has about the same gravity as Promeii 7."

Promeii 7's gravity had been a little stronger than Earth's. If a human or *gifted one* immigrated there, they would feel wearier at the end of each day and build muscle faster. But thanks to her enhanced strength, it hadn't bothered Simone.

"Which side are we headed to?" As pretty as the bright side was with its blanket of ice, she didn't want the sun to burn her skin. And she sure as hell wouldn't remain behind. If she had to use preternatural speed to dart from icy overhang to icy overhang in search of shade, she would. She just wished she wouldn't have to. The *Tangata* had spoiled her with its fabulous faux sunlight.

Hmm. She wondered if Chief Medic Adaos could find a way around the photosensitivity that afflicted Immortal Guardians. He was already researching ways for them to safely conceive and bear children without infecting them with the vampiric virus. Perhaps she could talk him into researching both?

"The facility we'll infiltrate is on the dark side," Janwar announced.

"Yes!" she exclaimed with a grin.

When everyone regarded her with surprise, she shrugged. "I wasn't looking forward to the sun blistering my skin."

Janwar took her hand in his. "It wouldn't. T and I designed a new spacesuit for you. The helmet includes a special visor you can slide into place to protect you."

She stared at him, her heart turning over. "You did? That's so sweet." Stretching up, she stole a quick kiss. "Would you show me how to activate it so I'll be ready when the sun rises?"

"Yes."

"You won't need it," Elchan inserted. "Based on the speed of the moon's rotation, the sun won't rise again on that side for twenty-one ship days."

She smiled. "Awesome. Then I can relax and have fun."

"But not *too* much fun," Janwar warned. "Remember what happened the last time you fought those *grunarks*. I don't want another scare like that."

Her eyes narrowed as she recalled how close she'd come to death as a result of the *bosregi* poisoning. "Oh, trust me. I remember. But those bastards can't get me with their tail spikes if I remove those tails first."

That brought his smile back, though it failed to hide the concern in his eyes. "Just be careful, my little conqueror."

"You be careful, too." She kissed his tempting lips again, then leaned back and pointed to the others. "*All* of you. I mean it. Anyone who gets hurt will suffer a serious ass-kicking as soon as you recover."

They laughed.

It didn't take them long to reach the other side of the moon. As expected, it was dark. Dim light reflected from sister moons kept it from being pitch black, but most humans would still have to squint to make out structures. Simone, on the other hand, had no difficulty noticing the difference in topography with her enhanced vision. Whereas the other side of the moon was relatively flat and streaked with crevices, this side bore tall mountains locked in ice. Each jagged peak reached for the sky in disjointed chunks she found fascinating and beautiful.

Spotting something nestled at the base of the mountain range, she leaned forward. "Is that it?"

A long minute passed, perhaps because the others didn't have her sharper vision.

"Isolate it," Janwar ordered.

A clear viewscreen descended from the ceiling and projected the same image they'd spied through the windshield. Then the camera or scanner zoomed in.

"Enhance visual," Janwar murmured when it remained too dark for them to see clearly.

Elchan tapped commands into his console.

The image brightened without the graininess her most recent Second back on Earth had grumbled about whenever he tried to enhance dark photos.

Simone hated to admit it, but the Gathendiens had done a fantastic job creating a facility that would blend in perfectly with the ice. Backed up to the mountainside—perhaps even carved out of it—lay a complex web of structures partnered with a cave that she suspected was an aircraft hangar due to the flat, shuttered entrance.

She studied the interconnected buildings.

It looked as if the Gathendiens had either coated the whole place with ice or let nature do it for them. Nothing metal or bearing a different color from the moon stood out anywhere. The buildings may have begun as boxy shapes but now had taken on the same chunky uneven surface as the mountain behind them and blended seamlessly with the terrain. Anyone flying past on their way to Promeii 7 wouldn't notice a thing and assume the moon was a frozen, barren wasteland.

But Simone *could* see it. And one thing immediately stood out. "That's awful big for a research facility." Her gaze roved each structure, taking in every icy detail.

Janwar slowly shook his head. "That isn't your average research facility. That cave masks a hangar large enough to accommodate multiple craft."

Elchan nodded. "And I'm picking up a lot of life forms."

"How many?" Simone asked, anxiety creeping in. She really wanted this to be a quick and easy mission that would result in no serious injuries or loss of life. These men were doing this for *her*. For her friends. They might claim it was for whatever monetary reward the Lasaran royal family would pay them for finding Earthlings, Lasarans, or Yona, but that was bullshit.

Elchan stared at his screen. "More life forms than you would find on a standard military base." He glanced at Janwar. "At least two war-time contingents."

Janwar swore. "We may have just found one of their primary research and development bases."

Simone's gaze swept the men, then returned to Janwar. "Well, whatever they're researching and developing here must be pretty damn important if they have that many soldiers guarding it."

He nodded. "Scientists in the Gathendiens' viral research division are very competitive and often set up private, isolated labs they can work in without worrying about other scientists purloining their data. All covet the emperor's favor, so stealing and capitalizing on the work of others is a common issue. But this..." He motioned to the icy structures beneath them. "This goes far beyond that. Elchan, scan that hangar and see if you can tell us what's inside it."

Elchan went to work, tapping away and studying his screen. "Thirty fighter craft, a dozen of the larger troop transports, and... twenty ground combat vehicles."

"*Merde*," Simone whispered.

Janwar nodded, his face grim. "This is definitely one of their military's research and development bases."

"Which means...?" she prompted.

"Viral research isn't all they're conducting here. They're also refining and developing weaponry, ammunition, and combat-related craft."

She studied the base. "So in addition to having a shit-load of soldiers, they may also have advanced weaponry you've never encountered before?"

"Essentially."

This was worse than they'd anticipated.

She swallowed hard. "If you want to cancel the mission and wait for Segonian backup, I understand."

Janwar's hand tightened around hers. "We've already discussed the risks that would entail. The *Ranasura* and its troop transports can only hide from radar. They don't have the *visual* cloaking abilities we do. By the time they arrive, this side of the moon will be in daylight, and the Gathendiens would have no difficulty seeing them coming."

And if any *gifted ones* or Immortal Guardians were being held on that base, waiting would give the Gathendien researchers weeks to find a new virus that would succeed in killing every human, *gifted one*, and Immortal Guardian on Earth so the lizard bastards could swoop in and claim the planet for themselves.

"Okay," she said a little too brightly as worry clawed at her. "New plan. You all stay up here on the *Tangata* and create a diversion with the drones while I sneak inside with a T android and see whom I can find."

"*Drek* no," Janwar barked, his brows drawing down in a deep V.

"Look, this is more than any of you signed up for," she said, agitation rising. "*Way* more. I see that now, and I don't want you all to risk your lives."

He made an angry, scoffing sound. "So you want us to sit up here while *you* risk *yours*?"

"I told you, I'm very hard to kill—"

"But you *can* be killed!" he shouted.

Silence fell.

"You *can*... be killed."

Simone didn't know how to respond as she met Janwar's russet eyes. His emotions flowed into her where they still held hands, allowing her to feel the anguish hidden behind the anger.

He loved her and didn't want to lose her.

They were two peas in a pod then. The same sentiment had driven her to suggest the new plan. She couldn't bear the thought of him dying while helping her fulfill her quest to save her friends. The fact that they didn't even know if any of her friends were being held on that base just made things worse.

T spoke when no one else would. "Shortly after our last conversation, one of the Gathendiens mentioned they would not break for mid meal for another ship hour." And boy, did the AI sound disgruntled. "To alleviate Kova's boredom, I have been letting him listen to the happenings on the bridge."

To alleviate *Kova's* boredom or *T's*?

"Simone," T continued, "Kova has asked me to deliver the following message: *I don't know why you might need to be told this, but in case you do... You are* not *expendable. You are my friend. And I need you. We* all *do.*"

Well, damn if that didn't make her eyes well with tears.

Embarrassed, she sniffled and blinked them back. "You guys suck," she muttered.

Masculine laughter filled the bridge, alleviating some of the tension.

Simone wished she could simply use her telepathy to comb through all of the minds down on that base and see if anyone was thinking in English, but it wouldn't work from this great a distance.

Even if it did, a lack of "Earthling" thoughts wouldn't necessarily mean none of her friends were down there. If the Gathendiens drugged them and rendered them unconscious, she wouldn't hear any thoughts or dreams.

Searching the base was the only way to be sure.

"So what's the plan?" she asked finally. "How do we sneak in?" With that many soldiers on the base, they couldn't just rush in, guns blazing. As Janwar had heatedly pointed out, there *were* limits to her abilities as an Immortal Guardian.

Janwar looked at Elchan. "Map the base."

Her eyebrows rose as she glanced at the Segonian. "You can do that?"

"To an extent." His eyes remained on his screen as his fingers flew over his console. "I've found a way to combine ground penetrating radar with seismic waves and a scan for subtle changes in microgravity that can give us a somewhat accurate map. But the trick is doing all of that without the base noticing."

Could he do all of that without the base noticing?

"He's very good at what he does," Janwar said. "If that place has a back door or escape tunnels—and most Gathendien facilities do—Elchan will find them."

Simone just hoped he wouldn't trigger any alarms in the process. Had this just been a little private viral research lab manned by scientists, she wouldn't worry. But Janwar had admitted this base might contain weaponry and defense mechanisms he'd never encountered before.

Might some of those detect Elchan's efforts?

Time passed. Simone fidgeted as her patience began to wane.

"This is the best I can do without arousing suspicion," Elchan announced. A map appeared on the screen, superimposed over the base's icy exterior. It wasn't quite complete, as if Elchan had been interrupted while generating it. But it showed more than she'd hoped.

Janwar rose. "Send it to the war room." He waited for Simone to stand, then strode toward a door she had never noticed before. Unlike the others on the *Tangata*, there was nothing to distinguish this one from the wall, allowing it to blend in perfectly until opened.

She glanced around as they entered. The war room reminded her of the conference rooms she'd seen in network headquarters back on Earth. A long table dominated the center of it. Made of gleaming wood, it boasted grain patterns that were so colorful it almost looked painted. Several consoles—as clear as glass until activated—were embedded in its surface while viewscreens adorned the walls like paintings. Images of the moon appeared on the latter as the others joined them.

Though only six men crewed the *Tangata*, she counted eight chairs.

Had Janwar added two for Taelon and Lisa during their stay?

None of the men seated themselves. Instead, they gathered around the table. Krigara joined her and Janwar on one side. Srok'a, Elchan, and Soval clustered together on the other. When Elchan tapped several commands into a console, the largest one in the center of the table lit up with the map he had created.

Simone studied it.

A series of boxy rooms and hallways lit up as he pointed to them. "On first look, the base only has one entrance: this one here in the front. I'm running into some weather interference and won't have a clearer life-form scan until we approach it in the transport, but I'm sure it will be heavily guarded. These rooms here are large but have low ceilings. They're also long and narrow, so they're likely where the soldiers bunk. Based on their size, this room is probably a mess hall and this one used for training because the ceiling is a little higher. These two, though, have *significantly* higher ceilings."

Janwar leaned forward. "That's where they'll be doing the weapons development and testing."

"Agreed," Elchan said. "I suggest we bring T-2 with us to see if he can hack their system and tell us what they're working on in there."

"I am a very efficient hacker," T announced proudly. "If the Gathendiens we're monitoring didn't insist on remaining for their full shift, I would've already hacked this ship's system."

Simone smiled. "Hang in there, T."

Elchan shook his head and continued. "The hangar is obvious. That's where they store their craft, unload cargo deliveries, and build the new craft. Judging by the energy radiating from these two, they're engineering. These rooms here, clustered together near the back, look like private quarters reserved for military officers. These are similar but smaller."

"Likely the scientists' quarters," Janwar mumbled.

"That's what I was thinking. These rooms over here are positioned farthest from the others, way in the back. I had difficulty mapping them, which can sometimes indicate thicker walls or added layers of protection."

Janwar grunted. "Like the kind one might use to prevent potentially deadly bioengineered viruses from escaping and infiltrating the rest of the base."

"Exactly. This is most likely the primary lab. There's a long, vertical duct that extends from the ceiling to a hatch in the roof that I'm guessing only opens if they need to vent whatever bioweapons those idiots accidentally release. I also detected a second entrance to the base—much smaller than the one in front—that's close enough to provide the scientists with an emergency exit. This room appears to be a smaller secondary lab with another ceiling hatch. There's also something over here by the officers' quarters that I *think* could be another emergency exit."

Simone scowled. "So in the event of an attack or biological catastrophe, the officers can run away and leave the others to deal with it?"

Elchan nodded. "That would be my guess. It looks like a passage of some sort but is much narrower than the rest, with a ceiling so low that Soval would have to duck. It leads to this space here. I couldn't get a clear reading of it. But it may be large enough to hold a single transport capable of getting the officers off-planet."

She studied the fuzzy blob. "Is it connected to the hangar in any way?" If not, whatever craft waited inside must have been hidden there during the base's construction because she didn't see anything resembling a garage door.

"No. And though it's near the outside wall of ice, there doesn't appear to be a bay door."

"Then how would they get it out?"

"If the transport is armed, they should be able to blow their way out."

"Or we could melt our way in," Janwar mused and glanced at the others. "Looks like we have our choice of entrances."

Elchan pointed. "I think the one least likely to be manned by guards is the last one."

"The one that leads to the officers' quarters?" she asked.

He nodded. "I doubt the rest of the base knows about it. The exit by the primary lab will probably be heavily guarded, especially if they have lab subjects they worry might try to escape."

"What about the ceiling vent in the primary lab?" Simone asked.

"I don't know. They wouldn't expect anyone to use that to escape because it goes straight up, but there may be surveillance cameras on the roof."

Or the ice that passed as a roof. "Would they have cameras on the icy wall outside the officers' escape route?" she asked.

Janwar shook his head. "If they did, anyone who monitored the security feeds would know something was there. And I doubt the officers would want the lower ranks to see them sneaking away during an emergency. Krigara, once you're inside, can you tap into their security feeds and keep them from seeing the roof?"

He nodded. "All I need is terminal access. Once I override their protocols, I can put the rooftop footage on a loop. T can help me if I run into any trouble with it."

Janwar highlighted a corridor. "There should be a terminal in the officers' wing."

"Several, I would think," Elchan added.

Janwar pointed to the map. "Krigara, I want you, Soval, Elchan, and T-2 to enter the base through the officers' escape tunnel. Elchan, if your camouflage is working, stand guard wherever you have the best line of sight and warn the others of anyone heading their way. If it isn't, position yourself at the nearest corner and kill anyone who comes around it—quick and clean—before they can sound the alarm. Soval, position yourself in the middle of the corridor and do the same with anyone who steps out of those officers' quarters. Keep it quiet, and toss the bodies in the escape tunnel."

Leaning over, Janwar tapped Elchan's console, then touched a spot on the map. A red dot appeared on the mountain's icy side, far above the base. "Simone and I will standby here until you can loop the rooftop security feed. If you can loop the hallway feeds near the labs, do it. As soon as you give us the all-clear, Simone and I will enter through the primary lab's rooftop hatch and begin our search. While we do, I want T and Krigara to find out everything they can about the research the Gathendiens are conducting on this base, both viral and weapons. Once that's done, all of you should retreat to the escape tunnel and standby in case Simone and I need you."

He straightened. "Srok'a, I want you to monitor everything from up here. If Kova runs into trouble on the Gathendien ship and the drones I sent after him aren't enough, send T-3 and T-9 in with whatever else he needs to get his ass and whomever he finds out of there safely. If we run into trouble planet-side, have T attack the front of the base with K-6s. We'll be in the back, so drawing the bulk of their forces to the front should help us out of whatever situation we land ourselves in."

Simone waited for T to chime it and remind them that he was an extraordinary drone operator, but he seemed to understand the gravity of the situation and remained silent.

Janwar glanced around. "Everyone good with that?"

While the others nodded, Simone raised an index finger to get their attention. "I have a question."

All turned curious looks her way.

"Once T and Krigara have ferreted out all the information they can," she said, "and we've hightailed it back to the *Tangata*, any chance we could nuke the place from orbit?"

Janwar blinked. "My translator defines nuke as a weapon of mass destruction used on Earth that leaves up to twenty *kells* of land uninhabitable for many years after being deployed. By nuke, I assume you mean bomb?"

"Yes." She met all their gazes and shrugged. "I'm a you-reap-what-you-sow kind of girl and believe in an-eye-for-an-eye justice. The Gathendiens tried to commit genocide on Lasara. When they failed, and the Lasarans and the rest of the Aldebarian Alliance kicked their asses, that should've been the time the Gathendiens rethought their actions and resolved to change their ways. But they didn't. They're still trying to commit genocide on Earth and now want to do it on Purvel as well. For all we know, they may still have designs on Lasara. And those are just the civilizations and planets that we know of. As far as I'm concerned, anyone that full of greed and avarice with so little regard for life deserves the fate they wish to deal to others."

"Genocide," Janwar said.

Again, she shrugged. "Or in this case, a massive ass-kicking. If this is one of their primary research and development bases, taking it out would be a substantial blow."

Janwar looked at the others. "I'm good with that."

The rest voiced their agreement.

When he turned back to her, Janwar smiled. "But we'll use weapons that won't render the area uninhabitable. Someone may want to tweak the atmosphere later and terraform the moon."

She grinned. "Terraforming is so cool. They can only do that in entertainment vids on Earth."

He curled an arm around her shoulders. "Well, the Sectas and Lasarans have perfected the process. Once we're done here, I'll show you accelerated footage of the last moon the Lasarans terraformed."

Rising onto her toes, she kissed his chin. "It's a date."

CHAPTER SIXTEEN

T ENSION THRUMMED THROUGH JANWAR as he helped Simone don the white armored suit he and T had generated for her. He would rather she wear exo-armor like his. But with her exceptional speed and strength, he wasn't sure whether the armor would aid her or slow her down.

It certainly aided him and his men, enabling them to run faster, jump higher, and lift weight they ordinarily couldn't. It also protected them from extreme temperatures, toxic gases, and bioweapons and could take direct hits from blasters without suffering any damage beyond discoloration... unless it took too *many* hits. All armor had its limits.

"This is much better than the Lasaran suit," Simone declared happily as she pushed her hand through a sleeve. Once she did the same with the other, Janwar tugged the front halves together over her breasts and applied pressure to the front collar. The two seams instantly adhered to each other as though with magnets, sealing the front of the suit from her neck down to her hips.

When she tugged on the tight gloves, he showed her how to seal them to the wrist cuffs of the suit. "Now, my daggers," she said.

Janwar grabbed a belt that sported multiple sheathed blades and helped her fasten it around her hips. Then he stepped back to inspect her.

Simone did a few experimental knee lifts and jumped up and down several times. Then she swiveled from side to side at the waist before nodding. "This will do. There's almost no movement restriction, and even the shoes fit perfectly."

He glanced down at the boots that encased her tiny feet. "Both the suit and the boots will keep you warm in freezing temperatures."

She smiled. "Even if they didn't, I'd be okay. I can regulate my body temperature."

He stared at her, surprised that there were still things he didn't know about her considering their tendency to snuggle after sex and talk long into the night. "Truly?"

She nodded.

"That's a useful talent."

"All Immortal Guardians can do it," she said with a shrug. Then her expression sobered. "Which reminds me..."

Trepidation joined the tension that gripped him when she nibbled her lower lip. "What?"

"If things go wrong and this mission ends up fubar—"

"What's fubar?" His translator didn't even *try* to provide an alternative to that.

A faint smile tilted her lips. "It stands for fucked up beyond all recognition or repair."

"Ah." He sure as *srul* hoped it wouldn't.

"If all hell breaks loose and something happens to me," she continued, "as long as I'm still... me... don't write me off even if you think I'm dead."

Tamping down the anxiety spawned by the thought of her dying, he turned her words over in his mind. "I don't know what that means. If you're still you?"

She wrinkled her nose. "You may find what I'm about to tell you disturbing. Most do. But the virus the Gathendiens created and infected us with behaves like a symbiotic organism. It makes us stronger so it can survive even though it's been programmed to corrupt the brains of vampires. So when Immortal Guardians—and vampires—die, the virus begins to consume us from the inside out in a desperate bid to continue living, and we... shrivel up like a mummy, for lack of a better description, until there is nothing left but our clothing."

Appalled, he could find no response for several minutes.

Even then, all he could come up with was, "What?"

"We rapidly decompose until there's nothing left."

His heart began to thunder in his chest. "How rapidly?" Too rapidly for them to try to revive her?

"Within minutes." Her features full of concern, she stepped closer and touched his arm. "I told you because..." She sighed. "We don't know what will happen down there. If I suffer wounds that would kill anyone else or if something happens outside the base and I'm exposed to the atmosphere and freeze like a popsicle, I wanted you to know that as long as I still look like me and don't start shriveling up, there's a chance I can be saved. Just get me back to the infirmary here on the *Tangata*, contact Eliana, and do whatever she tells you to, which I imagine will begin with giving me a transfusion. I've followed her example and stored some of my blood in Med Bay in case something bad enough happens that Elchan's won't suffice."

If Simone were Akseli, died, and *didn't* decay as she'd described, Janwar would still lose her, so he wasn't sure why the notion of her shriveling up until there was nothing left disturbed him to such an extent. But it did.

Wrapping his arms around her, he hugged her tight. "Don't die, Simone."

Her arms crept around him, but his armor didn't let him feel much of the press of her body against his. "I don't intend to." Tilting her head back, she raised her lips for a kiss tinged with the trepidation both felt. "Don't *you* die either, Janwar," she whispered when he lifted his head. "I've waited seven hundred years to find love. I want to spend the rest of your life—however long it may be—playing pirate with you."

His heart beat faster at the declaration. "The Sectas value love above everything else. They can extend my life to match your lifespan if they find me worthy."

Her eyes widened as her features lit with excitement. "They can?"

"Yes. *If* they find me worthy. With my background—"

Arms still wrapped around his waist, she started jumping up and down, startling a laugh out of him when she took him with her, exhibiting some of that impressive strength. "Why didn't you tell me that before? Now I don't have to worry about losing you to old age."

Pushing out of her arms so she'd stop bouncing him around, he quelled his laughter. "I said *if they find me worthy.*"

"*Pfft.* Of course, they will. If they have any doubts, I can convince them."

She seemed so confident that he found himself feeling hopeful.

Then she scowled and shook a finger at him. "So don't get killed. I want eternity with you."

"Yes, ma'am," he agreed with a grin, using the Earth term instead of the Alliance Common term. He snuck another kiss. "Activate your helmet, honey."

"Honey?" She grinned. "You love using Earth terms, don't you?"

"I do." He winked. "Perhaps because I love a certain Earthling."

Face flushing with pleasure, Simone glanced down, found the button on her suit's front collar, and pressed it. A transparent bubble sprang up from the collar at the nape of her neck and swept forward to enclose her head, hissing as it sealed in front. "What if a Gathendien hits that button? Will the helmet automatically pop off?"

"No. There's a failsafe in place. The button only responds to sensors in the fingertips of your gloves."

"I love alien tech. And if something damages my gloves?"

"You can unlatch it verbally by saying, *Voice override. Simone the Conquerer. Retract helmet.*"

Laughing, she repeated his words. Another hiss sounded as the helmet's seal broke, and the clear bubble retreated to her collar. "You are so freaking awesome."

He grinned and grabbed his helmet.

As Simone scrutinized his armor, her smile faded a bit. "Aren't you going to stand out against the ice in that?"

His armor still bore the black tint his last mission had required. "No." Raising his wrist pad, he tapped a command into it. Within seconds, the dark armor turned white.

Her eyes widened. "Absolutely brilliant!"

He shook his head. "Our armor can only assume solid colors. You should see Elchan's. He wears Segonian armor that detects the chemical changes in his skin and camouflages him as well as his chromatophores do."

"I am so jealous! If I could do that, I would be unstoppable."

"You already *are* unstoppable. Just ask the Dotharian."

Laughing, she grabbed her sheathed katanas.

In short order, they joined Soval, Krigara, Elchan, and T-2 in a transport. Tense silence engulfed them as Krigara claimed the pilot's seat and headed for the moon.

Usually, on a mission like this, adrenaline would run high, and he and his friends would trade insults and jokes as they looked forward to any fights that might erupt.

Because fights almost always did.

But they had a newcomer in their midst. One they considered a precious member of their makeshift family. And all knew that—despite her bravery, strength, and outstanding skills as a warrior—Simone *could* be injured or killed if they *drekked* up.

Janwar found the anxious, uneasy feeling that plagued him unsettling and suspected the others did, too. Hence the silence as Krigara expertly navigated the darkness.

Though the transport was equipped with the same radar and visual cloaking as the *Tangata*, his cousin hugged the mountainside while approaching the base.

"It looks even bigger up close," Simone murmured behind him. "As big as one of the mercenary bases my Immortal Guardian brethren blitzed back home."

No alarms sounded at their approach. Strong winds whipped across the glacier and pelted the windshield with snow and ice, rendering visibility low.

Strapped into the co-pilot's seat, Janwar studied the base, then pointed to a rough ledge on the mountainside above it. "There." Jagged points lined the edges like stalagmites, extending high enough to offer them something to hide behind.

Krigara guided the transport as close as he could get without the stronger gusts slamming them into the mountainside.

Unfastening his harness, Janwar rose and stepped into the back where the rest of the seats hugged one wall.

Wedged between Soval and Elchan, Simone unclasped her harness and joined him near the hatch. "Time to go?"

He nodded, unable to quell a nervous flutter in his stomach. "Helmet up. We'll be able to talk over comms, but the storm may make it harder to hear each other."

"That's okay. I remember the plan." Smiling, she slipped her katanas onto her back and activated her helmet.

Janwar donned his own and slid the visor into place. The feed instantly lit up, enhancing visuals. Cameras embedded in the back of the helmet gave him a view of everything behind him. A running display on one side kept him apprised of his vitals and oxygen supply and could provide further information on command.

While the rest of the crew donned their helmets, Janwar looped an *osdulium* rifle over one shoulder. Next, he drew the strap of a bag over his head and the other shoulder, settling its bulk against his back. He didn't know what they might find inside that base, so he'd packed the bag with decontamination suits for anyone they found who might be infected with the Gathendiens' viral concoctions. He'd also added several *lekadis* that could serve as both stretchers and decon tubes for those too ill to walk. Or to transport the bodies of any who might have been killed before the rescue attempt.

He hadn't mentioned the latter to Simone.

Once everything was adjusted to his liking, he reached into one of the many pockets magnetized to his armor and withdrew a *kada*.

"What's that?" she asked, her voice emerging from the speakers in his helmet as she peered at the *kada*.

Janwar snapped one corner off the small rectangular device and dropped the rest. As it fell, the tech expanded into a board about the length of his arm that was just wide enough to accommodate his feet if he stood with them braced a shoulder's width apart.

The *kada* halted without hitting the deck and floated a hand's span above it.

Her eyes lit with delight. "Is that a hoverboard?"

He nodded and held up the corner piece. "We call it a *kada*. I control it with this."

Judging by the excitement that brightened her pretty features, she would want one of her own once they returned to the *Tangata* and would no doubt spend hours using it to fly through the corridors.

"What other cool goodies are you carrying?"

He patted his pockets. "Emergency medic supplies in this one. Bex-7 stun grenades in this one. And Z-12 e-grenades in this one."

She smiled up at him. "I am so turned on right now."

The other men chuckled.

Laughing, Janwar stepped onto the *kada*. Since the winds were so fierce, he took the added precaution of activating the magnets in his boots to ensure the *kada* wouldn't be swept out from under them, then held out a hand.

Simone eagerly clasped it and held on while she stepped up and positioned her feet between his. Her balance was perfect as she slid an arm around his waist to anchor herself to him.

He should have known it would be. Everything about her was perfect. "Ready?"

A wide grin lit her features as she nodded. "Let's do this."

Reaching over, he hit the release button beside the hatch.

Wind rushed inside as it opened but failed to tear Simone from his arms. Little taps sounded as ice pellets struck his armor.

"Wow," she said over the comm. "That wind is *really* blowing. Are you sure we can fly through it on the *kada*?"

"Yes. There are small jets strategically positioned on my armor that I can use to keep us on course." Janwar glanced over her head at his men. "No casualties."

"No casualties," they repeated.

"Happy hunting!" Simone called, then squealed and clutched him tighter as they shot out of the transport.

Janwar immediately had to employ the rockets on his armor to keep them from slamming into the mountain. His heart jumped into his throat, pulse spiking, as he fought the constant barrage and navigated them over to the outcropping he'd targeted.

A sigh of relief carried over the comm in his helmet once they ducked behind its jagged edges.

"Whew! That was close. Good flying," Simone praised with a smile.

"Careful," he murmured as he helped her step off the *kada*. "The ice is slick." He showed her how to access the control panel on her wrist and call spikes forth from the soles of her boots.

"That's handy."

"We're good," Janwar told Krigara.

The transport's hatch closed, hiding the interior and rendering the craft virtually invisible once more.

Janwar tucked the *kada* under his arm, then he and Simone settled in to wait for the transport to land outside the officers' escape tunnel.

The wind wasn't as bad here. The icy ridges blocked more than he'd expected.

"Boots on the ground," Krigara muttered over the comm. "Soval, T, and Elchan are cutting their way in."

"Any indications the Gathendiens know you're there?"

"None."

Good.

Janwar glanced at Simone.

A wide smile lit her features as she peered over the chunks of ice that hid them and studied the frigid surface below.

He shook his head as affection welled up within him, dampening some of his worry. "You're enjoying this, aren't you?"

"Absolutely," she answered, her voice full of enthusiasm. "I have now visited an alien planet *and* an alien moon. I've become an honest-to-goodness space explorer."

He loved this sweet, innocent side of her. If she weren't wearing a helmet, he would smooth a hand over her hair and lean in for a kiss. "What are you thinking?" he asked, curious to know what thoughts tumbled through her sharp mind as she studied the landscape.

"Right now? Part of me is imagining you naked inside that armor."

Surprised, he laughed. Perhaps innocent wasn't the right word. "And the other part?"

"I wondered if there might be any Dotharian-sized creatures lurking in the ocean beneath the ice."

Still smiling, he nudged her. "Already looking for a new challenge?"

"Perhaps," she admitted with an impish grin. "Some of my immortal brethren can communicate with animals and coax them into doing their bidding. I was thinking how cool it would be if I could raise an army of giant sea creatures and sick them on the base."

He grinned. "That would be one *srul* of a distraction." And vastly entertaining.

"I bet we'd be able to get in and out without anyone noticing us."

"And have quite a story to tell afterward."

Her laughter filled his helmet and soothed his nerves.

"We're in," Krigara announced. "Elchan was right. There's a transport in here, outdated but still functional by the looks of it. There's also a tunnel leading toward the base. We're entering it now."

Janwar and Simone shared a somber look.

A few minutes passed.

"Found the door," Krigara said. "T and I are trying to override the access code." A beep sounded in the background. "Done." What sounded like metal grinding against metal carried over the comm. If that door hadn't been opened since the base's construction, the cold could have adversely affected the hardware, robbing them of the quiet entrance they'd hoped for.

Krigara swore. A couple of pulses carried to Janwar's ears, followed by two thuds. "Two hostiles down."

"Did they know you were coming?" Janwar asked. If the soldiers had been standing there, waiting for the door to rise—

"No. They just happened to be in the corridor when we opened the door. Both were so shocked that they didn't even reach for their weapons before we stunned them."

"Drag them into the tunnel."

"Soval's already doing it."

Simone caught Janwar's gaze. "What happens when they wake up?"

"They won't. They'll freeze to death within minutes once Krigara closes the door."

"Really? It's that cold out here?"

He nodded.

"T found a terminal," Krigara whispered. "We're looking for a way into their systems. Elchan is positioned at the end of the corridor in full camouflage. Soval is halfway between us, ready to take on anyone who steps out of the officer's quarters."

A moment passed.

"Incoming," Elchan whispered. A thud followed. "Put him with the others."

Metal ground against metal.

Simone winced. "That thing needs some WD40."

Janwar didn't know that that was. "Can't you do anything to quiet that?"

"Soval," Krigara whispered.

"Two more incoming," Elchan murmured.

More thuds.

The grinding metal sound wasn't as loud this time but still concerned Janwar.

T spoke. "The Gathendiens have detected a change in atmosphere in this sector and are sending a crew to investigate it."

Janwar swore. "The base doesn't have an atmospheric barrier?" That was usually the first thing erected on planets and moons that lacked a breathable atmosphere so no one would die if an equipment failure or unexpected breach occurred.

"It does not," T informed them.

Simone scowled.

"They must monitor nitrogen levels," Krigara added grimly, "so they'll know if the shifting of the glacier beneath them or the ice above them fractures the base's exterior."

"Leave the exit door closed until further notice. If you have to kill anyone else, just pile them in a corner." Hopefully, when no new nitrogen influxes occurred, the Gathendiens would believe the sensor was malfunctioning. But...

He looked at Simone.

She nodded. "Even if we don't trip any security alarms, the nitrogen sensor will alert them the moment we open the hatch above the lab."

"Yes. We'll have to work fast."

"I can do that," she boasted with a wink. But her smile had lost some its former ebullience, betraying her concern.

"T," Janwar said, "see if you can shut down their atmospheric monitoring system."

"Yes, commander."

Fortunately, the AI could execute multiple tasks at once without slowing down.

"Srok'a, you getting this?" Janwar asked.

"Yes."

"Ready the drones."

"Already doing it."

Janwar hoped like *srul* they wouldn't need them.

***

S IMONE'S NERVES JANGLED OVER the increasing certainty that this mission was not going to go smoothly. "I take it most bases like this have the same atmospheric barrier that ships use?"

"Yes." Janwar looked as grim as she felt. "But when those in charge prefer to allocate funds elsewhere, cheaper atmospheric monitors are sometimes used instead."

Damned Gathendiens.

Simone studied the base below. If T couldn't disable the atmospheric monitors, then shit might hit the fan as soon as she and Janwar opened the ceiling access. What if the soldiers on the base thought the *scientists* had opened it because they'd screwed up and released some deadly contagion? Alarms would blare. Chaos would erupt. The officers would all head straight for Krigara and the others, intending to make their cowardly escape. And she didn't know *what* would happen to whoever might be incarcerated in the cells adjoining the lab.

Anxiety rising, she caught Janwar's gaze. "When we open that hatch, will everyone in the lab die from a lack of oxygen?" What would prevent it if the base had no atmospheric barrier?

Reaching out, he touched her arm with a gauntleted hand. "No. It will only be open long enough for us to duck inside."

"But they *will* detect the rise in nitrogen."

"Yes, unless T can prevent it. Srok'a, map us a route from the labs to Krigara's position and send it to my helmet."

"Mapping it now."

She arched a brow. "New plan?"

He nodded. "An atmospheric barrier would've allowed us to slip in unnoticed, take out the scientists, and handle whatever we find in terms of çaptives. We would've been able to render aid and get anyone we rescued into protective gear, all while giving T time to download every bit of information he could from the ship's databases. And even though I know it would be awkward, I hoped we could take whomever we find back through the ceiling vent and have the transport pick us up on the roof."

"But the nitrogen sensors will likely send the soldiers straight to the lab."

"And possibly to the roof to check out the vent's exterior if they think it's a malfunction, so we may either have to take our chances with the guards that man the emergency exit near the lab or rendezvous with the rest of the team and evacuate through the officers' escape tunnel."

Krigara spoke before Simone could respond. "I disabled the alarm on the lab's vent access. And T looped the security feeds on the roof, in the lab, and in the corridors leading to it. You're good to go."

"What about your area?" Janwar asked.

"We looped those, too."

"Any luck with the atmospheric monitors?"

"Not yet. Too many eyes on it right now, so we have to be doubly careful. But life-form scans are operational. I'm going to send you a live feed."

A translucent map popped up on Simone's helmet, surprising her so much that she jumped. When she looked down at the base, lines representing walls and red dots indicating life forms now overlaid the icy structure.

"That's more guards than I'd hoped," Janwar murmured.

"Where?" There were red dots everywhere, though most were concentrated in the front half of the base.

"At the primary lab's exterior emergency exit."

She followed his gaze. While several dots littered the corridor outside the lab, at least twice their number inhabited a room around the corner that she assumed someone would have to pass through to use the emergency exit. "Oh. Wow. Yeah, that's a lot of guys to get through." There were so many they formed one big blob instead of a cluster of smaller dots.

Krigara spoke. "If you can't exit through the roof, are you going to head our way instead?"

"Yeah," Janwar responded, "unless we don't find anyone. Then Simone and I will head back up through the roof and meet you on the mountainside where you dropped us off."

"Understood."

Janwar stepped up onto the *kada* and extended a hand.

Shutting down all fear and apprehension, Simone clasped it and joined him. *This is no different from blitzing that military base back on Earth*, she told herself. This time she just wore atypical clothing and would be fighting reptilian aliens instead of vampires and mind-controlled soldiers. She could do this.

They all could.

And she would make damned sure every one of them made it out alive.

"Ready?" Janwar asked.

She nodded. "Let's go."

They flew toward the base, the wind howling as it whipped around them.

Undeterred, Janwar expertly guided them down to the roof.

The ice was so slick and the wind so strong that they had to activate the spikes in their boots once they stepped off the *kada* to keep from skidding across the surface. The translucent map on their helmets then guided them over to a patch of thick ice that looked no different from the rest.

Simone bit her lip, wondering if she should draw her swords and start hacking away at it.

Janwar shifted the pack on his back, drawing it around to the front and opening it. He really did look kick-ass in his armor, which anchored him in place so well that he didn't even sway as he withdrew what looked like four shining metal coins.

Simone, on the other hand, had to employ some of her preternatural strength to remain in place while hurricane-force winds pushed and shoved her. *Sheesh*, they were strong!

Kneeling, Janwar set the coins on the ice about a foot and a half beyond each corner of the lab's vent. When he tapped one coin, a red laser shot from it, connected to the next, then to the next, and to the first again, forming a square.

Her eyes widened when dozens of red lines stretched across from the sides to form a grid pattern inside the shape. Seconds later, the ice inside the square began to melt, the coins sinking down yet maintaining a pristine quadrilateral shape. Steam rose as the meltwater heated up and boiled away.

Leaning forward to watch, Simone marveled over how quickly the ice separating them from the vent disappeared. There wasn't even any water at the bottom when it finished.

She sent Janwar a smile. "You know what I'm going to say."

He grinned. "That's awesome?"

"Hell yes."

He chuckled. "T, are you having any success with the atmospheric monitors?"

"Not yet. But I succeeded in scrambling their comms so the base can neither receive nor send messages."

"Five hostiles incoming," Elchan murmured.

Rustling, grunting, and a couple of yelps ensued.

"Targets down," Soval muttered.

"*Drek*!" Krigara hissed.

More thuds and grunts.

"Report," Janwar ordered.

"One of the *grunark*'s cries drew an officer out of his quarters," Krigara said, "but we took care of him."

Simone studied the ice around them. This close, the life-form scan provided a little more detail. Quite a few red figures inhabited the lab beneath them. When she listened intently for the thoughts of those below, a jumble of different alien languages bombarded her in a mass of masculine gibberish. "I'm picking up more than one alien language but don't hear any English. Should I reach out telepathically to see if some of my friends are here?"

He shook his head. "We don't want anyone down there to exhibit a reaction that might tip off the Gathendiens that we're here."

She pointed to several figures that were stationary. "Do those have tails?"

Janwar followed her gaze. "I don't think so."

Hope rose. "Why aren't they moving?" Were they ill? Unconscious? Dead?

"I don't know. Krigara, we may have found what we're searching for. Do we wait, or do we move in?"

A pause ensued. "We're looking at the code for the atmospheric monitors now. I think shutting them off would take too much time, but we may be able to send up false flags elsewhere to reduce suspicion."

Janwar glanced toward the front of the base. "Send one up inside the primary entrance's security checkpoint. It's large enough that they would know instantly if there were an actual breach. So when the atmospheric monitor claims nitrogen levels have risen, they should assume it's malfunctioning. On my mark, send another to one of the engineering rooms and a third to one of the barracks' lavs."

"Sending one to the security checkpoint," Krigara confirmed.

Simone studied the front of the base, expecting an alarm to blare or a red light to flash.

Nothing happened.

"Anything?" Janwar asked.

T answered. "The security officers are contacting maintenance now and telling them the sensor is malfunctioning."

Janwar met Simone's gaze. "Let's go." He lowered himself into the hole in the ice.

Simone followed and had barely enough room to squeeze in next to him as he knelt and attached a gadget to a passcode entry pad next to the vent, which she thought looked more like an ordinary hatch.

Numbers and letters in an alien alphabet she couldn't decipher scrolled across the surface of Janwar's device.

While he waited, he turned to her. "According to the life-form scans, there are five almost directly beneath us. Four are unquestionably Gathendien. You can see their tails. That'll be the scientists and their assistants. This one they're clustered around may be a lab subject. The others you noticed that don't appear to have tails are over there." He motioned with his hand to an area about twenty feet away. "Their grouping suggests they're likely being held separately in cells." He pointed to the right. "And those are the guards."

Simone pursed her lips. "That's a hefty number."

He nodded. "I'll take out whoever stays in the corridor with a stun grenade but can't use one in the lab without risking the welfare of anyone being held captive if they're in poor health. So we'll have to contend with the scientists and the guards who rush inside—"

"As quickly as possible to keep them from sounding the alarm," she finished for him. "Got it."

He touched her arm. "I know if you find some of your friends, you may want to remove your helmet, but keep it on and your visor sealed. We don't know what viruses they may carry."

She nodded, realizing that her first instinct *would* have been to yank off her helmet and put them at ease. "Thank you. I will."

The text on the device ceased scrolling. The light on the passcode entry pad changed color.

Janwar gave her arm one last pat, then tucked the device back into one of his pockets. "Retract your spikes."

Oh. Right.

They retracted the spikes on the bottoms of their boots.

"Krigara, send the other atmospheric alerts."

"Sending them now."

Simone backed up as much as she could to clear the hatch.

"There's the one in engineering," Krigara muttered. "And there's the one in the lav. Done."

Janwar met Simone's gaze. "One. Two Three." Quietly opening the hatch, he dropped inside.

CHAPTER SEVENTEEN

D ARKNESS SWALLOWED JANWAR.

Simone grabbed the inner handle on the hatch and slid in after him, her heart thumping as adrenaline flooded her veins. At the last second, she threw her free hand out, clutched the rim to slow her momentum, then closed the hatch silently behind them.

No ladder waited inside, just a dark, narrow tunnel with smooth walls that were climate controlled by the lab beneath and fortunately weren't slick with ice.

Dangling by the hatch's handle, she glanced down. A faint light shone somewhere below, but she couldn't see past Janwar, who waited just beneath her with his back pressed to one wall and his feet braced on the other to keep him from sliding down.

Pressing a hand to one wall, she reached for the other with her feet. As soon as she felt stable, she released the handle and mimicked his position. It reminded her of a vampire she'd had to chase down a chimney in Paris a couple of centuries ago.

Oddly enough, that hadn't been the only time.

While Janwar's knees were bent, Simone was short enough that she had to lock hers and keep her legs as straight as boards to reach the other side. Once settled, she glanced down at Janwar, whose armor abruptly turned black.

Reaching up, he took her arm and tapped the control pad on her wrist.

Her suit turned black as well.

So cool.

Loud voices carried up to them. Both smiled, relieved that their entrance had gone unheard.

"...asking if we've opened the emergency vent," a male grumbled in Gathendien. Fortunately, the earbud thingy Simone wore translated everything for her.

"Did you see me open the vent?" another male snapped.

"No. But the atmospheric sensor inside it detected a rise in nitrogen."

The tunnel went dark as the dim light beneath them vanished.

Were the scientists peering up at them?

She tensed.

Dim light flared again as the second male spoke, his voice full of aggravation and growing quieter with distance. "Give me that. It's closed."

"Should I send a decontamination unit?" a third voice asked, fainter than the others. He must be talking to them over a comm.

"No," the second growled. "We don't need a decontamination unit because nothing happened. The *drekking* sensor must be malfunctioning."

"According to the sensor, the vent opened."

"If the vent had opened, it would've shattered the ice above us and sounded like a *drekking* Z-12 exploding. Snow and ice would be pouring down on us. And we'd be scrambling for masks. But it didn't, it isn't, and we aren't. The vent is sealed!"

"We've been alerted to breaches in engineering and one of the lavs, too."

"Are there leaks in engineering or the lavs?"

"Those we've spoken to say there aren't."

"Then the atmospheric monitoring system is malfunctioning. Do whatever you must to fix it, and don't interrupt my work again."

Mumbling ensued that her translator either couldn't or wouldn't interpret.

She smirked. Looked like the Gathendiens' a-hole nature would work in their favor.

Janwar reached up and tapped one of her hands, drawing her attention. When she looked down, he raised his eyebrows.

She nodded, indicating she was ready.

He palmed a Bex-7 stun grenade and fiddled with it. What looked like a countdown began on its surface. Winking, he held up one finger on his free hand. Then two. On three, he dropped his legs and plummeted to the floor twenty feet below, landing in a smooth crouch with nary a wobble thanks to his exo-armor.

Gasps sounded as he stepped aside and tossed the grenade.

Simone followed, landing just as smoothly behind him, and took in as much as she could with a glance. The lab was long and rectangular. A bare-chested male was strapped down to one of three operating tables. Two tall Gathendiens wearing the equivalent of white lab coats hovered over him with bloody instruments and gaped as Janwar raised his O-rifle and aimed it at the guards rushing in the door. Another scientist spun away from a screen that displayed something resembling microscopic bacteria.

Five containment cells adjoined the lab, antiseptically clean and bearing metal bars. In front of them, a smaller Gathendien garbed more simply than the others jumped and dropped an armful of beverage containers.

Before Simone could catalog the prisoners behind him, brilliant light flooded the room from the hallway as the stun grenade detonated with the faint sound of crackling electricity.

Drawing her swords, she burst into action. Blood sprayed as she shot around the lab with preternatural speed, decapitating all three scientists before they could activate their comms.

Thuds sounded as some of the guards out in the hallway collapsed. But several made it far enough inside not to be taken out by the stunner. Janwar fired his O-rifle, engaging three of them.

When Simone saw a fourth reach for his comm, she dropped a sword, palmed a dagger, and let it fly. The blade pierced the Gathendien soldier's hand with such force that he stumbled backward. Darting forward, she snapped his neck, then took out two others with her blades as more fell beneath Janwar's fire.

Thank goodness O-rifles made little noise. The automatic weapons sometimes used by the human network that aided Immortal Guardians tended to hurt her sensitive ears and attract unwanted attention.

As the last hulking Gathendien fell, Janwar swore and turned to glare at her. "Are you insane? I could've shot you! Give me some *drekking* warning next time!"

She stared at him in surprise. "I was careful to avoid your fire."

"You wouldn't *have* to avoid my fire if you'd use the *tronium* blaster I gave you!"

Aware that his anger stemmed from fear for her safety, she wrinkled her nose in chagrin. "I know. Sorry about that. I'm just more accustomed to fighting with swords and daggers." She winked. "As you know, I'm quite good with them."

Rolling his eyes in exasperation, he turned to face the lab's interior.

All three scientists were dead on the floor, their heads scattered between them. The lab assistant was now flattened back against the bars with a beefy arm locked around his neck and a second locked around his chest.

Simone sheathed her sword and glanced at the Yona warrior who restrained him. "Thank you. I forgot about that one."

He nodded. "Do you need him alive?"

She glanced at Janwar. "Do we?"

"No."

The Yona shifted his hold and broke the man's neck.

"Krigara," Janwar said, "we've breached the lab. All hostiles are down."

"Any injuries?" his cousin responded.

"No." He met her gaze. "Help me drag the others inside."

Simone did so in a blur of motion, managing to pile them all inside the lab before he'd taken more than a few steps.

Laughing, he closed the door. "Well, that was easy."

She grinned.

"Simone?"

Her breath caught, and her smile vanished at the sound of the tentative female voice. Spinning around, Simone visually searched the cells. A Purveli male stood in one. Two Yona warriors each had a cell. And... "Allie?"

The woman shuffling toward her inside the farthest cell bore little resemblance to the *gifted one* Simone had come to know so well on the *Kandovar*. Allison's colorful clothing had been replaced with a wraparound shirt and shorts that revealed arms and legs that were almost skeletal and bore numerous scars and raw patches.

Her long raven hair was a mass of tangles and bracketed a face that no longer glowed with youth or boasted the perpetual smile Allie was known for. Instead, her brown eyes were dull and haunted, and dark shadows painted the skin beneath them. She clamped chapped lips together, a muscle in her jaw jumping and accentuating hollow cheeks. Sweat beaded on her forehead as she reached the bars and clutched one.

Simone quickly closed the distance between them and placed her hand over Allison's. "Allie." Tears well in her eyes. What had the Gathendiens done to her? "I'm here."

Frustrated by the glove that kept her from feeling her friend's flesh, she started to tug at it.

"Simone," Janwar warned.

Right. She stopped. Allie might be infected with something that could harm Janwar and his crew. And maybe even Simone, since the Gathendiens were trying to manufacture a virus that would work more efficiently on Earthlings than the previous one they'd created.

She patted Allie's hand. "Everything's going to be okay. I promise."

The Yona warrior who'd spoken to them earlier nodded toward the Gathendien he'd killed. "The assistant has a chip in his wrist that will unlock the cells."

Simone stepped over several bodies to retrieve the sword she'd dropped earlier. When she turned toward the assistant, intending to extricate his chip, her eyebrows flew up.

Janwar stood over him, the assistant's severed arm in one hand. "I got it." Crossing to the gate on Allison's cell, he waved the assistant's wrist in front of a shiny access pad about the size of a credit card. A clunk sounded, then the gate swung open.

Simone hurried inside and dragged her friend into a hug.

"Is it really you?" Allison whispered, wrapping her arms around Simone. "Are you here, or am I hallucinating?"

"It's me," she said, blinking back tears. The younger woman's hold was so weak. "If you were hallucinating, I doubt I'd be wearing anything this weird."

A sound that was half-laugh and half-sob escaped Allie. And when she drew back, tears flowed freely down her gaunt cheeks.

"Let's get you out of here," Simone said softly. Wrapping an arm around her, she guided Allie out of the cell.

Janwar had already liberated the two Yona soldiers and moved on to the Purveli.

Simone studied the Yona. "You were on the *Kandovar*." She remembered seeing them but didn't recall interacting with them the way she had with Valok, Ari'k, and some of the others.

They nodded. "You are one of the Earthlings," one said.

"As is Allison," the other added. "Did Prince Taelon, his lifemate, and his heir survive?"

"Yes." She motioned to the armored man releasing the Purveli from his cell. "Janwar rescued them and ferried them safely to Lasara. He's helping the alliance search for my friends and other survivors." She thought it best to put that out there in case they recognized him as the infamous and often scorned Akseli pirate.

They shot Janwar a considering look.

"The Gathendiens attacked the *Kandovar* solely to capture the Earthlings aboard it," the taller one said.

"Yes," she acknowledged. "We realize that now."

"They opted to capture us, too," the second added. "Lasarans and other members of the Aldebarian Alliance rely heavily on our protection. The Gathendiens believe eradicating the Yona will weaken alliance nations and reduce the risk of retaliation."

Janwar joined them and handed Simone his bag. "Would you give them all protective suits while I free the one on the table?"

She glanced over her shoulder, lips tightening as she realized the unconscious male was Purveli. "Of course." That brought the count to five Purveli males they knew the Gathendiens had snatched, confirming Purvel was definitely on the list of worlds Gathendiens wished to conquer.

Releasing Allie, Simone squatted and dug through the bag.

Allison sank to her knees beside her and clutched one of the katana sheathes that dangled down Simone's back as though terrified of losing contact with her.

"Here." Simone held a rectangular packet out to one of the Yona. It didn't look large enough to contain a suit but had an image of one printed on the outside. "I'm Simone."

"Vedon," the taller Yona said as he took it.

"Denu," the second Yona said.

When they broke the seal on the packet, a white suit that reminded her of a hazmat suit popped out and expanded.

"M'kor," the Purveli said. Like Allie, he looked skinny, pale, and unwell. "My friend is Luft'a."

She nodded. "When you're finished, would you help Janwar get Luft'a into one of these?"

His eyes widened. "Did you say Janwar?"

She smiled. "The one and only."

Nodding with more enthusiasm, he shook out his suit. "I'll help him." He must fall into the category of rebellious young fellows who admired the notorious pirate.

While the others donned their suits, Simone turned to help Allie. "This will probably be way too big on you. Guys out here in space tend to be huge." She kept her tone light even as her heart broke for her friend.

Allie had to rise to step into the suit and wove on her feet.

Simone did her best to brace her as she tugged the suit up over Allie's bony form. As expected, it swallowed her, making her appear even more fragile. But the gloves and attached foot coverings were made from material meant to stretch to fit and weren't too bad. "There's a button here on the collar that will make a helmet like mine spring up from it. Once you activate it, don't remove it until we give you the go-ahead. It will provide you with oxygen and protect you from the hostile atmosphere outside. And the men who are helping me need protection from whatever virus you may be carrying. Understand?"

She nodded like a lost child who was so relieved to have been found that she would agree to anything.

"Okay. Activate your helmet."

Allie raised a trembling hand and fumbled for the button. When the helmet sprang out of her collar and swooped down to close in front, she jumped, eyes flying wide, and gripped Simone in panic.

"It's okay," Simone said gently. "It's supposed to do that." She forced a grin. "Awesome, isn't it? Mine has all kinds of fancy tech stuff flickering on the inside. I can't wait to show it to you later."

That managed to spark a faint smile.

Heart breaking for her, Simone turned back to the others.

Janwar and M'kor had managed to stuff Luft'a into a suit and activate his helmet, but the Purveli male remained unconscious.

Denu stepped forward. "I can carry him." Unlike the others, the two Yona warriors appeared to be in good shape, their muscles bulging.

Simone glanced around at their group. They'd gone from two people to seven, and only four of them were in prime fighting condition.

"No need," Janwar said as he retrieved his bag and looped it over his head again. "I have a *lekadis*." He drew out what looked like a sizable *kada* and broke off a corner. When he dropped the larger piece, the thing lengthened into a hovering gurney big enough to carry someone Soval's size.

They swiftly transferred Luft'a to the gurney. When Janwar tapped the corner he still held, a bubble emerged from one side, swept across the prone male, and encased him.

Janwar caught her gaze. "Are you comfortable enough with the map in your helmet to take point so I can cover the rear?" They still needed to check out the other lab.

"No need," Vedon said. "If you arm us, we'll cover the rear and eliminate anyone who follows."

Janwar hesitated.

Simone drew her *tronium* blaster and held it out to Vedon, grip first. "Janwar is a friend of Prince Taelon. Don't betray him."

"We have heard rumors of their friendship and will not betray him," Vedon stated, taking the weapon.

Janwar drew another *tronium* blaster from his bag and passed it to Denu.

Simone turned to M'kor. "Will you help Allison so I can take point with Janwar?"

He nodded.

But Allie didn't want to let go of her.

"It's okay," Simone said in the most comforting voice she could muster as she pried her friend's hand loose. "It's okay, Allie. I just need to keep my hands free so I can kick ass. You remember how good I am at kicking ass, right?"

Eyes wild, Allie nodded. "I'm afraid you'll disappear," she admitted shakily.

Those fucking Gathendiens. Allison still worried all this was a hallucination. "I won't disappear. I just need you to do me a favor and help M'kor." Leaning in, she said in a conspiratorial whisper everyone could hear, "I didn't want to mention it in front of him, but he isn't looking so good. I'm not sure he can make it on his own. Do you think you can keep him on his feet long enough for us to get him out of here?"

Over Allison's head, she saw M'kor's eyebrows fly up. But when Allison turned to look at him, he slumped his shoulders and staggered to one side with feigned weakness.

Allison threw a gloved hand out to steady him and glanced back at Simone. Her bony shoulders straightening, she nodded. "I can do it." Moving to stand beside M'kor, she looped an arm around his waist and held on tight.

When Simone looked up at the Purveli, he winked.

Both looked ready to topple over, but she felt confident they would keep each other on their feet as she turned to Janwar. "Let's do this."

J ANWAR LED THE WAY to the door, stepping over the fallen Gathendiens.

"How close is the other lab?" Simone asked.

"Just up the corridor on the ri—"

"You won't find more captives there," Vedon interrupted.

Janwar turned to face him. "Are you sure?"

The Yona male nodded. "They're conducting other experiments in there."

Simone frowned. "What kind of experiments?"

"They're creating Gathendien cyborgs."

Her jaw dropped.

Janwar stared at the Yona. "Are you sure?"

Vedon nodded. "One of the scientists you slew performed the necessary surgeries. And the assistant was a braggart. He claimed he was slated to enter the program upon its completion. If all he said was true, the Chancellor of Aksel sold the Gathendiens the research they needed to create cyborgs."

Fury consumed Janwar. That mother *drekker* Astennuh would sell out anyone or anything for a profit. And he was either too stupid to realize the Gathendiens would eventually turn those new cyborgs against the citizens of Aksel or too twisted to care. "Krigara, what's your status?"

"T is downloading everything he can from the research and development files while searching for information on any other Earthlings they've captured."

"How close is he to finishing?" Getting the *lekadis* and everyone else up the long vent shaft and onto the roof would be awkward, but Janwar thought that would be their wisest move now that they didn't need to search the other lab. It was only a matter of time before someone noted the guards' absence outside the lab and sounded the alarm. Then those positioned at the emergency exit around the corner would swarm inside.

Janwar glanced around. There was nothing to hide behind in here. And if they were making their way up the shaft when the alarm sounded, all the guards would have to do to kill them all was toss a grenade up it.

"I am forty-three percent finished," T responded.

So it would probably help if Janwar bought them some time. "Work faster," he ordered grimly. "Is maintenance headed our way?"

Krigara snorted. "Not inside. It looks like they opted the check the other malfunctions first so they could put off having to deal with the *grunarks* in the lab."

Simone laughed.

"But they *do* plan to send a group up to the roof to check the exterior access."

Which meant he and the others could be attacked from both above and below if they tried to exit that way. Janwar swore and met Simone's gaze.

"If they reach the hatch before us," she whispered, "all they'd have to do is drop a grenade down on us."

He nodded. Their chances would be better if they navigated the hallways here in the base. More corners to hide behind. No ice or wind to hinder Simone's movements.

"The ones inside will probably come here first," Krigara continued, "since the officers will want to ensure their domain is safe. But don't worry about us. We'll take care of them."

"Understood. We're going to head your way now with five captives: one in a *lekadis*, two limping, and two Yona we've armed. Monitor our progress and loop the feeds in the corridors as we go so security won't see us."

"Already monitoring you. I'll highlight the corridors as I loop the feeds."

"The Yona said the Gathendiens are creating cyborgs in the other lab, so be prepared to combat those once the alarm sounds."

Swears filled his ears. "Understood."

Janwar stepped over the downed Gathendiens and opened the door, his rifle at the ready.

An empty hallway greeted them. Hard to believe only a few minutes had passed since they'd taken out the guards. Since none had managed to call for help and the security feed was on a loop, maybe no one would check the hallway until either the next shift change or maintenance arrived.

He and Simone exited first. Janwar moved forward with military precision, his O-rifle at the ready.

Simone stuck close to his side with a katana in one hand and a dagger in the other, looking absolutely fierce. "When we encounter hostiles," she whispered, "You go left, I go right. You go low, I go high."

He nodded, hoping like *srul* he wouldn't accidentally shoot her. He'd never seen anyone move as fast as she could.

M'kor and Allie followed with the *lekadis* while the two Yona brought up the rear.

With the help of the real-time life-form scans in their helmets, they navigated three turns without running into anyone. Perhaps most of the personnel on the base were wise enough to give the lab areas a wide berth. *He* sure as hell would if he were stationed here.

Then their luck ran out. Three red blobs headed toward the next intersection, and he and his group were too far from the corner they'd turned to retreat and duck behind it.

"Simone," Janwar whispered. "Can you take them out quietly?" Now that they were venturing into less isolated hallways, the bright flashes of light spawned by O-rifle fire would surely draw attention, as would the brilliant flash of a Bex-7 stun grenade.

"Yes," she whispered back. "And I love you even more for asking me to do it." Before he could respond, she shot forward in a blur and disappeared around the corner. Several grunts and thuds later, she returned with a broad smile. "Done."

"What the *drek*?" M'kor whispered.

Janwar shook his head. "No time to hide the bodies. Move faster and let us know if you start to fall behind."

M'kor and Simone's friend nodded.

They hurried forward at just short of a jog, down one corridor and up the next. *Drek*, this was a big base.

Wee-wonk! Wee-wonk! Wee-wonk!

He and Simone shared a look. Then they all took off running.

"T," he ordered, "send the drones to the front of the base."

"Yes, commander," T responded. "Drones arriving in thirty, twenty-nine, twenty-ei—"

"I don't need a countdown. Just blow *bura* up."

"Yes, commander."

Simone laughed.

Blaster fire erupted behind them as the Yona defended their rear.

A door up ahead opened, and Gathendiens poured out.

Janwar fired at those on the left, aiming for their torsos as Simone's words rang in his head. *You go left, I go right. You go low, I go high.*

And *drek* did she go high, so quickly that all Janwar noted on the periphery was a black blur racing up the wall on their right and flipping over the soldiers' heads, one of which toppled to the ground.

"Get behind me," Janwar ordered Allie and M'kor as return fire struck his armor.

He took down four Gathendiens while Simone's blades flashed and eliminated the rest. Once the bodies fell, she stood facing him, her suit and helmet splattered with blood. But she sported no injuries.

Relief brought a grin to his face.

Janwar spun to check on the others.

Everyone in the group still stood.

Several soldiers lay unmoving at the other end of the corridor.

He gave the Yona warriors a nod of thanks before they resumed their race to the officers' wing.

Explosions shook the building as the alarm continued to blare.

Janwar swore when multiple red dots on his visor indicated that a relatively large number of Gathendien soldiers approached the intersection up ahead. "Simone."

"I see them."

"Here." He activated a Z-12 grenade and tossed it to her.

Catching it, she rushed forward in a blur, hurled the grenade at the oncoming soldiers, and continued past the intersection. A shout sounded just before the grenade exploded, sending flames and remains in all directions.

When the fire receded, Simone grinned at him. "That was awesome!"

Shaking his head, he caught up with her.

Allie and M'kor's breathing grew ragged behind him as the small group made their way through the base. The Gathendiens' torture had not left them in prime running condition, but they were toughing it out.

According to the life-form scan, utter chaos had erupted on the base. Explosions continually rocked the structure as soldiers scrambled to figure out what the *drek* was happening and combat attacks from within *and* without. Janwar and Simone worked well together, defending their front, while the Yona warriors industriously fought off anyone who approached from behind.

A warning light flashed on his visor. He'd taken enough hits to weaken its defenses. A few more, and he'd lose protection, enabling enemy fire to damage the suit *and* him. But they had almost reached Krigara and the others.

Another cluster of Gathendien soldiers moved to intercept them from the left at a T-shaped intersection ahead.

Janwar tossed Simone another Z-12 grenade.

She shot forward in a blur.

Light flared as a blast from an O-rifle streaked from the other hallway.

Janwar's heart stopped when Simone abruptly flew sideways and slammed into the wall on the right. Her body slumped to the floor, one shoulder smoking as the grenade she'd dropped rolled slowly toward the lurking soldiers.

"No!" Racing forward, Janwar dove for the floor, looped an arm around her as he passed, and dragged her with him as he skidded away from the intersection. Fire exploded from the other hallway, just missing them. "Simone?" When he sat up and looked at her, she appeared to be unconscious. Though the shoulder of her suit was scorched, it remained intact.

He gave her a little shake. "Simone?"

She didn't respond.

Heart pounding, Janwar pushed her against the wall and backed up to her, covering her as well as he could while he aimed his O-rifle at the smoke pouring into the intersection.

Moments later, the biggest Gathendien he'd ever seen stepped from the flames and turned to face him. Unlike the others, this one wore exo-armor like Janwar with multiple weapons attached to each limb.

Ah drek. This must be one of their cyborgs.

The Gathendien's right shoulder was scorched black. Part of his face was singed, too, indicating a weakness on that side of his armor. And his right eye glowed red when he turned toward them.

Janwar fired at that eye, the sharp *osdulium* blasts bouncing off the *grunark*'s face shield. If he could just get him to turn his head and expose more of that weak side...

A moan carried over the comm in his helmet.

"Simone?" He shifted his aim to the cyborg's arm as it rose to fire a weapon at them.

They were utterly exposed here. And he doubted his armor would be able to withstand much of whatever the *grunark* fired.

"Bastard shot me," she muttered.

"I know. But we have a bit of a situation here, honey."

The cyborg fired.

Janwar grunted when the blast hit his side with the force of an android's punch. *Osdulium.* He could take a few more of those but needed to figure out how to kill the *grunark* before he flung anything more deadly at them.

"Did he just shoot you?" Simone demanded, sounding more alert and outraged.

"Yes. As I said—" He grunted, taking another round as he continued to fire at the cyborg to weaken his armor. "We have a situation."

"He shot you *again*? Oh *hell*, no!"

When she squirmed beneath him, he tried to hold her down. "You won't be able to penetrate his armor. And he'll see you coming no matter how fast you move."

"I penetrated a fucking transport," she declared furiously. "I can damn well penetrate his armor."

Oh. Right. "But he'll still see you coming, and you won't be able to decapitate him or break his neck as easily because they've probably reinforced his skeletal system with *alavinin*." The next time Janwar took a hit, red warnings flashed urgently across his visor, and he was pretty sure the impact cracked a rib.

The cyborg jerked suddenly and glanced over his shoulder.

Through the smoke, Janwar could just make out the two Yona warriors firing *tronium* blasters while Allie and M'kor ducked behind the *lekadis* that shielded the unconscious Purveli male.

The cyborg turned toward the Yona.

Simone shoved Janwar off and stuffed her hand in one of his pockets. Before he could shout a protest, she raced forward with that exceptional speed of hers and leaped up high.

His mouth fell open when she landed on the cyborg's shoulders, tucked her ankles under his arms, and started stabbing at the edge of his helmet with a dagger.

The cyborg staggered backward, caught off guard.

The Yona lowered their fire to his legs.

Janwar stumbled to his feet and shot the *grunark* in the ass and tail, every hit weakening the cyborg's armor further and diverting his attention from the woman wobbling on his shoulders.

Suddenly, the cyborg's helmet flew off.

Grabbing the Gathendien by the forehead, Simone yanked his head back. When his jaw dropped open in surprise, she shoved a Bex-7 stun grenade inside his mouth and clamped both hands over it.

Janwar's eyes widened. *Oh, drek.*

He waved at the others. "Get back! Get back!"

The Yona warriors tackled Allie and M'kor, taking them to the floor.

Janwar raced forward, intending to do the same to Simone as soon as she leapt free.

But she didn't leap free. She clung tenaciously to the struggling Gathendien, never relinquishing her grip.

Blue light erupted from the cyborg's eyes and nose and poured through the fingers Simone clamped over his mouth. As the Gathendien jerked and spasmed, more crackled over the surface of his armor, which seemed to contain most of the Bex-7 stun grenade's blast.

Atop his shoulders, Simone stiffened as the blue light swept up her arms and legs and everywhere else she touched him.

Janwar ran toward them, absolute terror infusing him. A stunner could incapacitate soldiers twice and thrice her weight. She was so much smaller. Would it harm her more? Would it stop her heart? She'd said if she died, her body would deteriorate within minutes. If this stopped her heart, would he even have time to try to revive her before—

The blue light vanished.

The cyborg wavered, then toppled forward, taking Simone with him.

Janwar grabbed her before she hit the floor and sank to his knees. "Simone?"

Her body twitched in his arms, muscles convulsing from the electricity zipping through her.

Why the *srul* had he tuned all the Bex-7s to the highest settings?

"Simone?" He was on the brink of breaking his own rule and removing both their helmets when her eyes fluttered open.

Bright amber irises locked with his. "*M-merde*," she gritted with a final twitch. "Th-That hurt l-like a bitch."

Laughing with relief, Janwar hugged her as close as his armor would allow.

"Did I get him?" she wheezed.

"Yes, you got him. Even though it scared the *srul* out of me, shoving the Bex-7 in his mouth was brilliant." It had likely fried all of the cybernetic implants in his brain and taken him down much faster and more efficiently than trying to penetrate his armor would have.

"Good. Help me up, will you?" she said, sounding more like herself, if a little cranky.

Janwar ignored the painful protest of his ribs and rose, pulling her up with him.

Grimacing, she placed her hands on her lower back and arched it, pushing her chest out. "Damn, I feel old."

"Me, too." He felt as if he'd aged thirty solar orbits in just the past few seconds. "But we aren't safe yet."

She looked around a moment, then retrieved the sword she'd dropped when she'd been shot and—just like that— was ready to dive back into battle.

Drek, he loved her.

On the other side of the downed cyborg, Denu helped M'kor and Allie up. None of them appeared hurt. And the *lekadis* still protected the unconscious Purveli.

Vedon walked over to the cyborg, aimed his *tronium* blaster at the back of the Gathendien's head, and fired. "In case his cybernetics are stronger than the Bex-7."

Janwar nodded.

Krigara's voice carried over the comm, accompanied by rifle fire. "Janwar? Why did you stop? Do you need backup?"

"No. Simone just needed to kick a little ass. You taking fire?"

"Yeah. But we're handling it. T just completed the download."

Janwar waved for the others to follow him and took off jogging again. "Good. We're almost there."

"Keep an eye out for the officers. It looks like almost every one of the cowardly *grunarks* is heading this way, ready to flee the base."

Janwar grunted.

They did encounter a couple of officers but took them out quickly. The only other soldiers they ran into attacked them from behind and were swiftly defeated by Vedon and Denu.

At last, they swung around a corner and found Krigara, Elchan, and Soval waiting in front of the opening of a tunnel that looked as if it had been carved out of ice.

Elchan's armor flickered as his camouflage fluctuated. One second, he appeared to be there. The next, he faded into the background and seemed to vanish. Then he reappeared again.

"Where's T?" Janwar asked as they tromped toward the trio.

"Firing up the transport."

"Any hostiles outside?" Janwar positioned himself on one side of the tunnel and gestured for the others to enter ahead of him.

"No." Krigara grinned as Vedon pushed the *lekadis* into the tunnel. Denu urged Allie and M'kor to enter, then ducked inside behind them. "T is attacking with more enthusiasm than we anticipated. I think this is the only entrance or exit to the base and the hangar that hasn't been completely demolished."

Shaking his head, Janwar rested a hand on Simone's back and drew her with him into the narrow passage. Firing erupted behind them.

"Grenade," Soval called. As he, Krigara, and Elchan joined them in the tunnel, an explosion rumbled through the corridor they'd just left.

Cracks crawled across the surface of the ice above their heads as fine white powder sifted down.

Janwar swore. "Don't blow up the *drekking* mountain while we're still under it!"

His friends laughed as they reached a broader space that housed the outdated officers' transport. Krigara had melted a sizable hole in the exterior wall to gain access.

Janwar and the others hustled through it and stepped into a blizzard. The transport that had carried them from the *Tangata* waited outside, engines running. But the only part visible was the glimpse of the interior the lowered ramp revealed.

He glanced toward the front of the base. Flames reached for the sky as K-6 drones zipped back and forth, firing at targets he couldn't see through snow and heavy smoke the wind tossed around.

Return fire was sporadic at best.

Once they all piled into the transport, he and Vedon secured the *lekadis* to one wall. Then everyone found seats and strapped themselves in. Simone sat beside her friend while Krigara replaced T-2 as pilot. Janwar claimed the co-pilot's seat.

No one fired on the transport as it lifted off and sped away. The Gathendiens likely had never even been aware of its presence, cloaked as it was. But Janwar didn't allow himself to breathe a sigh of relief until they left the moon's atmosphere and approached the *Tangata*'s bay.

He glanced back at Simone, who murmured reassurances to Allie as her friend clung to her as much as their harnesses and suits would allow.

She met his gaze. "We did it."

And they'd all made it out alive.

He smiled. "We did it."

CHAPTER EIGHTEEN

S IMONE BIT HER LIP as she paced the bridge and stared through the *Tangata*'s windshield.

As soon as they had made it back on board, Janwar had bombed the crap out of the base, reducing it to a smoldering pile of rubble and kicking off one hell of a landslide in the mountain behind it that completed the base's obliteration.

Chalk one up for the good guys. They'd struck quite a blow with their little rescue.

Almost forty-eight hours had passed since then. Everyone they rescued had visited Med Bay, received treatment, and settled in. Thanks to several consultations with Chief Medic Adaos on the *Ranasura*, Luft'a was recovering from the virus he'd been infected with and posed no threat to them. Allie was, too. The rest had been cleared medically after undergoing standard decontamination procedures.

Since Simone spent all of her nights with Janwar, she offered Allie her former room. The Purvelis assured them they'd be comfortable staying in Med Bay. And the two Yona opted to bunk in the training room, which was the only other chamber that had a connecting lav with showers.

The *Tangata* would never qualify as a cruise ship. As far as Simone knew, this was only the third time Janwar had had guests.

At this point, Simone would've thought she, Janwar, and the rest of the *Tangata* crew would be able to breathe a giant sigh of relief, having successfully infiltrated the base and completed their mission without suffering losses or serious injuries. Simone's bruised shoulder had healed after a transfusion. And Janwar's ribs were mending swiftly, thanks to a *silna*.

But they hadn't heard anything from Kova since their return.

Even more worrisome, T couldn't tell them where Kova was.

According to T, all hell had broken loose after Kova found Liz, one of the missing *gifted ones*, and liberated her from her cell. A battle had ensued. The T-4 android that accompanied him had been destroyed, as had the T-7 in the backup fighter craft. And the Gathendiens had blown up the drones when they attacked the ship to create a diversion while Kova and Liz escaped.

"You don't know what kind of craft they're in or which direction they went?" Simone asked for the fourth or fifth time.

"I do not," T repeated. "Prior to the destruction of my T-4 android form, I was only able to infiltrate the warship's comms, not those of every craft aboard it."

She looked at Janwar, who lounged in the commander's chair.

"I'm sure they're fine," he said.

"Then why hasn't he contacted us?"

"If he's in a Gathendien craft, he may not want to use the comms until he modifies them enough to ensure other Gathendiens won't hear his messages."

She bit her lip. Yeah. That would be pretty bad. A Gathendien warship against two people in—what—a transport? Escape pod? T seemed to think the stealth craft they'd arrived in had been destroyed. "Well, why haven't we caught up with them?"

"Gathendiens have many enemies. Their transports and escape pods tend to be faster than the norm."

"So anyone they piss off won't catch them when they run away?"

"Yes."

She resumed pacing.

Wondering how Janwar could be so calm when one of his men was missing, Simone reached out with her gift and realized he was far more concerned than he let on. He was just manifesting a relaxed façade to try to ease her worry.

Elchan stiffened suddenly and touched his ear. "I have them!"

She was beside him a heartbeat later.

Eyes wide, Elchan jumped about a foot. "*Drek!* Don't do that."

Simone winced when she heard the rapid pounding of his heart. She hadn't meant to startle him. "Sorry. Did you find Kova?"

"Yes. Krigara, I'm sending you their coordinates now."

"Are they okay?" she pressed.

Elchan smiled. "They're okay. The Gathendien language isn't Kova's strength, so it took him a while to work his way through their coding and alter it to ensure all messages he sent out would remain private."

"And Liz is with him?"

"Yes. He said she'll need some time in Med Bay but should make a full recovery."

Tears welled in her eyes as Simone turned to face Janwar. "She's going to need time in Med Bay." What had those bastards done to her?

He waved her over. "But she'll make a full recovery."

As soon as she was within reach, Janwar drew her down on his lap.

Simone leaned into him, tucking her head beneath his chin. *Would* Liz make a full recovery? Every time Allie dozed off, she woke up screaming, something Simone's superlative hearing allowed her to hear from down the hallway. And it would take weeks for Allie to reach a healthy weight again.

Simone hated to think how close her friend had come to dying and worried about the long-term detrimental effects her torture and confinement would have, not just on her body but on her mind.

Eliana had told her Ava still suffered terrible nightmares that only Jak'ri's presence seemed to quell. Would Liz suffer the same now that she was free?

"How long will it take us to reach them?" she asked, wanting Kova and Liz safe. Right now.

"At top speed, we'll reach them in five hours," Krigara said.

Three hours later, they had to veer around a vast debris field they ultimately concluded was all that remained of the Gathendien ship Kova and Liz had fled. That brought the tally up to three Gathendien warships and one primary research and development base that Earthlings and Aldebarian Alliance members had either destroyed or commandeered since the bastards had attacked the *Kandovar*.

If you mess with the bull, you get the horns, assholes, Simone thought with relish.

Another two and a half hours found Simone standing in the *Tangata*'s largest docking bay, shifting her weight from foot to foot. Janwar waited patiently on one side of her while Allie stood on the other, just as restless as Simone. Both women were garbed like Immortal Guardians in the *Tangata*'s closest equivalent of black cargo pants, T-shirts, and boots.

The rest of the *Tangata* crew and the two Yona—Vedon and Denu—formed a semicircle behind them. M'Kor had chosen to remain in Med Bay and keep Luft'a company.

When the massive bay doors opened, Allie's jaw dropped. "Wow," she breathed as deep space was revealed in all of its stunning glory.

Simone found a smile as she took her friend's hand. "I know. It's beautiful, isn't it?"

"It really is."

The transport that eased inside, on the other hand, was as ugly as the Gathendiens' nature. Simone had grown accustomed to the sleek designs of Janwar and Taelon's warships, transports, and assorted craft. This looked like a junky, clunky piece of crap by comparison. It was hard to believe a dungheap like that could travel so swiftly.

And what was with the pukey yellow color?

As the bay doors closed, the transport lowered to the deck. Docking clamps rose and secured it with a thunk.

Allie's hand tightened on Simone's.

A minute passed. Then another.

"What's taking so long?" Simone exclaimed, ready to race forward and pound on the hatch.

Beside her, Janwar frowned. "I don't know. Perhaps they're more injured than Kova led us to believe and are moving slowly."

Well, hell. That wasn't what she wanted to hear.

Finally, the transport's hatch opened, and a ramp lowered to the deck.

Kova strode forth from the darkness.

She frowned. No, not strode. Limped. He hadn't mentioned that *he* had been injured.

The fact that he retained that limp made her wonder how badly Liz had been hurt. Liz was a healer. She could mend many wounds with a touch of her hands and wouldn't have hesitated to heal Kova if she'd been capable of it.

The only reason she *wouldn't* have been capable was if her own injuries were either too severe or too numerous.

Releasing Allie's hand, Simone strode forward and wrapped Kova in a bear hug. "You made it."

After a momentary surprise, he hugged her back. "So did you."

Stepping back, she smiled up at him. "How could I not after T delivered your message?"

A flush crept into his scarred cheeks.

But she didn't tease him about it. "Where's Liz?"

"She's coming. But you'll want to step back and give her some room."

Give her some room? What the hell did that mean?

At his direction, she returned to stand between Janwar and Allie.

Rhythmic thumps sounded inside the transport, almost like footsteps but much louder.

Simone's eyes nearly popped out of her head when a huge, hulking figure emerged from the shadowy interior and ducked to make it through the exit.

Her mouth fell open.

It had to be at least eight or nine freaking feet tall and looked like a massive metal warrior. Or robot. Or… hell, she didn't know.

Dismay hit her with the force of a fist. Had the Gathendiens turned Liz into some kind of robowarrior? Was that possible? Was that even a thing?

The Gathendiens on the base had been creating cyborgs, but the one she'd seen had been an ordinary Gathendien with enhancements and had looked *nothing* like this.

Clunk. Clunk. Clunk. Down the ramp, it marched.

"What the *drek*?" Janwar muttered.

Merde. If even Janwar didn't know what this was, how could they hope to undo it?

The warrior machine halted at the base of the ramp. A long moment passed, during which Simone's heart pounded in her chest. Then the visor on the machine's helmet rose, revealing Liz's sweet face.

Was that *armor*? "Holy Lieutenant Ripley," Simone breathed in awe.

Liz faked a scowl and snarled, "Get away from her, you *bitch!*"

The men all gaped.

Well, all of them but the Yona.

But Simone burst into laughter at the quote from *Aliens*, one of her all-time favorite sci-fi movies. Liz *did* sort of remind her of Ellen Ripley in the mechanical armor or whatever. "That is so freaking awesome!" she shouted and skipped forward.

Liz grinned as the warrior machine's torso, upper arms, and legs peeled open, revealing the rest of her.

Like Eliana, Liz was petite and stood only an inch or so above five feet. Surrounded by the machine's bulk, she looked even tinier. She was also almost as emaciated as Allie and bore multiple wounds and scars on the arms and legs bared by her shorts and wraparound shirt.

Simone struggled not to frown. *Gifted one* and immortal healers always recovered at an accelerated rate. Why did Liz still sport those wounds? What had the Gathendiens done to dampen her gift and keep her from healing?

Stepping between Simone and the machine, Kova reached up and lifted Liz down.

Once her small feet—encased in socks Simone suspected were Kova's—touched the deck, she smiled up at him. "Thank you."

Nodding, Kova stepped aside so Simone could drag her into a hug. Then Allie joined them, and the three women clung to each other, bursting into tears while the men stood around, looking awkward.

Except for the Yona. Those guys *never* showed emotion. Only Valok ever had, thanks to her empathic gift. But Simone couldn't let herself think of him right now or she would never stop crying.

"I can't believe you found me," Liz muttered, her voice thick with tears. "I'd almost given up hope."

"Same here," Allie admitted. "They found me on a Gathendien military base."

Liz drew back and wiped her eyes. "The Gathendiens captured you, too?" Concern darkened her features as she took in Allison's fragile appearance.

Allie nodded.

Liz turned to Simone. "What about you? Did they capture you, too?"

"Nope." She forced a cocky smile to hide her concern. "I kicked their asses."

Both women laughed. "Of course, you did," they said in unison.

Janwar joined them now that their tears had ebbed. "She also commandeered one of their ships."

Liz stared up at him, blinked twice, then leaned closer to Simone and whispered, "Am I losing it, or did Jack Sparrow just walk up and put his arm around you?"

Simone laughed at the pained look that crossed Janwar's face. "He isn't Jack Sparrow. This is Commander Janwar of the *Tangata*. He and his crew just destroyed the military base that held Allie, two Yona, and two Purvelis captive."

"With Simone's help," he added, his smile returning. "We couldn't have done it without her."

Aww. He's such a sweetheart.

Expression somber, Liz shifted her gaze to Simone. "Who else made it? The Gathendiens said they destroyed the *Kandovar*."

"They did," Simone confirmed. "We're still trying to determine how many survived. Most of the escape pods deployed safely before the explosion, but they were scattered throughout vast sectors of space. And we don't know how many—if any—fighter craft made it through the battle. A massive alliance-wide search and rescue operation is currently underway, and they're steadily finding Lasarans."

"What about Earthlings and Yona?" she asked.

Simone sent Vedon and Denu apologetic looks. "So far, the only Yona warriors recovered alive have been the royal guard. Janwar and his crew rescued them along with Lisa, Taelon, and baby Abby. They're all safely on Lasara now. The Segonians found Eliana and Ava a while later. There's quite a story to tell there. We just found

Allie two days ago. But the rest of us from Earth we aren't sure about."

Liz swallowed hard. "So ten of us are still missing?"

"Yes."

Somber silence fell.

Janwar rubbed Simone's shoulder. "Don't forget: T is scouring the information he downloaded from the Gathendien ship. We're hoping it will lead us to the others."

"Wait," Allie said all of a sudden. "Are you *the* Janwar? The pirate I heard a couple of Lasarans whispering about?"

Janwar glanced at Simone. "Yes."

Allie smacked herself in the forehead with her palm. "How did I not realize that before?"

Liz looked back and forth between them. "Seriously? That's a thing? There are space pirates?"

Simone laughed. "Yes. But don't worry. He's the good kind." Rising onto her toes, she kissed his bearded cheek. "And he's *my* pirate."

Janwar grinned down at her.

"Uh-huh," Liz said, her eyebrows nearly touching her hairline. "I see we have some catching up to do."

Janwar sent her a kind smile. "Let's get you to Med Bay first. I see you've some wounds that need tending."

"Thank you. I would appreciate that."

They turned toward the exit. Simone carefully kept her smile in place when Liz limped along beside her.

As they came abreast of Kova, Liz reached out and snagged his hand. "You, too," she said.

Much to Simone's surprise, Kova let her tug him along after her.

Simone glanced up at Janwar and raised her brows.

Pursing his lips thoughtfully, he shrugged.

Maybe Simone and Eliana weren't the only ones with stories to tell.

S ITTING AT A TABLE in the lounge, Janwar sipped his drink and smiled as he watched the activity taking place in front of the large vid screen.

The chair beside him slid back, and Segonian Commander Dagon dropped into it.

Two Purveli males—Jak'ri and Ziv'ri—joined them.

Dagon smiled. "They're something, aren't they?"

Janwar nodded. "Something special."

Another highly emotional reunion had taken place when the *Ranasura* at last docked with the *Tangata* three days ago. Now five Earth females sat shoulder-to-shoulder on the cushy sofa, passing snacks back and forth and chattering happily as they watched an Earth entertainment vid called *Aliens* that Kova had successfully transferred from Simone's phone to the large view screen.

Dagon and the Purvelis were the only males from the *Ranasura* present. Janwar had insisted all others remain aboard the Segonian warship, not wanting anyone curious about his unusually advanced technology to wander around, snooping.

The two Yona—Vedon and Denu—were sparring in the training room, as were M'kor and Luft'a, who struggled to regain the strength they'd lost at the Gathendiens' torturous hands. But the rest of the *Tangata* crew loitered in here with Janwar and the others, enchanted by the boisterous behavior and laughter of the Earthlings in their midst.

Jak'ri, Ava's lifemate, nodded at the vid screen. "If *that* is Earthlings' conception of aliens, I'm surprised their leader allowed the females to venture into space."

All laughed as they regarded the revolting, drooling creature with its jagged teeth.

"Do you think he'll send more?" Ziv'ri asked, his tone a bit wistful.

Janwar shook his head. "I've spoken with him several times. Seth is unwilling to risk the females' safety and made it very clear that no more Earthlings would travel to Lasara until the Gathendien threat is under control."

Dagon snorted. "I'm not certain that will ever be the case. Those *grunarks* are tenacious."

All nodded.

Krigara joined them, taking the seat on Janwar's other side. "*We could get them there safely.*"

Janwar turned to him in surprise. "What?"

"We could convey Earthlings safely to Lasara." His cousin shrugged. "We've defeated the Gathendiens at every turn and are the only ones in the galaxy with the balls to actively seek confrontations with them."

Janwar grinned at Krigara's use of the Earth word for *insisas*.

"Oh no, you're wrong there," Ziv'ri said with a chuckle and pointed to the women who appeared unfazed by the gory violence transpiring on the screen. "I believe those women have bigger balls than all of us."

What could the men do but laugh and agree?

Janwar shook his head as he eyed his cousin. "You think turning the *Tangata* into a cruise ship is the answer?"

Ziv'ri grunted. "I think Krigara is simply looking for a means to meet more Earth females. And I don't blame him." He met Janwar's gaze. "If you end up doing it, I would happily join your crew."

Jak'ri shook his head. "You have to help me convince our government to quit *drekking* around and join the Aldebarian Alliance... *and* their fight against the Gathendiens. There is no question now that Purvel has become a target."

Ziv'ri swore foully. "True. But after that—"

"You have to help me terraform Purvel's moons," his brother reminded him.

More cursing.

Janwar laughed.

Simone grinned at them over her shoulder. "You've been spending too much time around Eliana, Ziv'ri. You curse like a sailor."

Eliana laughed and gave Simone a playful shove. "Shut up."

"Hey! Don't make me spill my *jarumi* nuggets," Simone protested with a chuckle.

Dagon turned to Janwar. "You do realize you're going to have to fill one of your cargo bays with bags of *jarumi* nuggets now. Earthlings *love* them."

He smiled. "No need. We make our own."

Dagon stared at him. "What?"

"We have the company's recipe."

"How the *srul* did you get that?" the Segonian asked in astonishment.

Janwar shrugged. "I'm a pirate." Though he knew the guests present would all assume he had stolen the recipe, it had actually been a gift. The producer of *jarumi* nuggets had rewarded him with it after Janwar and his crew located his son and saved the boy's life after the idiot made a series of unwise wagers, racked up too much debt with the wrong people, and went missing.

His lips turning up in amusement, Dagon shook his head. "Any chance *I* could get that recipe?"

Janwar feigned a sigh full of regret. "I'm afraid you law-abiding folk will have to acquire *jarumi* nuggets the usual way. I wouldn't want to corrupt you, after all."

Dagon laughed. "Or deprive the company of business. Eliana's appetite will probably double their profits."

"Damn straight," she called without looking back.

They laughed.

Liz twisted around on the sofa and searched the room. "Kova," she called, "come watch. This is the scene I was telling you about—the one where Ripley gets into the machine thing like me." Switching places with Allison, she settled at the end of the group and urged everyone to scoot over and make more room. Then she smiled at the Rakessian and held out her hand.

All eyes went to Kova, who tensed. Leaning against a wall in the back corner, he did *not* like being the center of attention.

"Hurry up," Liz urged with a grin and waggled her fingers. "You're going to miss it."

Rubbing his hands on his pants, he hesitantly strode toward her, as unable to resist the Earthlings' lure as the rest of them, it would seem. But *vuan*, he looked awkward.

Liz didn't appear to notice as she grabbed his hand and tugged him down to sit beside her. "Watch."

Still silent, Kova obediently watched the Earth female onscreen climb into something resembling a loading machine that was as large as Liz's monstrous mechanical armor but far more primitive.

318

Eyes glued to the screen, Simone passed Kova a bag of *jarumi* nuggets.

Janwar turned and caught Srok'a's gaze.

Expression stunned, Srok'a mouthed, *What the* drek?

Janwar couldn't help but smile.

Hours later, he and Simone bid her friends goodnight and retired to their quarters.

"What did you think of the movie?" she asked, all smiles after spending time with her friends.

"I think you could kick those aliens' asses."

Laughing, she rose onto her toes and looped her arms around his neck. "I think you're right."

Hugging her close, he rocked her from side to side. "Are you sad that your friends will leave tomorrow?"

"A little," she admitted, her smile dimming.

In the morning, Allison, M'kor, Luft'a, Vedon, and Denu would join Eliana, Dagon, Ava, Jak'ri, and Ziv'ri on the *Ranasura* and depart.

"Thank you for letting Liz stay on the *Tangata*," she murmured. "I know you don't like having strangers aboard, but you can trust her. She won't betray you."

If Simone trusted Liz, Janwar would, too. "I understand her reasons for asking and know how difficult it must have been for her to admit them to me." The smaller Earthling valiantly tried to hide the trauma she'd endured behind smiles and teasing comments, but sometimes it bled through. After being in the Gathendiens' cells for so long—first on the ship and then on the base—she now had trouble with confined spaces.

Simone sighed. "Those assholes on the ship that was taking her to the base kept her in a room so small she could barely stretch out in it when she lay on the floor. It's why she spends so much time in the park. Kova said the vast openness of it helps her."

Janwar dipped his head and nuzzled her neck. "Then she can remain with us for as long as she wishes."

Turning her head, Simone brushed his lips with a kiss, feather-light at first, then deeper and more ardent. "How did I get to be so damn lucky?" she whispered. Her body brushing his, coupled with the touch of her lips and stroke of her tongue, sent heat racing through him.

Janwar pressed her even tighter, aligning their hips. "Hmm?" He buried his face in the long hair she'd left loose tonight, loving her scent. Even a *scleruvian* aphrodisiac couldn't affect him as strongly.

"I ventured into space to watch over my friends while they fell in love and ended up falling in love myself instead."

Raising his head, he met her gaze and found glowing amber eyes assessing him.

"I love you, Janwar. More every day."

Joy filled him as it always did when she spoke those words. "I love you, Simone."

She claimed another scorching kiss, then gave his chest a little pat. "Now back your handsome ass up so I can tackle you to the bed."

Laughing, he took a few steps backward, taking her with him.

But a package resting atop the covers drew her attention.

"What's that?" Releasing him, she picked it up.

"A gift."

Her smile stretched as her features lit with pleasure. "For me?"

He nodded.

"Awww. Thank you." She gave him a quick kiss. "Wait. It *is* from you, isn't it?"

He laughed. "Yes."

"Awww. Thank you," she repeated and kissed him again before eagerly tearing into the package.

A shirt fell out. Puzzled, she grabbed it by the shoulders and held it up for inspection. Her eyes widened. A huge grin blossomed. Splashed across the chest was an image of Simone riding the Dotharian with the words *Simone the Dotharian Conqueror* scrawled above it in Earth English.

"I love it!" she shouted with glee. "It's perfect! You are so freaking awesome!" Still clinging to the shirt with one hand, she drew him down for a more exuberant kiss. "I am so wearing this while we make love."

"Oh no, you're not." Janwar grabbed the shirt and tossed it on the bedside table. When she laughed and lunged for it, he growled and looped his arms around her waist, lifting her off her feet. "You aren't wearing anything." He kissed her long and hard, his body already burning for her. By the time he lifted his lips, both were breathless and eager for more. "Beginning in two minutes."

She nodded. "Let's make it one. I'll just have to wear the shirt tomorrow."

Grinning, Janwar fell back on the bed with her.

EPILOGUE

"COMMANDER JANWAR."

Janwar's eyes flew open at the faint call.

He glanced down at Simone. Curled up beside him, she slept deeply with a hand on his chest and a thigh draped across his.

"Commander Janwar," the low voice came again.

Reaching over, he grabbed his ear comm off the bedside table and inserted it. "T?" he said softly.

"Yes, commander. You have an urgent incoming communication."

Frowning, Janwar carefully extricated himself from Simone's pliant form and slipped out of bed.

"Did I wake Simone?" T asked.

He stared down at her.

Brow puckering, she slid a hand over the sheets, then rolled into the spot he'd occupied and sighed.

He smiled. "No. Give me a minute and send the communication to my office."

"Yes, commander."

Once he donned a loose shirt and pants, Janwar padded barefoot to his office.

A transparent panel hovering above his desk lit up as he sank into his chair.

Incoming Communication

Code 39712
Designation: Urgent
Frowning, he opened communications.

A familiar face filled the screen. The male's features were Akseli, but his dark hair was cut short. A scar marred one cheek near his ear where he'd either cut or burned away the ident bar he'd been labeled with. A couple of thinner scars formed slashes beneath it to deter suspicion. Though the male was twenty or thirty solar orbits older than Janwar, they appeared to be the same age. Aside from the scars, Wonick hadn't changed at all since the day Chancellor Astennuh had deemed Janwar and Krigara terrorists and sent Wonick and Savaas to bring them in for execution before they'd fled Aksel.

"Wonick? What's up?"

The male glanced to one side as though ensuring none were listening.

Janwar had always found the cyborgs who had secretly escaped decommissioning—some with his aid—to be a somber lot. With good reason. If anyone discovered they'd survived, the Akseli cyborgs would be hunted as mercilessly as the Gathendiens now hunted Earthlings and would never know peace again.

But today, Wonick seemed anxious, his expression more animated than usual. "You told us to monitor every communication that passes through our sector and keep an ear out for any mention of Earthlings."

Surprised, Janwar leaned forward. "Did you find something?"

"Yes. An Earth female in a Lasaran escape pod is headed our way."

Excitement shot through him. Simone would be thrilled that another of her friends had survived. "Is she well?"

"Yes." His face twisted in a scowl. "And very loud. If she doesn't shut the *drek* up, she will attract every predator in the galaxy."

"What do you mean?"

"She's broadcasting on every channel—*every drekking* channel, *every drekking* night, sometimes for hours at a time. And last night, she dared the *drekking* Gathendiens to try to capture her!"

That was a lot of *dreks*. And if Wonick weren't trying to keep his voice down, Janwar suspected he would've bellowed the last.

Interesting. Wonick usually only got this worked up when they failed to rescue one of his fellow cyborgs or succeeded but found the cyborg in horrific condition.

"She did *what?*" Janwar asked belatedly.

"I told her not to. I warned her that the Gathendiens would kill her if they found her, and the female just laughed and said, *They can try.*"

"Wait. You've been talking to her?" As far as Janwar knew, he was the only one the cyborgs ever communicated with. Understandably paranoid, they kept their location and the fact that they still lived and breathed a secret from the rest of the galaxy.

Wonick clamped his lips together and seemed to wage an internal battle before admitting, "We've also been monitoring a Gathendien ship that will soon be close enough to pick up her transmissions. I had to warn her."

"I'm surprised Savaas let you."

Savaas was the self-proclaimed leader of the few remaining cyborgs. He had been one of the first soldiers to volunteer for the program. The first to survive the excruciating surgeries. The first to be touted as a success. And the first to refuse to obey orders when he'd been sent to kill Janwar and Krigara but chose to listen to them instead. Savaas had led the ensuing cyborg rebellion. And when the government had hurled so many soldiers at them that even cyborgs with their many enhancements couldn't hope for victory, he had gotten as many off-planet as he could and led them into hiding.

Tragically, a majority had been slain.

Savaas had considered every death a personal failure and became obsessed with keeping the rest safe. Had the life they'd eked out afterward not been so stark—their struggle to survive on their own one full of deprivation and despair—Janwar thought they would've disappeared into the ether with no one ever knowing they still existed.

But Savaas wasn't satisfied with merely keeping his fellow cyborgs alive. He couldn't bear their suffering and wanted them to find contentment if that were all they would be allotted. So mere days after Hanon had died and Janwar had become a cargo ship captain, Savaas had contacted him.

Naturally, Janwar had jumped at the chance to repay the kindness Savaas and Wonick had paid him by sparing his life. He and Krigara immediately began making cargo deliveries to the cyborgs, who had sought refuge in an abandoned mine on a *srul*-hole planet no one looked at twice. And in the years since, Janwar had found a habitable planet halfway across the galaxy they could call home and procured whatever supplies, tools, and technology they needed to build their community. He'd also carefully dispersed rumors over the galactic net that the planet was a hostile wasteland with neither a breathable atmosphere nor profitable resources.

No ships went near the place. And the cyborgs wanted to keep it that way.

A muscle in Wonick's jaw jumped, making his scars twitch. "Savaas doesn't know."

"That you've been talking to her?"

"Yes."

"How is that even possible?" The two cyborgs were like brothers.

They *all* were like brothers. Shared trauma tended to forge strong bonds. If one knew something, the rest usually did, too.

Again, that twitch. "I talk to her while the others sleep," he grumbled reluctantly.

Janwar stared. "That makes it sound like you've spoken to her more than once."

The guilt that suffused Wonick's face confirmed it.

"How many times have you talked to her?" Janwar asked curiously.

Wonick's brows drew down in another scowl. "More than once," the stubborn *grunark* said, refusing to give a more informative answer.

"Well, if you two have become best buddies," he offered dryly, using one of Simone's terms, "tell her to haul ass to your homeworld and keep her safe. She's probably just trying to provoke someone into coming to get her before her oxygen supply runs out. There can't be much left at this point."

"There isn't. And I can't. No one is allowed to land here. You know the rules. We can't risk discovery."

"You won't risk anything if you help her. The Earth female will keep your secret. Trust me."

"*You* we trust. Others we never will."

"Wonick, I'm telling you she won't betray you. She won't share knowledge of either your existence or your location with anyone else. I'm certain of it."

"You don't even know her."

"No. But I have an Earth female on board the *Tangata* whom I would trust with my life. *Everyone on this ship* would trust her with our lives. And we're as paranoid as you are." He leaned back in his chair. "I've also met four others who are just as honorable. I guarantee you every Earth female who was aboard the *Kandovar* will keep your confidence. One of the reasons they left Earth was because they're different from ordinary Earthlings. Like you, they're unique and were treated harshly because of it. Hunted even. They know how *drekked* up that is and will empathize with you. Contact the female and guide her to your home."

"Savaas has ordered us to destroy any craft that breaches our atmosphere. He will not change his mind. You need to come get her."

Frustration burned through Janwar. "I can't! We're docked with the *Ranasura*."

"The Segonian warship?"

"Yes."

There was no question that he had astonished his friend. "Why?" He scowled. "Do they intend to commandeer your ship and turn you over to Chancellor Astennuh?"

Janwar snorted. "As if *anyone* could commandeer my ship. No. We recently infiltrated a Gathendien warship, then took out one of their primary research and development bases."

Wonick could not look more astonished. "You and the Segonians? You're working together?"

"No, just the *Tangata* crew and Simone."

"Who is Simone?"

"The Earth female I told you we'd trust with our lives. Our missions enabled us to rescue two Earthlings, two Yona, and a couple of Purvelis."

"The Gathendiens are targeting Purvelis and Yona now?"

"Undoubtedly. One of the Earth females has chosen to remain with us. The rest will transfer to the *Ranasura*. We'll undock tomorrow."

Wonick studied him with something akin to fascination. "You intend to keep two Earth females aboard the *Tangata*?"

"Yes."

He issued a decisive nod. "Then contact this one so she'll stop daring Gathendiens, mercenaries, and every other *drekker* out there to *come and get her*." The last four words reeked of frustration, as though Wonick were repeating the female's dare word for word.

It *did* sound suspiciously like a challenge Simone would issue.

Janwar threw up his hands. "Contact her and tell her *what*? That we're too far away to reach her before her oxygen supply runs out?"

The cyborg speared his fingers through his hair, his agitation growing. "Well, you have to do *something*!"

"No, *you* have to do something. Change Savaas's mind. Talk him into bringing her to your world. The AI in her pod has probably already told her the atmosphere there is toxic." All *bura*, of course. In reality, it was a lovely planet that teemed with life. But the cyborgs could hack any database in the galaxy and had filled them all with false information to deter visitors and explorers. "If you don't contact her, she'll think the Gathendiens are her only option."

"I spoke to Savaas when she first came into range. He adamantly refused to let her land here. He isn't going to change his mind. You know how fanatical he is about maintaining our safety."

"And he was just as fanatical about obeying orders until *I* changed his mind. You can change his mind, too. Tell him I'll vouch for her and—" He broke off when the office door slid up.

Simone stood on the other side, her lengthy hair rumpled and her eyelids a little heavy. She looked as if she had just woken up, tugged one of his shirts on, and come looking for him. He would bet quite a few credits that she wasn't wearing anything under that. Fortunately, his shirt covered her petite form almost to her knees.

He smiled.

She was so *drekking* adorable. How had he come to be so fortunate?

Giving him a sleepy smile that eradicated his irritation, she entered. "Hi, babe. What are you doing?"

Janwar debated a few seconds before announcing, "Another Earthling has been located." He knew Simone would never betray the cyborgs. Let Wonick and Savaas try to refuse *her* entreaties and see where it got them.

"What?" Hurrying around the desk, she plopped down on his lap and peered at the screen. "When? Where'd you find her? Who is it? How is she? Is she okay? Is she hurt? Are you the one who rescued her? Is she safe?"

Wonick froze, his eyes as wide as Janwar imagined they would be if someone had just tossed a grenade and he'd caught it thinking it a harmless *doba* fruit.

Silence fell... and stretched.

Simone frowned. "What's wrong?" She leaned closer to the screen. "Did we lose the connection?"

Janwar hastily grabbed her hands before she could start poking at the console and accidentally close comms.

"You didn't lose the connection," Wonick intoned.

"And you're back!" Simone exclaimed brightly, throwing her arms up in celebration. "Hi. I didn't introduce myself. I'm sorry. That was rude of me. I'm Simone. It's nice to meet you."

Wonick stared.

Her brow furrowed. "Damn it. He froze again. What's happening? Is it buffering? Because if it is, I have to tell you my admiration for alien technology just took a nosedive."

Amusement wrung a smile from him. "It isn't buffering. He's just shocked."

"By what? My appearance?" Glancing down, she tugged his shirt over her knees. "Well, if I'd known you were video conferencing, I would've donned something more appropriate." She combed her fingers through her hair to tidy it, but it still looked delightfully rumpled.

"It isn't that," Janwar said. "He's never seen an Earthling before." If Wonick had been videocomming the other Earthling instead of just using audio, he wouldn't look so flabbergasted.

Wonick studied her with avid curiosity. "You look Lasaran."

"So I've been told," she responded with a smile. "But I don't think a Lasaran woman would walk the *Tangata*'s hallways garbed only in a man's shirt."

The cyborg's eyes narrowed. "You're too small and pale to be a Segonian. But you could be a Segonian/Lasaran half-breed."

She wrinkled her nose. "Really? Half-breed? Is that term still used out here?"

"Wonick has trust issues," Janwar inserted. "He's doubting you're an Earthling."

Simone rolled her eyes. "Oh, brother. Is he your friend? Do you trust him to keep a confidence?"

"Entirely."

She turned back to the screen. "Then Wonick, can Lasarans or Segonians do this?" Those big brown eyes of hers flashed bright amber. Then she bared her teeth in a silent snarl.

Janwar's eyebrows flew up when pointy fangs descended from her gums, looking as dangerous as those of the large jungle predators on Aksel. "You have fangs?" he blurted.

Eyes widening, she clamped a hand over her mouth and turned sideways on his lap so she could face him. "Yes," she said hesitantly behind her fingers. "Retractable ones. I didn't think to tell you because... well, I forgot. I haven't had to use them since coming aboard the *Tangata*. If I need a transfusion, I just get one from the Med Bay thingy." When she lowered her hand, the fangs were gone. But her eyes continued to glow.

"There *have* been a few distractions." He rubbed her back soothingly. "You use them to infuse yourself when you need blood?"

She nibbled her lower lip. "Yes."

"Why do you look so worried? You think I'm going to love you less now that I know your teeth are different?"

"No." She smiled sheepishly. "Sorry. Force of habit. The fangs never went over well on Earth."

"Then you *are* an Earthling?" Wonick asked, leaning forward. "Do all Earthlings look like you?"

"Do all..." She glanced at Janwar. "What is he?"

"Cyborg."

She swung back to Wonick. "Do all cyborgs look like you?"

Wonick's eyes widened.

So did Simone's. "Wait. You're a cyborg?"

The look of betrayal on Wonick's face made Janwar's stomach clench.

But Simone didn't seem to notice it. Nearly bouncing with excitement, she studied his friend. "It's so nice to meet you," she gushed. "Are you *the* cyborg? The one who was supposed to execute Janwar but didn't?"

"One of them," Wonick growled.

"Oh, my goodness! Then it's doubly nice to meet you. Thank you so much for saving his life. I owe you a great debt."

Both males stared at her.

"What?" Janwar asked.

"If you hadn't saved him," she continued, "I would never have met him. He wouldn't have saved my life. The damned Gathendiens would've succeeded in killing me. And I wouldn't have fallen head over heels in love with him. If you knew how long I've waited for the last, you'd understand how much that means to me. And now you've found one of my friends? I can't thank you enough."

Wonick shifted uncomfortably, his gaze sliding to Janwar.

Smiling, Janwar arched a brow. *That's right. Let's see how easy it is to say no* now.

"Who is it?" she asked. "Did she give you her name?"

"Rachel."

Simone's eyes welled with tears and began to glow again. "Is she okay? What kind of condition was she in when you rescued her?"

"I haven't exactly rescued her. I just... located her."

"Is she okay?"

"Yes. She's still in the Lasaran escape pod and said she is unharmed."

Her brow puckered with worry. "She must nearly be out of oxygen. How soon can you reach her?"

Again, Wonick shifted. "I am unable to leave the planet at this time."

"Unable," Janwar prodded, "or unwilling?"

Wonick shot him a glare.

"I don't understand." Simone's gaze darted back and forth between them. "You don't have a ship? Can *she* reach *you* then?"

Wonick looked everywhere but at Simone while he searched for a response.

Janwar cleared his throat. "It took the remaining cyborgs a long time to find a planet they could call home. They're fiercely protective of it and can't let anyone know its location."

"Rachel won't tell anyone." Shaking her head, she addressed Wonick. "Why would she? Do you know how many people have tried to kill me and my friends in the past because we're different? How many have hated us? Feared us? Called us evil? Dangerous? Wanted to eradicate us? How many have tried to capture us and force us to use our special gifts to help them gain power and wealth or harm others?"

All of which should strike a chord with Wonick.

"That's why we left Earth," she continued. "To get away from that bullshit. If you save Rachel and don't mistreat her, you will have a friend and ally for life. Should anyone approach her in the future and ask if she's ever seen a cyborg, she will laugh it off. If they persist, she'll tell them to go *drek* themselves. And if someone ever locates you through other means—because they sure as hell won't find you through us—and harms you?" A grim smile curled her lips. "She will hunt them down and ensure they can never hurt you or anyone else again. And I'll help her. We've been in your position. Had to hide our existence. We know how crappy that is. And we're loyal to our friends."

Love burned through Janwar, coupled with a determination to keep her from ever having to deal with that *bura* again.

"Save my friend's life," she vowed, "and if yours is ever threatened, I will risk my own to aid you."

"I will, too," Janwar added.

Wonick's shoulders slumped in defeat. "You won't be *able* to aid me because Savaas will kill me for this."

Grinning, Simone punched the air with a fist. "Yes!"

Wonick's expression questioned her sanity.

She laughed. "Not *yes*, Savaas will kill you. I meant *yes*, you're going to save Rachel. Keep Savaas at bay until we get there. I'll deal with him myself."

Wonick caught Janwar's gaze and shook his head in bafflement. "Who *are* these females?"

Wrapping his arms around Simone, he hugged her. "Worthy allies and true treasures."

"Awwww." Cupping his jaw in one hand, she brushed a kiss across his lips. "You say the sweetest things."

Over her shoulder, Wonick shook his head. "I am so dead," he muttered and cut the connection.

"Shoot." Leaning back, she frowned. "I didn't get to say goodbye."

"I'm sure he'll comm us again once he gets Rachel to safety." Keeping one arm around her back, he tucked the other under her knees and rose with her in his arms. "Right now, I'm more interested in exploring what's under that shirt."

Smiling, she slipped her arms around his neck as they left his office and headed back to their quarters.

His pulse quickened when she nuzzled his beard and drew a finger down his chest in a teasing caress.

"Do you think we would scandalize the *rinyas* if we made love in the park?" she murmured.

Grinning, Janwar turned and headed for the park. "Only one way to find out."

Laughing, she snuggled closer.

FROM THE AUTHOR

Thank you for reading *The Akseli*. I hope you enjoyed Simone and Janwar's story. I had so much fun writing it. If this is the first Aldebarian Alliance book you've read, you can see firsthand how these daring women ended up in space in *The Lasaran*, Prince Taelon and Lisa's story. If Eliana intrigued you, you can find her adventure in *The Segonian*, which I was thrilled to learn was deemed on of the Best Audiobooks of 2021 by *AudioFile Magazine*. You can also see the mischief she got into back on Earth in *Broken Dawn*, part of my Immortal Guardians paranormal romance series. And you can see Ava come into her own with Jak'ri in *The Purveli*.

If you enjoyed *The Akseli*, please consider rating or reviewing it at an online retailer of your choice. I am always thrilled when I see that one of my books made a reader or audiobook lover happy. Ratings and reviews are also an excellent way to recommend an author's books, create word of mouth, and help other readers find new favorites.

ABOUT THE AUTHOR

Dianne Duvall is the *New York Times* and *USA Today* bestselling author of the acclaimed Immortal Guardians paranormal romance series, the exciting new Aldebarian Alliance sci-fi romance series, and The Gifted Ones medieval and time-travel romance series. She is known for writing stories full of action that keeps readers flipping pages well past their bedtimes, strong heroes who adore strong heroines, lovable secondary characters, swoon-worthy romance, and humor that readers frequently complain makes them laugh out loud at inappropriate moments. *AudioFile Magazine* declared *The Segonian* (Aldebarian Alliance Book 2) one of the Best Audiobooks of 2021 and awarded it the AudioFile Earphones Award for Exceptional Audio. It was also a Barnes and Noble Top Indie Favorite Pick. Audible chose *Awaken the Darkness* as one of the Top 5 Best Paranormal Romances of 2018.

Reviewers have called Dianne's books "fast-paced and humorous" (*Publishers Weekly*), "utterly addictive" (*RT Book Reviews*), "extraordinary" (*Long and Short Reviews*), and "wonderfully imaginative" (*The Romance Reviews*). Her audiobooks have been awarded AudioFile Earphone Awards for Exceptional Audio. One was nominated for a prestigious Audie Award. And her books have twice been nominated for RT Reviewers' Choice Awards.

When she isn't writing, Dianne is active in the independent film industry and has even appeared on-screen, crawling out of a moonlit grave and wielding a machete like some of the psychotic vampires she creates in her books.

For the latest news on upcoming releases, sales, giveaways, and more, please visit **DianneDuvall.com**. You can also connect with Dianne online:

Subscribe to Dianne's Newsletter
eepurl.com/hfT2Qn

Join the Dianne Duvall Books Group
www.facebook.com/groups/128617511148830/

Dianne's Blog
dianneduvall.blogspot.com

Facebook
www.facebook.com/DianneDuvallAuthor

Instagram
www.instagram.com/dianne.duvall

Twitter
twitter.com/DianneDuvall

Follow Dianne on BookBub
www.bookbub.com/authors/dianne-duvall

Pinterest
www.pinterest.com/dianneduvall

YouTube
bit.ly/DianneDuvall_YouTube

Printed in Great Britain
by Amazon